Vaelift

Benjamin Wesley Atwood

DEDICATION

For Irving Degraw Smith for always inspiring the grand old adventure and Catherine for being a rock solid companion.

CONTENTS

Chapter 1
Newbers

Bendin Slight awoke. Bendin, 1.85 meters tall and sixty-eight kilograms, was eight years old today. He was very proud that he was just taller than the Commander. Even though it seemed like it was just another day, it was a good day; the day before *the* day.

It was the day before it would be determined where he was going to be for the rest of his life. This year, he would be the one picked. He knew it, and he was ready. He was going to be one of Odge's Vaelift. Among other problems Bendin had in his chances, only one person was picked per year. Bendin rubbed his bright blue eyes and scratched his medium-length wavy blond hair.

His roommate, Tyler Thurber, who had a rounded face, brown hair, and brown eyes snored in the bunk above his head.

Tyler probably had a long night. He'd been up for hours into the night for weeks trying to catch up with the rest of the group's knowledge of the ways of Odge; however, even with all the extra time, he was still the bottom of the class. Bendin felt sorry for him.

Bendin pushed back the red blankets, smiling to himself as he grabbed a brush and wiped the dust that had gathered overnight off his Vaelift-style uniform. They were so standard and common he hardly thought about it. It's not like everyone in the temple was wearing exactly the same thing. It was more like the color and styles were very similar. His consisted of a comfortable soft lower layer make of a cotton polyester fiber mesh, a middle layer of a thin style of dark rayon, and the outer layer was made of a durable material. He really didn't know what it was made of, but it seemed to not fade or wear for anything. It rested on him so as to be loose fitting with a pair of drawstrings that crisscrossed up the middle and part way in the back. He despised the white ovals embroidered on the bottom tails that hung on the front and back parts of the outfit.

Bendin's room was small, hardly enough space for the two of them. But, regardless of its size, he felt that it was a blessing from Odge; most people had smaller rooms to share than his. All rooms had a small shower and bathroom attached to them. There were small bins, dressers, and most importantly two desks for automation and work.

The desks revealed history. The bottom parts were made of wood, but as you went up the desk the materials changed; it went from wood parts to iron parts to glass, plastic, steel, till you reached the top where you found the crystal displays and the laser projections. Bendin looked at the desk fondly and tapped his fingers on the leg. It was like seeing a little of what his people had been able to discover, put together, and use through the years. He was quite proud of it.

Every student had one of these desks with a customized Automated Desk Advisor. Bendin found ADA very annoying. ADA felt like having a wonderful dream interrupted by incredible static and waking up to find that you had been sleeping on a pebble all night, digging into your side.

Bendin sat in the chair and pulled out a small writing utensil and waved it, rather lazily, at the crystal displays. They snapped to life and the lasers projected a small red holographic image of a woman. A female voice radiated from the image.

"Good morning, BD3. Thank you for being on time."

"As usual. Ada, I've told you, let's see how many times has it been since I started keeping track," Bendin glanced at the counter on his screen, "six hundred eighty-eight times now that my name is Bendin?" Bendin clicked the counter. It now read, "Six hundred eighty-nine."

The hologram laughed. "It's formal, but perhaps when you graduate I'll reconsider the policy."

Bendin smirked in triumph. "Thank you, Ada. Review schedule again please."

"Breakfast at 08:00, History at 09:00, break at 13:00, Competition at 13:30, Cycles at 15:00, dinner at 17:00, --"

"I've heard enough; copy all of it to watch."

Four small lights at the corners of the display blinked from red to green before going dark on Bendin's sleek black colored watch.

"Have a good day, BD3."

"Thanks, Ada."

Bendin stretched and walked out of the room.

The halls were gray, etched, and tall. If it wasn't for the red carpets and red tapestries, as far as color goes, they'd be the most dull and boring hallways ever. The walls were so high you could barely make out the ceiling. Even though the walls were very high, they were only wide enough to fit two people standing side by side.

After traversing many halls and being greeted by some

of the top students, Bendin found himself smelling the delicious aroma of the large Feed Hall. Unlike the walking-halls, the Feed Hall had a low ceiling only three meters in height. Despite its relatively low ceiling, the room was enormous. It was twice as long as it was wide and could fit well over four hundred students during rush hours.

It was rush hour. People were accidentally bumping into each other, dishes clattering, and food being consumed. Unlike the feed hall in the lower temple, this temple was the best at having plenty of lines for students to fill. It made for a quick run through to pile on the food. Bendin hungrily grabbed his favorites: eggs, bacon, ham, turkey, and gravy.

"Good morning, sunshine."

"Good morning, Mister Lacak." Bendin sat down next to a blond haired man who was one of the temple janitors. He was here every day and loved to talk and kid with the students. Bendin thought he was the nicest man he'd ever met. Everyone knew Ladak wanted a teaching position, but the organization hadn't let him. If he wasn't cleaning, he was painting.

"Been studying hard, I see. I had a question for you."

"Yeah?"

"That girl over there, see her?" Ladak grinned. Bendin knew. He flushed slightly but continued to eat.

"Yes, I know, I know, I know." Bendin poked his ham nervously.

"I was just pointing her out that she is a girl. Just so you know." Ladak winked at him and moved down the table talking with other students as he went.

Bendin sighed. Lyla Shovek, blonde with curls, a year younger than him had been very interested in him for weeks now. It might have been months, he had forgotten now. There was only one really big problem with Lyla and him--he wasn't into her. It's not that she wasn't cute, she was a parasite. It wasn't like he didn't like girls either. No, it was far from it, just not her. Not her. Not her. He thought if he ignored her enough she'd just go away, but she was there, all the time. She would shadow him in the hallways, peek at him in the class rooms, and always try to out shoot him on the range. Why did she have to be in his group? People like Lyla were annoying. The only person who could compete with her for being the most annoying was Radu Landus.

Bendin noticed Radu glaring at him wickedly. Radu was small, ruddy, and had piercing black eyes. Radu had an appetite for being mean. He did not like Bendin one bit, and anything he could do to mess him up or interrupt him in any way, he was there. If there was a way for him to get rid of Bendin, Bendin was pretty sure Radu wouldn't hesitate. Just last week, in Cycles, Radu had somehow gotten all the machines to target him. Radu's friends were abnoxiously supportive of Radu's efforts. They were well known as bullies among the students, but decent among the teachers. How the teachers could not notice was beyond comprehension. Bendin's best guess of Radu's motives were that he was jealous of Bendin's skill and position in the class. Bendin smartly ignored Radu's glare.

"Morning, Bendin." Tyler sat down with a full plate.

"Hi."

Tyler glanced over and saw Lyla quickly turn her head away. "Lyla again?"

"Yeah." Bendin seemed to have lost his appetite, for a second.

"She really likes you. At least you got someone who really digs you. Ain't nobody likin' me." Tyler beamed a huge grin on his round face scanning the room. No one seemed to notice him. This confirmed his suspicions and he frowned even more. "The newbers 'ere yet?"

Bendin lifted his eyes and flashed a huge smile at Tyler. "You're right. It's newber day!"

Almost as if on cue, the main double doors opened and in came the newbers. Everyone clapped and cheered enthusiastically. The newbers were led by none other than the head Vaelift master himself, Findall Quin. He wore almost the same attire as the students, but carried a blue ribbed Vaelift staff that had beautiful black carvings on one end of it. Bendin wanted to be just like him. To be under Findall was the highest honor and rank in the kingdom. Some of them even personally guarded the queen herself. It was the best that any of Bendin's group could hope to achieve, and he wanted it. The newbers were dressed in class one Vaelift-style uniforms with the same layers but with different markings. The group marched straight through the middle of the room and ended in a line in front of Findall. They would now be assigned new quarters and an exemplar for the rest of the day.

Findall Quin smiled at all the students and said simply, "Behold, I bring you the newest of our Vaelift trainees!" Findall twirled his staff, and with a bright blue streak accompanied by a loud electric crashing sound, he was gone.

"That was *so cool*," Tyler said.

"I want to do that!" Bendin cheered. Most other students were clapping and cheering as well. Even Radu folded his arms, smugly impressed.

"Newbers, Tyler. They could pick you!" Bendin nudged Tyler teasingly with his elbow.

"Why me? Why not you? I'm the worst pick!"

The names of the newbers were read along with the department they had chosen as well as the name of their exemplar. Bendin loved his group. He'd chosen the Defense of Odge Department or DOOD group on his arrival. It had seemed like it was the most honorable and fun; he'd been right.

"CT4, to Agriculture Industries . . . Exemplar is Alexander Pumble."

One of the visiting graduates pulled CT4 out of the line.

"Ha, poor Alexander Pumble. He was hoping he didn't have to do that today," Tyler said and laughed.

"You knew that?" Bendin said curiously.

"Ran into him in the hall today, and he was grumbling about the chances of having extra dead weight on him today."

"No kidding. They'll do anything with visiting graduates nowadays," Bendin mumbled.

"Nope, not kidding," Tyler remarked with a sly grin.

"DA2, to Aviation Department . . . Exemplar is ET7."

"Why don't they use *our* names? Is so stupid to do that," Tyler ranted.

"I agree. Waiting after graduation to use full names is so stupid. I tell Ada that every day. Some rules are so dumb." Bendin was almost done with his breakfast.

"SU1, to Defense of Odge cepartment; Exemplar is TY4"

Tyler looked like he'd been shot. (Bendin knew that look, because Tyler was accidentally shot last week. This, however, wasn't a bullet.)

Bendin stopped eating in surprise.

Tyler shook himself, stood up, went to the front, bear hugged SU1, and carried him in the air all the way back to the table.

"Way to get one!" Bendin cheered.

The other students exploded in laughter at Tyler's unusual way of greeting the newber. Tyler planted SU1 on the ground next to the table and sat down. "I'm not going to have time to do all the laps I wanted; especially not if I have to tote this guy around." Tyler flipped his thumb at SU1.

"It's only for today," Bendin offered.

"I know, I know, but why me?" Tyler glanced from his plate to Bendin and back again quickly three or four times.

"Stop that. You'll be fine. You'll see."

"That's easy for you to say." Tyler frowned miserably. "You ain't had one."

It was true. Bendin had never had one and he didn't really know what to think about it. Was it a sign of incompetence? Or was it the leaders poking fun at him? Bendin could easily imagine them behind the comfort of their monitors and data laughing and keeping people like him from training newbers.

"Guys, I can hear everything you are saying," SU1 softly spoke up eyeing them nervously.

"Sit down, SU1, you're giving me the amateur look here," Tyler said tapping SU1 on the leg with his fork.

SU1 sat down, throwing his backpack onto the ground. He was below average height, with glossy black hair and dark brown eyes. His breakfast plate was full of food. Bendin checked to see if there were any remaining newbers. He didn't see anymore, sighed, and turned back to SU1. His plate was unbelievably already half empty. A few moments later SU1 just stared at his plate, and then over to Tyler's plate, and then back again. And again. And again.

"Hungry?" Tyler asked.

"Yes." SU1 grabbed the plate Tyler offered him and skillfully sucked the food off right in front of their eyes. SU1 peered up at their curious expressions.

"I'm hungry."

"We see that," They both said.

"Okay, SU1, the first thing that we do here is give you a real name," Tyler stated and winked at Bendin. "Is there anything you'd like to be called?"

SU1 paused and scratched his chin. "Steve."

Tyler's mouth opened in surprise. "Steve?"

"Sure, Steve. Traditionally we give you your last name, and we'll have it for you in a little while," Bendin said.

"Okay. Are you going to eat that?" Steve pointed to the last of Bendin's eggs.

"No, here," Bendin said carefully sliding his plate in front of Steve.

"Ah, thanks. It was a long ride," He said it as if it explained everything. Bendin remembered his long ride to the upper temple and knew exactly what he was talking about.

The side doors burst open with a loud crack and two figures appeared, one was being dragged across the floor by the feet.

Silence immediately fell over the entire Feed Hall. Radu watched eagle-eyed. Bendin knew that Radu loved these kinds of displays.

It was Commander Zist. Tall, firm, huge body, thick black hair with bushy eyebrows, and a gaze that would set your soul on fire. He was the most dangerous person that Bendin knew of, except for D-men (but he'd never seen one, only heard tales of their unbelievable acts). He had no idea why Zist would be here, but it certainly couldn't be good.

"I caught this young man, VD7, stealing!" Zist's booming voice shook the entire room.

Bendin knew that VD7 might have to scrub or paint the walls, or carry the disposables for a month for that kind of crime.

Zist wasn't finished. "He was stealing from the R-limiter storage systems in the *Defense Of Odge Department.*"

An audible gasp from the students echoed through the room and then it was deathly still. R-limiters were common around the temple departments, but no one, absolutely no one, was allowed to access that particular R-limiter except under executive orders and under the strictest supervision. It held coveted temple data statistics, location specific data on students, keys, codes and such. The actual unit itself wasn't guarded fiercely because that R-limiter was in the back of the control center, and Bendin knew of no one who had successfully stole from that specific R-limiter without being caught.

"He could have just said the control center, same thing," Bendin muttered to Tyler.

"Is he going to die?" Steve's voice carried a little bit too far and several students around them turned and stared at Tyler and Steve.

"Shhhhhh!" Tyler placed a finger to his mouth.

Commander Zist's eyes flared as he scanned the faces of the students, workers, and teachers.

"Do your duty, or it will come to this." Commander Zist kicked VD7 painfully till the students could not hear VD7. Bendin turned away as the groans and whimpers died down. Commander Zist gripped VD7's feet and stomped out the doors dragging the guilty student behind him. Bendin felt a cold shudder as the echo of a shot bounced down the hall into the room. Bendin wondered what must have driven VD7 to risk his life to try to swipe information out of the DOOD R-Limiter.

Radu caught Bendin's attention and mouthed one word, "You!" He laughed and made shooting gestures at Bendin while all his friends patted Radu on the shoulders and laughed with him.

Bendin pursed his lips and shook his head sadly.

Tyler turned to Steve and eyed him seriously. He spoke very quietly, "We can do whatever we want, as long as we follow the rules."

"Same as the lower temple?"

Tyler tapped his watch, "Yeah, pretty much. Be punctual, speak in turn, listen, and don't steal. Do that and you'll be fine."

Bendin's watch beeped at exactly the same time as Tyler's.

"Ha!" They both chuckled and pointed fingers at each other.

"On time in time to be on time as usual. Come on, Steve." Bendin motioned with his hands, beckoning him.

"Hey, when do I get one of those?" Steve asked pointing at Tyler's watch.

Tyler grabbed Steve's backpack and pulled him out of the chair. They quickly followed Bendin into the hall.

Bendin walked and navigated the halls, half paying attention. Normally, it was an easy thing to traverse the many halls leading from room to room.

Not today. Steve and Tyler hardly kept up, and when they did catch up, it was disaster. They constantly bumped into people and accidentally pushed them over, which caused all sorts of bottlenecks and problems. It was very amusing to Bendin who, even with people falling all over, was unaffected.

"Who is she?" Steve managed to ask Bendin during one of his catch-up attempts.

Bendin didn't even glance back. "Lyla."

"She's cute." Steve's excitement was not contagious.

"Sure." Bendin waved his hand away in annoyance.

Steve opened his mouth to respond, but he saw Tyler shaking his head vigorously as he led him away into the classroom.

The classrooms were fairly proportional in size, depending on the number of students that it seated. They ranged anywhere from thirty to one hundred students. This six meter high room seated about thirty. The illustrious red carpets and red drapes were also here. Lights shined in the room from cube-shaped etched holes in the walls, ceiling, and floor.

The teacher, Professor John Goldbarm, was a bald, stoutly man who had a wit half as tough as his rippling muscles. The students each had their own desks. They were exactly like the desks found in their respective sleeping quarters. Bendin sat in his own desk while Tyler went to the front where two desks had been shoved side-by-side for the Exemplar and the trainee.

Prof. Goldbarm had written "Odge" on the green-on-black screen behind him. Bendin sighed. He had seen this topic before countless times and he hoped that they would expand beyond the information that they already knew.

"Good morning, students. I have been told by Master Findall himself that we are to review the basic information we know of Odge." Some students groaned audibly throughout the room.

"This again?" A student behind Bendin asked.

It simply meant it was going to be boring. Maybe if Bendin participated actively enough, he'd be able to remain focused and avoid the problems of waning attention due to repetition.

"In light of our newest addition to our group, "Goldbarm gestured to Steve with his thick fingers, "I think it fitting to change from the topic, 'The Duties of the Elect', to 'Who is Odge?' tap in anyone."

Bendin quickly tapped a button on his desk causing a small green light to light up on the desk and a popping sound to emit from it. "Odge is everything." The words appeared on the screen up front as he spoke them.

"Correct. Odge is everything. Anything else?"

Lyla tapped the button and shouted confidently, "Odge can do anything!" This was again written automatically on the board up front.

Bendin knew this, but certainly didn't understand it. No one did. Odge was so great that no one knew who or what he, she, or it was. He'd heard this stuff so much that his concentration began to waver and his well thought-out plan was beginning to fail.

"Odge cannot be known," Another male student with rich red hair in the back put in.

"What?" Steve said rubbing his chin furiously, "They didn't teach us that!"

"SU1, we are the keepers of the true knowledge of Odge. They don't teach advanced concepts at the lower temple, and we know that Odge is so powerful and all-knowing and beyond our comprehension and skilled and benevolent and he saved all of us from anything we might do that is wrong ever," Prof. Goldbarm said firmly. His words appeared on the board word for word.

"He didn't save us from the horrid grammar in that sentence," Lyla noted pointing to several mistakes in the sentence that had appeared on the board. Her sentence appeared word for word under Golbarm's sentence with one alteration. It read, "He did save us from the horrid grammar in that sentence." Several of the students near her snickered till Prof. Goldbarm stared at them angrily, turned, and pointed at the board. The sentence mystically adjusted itself on the board to be grammatically correct.

"Odge," Prof. Goldbarm said simply.

Steve's furrowed brow was so pronounced he looked like he had a thin black line across the top of his head.

"Yes?" Prof. Goldbarm smiled at Steve.

"Saved . . . from anything we do wrong?"

"Yes, anything against the rules."

Steve's mouth opened as large as a frog's mouth. If a fly had been buzzing nearby, Bendin wouldn't have been surprised to see Steve's tongue flick out and catch it.

"Meaning if we do not do our rituals, we lose favor with him. We do wrong," Prof. Goldbarm said carefully, trying again.

Steve's mouth snapped shut, his eyes glowed slightly, and his furrow disappeared.

Prof. Goldbarm knew Steve had figured out somewhat of what he said because he continued, "Going along with the topic of preservation, who helped us win the Great War?"

Radu tapped in. "It was Zadok who helped turn the tide of the war and win it for the Vaelift."

"Correct, without the wisdom of Zadok it would have been impossible to defeat the uprising of that day and age."

Bendin knew about the Great War, blah, blah, blah. They had more people fighting than ever before, but then who cares? It's in the past. It wasn't heroic defense of the queen or protecting the name of Odge then. His thoughts began to wander as he heard the teacher continue from the Great War and give the rest of the Odge lesson for the millionth time.

"Odge is incomprehensible, unknowable . . . This makes

him the great, grand wonder of the universe . . . We love him because he is so mysterious . . . He gave us Vaelift leaders till we reach Findall. He gives us . . "Bendin fell asleep finally succumbing to the power of Prof. Goldbarm's golden droning voice.

The next thing Bendin knew he snapped awake at something light, soft, and damp, brushing up against his cheek. Lyla's whole face obscured his vision. The moment he realized she'd kissed his cheek, Bendin reacted impulsively with an uncanny jerk away from her, and he fell onto the floor.

Lyla tapped his desk and grinned as though she had won some sort of contest.

Bendin saw those near him laughing and pointing fingers at him. He frowned, got up, and noticed almost everyone else was getting up and leaving. Some were still talking with Prof. Goldbarm. How had Prof. Goldbarm not seen that Lyla had stolen a kiss and prevented it? All Bendin could tell was that he was occupied up at the front with the other students.

"May I walk with you this time?" Lyla asked twirling her drawstring between her fingers.

"What? Instead of following me? What do you want?" Bendin looked past her at Tyler waving his arms, and pointing to the heavens. He was visibly trying to explain the great mystery to Steve.

"Please?"

"Oh, all right."

Once again she looked as if she had won again because she looked over her shoulder at a group of girls and grinned.

Bendin let out a soft snort, put an arm out, and Lyla hooked her arm around it. He led her out of the room, getting goofy looks and raspberries from the other students. Tyler was so immersed with Steve, he didn't notice anything else.

"So what is it? What do you want?" Bendin asked when they were out of earshot from the other students.

"You," She replied eagerly.

Bendin watched her a little puzzled, but mostly too nervous to say anything anyway.

"You are the only student who doesn't engage in--"

"What? That I've never been with anyone?" Bendin sighed. It was his break right now and he was looking forward to seeing the frogs but here Lyla was. He was trying to figure out some reasonable way to ditch her because saying he was planning to sit by some frogs certainly wasn't going to work as something to get her to go away; he feared if he said anything about the frogs it'd be more like an invitation. Bendin ran his hand through his hair nervously. Throw her aside? Make an excuse? Maybe faint? He couldn't think of anything reasonable.

"Yes, but also, no." Lyla's eyes were so focused she looked like she had been thinking of this question for years. She tugged his arm and forcibly pulled him into a classroom that just happened to be very dim and empty. "Look. Bendin. Look at me." Lyla grabbed Bendin's face and forced him to look at her.

Bendin had been looking at what was stenciled on the screen, "Hearing for beginners."

She gestured for Bendin to sit.

Bendin sat, rather reluctantly. Lyla sat gingerly next to him grinning rather peevishly.

"Bendin, I really like you, and I wanted to know," she paused and spoke fervently, "if I have a chance."

She was pretty bold. Bendin had been telling Ladak and Tyler how he felt for years. How could she know how he really felt, unless he told her?

"I don't like it."

Lyla flinched as if hurt. "Why don't you like it?"

"No, not you," Bendin smiled very nervously.

"Then what?"

"It's just, the second rule of Odge. Nothing ever lasts."

Lyla looked at him as if what he said didn't matter at all, "So? That's *why* we engage in linking--"

"No," Bendin interrupted, "it's not you! I personally don't like the second rule of Odge. It's just, I don't want to waste something as valuable as linking with anyone, when it isn't going to last."

Lyla spread her arms out in confusion, "Bendin it never lasts for anyone; when do you see that it doesn't? The way it is now fits the laws of Odge perfectly."

Bendin sighed and shrugged. "I don't know. I just thought of it one day, when our social science teacher was explaining the value of the perfection of bonding and linking with as many different people as you could." If only Tyler could see him now. He probably would have been so disappointed in him. He'd have linked for sure. Not to mention Ladak. He'd been concerned almost immediately for Bendin from the time Bendin had put off hooking up with anyone.

Lyla was crushed. "No then?" Lyla's eyes filled with tears.

Bendin shook his head, stared at the ground, and started pacing. "No, but maybe we could be friends?" When Lyla didn't answer, Bendin looked up, and he was surprised to see that she wasn't there. She was gone.

Bendin had a problem with linking. This much was true, but it wasn't because he didn't think it was valuable. That was the problem. No one was allowed to link with another person a second time. Period. People who had tried in the past were annihilated. Students could hold hands, hook arms, talk to another person; but linking, could only be done once with that particular person. The truth was, he was scared of wasting it.

Bendin rushed off to the frog pond. It was a four by four meter square room with a high ceiling that had a skylight at the top of it. This was the only sunlight that Bendin knew of in the upper temple. Inset in the floor, so that it occupied almost a quarter of the room, was the frog pond. Aside from the bugs and squeaking mice that roamed the temple darkness, these were the only animals that Bendin was familiar with.

He picked up a frog, enjoyed its movement, the glow from the natural light above, thought about the upcoming competition, and wondered how good Steve was going to be. He hoped that no matter how good Steve was, that he'd be better!

Bendin left the pond and went to the range where they were going have the competition.

The range was a large room with a huge concrete wall that spanned about a hundred meters down the middle. One side was designed with seating facing the range. On top of the concrete wall was a blast-proof glass window that went almost to the ceiling. The range had every type of weapon that had been invented for the use of defending the great name of Odge.

Bendin briskly entered the room as he was close to being a minute late.

"Bendin!" Prof. Grey shouted, "Get your gear on and join the others!"

Professor Harry Grey was the oddest person Bendin knew. She was a short woman with crooked knees, bowed feet, squat build, and she had bumps everywhere. The most distinctive feature about her was her pair of large, glowing, blue eyes. Bendin thought that was why she never missed. Never.

Prof. Grey was trying to explain the importance of the unique weapons to Steve, "For seventeen hundred years these weapons have kept the name of Odge safe. What do they teach you guys at the lower temple anyway?" Bendin couldn't stand Prof. Grey's squeaky voice. He tried really hard to focus on the competition at hand instead.

Bendin hurried over to the shooting area where his classmates were waiting to start.

Radu stood confident. Bendin cheerily offered his hand for a handshake.

Radu took it and Bendin said, "May the best man win." Radu smirked.

Bendin looked at the stadium-style seating and watched as thousands of students filled the chairs. Bendin was always amazed to see so many students in one place. The building just never felt this full at any given day or time, but when you got most of the students together it was always a breathtaking sight.

Findall, Marshall Harbreaker, Zist, and others he didn't recognize were sitting in the front row. Ladak and the other janitors were even there waving and smiling at him. It wasn't completely unique, but competitions normally didn't have the entire janitorial staff in the audience.

It was time.

Colorful flags were raised, a bell sounded, and sparks shot off in every direction. Bowl shaped targets appeared from behind large concrete structures in the range. The goal was to shoot a bowl before the others did. There was always one less bowl than the number of entrants.

Bendin didn't even breathe and nailed the first bowl that appeared in the back with his pistol only a second after the flags went up. The bowl exploded in a massive firework of bright blue and white sparkles. The other students, frantically shot and claimed their bowls as quickly as they could till there was only one person who didn't hit one. It was Tyler.

The students cheered while the leaders watched and nodded their approval.

Tyler was so horrified and nervous he dropped his pistol and it shot a round towards the audience. Bendin knew this was against the rules. Tyler was removed by Prof. Grey and left the range dejected. Bendin felt sorry for Tyler and wanted to help, but he needed to focus on the task at hand. He would chat with him later.

As the rounds progressed, the size of the bowls shrank and the targets began to move across the range at high speeds.

Bendin claimed a bowl first with his bullet nearly every round and felt very confident.

Soon there were only Radu, Lyla, Bendin, Shari, and two other students left.

The next round started and a furious wind belted at them. The air was moving so fast that Bendin's eyes watered, even behind the glasses they wore. Radu shot the first bowl but a sudden gust of air flipped Radu over and another shot rang out, glancing off the blast-proof glass. He must have been embarrassed because Radu didn't move, or open his eyes. Prof. Grey couldn't carry him by herself and had to have other students carry him out. Bendin had been so distracted by Radu's debacle that he barely caught the last remaining bowl which exploded in a beautiful display of pink and red. Shari gave him a smile and an encouraging nod as she dropped off her pistol with Prof. Grey.

Two rounds later only Bendin and Lyla remained.

Lyla nudged Bendin, smiling at him.

"Lyla," Bendin began, but the flags were raised up, sparks shot off, and the next round began.

Bendin grinned as he shot the target and watched it burst into magnesium sparks.

He turned to see Lyla grinning too.

The audience was insatiable and the roar of the crowd was tremendous. Bendin could tell they wanted to know what had happened too. A large screen was brought down and everything dimmed. Footage of the bowl they shot appeared. Bendin watched open mouthed as two bullets simultaneously entered the bowl. It seemed impossible, but it was true.

They had tied. This had never happened before, and Bendin wondered what was going to happen.

"Make it harder!" shouted Commander Zist, who had risen from his seat and pumped his fist into the air. He shouted, "Harder!" with every fist pump. Soon the entire audience was screaming the word "harder" with him.

Prof. Grey showed off a grizzly smile and hushed the crowd with a wave of her hands. She disappeared into the large armory and returned a few seconds later with two pistols so small you could hardly hold it, much less aim it at anything. They were tiny weapons, but very rare. Bendin had only seen these weapons once before during his first year in the Defense of Odge Department. There were only a few in existence and they were one of the few things the Vaelift hadn't figured out how to remake. They had been designed by Vaelift during the Great War but hadn't been duplicated since. They seemed magical, just pull the trigger and the pistol would incinerate anything in front of it.

Prof. Grey explained seriously, "Do not, I repeat, do not shoot those at anyone. Good luck."

The roar of approval from the crowd was deafening, and that was *with* earplugs.

Bendin gripped the valuable little gun knowing that it was time to impress.

Lyla clenched her teeth.

The round began as normal. Bendin couldn't see anything. He glanced at Lyla and she seemed to be thinking the same thing.

"Shoot the target!" Prof. Grey's voice boomed over the speaker.

Bendin focused again on the range, and scanned for the target. He saw something, it might have been a blur it was moving so fast, but it was definitely the smallest target he'd ever seen. It was a dot sized target and it was moving so fast if you didn't watch it closely, you'd miss it entirely.

Bendin took aim and just before he shot he heard a cry of exclamation.

"I see it!" Lyla screamed and fired her tiny pistol which made a loud elongated whine.

Bendin smiled as the look of horror crept over her face at the strange sound of the pistol. He knew what they sounded like, he'd heard them before. Scanning the field again and for the first time during the competition, he feared he might not win. He saw it again, took aim, and fired. The biggest explosion of all the targets erupted knocking both of them flat on their backs. While Prof. Grey chuckled at them from the door of the armory, they felt the heat from the blast waft overhead.

The match was over.

The crowd cheered triumphantly for the win and Bendin watched his shot being replayed over and over again on the screen. He felt fabulous. He had won!

Bendin turned and helped Lyla up off the ground to congratulate her. Bendin felt perfectly assured in his chances of being picked tomorrow.

Lyla shook Bendin's hand till Bendin frowned.

Bendin looked around for Tyler, to see if he had come back yet, but he couldn't see him. Bendin felt incredibly happily satisfied and even shook hands with Findall on his way out.

Chapter 2
Cycles

The classroom used for cycles was more of a training arena than for anything else and Bendin didn't know why it was called cycles. The room itself was very large, one of the biggest ones Bendin knew of with extremely high ceilings and wide open space. The middle was usually jam packed with buildings and pathways. Most of the time cycles consisted of solving puzzles and problems, and Bendin felt some of the puzzles were getting old.

Bendin hoped to be teamed up with someone like Shari or Steve, but cringed at the thought of being with Lyla.

The instructor for the class, Professor Roger Garret, was a balding grey-haired man with one blue eye. His other eye was lost in some freak arena accident, or so he had boastfully claimed. He was short, about one and a half meters tall.

Radu shouldered Bendin as he passed, knocking Bendin off balance. Bendin locked his eyes angrily with Radu, who had cleverly taken advantage of the teacher's conveniently occupied attention. "You don't have a prayer, Radu. I've got tops for cycles today."

"You wish, born loser," Radu bantered withdrawing from Bendin to the other side of the class.

"Bendin, good job out there, son!" Bendin jumped around in surprise to see Ladak.

"What are you doing here, Ladak?" Bendin asked. Ladak wasn't usually down in cycles.

"Just wanted to congratulate you for your success. You're doing exceptionally well. Don't forget the girls. They look prettier than you do."

"Hey!" Bendin frowned.

Ladak shook Bendin's hand, pointed at the girls in the room, winked, and left smiling.

"Okay, thanks," Bendin called after him feeling a little exposed. He saw Lyla with Steve, and it appeared as if she was trying to explain the differences in the cycle procedure versus the lower temple versions. Bendin went over to them and discovered he was right.

"What happened to Tyler? Where is he?" Bendin asked

interrupting their conversation.

"He said he was sick and got special permission to go to the Health Systems. He said he'd be right back," Steve explained.

"I've been assigned to work with Steve until he returns." Lyla grinned at Steve. "He's brilliant!"

Steve tapped his foot on the ground sheepishly and turned away.

Bendin was secretly pleased at her special attention to the word "brilliant."

Professor Garret clapped his hands together sharply and cupped them to his mouth. "Class! Today we are going to learn about awareness and self-projection, and then later you all will have the opportunity to demonstrate your ability to collaborate in pairs, to ensure protection of your team, and finish the cycle."

Prof. Garret grabbed a student up at the front and rasped sharply, "Here. Stand here, and allow yourself to self-project." The student was a girl named Harmon Greystead, and her slouched posture made it appear like she was about to tumble down the small platform that the teacher was standing on.

"This is an example of poor self-projection." He paused and gestured at Harmon. "I'm sorry, Harmon, but could you just straighten your back? That would help you out immensely."

The effect was instant. Harmon straightened her back; she appeared visibly more confident. Bendin yawned. Like he had never seen this before? Bendin was looking forward to doing the assertive tactical work of the class. After a few more words times one thousand, the teacher finally assigned teams.

Bendin was paired with none other than Harmon. Harmon was in her second year at the DOOD and had red hair that rivaled the color of the tapestries of the temple.

"How is your knowledge of science working out for you in our department?" Bendin asked.

Harmon beamed as though she'd been offered a priceless gem. "It's fascinating! I mean working to prove through sciences the works of Odge is just . . . unprecedented!"

"And that's possible?"

"It certainly is. It's just using the right experiments and adjusting your knowledge as we gather new sources and results for the tests."

"Nice," Bendin said as a small smile slowly crept over his face.

"We're working in pairs today?" Harmon asked as they moved toward the compartments along the wall.

"It appears so," Bendin said as he gathered up his gear from his compartment.

"Isn't this uncommon? I mean, I've only worked with quads."

Bendin grinned slightly again in spite of himself, thought better of it, and gave her a huge smile.

"They don't make us do single runs do they?" Harmon asked nervously.

Bendin continued to smile.

"You're making me nervous, could you stop that, please? Really, *really*!" Harmon said blinking her big blue eyes at him. Harmon was fair skinned, slender for her medium height, but was not as athletic as the other girls in their class. She nervously tucked her hair up inside her helmet so that her hair would not be getting in the way.

"Do you think I'll do well?" Harmon asked.

"Yep, of course you'll be fine. I'm going to enjoy working with a scientist."

"I hope so. Normally I just follow along and offer advice to the others. But, now it's just us. What if something dreadful happens to you?" Harmon gripped her helmet with white knuckles.

"Relax." Bendin placed his hand on her shoulder. Harmon let out a long breath of air and released her grip on her helmet.

Bendin and Harmon joined the long line of students in front of the entrance and waited their turn, listening to the booms and explosions echoing from inside the area. They could hardly see what was going on because the tempered glass and the dim lights obscured their vision.

Harmon whispered, "Any ideas on what to expect this time?"

"I thought we'd wing it," Bendin shrugged and continued, "but it can't be anything they haven't tried before."

"Then you're leading out."

"Sure. Don't worry. I think I can handle it," Bendin stated securely.

"Will there be others in there at the same time as us do you think?"

"One hundred percent sure. Look, notice his assistant sends people in before others get back? Looks to be about two maybe three tea--"

Harmon gasped, gripped his shoulder, and pointed at the exit. The first team was wheeled in from the other side on stretchers and out of the classroom, clearly headed for Health Systems.

Bendin reassured Harmon with a clasp of his hand on her arm, "We can do it. You're smart; I'm experienced. Come on. What can they do?" Bendin grinned.

"They can kill us one hundred percent sure," Harmon muttered utterly unconvinced.

After a few more students went through, it was their turn. The flap was thrown up and they were in.

The buildings for this run were tall and brick, but the brick was chipping and falling off in several places. The cobblestone roads were in disarray, and there seemed to be no way to move around the edges of the building to their immediate right or left so they had to go down the straight road in front of them. There were pockets of smoking holes all over the place, and despite wreckage littering the road, there was no sound at all.

"Where are the other teams?" Harmon asked.

Bendin had only a second to pull Harmon down out of the way of a turret, which had popped out from the side of the building that was going to shoot her in the face. The turret shot the space she had been with an echoing blast.

Bendin put a finger to his lips and motioned her to follow him. He backed them into the building away from the turret.

Once inside, Bendin pulled drawers open and ripped boxes looking for anything that might be useful.

Harmon found a couple of small pouches and a belt. After a minute of searching, Bendin found something he didn't recognize. It was a small device with a curved shaped handle, and he showed it to Harmon, who almost giggled in glee. She made several motions with her hands, but Bendin didn't know at all what she was saying. Instead of trying to figure it out, he gave her the device and picked up a sturdy pole that was equal to his height. Harmon followed him with surprising eagerness. They sidestepped the turret, went down a couple alleys, and found a small opening in a wall. Through the opening there was another alley with a very large wall at the back, something Bendin did recognize. He made several gestures with his hands meaning "do as I do". She watched in perplexed anticipation. Bendin ran straight at the wall, and just before he hit it, he tucked his body into a ball, and rolled through. Bendin waited for Harmon to appear, but he heard another team shouting at her instead.

Idiots.

"Hey!"

"Wait!"

Bendin heard the sliding of the metal turrets popping up and shooting. Shrugging, he got up and prepared to roll back through. Before he could, Harmon rolled into him, and both of them sprawled out on the floor.

Harmon picked herself up off the dusty floor, and Bendin watched her gaze at a room big enough you could fit a large vehicle in it.

"You made it. Swell." Bendin dusted himself off and sat in a chair behind a table.

"We can talk?"

"In here it's okay." Bendin tapped the camouflaged walls.

"What is this?"

"It's used for hiding Vaelift units."

"How did you know it was here?" Harmon asked.

"If you study the wall carefully, you can see the ripples in the fabric that give it away. It's the only flaw in this design."

Harmon dusted herself off with her hands and said, "Do you think it's really all stone and bricks outside?"

"I hear that is what most of the outside world is like."

"Ever been there?" Harmon's eyes expressed curiosity.

"Heard. Never seen. Maybe I will, though. I'm hoping to get picked tomorrow."

"For Odge's Vaelift?"

"Yeah." Bendin flipped the bar he was holding several times.

"Wow. Sounds really nice." Harmon crossed her arms. "Even those who qualify don't end up as Odge's Vaelift. They normally get a lower rank."

"I know. What is that?" Bendin pointed his pole at Harmon's mechanical instrument.

"It's the highest class of welder."

"A welder?" Bendin scoffed. "You have got to be kidding me. Let's finish our run." He had been hoping for something else.

Harmon motioned for him to go first. Bendin smiled and parted the seams of camouflage on the side opposite they had come in. They passed through the seam into a courtyard. It was connected to another sad excuse for a street. Bendin scouted a difficult path around potholes, metal, and other twisted configurations of debris, till they made it halfway across.

Loud rumbling echoes bounced to them from down the street. Steve and Lyla sped around the corner up ahead, running at top speed towards them. Burned, battered, and bruised they desperately waved their arms for Bendin and Harmon to run the other way.

Bendin didn't need to see what followed to know what their signal meant. He grabbed Harmon by the hand and pulled her safely out of the way and into a building. Steve and Lyla didn't seem to think that was a good idea as they passed them and continued down a nearby alley. The ground shook as eight large, mechanical machines rolled by. The machines were box-like, with wide treads, and an intimidating large gun.

"Bendin, who let *tanks* on the cycle's floor?" Harmon mumbled.

Bendin turned around from the wall he was studying in time to see a couple of the tanks at the end of the line skid to a halt and begin to turn on their wheel treads towards them. He heard Harmon gasp as she swiftly put her hands over her mouth. He hastily turned around and pressed his hands up against the wall. He felt quickly, but carefully, searching for something.

The tanks fired simultaneously, and the shells broke through the front and rear windows spraying glass everywhere. The building directly behind theirs exploded rocks, chunks, and dust into the air. Bendin saw Harmon cringe out of the corner of his eye as they sped towards them inside the building. Bendin heaved a sigh of relief as he found what he was looking for. There was a brick that was slightly a different shade of grey which he pounded on with his fist.

The two tanks crashed through the front of the building and Harmon screamed.

The wall next to Bendin slid open with a thud. He grabbed Harmon by the elbow and yanked her into the revealed pathway. The wall slid and sealed shut as a loud crushing noise and explosion sounded on the other side of the wall.

The wall shook, but it held. There was an odd clicking noise, and light from outside the room filtered in through holes in the ceiling.

"You got lucky, Harmon," Bendin mused pulling small pieces of glass out of his arm and shaking any remaining pieces from his clothes. He reached out his arm to help Harmon, but she pulled back impulsively.

She stood in shock for a second, then flared, her blue

eyes sparkling viciously, "We almost died! None of the other cycles have ever been this violent! It's always been 'fix this' or 'cause this to go away', 'heal this man', 'which path should we take', 'a pit not to fall in'. This, this is insanity!"

Bendin grabbed her arm and pulled her a few paces down the passage, "I'm guessing they want us to be ready for the occasional skirmish that happens every now and then. It's happened before you know--"

"How'd you know about this passage?" Harmon fumed pulling her arm back and folding her arms across her chest.

"This? Actually, Ladak told me about this kind of passage about fifty cycles ago." Bendin tapped the floor with his pole and the walls vibrated and shook.

"Really?"

"I know. Ladak likes to see the students succeed," Bendin shrugged as they moved further along, "I wonder if these cycles are harder than what it's like outside."

"Not likely. Unless you were here like a thousand years ago."

"I'm not referring to that. That was full scale. I'm talking about the small skirmishes that we are going to be expected to face in the line of duty, protecting the kingdom in the name of Odge."

"But tanks can't be common!"

"I've seen this cycle at least four times. Granted, though, this one is a little crazier."

Harmon brushed the glass from her pants and shirt. "Do you think there's something outside that they're not telling us?"

Bendin thought for a few seconds. "Harmon that is an interesting question. I don't know."

The walls shook again as another explosion went off outside the walls.

"Where does this end?" Harmon asked.

"I don't know. Let's find out," Bendin replied.

After walking what seemed like forever, not to mention twists and turns, they came to a door.

Bendin pushed it open without hesitation. Inside was a circular room that seemed to have no ceiling. Chains hung in the middle of the room and lined the walls, and there was a pile of broken furniture piled up near the far wall. A behemoth of a man with a helmet and rippling muscles walked into the light from behind the huge pile of furniture. He was laden with axes, a drawn pistol, and a collection of knives. Bendin instinctively threw his pole at the man with such dizzying accuracy that it collided with the man's pistol and knocked it out of his hands. The man impressively threw his axe at Bendin, and there was a sharp crack as the axe lodged in Bendin's helmet. The force of the collision slammed Bendin's head into the wall, and he collapsed onto the floor unconscious.

Bendin was jostled awake as a piece of furniture ricocheted off the wall and bumped him in the head. He opened his eyes as Harmon grabbed chain after chain and she slung them around the man. There were knives and axes sticking out of the wall behind Harmon. How had she not been hit?

Bendin's vision swam for a second as he got up and held the wall to steady himself. Crazy temple cycles. It was common enough that if a person didn't survive the tests and classes it was just as well, no real loss lamented, because people were not expected to fail once they were out of the temples.

"Harmon! Here!" Bendin grabbed the chains nearest him and helped Harmon by throwing them around the other direction around the man. Harmon used her tool and welded the chains instantly around the man so he could not move.

When the man saw this, he relaxed and gave up.

"Stop," He grunted. "Cycle over. You've defeated me. The secret word is Paraxalope."

Harmon cut him free with the welder, and he pointed down the passage to the left of three entering into the room.

"We could have just run down this corridor and skipped this entirely?" Harmon panted, pointing down it.

"Yes and no," the man said staring up at the endless space above them. "That way heads straight back to the classroom." He turned to them and whispered, "If you had gone the other way there was a trap of boiling water that opens up, and I have the button that controls the way back to the classroom so that if you had just ran down it instead of facing me it would shift over and lead you back to a more dangerous part of the cycle arena.

Bendin waited patiently, as he already knew this. They reported back to class, worn but satisfied. They gave the word to their teacher, who awarded them high marks, and dismissed them from class.

Before splitting in the hall, Bendin held Harmon's shoulders for a second. "Thanks, Harmon. You really were brilliant back there."

Harmon couldn't hide her approval, a slight hint of pink crept onto her face. She fiddled with the device in her hands, "They let me keep it. You're the one that really deserves the credit; thank you for saving me."

She stole a kiss on his cheek and took off running in the other direction.

Bendin rubbed his cheek in surprise.

"Always so cute, aren't you, Bendin? Too bad you're too weak to link."

It was Radu. He had a cut above his eye and his clothes looked as though he'd been through a bombing run. His pants were torn, his body was bruised in several areas, shoes dusty, and his fists were clenched so tight there was no color left. "You didn't have to face demolitions." Radu took several steps toward him. "And you didn't have to see your partner get blown up!"

"There was no way for me to know," Bendin said taking a couple of steps backwards. "You know there are multiple endings to every cycle."

Radu was in his face now. "But, you didn't have to fight the toughest! You've always had it easy. You always cheat your way through the teachers, classes, and everything!"

Bendin felt strong hands fasten to him from behind, and he realized too late that it was one of Radu's friends. Radu grabbed Bendin and threw him against the hall wall, who hit it like a rag doll thrown down the stairs. The pain from the previous knockout surged through Bendin's head and he groaned. Bendin tried to push out mentally and physically, but before he could do anything or even say anything else, Radu kicked him in the head.

It went dark.

Bendin woke in Health Systems. Steve and Lyla's silhouettes loomed over him. When they moved back and the light illuminated their faces, Bendin saw the tears in their eyes.

"Guys, I'm not made of glass. It's okay," Bendin said rubbing his eyes with his hands and feeling the lump that was on his head where Radu had kicked him. "The people here are really good."

"But we found you lying on the floor," Steve exclaimed. "We thought you were dead."

"It was just Radu." Bendin frowned, sat up on the little bed, and scanned the area. Health Systems had the capabilities of holding many people. The stays for people were notoriously short, either you recovered quickly or you died quickly. There was no one that retained a stay for very long. At least anyone that Bendin knew. It was extremely efficient. The room itself was the same grey color with the same red tapestries. The only difference was this room was bigger, had many large columns holding up the ceiling which was too high to be seen, and there were a million different machines scattered throughout the room measuring various types of things and displaying various solutions and suggestions for the doctors.

"Where's Tyler? He should be here, right?" Bendin said pivoting his legs off the bed and throwing the blankets back. He noticed a few other students getting fixed up, repaired, or carted out.

"They sent him to dinner," Steve said.

"Oh, good. Then I'll be able to talk to him. Aren't you guys supposed to be at dinner?" Bendin stared down at his watch. "It's half past! We're late, and I'm starving!"

Bendin ran out of the room.

Steve and Lyla didn't move; they watched each other and burst out laughing.

A hungry Bendin had left his shoes.

Bendin grabbed dinner of steak and cabbage and searched the Feed Hall for Tyler. There were a lot of people, so it was sometimes rather difficult to locate a person if they didn't sit with their group. He walked up and down several rows, and he found most of the DOOD group sitting in one area. He sat next to Harmon, who looked up at him rather curiously.

"It's okay if I sit here, right?" Bendin asked with his eyebrows raised.

"Sure." As Bendin sat down, Harmon burst out laughing. "Where are your shoes?"

Bendin froze, blushed, and felt hands push him down onto the bench. Bendin's shoes plopped down on the table in front of him, and he quickly turned around in time to see Steve leave the Feed Hall with a huge grin on his face. Bendin's face was smug and he pointed at his shoes and said, "There."

Harmon laughed again as Bendin put on his shoes.

"Have you seen Tyler?"

"No, I haven't. He was in health systems last I knew." Harmon took a bite of her cabbage.

"He wasn't there." Bendin felt slightly agitated and asked the others nearby if they had seen Tyler.

"No," they responded. But Shari, sitting a table behind

Bendin, heard him.

Shari leaned him back and pulled him to her on the bench behind him with a firm but kind grasp. She whispered in his ear, "Tyler isn't here. He went to his room. I saw him on my way to Cycles. He seemed really tired, and he said the Health Systems recommended an early dinner and sleep."

"Thanks, Shari. I'll check there after dinner," Bendin said with a sigh of relief.

Shari gave him a sly grin and pushed him back over to the other bench sliding her hand down Bendin's back before letting him go.

Bendin was startled for a moment before he dived into dinner. Harmon monitored Bendin's reactions, and she must have been satisfied with Bendin's response to Shari because Harmon didn't say anything. Bendin thought it would be strange to listen in on his groups' conversation if you were not part of the DOOD.

"Did you see the trenches under the third building to the left?"

"No, I didn't, but the octagonal machine by the pincer's cabinet nearly killed us!"

"Yeah? That's nothing compared to the tanks almost crushing us in the alley on the third street!"

"I can't believe they would stick a translucent spike right in the center of the square!"

"How'd you get by it?"

"You could see just the bottom of it, it's the little shadow that gives it away."

Bendin thought how great it was to be a part of the DOOD.

Radu caught Bendin's attention with gleaming eyes. Bendin mouth the word, "What?"

Radu pointed at Bendin, pointed at his open palm, curled his other hand into a fist, and punched it into his palm.

Bendin shook his head. It didn't matter, tomorrow things would be different. He could feel it. He cleared his plate and left the Feed Hall.

Bendin felt as though someone had punched him in the gut the second he entered his quarters. The top bunk was shattered and the bottom bunk smashed. There were streaks on the walls in which someone had written something, but Bendin didn't understand the writing. There was some sort of amber gooey mess on the floor that he'd never seen before but was probably from one of the broken crystal displays, as Tyler's desk was sideways. Bendin's desk stood stalwart and untouched in the wake of the whirlwind that had blown through the room. Tyler must have had some killer nightmares. Bendin felt sick as he discovered an arm on the floor near the desk, with a watch on it. Bendin's watch and the watch on the floor beeped at the same time, and Bendin flinched remembering frightfully of Tyler's and his synchronized watches. Bendin could hear something. He nervously looked for the source of the sound. It sounded like sobbing and it didn't sound like it was coming from anywhere inside the room.

Bendin followed the sound into the quarters next to him and discovered a girl sobbing in the corner. Bendin went up to the small girl, and she jerked her head up in surprise.

"Hi, I'm Bendin. Who are you?"

The girl slowed her sobs and managed to say, "I'm Carly, from Agricultural Industries."

"Are you okay?"

"No," Carly squeaked out.

"What are you doing over in the Defense of Odge department's living quarters?"

"I came to see Tyler--" Carly broke into a fresh wave of sobs when she mentioned Tyler's name.

"Okay." Bendin felt sorry for Tyler, he had a follower and he didn't even know it. Bendin knelt down and sat next to her against the wall. Her markings revealed she was in her first year in the upper temple. "Did something happen while you were here?"

"Yes."

"Will you tell me what happened?"

Carly winced, but stopped sobbing, "Yes, or at least mostly what I could hear. Everything was already happening when I got here. I came over here because I saw Tyler heading this way. I thought since no one would be here that it would be a great time for me to introduce myself to him."

Bendin nodded.

"But, when I got over here, something was wrong. There were angry shouts and screaming coming out of the room, it sounded like things were being thrown and smashed. I was so scared I didn't go in."

"Could you tell what they were saying?"

"Someone wanted him, but he didn't want to go. I don't know why, but after all the noise it went quiet.

"Okay. What happened then?"

"I peeked out of here and saw four or five people come out of the room carrying bodies and go down the hallway." Carly peered up at him, tears glistening in her eyes. "One of the ones they carried away was Tyler. I didn't even get to know him!"

"How long ago did this happen?"

"Only like a minute ago. You just missed it."

Bendin let the air out of his body slowly as she finished.

"I'll go talk to some people to get this cleaned up and straightened out. I'm sure it will be alright."

"But you don't understand! When he wouldn't go, they killed him. He's dead. You can't bring back the dead."

Bendin wondered why Tyler would resist. "What were the people wearing that came out of the room?"

"They had on the regular Vaelift Uniforms."

"Was there anything else on the uniforms? Markings or colors?

"A couple had gold tassels. Angels, right?" Carly thought for a minute concentrating.

"Yes, those were some Vaelift Angels. Was there anything else?"

"Um, two others had blue embossed marks on the shoulders."

"Then it was definitely some Vaelift Elect. Thank you, Carly, please head back to Agricultural Incustries. I'll take care of this, and let me know if you see Tyler anywhere."

"Okay, Bendin, but he's dead. Berdin, he's gone."

Bendin successfully sought out Commander Zist in the most common place he'd be found, the control center. There were more monitors and gadgets in that room than one could count, and no one had ever determined the actual amount either. The room was wide and richly lavish with red carpet, fancy desks, and tables. More than that though, it was full of other officers and officials.

Bendin gave his formal announcement and request for time. Commander Zist led Bendin to a small, adjacent conference room which gave them privacy.

"Commander, I thought you'd like to know that Tyler is missing. Any idea what's going on?"

"Who?"

"Sorry. TU2."

Commander Zist pushed his skin on his face around like he was scrubbing away some dust, "I authorized the destruction of TU2. I sent three men in, and they took care of him."

"He's dead?" Bendin felt torn apart and miserable inside. Bendin let it sink in, and he didn't like the way it felt: Tyler wasn't just dead, he was destroyed.

"Yes, he is. There is something else you need to know, BD3, TU2 went criminal."

Bendin cringed. First death, and then something else?

"He broke codes 1, 2, and 3."

Bendin felt very clammy and cold. "Impossible. TU2 wouldn't have done that." Breaking codes 1-3 was inexcusable. They were simply not to defame the name of Odge, unequivocally support the leader of the Vaelift, and always give praise to Odge.

"See for yourself. Unfortunately, for him, this was one of many infringements." Commander Zist punched up a video on the monitor next to them. Bendin could see very clearly Tyler in the passage leading to the DOOD quarters cursing at the top of his lungs the name of Odge, cursing Findall, and praising a being called Pikuk. Pikuk was the spiritual adversary of Odge.

Bendin couldn't believe one of his best friends in the world was dead and had been breaking the fundamental codes that had been put in place by Odge since the beginning.

"Don't worry about it. We took care of him. I wanted to show you this as a warning for you and your fellow students. I look forward to the picking tomorrow. I have matters to attend, BD3. You are free to go." Commander Zist winked at Bendin as he walked away.

Bendin tried to sort things over in his mind as he trudged sadly back to his quarters. It was strange and odd to think that Tyler was so suddenly gone. He hadn't remembered Tyler being criminal. Very strange. Ahead in the hallway Bendin saw something that forced him to set aside the Tyler incident. There was a glowing blue light floating above the ground and he'd never seen anything like it before. The beautiful cobalt aura-emitting glowing ball bobbed up and down like it was trying to get his attention. Bendin nodded his head in the affirmative, and it moved off in a direction that Bendin had never gone.

It went up.

The walls of most of the halls were close enough that most students could shimmy up the sides by placing their hands on one wall and your feet on the other, and then with simple exertion they could climb the walls, if they were tall enough. Bendin had never thought of doing that himself, but he had never had a need till now. He was just tal enough to span the distance with sufficient force.

He followed the light up fo‑ about fifteen meters and he noticed the light in the hallway that was below him failed to reach this area. His hands were covered in dust and the wall turned from smooth into a mess of uneven engraved markings. He followed the bubble of blue light into an opening in the wall.

"Finally, someone actually follows my bubble. I've been trying for hours now," a voice said from the shadows. It was completely dark up in the small chamber except for the floating glowing blue ball, which cast a faint aura across the room. A huge man stepped into the light over a small grate; he was tall, dark-skinned, broad, and his hand gripped some sort of holstered weapon. "I haven't much time. The security in these places is extremely tight." He paused for a second then continued, "I'm Franklin. I serve the leader of the group of Alcs, Osmond Charles III. I need your help."

Bendin stared at him absolutely lost.

"I know you're confused, Let me explain. There is a war going on and we are trying to recruit as many people as we can. You could be on the inside, or with us on the outside."

Bendin shuffled his feet and folded his arms.

"We have better training than the temples for combat and intelligence. Our weapons are better than even the famous coveted Vaelift staffs. Here, I brought one with me." Franklin removed his weapon and handed it to Bendin.

Bendin took it, cautiously watching Franklin out of the corner of his eye, and held the cylinder shaped object in his hands.

"Push the button in the handle," Franklin instructed.

Bendin pushed the button, and with a loud crack the weapon activated. Rods extended to form a lightweight, strong pole that felt very impressive. Berdin swung it around and found it to be light and comfortable.

"It's satisfactory," Bendin conceded. He clicked the button again, which closed the weapon down, and handed it back.

"We have the best engineers in the world and are making rapid progress that has never been allowed outside the temple system. We want to share it with everyone."

"Even better than the Vaelift?"

"So much better it makes the Vaelift staff look like a

child's toy."

"What would I need to do?"

"You only need to join our cause immediately and help us."

"If I go, the Vaelift would kill me, not to mention Odge."

Franklin chuckled softly and responded carefully, "I am well aware of your situation and I promise you freedom and perfect safety from both. We can leave right now!"

Bendin hesitated. He wasn't sure what to do exactly. Embrace this man's offer? The weapons, technology, and training sounded appealing, but for Bendin, the promise of the picking was tomorrow.

"I'm going to have to say no, Franklin. I'm going to stay, the picking is tomorrow and I don't want to miss it. You had better leave quickly, security kills all intruders from the outside."

"I'm sorry to hear you say that. I'm not going anywhere without what I came for."

Before Bendin could even breathe, Franklin grabbed Bendin, flipped him around, and pulled Bendin's arms up behind his back.

"Let me go!" Bendin struggled, but it was useless against Franklin's superior strength.

"You are coming with me whether you like it or not."

Bendin felt the truth of his words creep into his heart and spread like frostbite. He was going to be captured. A thought came to him, and he thought he might have a chance. He said words that he had been taught for years, "Franklin, I'm warning you. I'm going to call on Odge, and I don't know what he is going to do to you."

Franklin pulled Bendin backwards past the grate and said mockingly, "Odge doesn't exist. I have nothing to fear from him."

Bendin shouted clearly, "Odge, help me!"

Instantly there was a slurping sound and an amber gooey substance shot up from a grate in the floor. It flowed up and covered Franklin's legs and Bendin's body. Franklin released Bendin's hands in a frantic attempt to brush the liquid off.

"What is this?" Franklin yelled.

This action only increased the amount of substance forming around him. The substance then quickly, and without warning, turned into a solid form of yellowish concrete. Franklin's arms and lower body froze solid.

"Impossible. I will break it!" Franklin struggled against the prison holding him.

The leftover substance flowed back down into the drain leaving Bendin miraculously dry as a bone. There was a jarring shake, and the roof of the room moved downward threateningly. Bendin watched a moment as Franklin struggled again and failed to break free of the concreted substance. Bendin leaped out of the room, narrowly escaping being crushed, as the ceiling slammed into Franklin, shattered the substance, and slammed into the floor.

Bendin panted. He was barely able to hold his weight horizontally between the two walls, but hold it he did. He told himself to relax and breathed deeply. Finally he felt his heart rate slowly decelerating. This didn't stop Franklin's daunting words from haunting him though: "Odge doesn't exist, I have nothing to fear from him." Bendin sighed. He found someone believing this to be very disturbing.

There were crashes down the full length of the upper section of the hall, and Bendin realized there must have been more spaces like the one the man had been in. He felt gratitude for being preserved by the power of Odge. Odge had saved him, and Bendin knew it. He carefully made his way back down to the floor and ran back to his quarters.

Chapter 3
The Picking

When Bendin entered his quarters, he was out of breath. The room was immaculate; all indication of the earlier tussle was gone.

"Hi, Bendin."

Bendin turned around to find himself face to face with Lyla Shovek, rolling a large case behind her.

"Oh, no. You can't be serious." Bendin realized with sudden dread. Unwanted fear flooded through Bendin.

"Yep! Isn't it great? I get to move in with you!" Lyla hugged Bendin in glee and slid him aside so she could roll her case to the corner.

"What happened to Steve?"

Lyla's eyes expressed sadness. "They moved him into my old room."

"So, no exemplar duties?"

"Nope. I got off early."

"I'm sleeping on the lower bunk. You can have the upper, and this is the desk I'm using." Bendin gestured, eager for her to know which things were not hers.

"Sure thing. Why weren't you at Infology class?" Lyla began unpacking her things.

"Some things came up and this room was all of sudden in need of a place to be filled," Bendin said gloomily.

"I was wondering why they pulled me out of class a little early to move me over here. What happened to Tyler?"

"I'm not ready to talk about it." Bendin sighed tiredly and said sarcastically, "You unpack, make yourself at home, and do whatever it is that you do to be comfortable. I'm going to meditate."

Bendin left and went to the frog pond. He needed to think and rest his mind. On the way, Bendin passed Ladak, who was humming and painting the walls with grey paint.

"Hi, Ladak." Bendin waved as he passed by.

"Bendin, you look like you could use some company," Ladak said and spun his paintbrush around professionally.

"Well . . . "

"I just finished a round of putty and paint. I've got some time."

"Sure, come along then. I'm just on my way to the frog pond." Bendin thought that having Ladak along might help him unclog his thoughts.

The frog pond was nice and the tiny frogs seemed almost delighted to see them.

"Nice pond, huh?" Bendin noted picking up a frog in his hands and showing it to the head janitor.

"Sure. Want to know something else? There are much bigger ponds filled to the brim with more creatures than you can imagine outside the temple." Ladak smiled knowingly.

"Is it really true that it would distract us so much that we can't go out to see them?"

Ladak knelt down and whispered in Bendin's ear, "Let me tell you a secret. It's because there is a great war going on. It's being led by the creature of the underworld himself."

Bendin nodded slowly. "You know what else, Ladak? Let me tell you a secret. Tyler praised Pikuk earlier today." Bendin turned in fear as if mentioning the name would summon Mr. anti-Odge himself.

Ladak clasped his hands warmly together. "I'm surprised it took him that long to choke. I noticed he was beginning to struggle with it weeks ago."

"Ladak, I'm concerned about what happened to Tyler. What could have caused him to defame the name of Odge so suddenly?"

"Pikuk has great power. Power enough to overcome students who let their guard down, especially Tyler. Tyler, as he told me, made a deal with him. That's why I'm not surprised about him defaming the name of Odge."

Bendin listened to him with eagerness. It must have shown because Ladak laughed in a deep, warm sounding way.

Ladak continued, "I've got your interest, my fine young man. He said that he had made a deal with him to help him get to the top of the list used in the picking."

"It didn't help him apparently." Sadly, Bendin placed the little frog back in the pond.

"No, he was betrayed by Pikuk who overcame him when he was ill and caused him to break the fundamental codes of Odge," Ladak explained further.

"Thank you, Ladak, for making me feel really secure," Bendin said sarcastically.

"Don't worry about it. *You* are no Tyler Thurber. Unlike him, you are going to be a true Vaelift." Ladak got up to leave.

"No, wait."

"Yes?"

"I met a man today. He said he was from the outside and was fighting in that war you were talking about."

Ladak moved back in the blink of an eye. His speech came out very precise, quick, and accurate. "Who was he? Who was he working for? What happened?"

Bendin took a deep breath. Both of them knew people like that weren't allowed inside the temple.

"He only said his name was Franklin, and that he worked for some guy named Osmond."

"Osmond," Ladak spoke softly. He brushed his hair with his fingers. "He's Pikuk's third in command. He runs his own group, the Alcs. Thank you for telling me this. Did you tell Commander Zist or Findall yet?"

"Not yet. Franklin was crushed, so I didn't think it was immediately urgent."

"Don't worry about it. I'll go take care of everything and tell Commander Zist about the intrusion. Thank you again for telling me this." Ladak got up again to move away.

"It was incredible. When I called out for Odge, amber gooey sticky stuff shot out of the floor and caught Franklin. It didn't catch me for some reason."

"Miraculous." Ladak's eyes shone with pride and mystery. "You are learning well. Odge truly has infinite power. His power comes to the aid of those who call for it."

Bendin pointed at Ladak, "Thank you, Ladak. Good luck with Commander Zist."

Ladak responded with a smile and pointed his fingers back at Bendin. "Good luck in the picking tomorrow. May you be one of Odge's Vaelift, I know it's what you've been hoping for. You better get to your room for your nightly worship exercises so you can be strong in the power of Odge for tomorrow."

"Bye, Ladak. Thanks for your advice."

Bendin departed and went back to his quarters.

For the third time this day, he didn't recognize his room when he entered it. It was entirely redecorated. The floors had pink rugs strewn all over, the upper bunk was pink with pink pillows and blankets, the walls were draped in pink, and pink towels were neatly stacked on the pink cloth covering her desk. Bendin rubbed his eyes and leaned back into the hallway to check if it really was his room. It was. Lyla was sitting in her bed wearing the innermost layers of her uniform, all in Pink. He thought his eyes and brain were about to explode.

"What's with all the *pink*? And you're not fully in uniform?" Bendin demanded.

"I like it, and I made sure that this," she pointed at her thin layer, "is allowed in the dress code."

"For quarters only," Bendin said with sudden realization.

"Yes, for quarters only," Lyla said prissily, "I'm *in* my quarters!"

Bendin quickly thought of something else that might win her over to wearing more than the very base of the quarters dress code. "That isn't the way to worship Odge. You are supposed to do it in proper attire." Bendin went to the space behind his desk where his only red rug was neatly laid, and he sat down in a cross-legged position.

"I will get to that when I get to that. Don't be a sour-flower." Lyla stuck out her tongue at Bendin.

Bendin only grunted unhappily and began his nightly worship practice.

It consisted of simple rote prayers and recitations, hand motions, and saying "praise Odge" about thirteen and a half times.

Lyla jumped off of her bunk, slid into her outer clothes, grabbed one of her pink rugs, and threw it down next to Bendin.

"Meditating here," Bendin muttered to her.

"It isn't just *your* room. I want to do it here as well."

Bendin grumbled unpleasantly.

Lyla watched Bendin do part of the circular hand motions for a few seconds.

"No, you're doing it wrong," Lyla commented, and she moved in and grabbed his hands.

"You need to do it more like this. Your circles are not completely circular." She moved his hands in a smaller but more circular arc. Bendin could feel his anger swelling and his blood boiling. He thought it was the stupidest thing he'd ever heard.

"Thanks, okay; but," Bendin pulled his hands away from her surprisingly firm grip, "I need a little breathing space."

Bendin moved his rug about a foot further down the wall towards the beds.

Lyla moved her rug a bit closer to Bendin but didn't interfere further with his meditations and prayers.

Bendin knew he needed to be ready for the picking

tomorrow, as tomorrow was a different day. Normally it was a day of worship only, with all day celebrations, worship ceremonies, some live video of the world around them, and all separated by three great meals. The celebration tomorrow was similar to the end of the year when everyone received recognition for another year completed. They congratulated and gave well wishes to those moving out.

Bendin finished his nightly worship and sat at his desk. He thought about pulling up ADA, but he checked a few things manually instead. It was better that way because it was less disturbing for Lyla who was still doing her chanting, motions, and ritual behind him on her rug.

He checked his standing in the class. He was still leading, but his absence from his last class didn't help him out too much. Radu was the only other contender for the top spot. At that, Bendin was a little surprised, considering that Radu was three or four under earlier in the week. Cycles class must have boosted Radu up, as well as the infology class. Thankfully there was a make up option for infology and Bendin was glad that infology wasn't one of his weaker areas. He spent the rest of the evening catching up on the science in regards to Odge and protecting his name in the kingdom.

Lyla woke Bendin by shaking him. Her nose was pressed up against his nose, and she was lying on the bed, wearing the minimal accepted clothes for quarters.

"Time to get up, sleepy head." She vigorously shook him again.

"Get out of my face," Bendin muttered sleepily. He rolled off the bed, nudging her away. He gazed at his watch. It revealed there was still thirty minutes till rising time.

"We still have time to sleep, why are you waking me up this early?"

"To do extra worship of Odge, of course!" Lyla smiled at him and made circular motions with her fingers.

"No." Bendin felt sick. He jumped back in bed and buried his face into his soft pillows.

Bendin heard Lyla dress fully, sit at her desk, and start to speak with ADA. She did so, loudly. That's all Bendin could hear. It made it impossible for him to sleep, so he grudgingly got up.

Bendin pulled on his uniform wishing there wasn't a curfew for the mornings and sat at his desk pondering the day. It was the day of the picking, and in a few minutes when the day started, it would be time.

Lyla crossed her arms and watched Bendin. Bendin smiled. Lyla's body posture fidgeted for a moment and relaxed. "Good luck today, Bendin."

"Thank you. Why are you so imposing on me?"

Lyla turned her head for a second before returning her eyes to Bendin's view. "I was just trying to help you."

A chime sounded from the desks.

"You are helping me," Bendin assured her, "Just, help me that way, less." They both shut their desks down and joined the throng of students going to the Worship Hall.

The Worship Hall was enormous. It was exceedingly wide and was certainly the largest room that Bendin knew about in the whole temple. You couldn't make out people who were on the other side of the room unless you had the aid of a monocular or binoculars. The sound system was good though, being wired and projected in such a way that all could hear. There was a stage, a podium, lots of seats to watch, two main aisles leading up to the front, a throne for the Queen, a place for Findall, for the high command, for Zist and his lower in command, and a place for the representatives from the other temples, at least one from each. There were six other upper temples dedicated to various different opportunities that they, as students, had to pick from initially.

Bendin couldn't contain his excitement, he was jumpy and his legs twitched. He found his seat about in the middle of everything. Most of the DOOD group were there right with him in the intensity and anticipation. Even with the horrible morning with Lyla, Bendin could hardly contain his energy.

The meeting started out with a choir singing in tumultuous praise, glorifying Odge in the light and glory of his infinite and almighty self. The crowd roared with thunderous applause when they were finished with the opening song. Findall rose and spoke the two famous starting words to any of the major meetings that they had in the worship hall.

"Praise Odge!"

Two large fireworks went off, bursting in the darkness of the upper ceiling and raining down the particles over the choir as torches lit up on either side of the podium.

"We are here," Findall proclaimed his staff waving in the air, "to worship Odge!"

The roar of the crowd surprisingly got louder. Two more large torches were lit next to the podium, lights lit all across the stage, and spotlights were shined down from the rear.

Findall's staff lit up in a brilliantly bright light, and the end of it shifted into a gavel shape with which he pounded on the podium. It gave off a loud, metallic, crystalline sound. The effect of this was instant silence from the crowd.

The words of the holy language were spoken. No one understood any of it, so most students simply referred to it as the unknown language for that reason. The doctrines that were taught in school were taught in their language, but the language of worship was of the holy language. So holy, only the Vaelift leader could read it and only Odge would be able to understand it.

In between statements, the crowd shouted cries of delight. Bolts of light shot across the ceiling as Findall finished the final words.

Smoke rolled out of grates that were on the stage. The choir, with the assistance of a band, rocked out next. Everyone rose up, threw their arms up, and sat down. Everyone repeated this about a dozen times till the song was over. Queen Vlasta rose elegantly from her throne and walked over to the podium.

The Queen's strong voice echoed throughout the entire room, "My students, I'm glad to bring you the hard work and dedication of our students who have moved on in the past few years. These are the things you hope to achieve in your lives. Please congratulate them for their fine accomplishments by making your own."

The roar of applause was such that she had to wait before she continued. "Your time is now. Your time is all you have to give. You are doing the greatest service you can, by serving yourself, and serving our great kingdom. Here are the works of those before you and the most recent works of those of the past five years."

A video flashed up on monitors all over the room, large ones up front and semi-large ones in the back. Bendin could even see smaller screens up front below the stage. The video displayed the outside world to which the students were going to be engaged in working after the temple graduations. There were grand ornate buildings, large arenas, labs and scientists, animals of all shapes and sizes, trees as tall as the temples themselves, and Bendin's favorite part was the section that showed the Vaelift in action with their staffs and their defense of Odge being proclaimed from the streets. The video was much longer this year than last year. The last parts of the video showed bits from the Queen's Hall and the students in other temples working very hard.

Bendin had to plug his ears because the students were so loud in their approval. They all wanted to be, in their hopes and dreams, a part of that big picture.

Queen Vlasta thanked them and sat down leaving the space for Findall to fill.

"It's time for the annual picking of the various ranks of the Vaelift."

This was it. Bendin smiled at Steve sitting next to him. Steve placed a hand on Bendin's shoulder and returned the smile.

"For the position of Odge's Vaelift rank, we call upon RC2 to please come forward."

In front of the entire group, Radu rose and crept up to the stage. He seemed as surprised as Bendin felt. Bendin then knew that Radu hadn't expected to get picked either which caused indignation to boil inside Bendin.

All the students in the DOOD groups' faces were turned towards Bendin and then to Radu.

"What's going on? This can't be right!" Bendin hissed to Steve.

Steve shrugged. "I don't know. This is my first one. Everyone said you were going to be the pick this year."

Findall shook Radu's hand and Findall placed his hands on Radu's shoulders and said, "By the power of Odge, be ye Vaelift!" Findall shoved Radu hard with his palms. Sparks flew out from all around Findall and the force threw Radu to the ground. Findall held out an Odge's Vaelift's rank blue and black ribbed staff. Radu picked himself off the ground and accepted his staff. He grinned and presented it to the crowd who cheered for him. Fireworks went off near the ceiling again, but for Bendin, fireworks were not just going off in the room, they were going off in his head.

Steve pulled him close, "Wait. Why?"

Bendin looked at Steve with tears welling up in his eyes, "I don't know, Steve. I don't know!" Bendin clenched his fists. Bendin wasn't just sad. He was jealous and angry that of all people, it was Radu who was picked.

Findall spoke again, "For the Elect, we will have acting positions this year in the temple. These need not get up, but are being noted for the sake of the records and that fellow students will know. These are BD3, LY365, DU87, and TP132. Thank you."

Findall spun his staff around which flared a fantastic bright blue, and with a flash he was gone. Radu beamed and did exactly the same thing, and with a flash, he was gone.

Bendin was devastated.

The Elect never wielded the cool blue-ribbed staffs or righteous responsibilities of defending the glorious name of Odge. They were more like glorified students with nothing more than guard duties.

The rest of the meeting went in a blur, and the rest of his classes melted together. Before he knew it, it was time for bed. Bendin mundanely went through his exercises and fell into a very rough sleep.

"See, Bendin? I told you, you were doing it all wrong! You should have listened to me." Lyla's words ran through his ears painfully as he woke up. She was next to his face again exactly like the day before.

"Lyla, please get off me!" Bendin complained.

Lyla sighed, frowned, and pouted. She sadly got off his bed and slowly put on her uniform.

"You are going to need to work with me eventually. Running away from me isn't going to be effective forever. It's not likely that they are ever going to let you be Odge's Vaelift unless you link with someone!" She plopped herself at her desk and ran through her morning preparation. She whispered, "I'm just trying to help you."

Bendin sighed irritably and rolled out of his bed. "That's not one of the requirements. It's just one of the cultural things that happens in the temple." Bendin was slightly afraid that she might be right, and it was really starting to bug him.

Lyla said nothing further and continued on with her morning exercises.

He pleaded with Odge from his usual cross-legged position with his morning repetitions, but he did so with a hope in his heart that things would turn out all right.

ADA was predictably annoying, and breakfast would have been eaten in silence if it weren't for Harmon. Harmon had taken to sitting next to him when she could and engaging conversation about some of the details of Odge and his principles or rules. This brought a smile to his face and warmth to the depressing start to his day.

He went to report to Findall's head of Elect, Mylin Samsove. Mylin was a beautiful woman with large green eyes and long flowing brown hair. The only thing that Bendin heard spoken about her was that she had linked with pretty much every single person she connected with during her years in the temples. She was the most active linker Bendin had ever heard of. Well, at least had been till her appointment to the head of the Elect last year. She wore the Elect Vaelift style uniform, and presented Bendin with the blue crested replacements that went on his shoulders. They also changed his class standing from his former position as a Vaelift in training.

"Congratulations BD3. You've been promoted into the ranks of the Vaelift Elect, with the duty of watching over your department while you finish your classes for the year. After graduation, you will then report back here to receive your new assignments."

"Thank you, Mylin. I will do that," Bendin said unenthusiastically.

Mylin reached down, as she was taller than Bendin, and touched his forehead. "BD3, I know personally that you were among the top picks for Odge's Vaelift, but do not be discouraged at this. Sometimes they override the 'one a year' rule and move a person up to the rank of Odge's Vaelift. Seriously, cut the depression. Cheer up . . and . . . you'll need this." Mylin handed Bendin a holster and a regular Elect issue firearm.

Bendin belted it on and prepared to go to class. As Bendin was leaving, Mylin pulled on his hand and whispered in his ear, "I'm available anytime if you want to engage in your one-time linking with me, my good sir."

Bendin recoiled from her hand, "Sorry Mylin, I'm not ready for anything like that, but thanks for the offer."

Mylin flipped her smooth hair, crossed her arms in displeasure, and turned back to her work. Bendin felt that he couldn't get out of that office fast enough. Once he was out of sight, he ran.

On the way to class, still grumbling to himself and moving swiftly, Bendin ran into recently promoted Radu Landus with two of his close friends. He was beaming now that he had the new authority given to him by Findall Quin. Bendin looked at him with pure envy and hatred which he felt was justified.

"Check out my new staff!" Radu twirled around the Vaelift staff and held it out so that Bendin could see it closer. It was slightly longer than Radu was tall, blue, and it was ribbed along the entire shaft so that each piece fit expertly into the next.

Bendin had never seen one this close before. There were many intricate variances along the shaft that gave Bendin the impression of supreme craftsmanship and comfort. He absent mindedly reached out to touch it but Radu defensively smacked Bendin's hand with the staff.

Bendin shouted in pain and swiftly leapt forward. He may not have been Odge's Vaelift, but he certainly reacted with the speed of one. Bendin shoved Radu to the ground, and Radu hit the floor with a smack. Radu's friends intervened roughly and pinned Bendin's arms from behind. Finding himself unable to move, Bendin suddenly feared the worst. Radu's face filled with a wicked smile as he flared up his Vaelift staff which gave off a flash of vibrant blue light and swung it as hard as he could at Bendin's shoulders. The swing connected, and Bendin's body landed hard on the ground. He held his freshly bruised shoulder with one hand, winced in pain, and used his other hand to push himself up.

Prof. Goldbarm strode around the corner.

"What's going on here?" He demanded.

"We were performing the ritual of the 17th day of Odge," Radu said quickly.

"You do not perform that on fellow students, RC2! Come with me. Findall needs you immediately."

Harmon walked around the corner and gasped when she saw Bendin getting up from the floor.

Prof. Goldbarm caught her attention and said swiftly, "Harmon, get him to Heath Systems."

Harmon nodded.

"Right, come with me, RC2."

Radu flashed Bendin a boyish smile as Prof. Goldbarm turned away and nudged Bendin in the ribs with his staff again. He then quickly followed Prof. Goldbarm down the hall.

"Bendin, what happened to you?" Harmon asked in such concern that she dropped her things carelessly.

"Radu was sharing his new toy with me. It felt wonderful." Bendin grimaced and reached down to help her pick up her things.

She stopped him. "Bendin, you need to go. Please let me help you."

"No, it's nothing."

Harmon pleaded, "Come now, Bendin, you know that's not true." Harmon pointed in the direction of Health Systems, but Bendin shook his head forcefully.

"No, I absolutely need to follow Radu so I can talk to Findall. I need to know from him why I wasn't picked. Can you please help me?"

"Anything. What is it?"

"I need you to tell Prof. Colloon in our next class I've gone to talk to Findall and will be there shortly."

"Okay," Harmon said nervously, 'but only because you are talking to Findall." Harmon nudged Bendin playfully on the shoulder he wasn't holding with his hand. "You know almost anything else results in cleaning the disposal units." Harmon stuck out her tongue and continued, "Anything else?"

Bendin admired her for a few seconds and said, "No, but . . . thanks for your help."

Harmon turned to go to class, and Bendin followed in Radu's wake.

It took a few minutes to find which direction Radu had gone, but after a while, Bendin noticed a trail of divots and dents in the wall that looked like someone has hit the wall with a pole. Bendin also noticed that in some spots, the divots and dents cracked the wall and stripped off the paint. In the gaps he could see shapes on the wall he'd never seen before. Bendin decided that those were what he had felt with his hands when he was up on the wall yesterday.

Bendin heard them before he saw them, and as he peeked around the corner, he saw Radu and Findall talking to each other. Bendin approached quietly from behind, and they didn't see him. They were talking seriously and walking down the corridor at a very slow pace.

A few steps closer and Bendin could make out some of it. "They've become increasingly stronger over the years. Some even say they're within the walls of the temples themselves." Findall was so focused on Radu he didn't hear or see Bendin walking closer to them.

"You think they've affected the students? Do you suspect some of the students are involved themselves?"

"Let us hope they are not. You must be the one to--"

A student came around the corner up ahead, and Bendin clenched his fist in frustration.

"Till then Master Findall," Radu said loud enough for the student to hear. Radu ran down the hall ahead of him.

"Don't forget, RC2," Master Findall called after him and spun his staff around so he could vanish away. Bendin managed to come up behind him and catch Findal 's staff in his hands and stop the spin. Bendin felt an electrical shock whip through his body, he was thrown backwards against the wall, and he crashed to the ground.

"What is this, BD3?" Master Findall harshly said, pulling Bendin off the ground. "You should know what kind of consequences happen to those wh--"

"Forgive my intrusion, Master, I only need to know why I wasn't picked!" Bendin cut in brushing himself off and marveling at the power he had felt.

Findall Quin sighed and irritably pushed Bendin's hand away like swatting a fly.

"You were one of the foremost ones to be picked, if not the first, but you didn't make the cut. You were not then, you are not now, and you never will be faithful enough, BD3. Now, I have other things that surely need attended to. Do not interfere with anything which you are not responsible for. Goodbye." Findall spun his staff and vanished in glittering sparks. Bendin felt Findall's words sink into him like a thousand rounds of bullet fire had been blasted into his body.

"He said I wasn't faithful enough," Bendin told Harmon, who was sitting in front of Bendin later during class. "I just don't believe that. I've done more in that area than anyone else I know. I never miss a prayer, a praise, I follow the rules of Odge, the principles, and I certainly haven't broken any of the codes."

Harmon was trying to pay attention to the teacher, who was rambling about the great wars of the past and the perfection created when Odge placed the Vaelift in charge.

Harmon turned around and said quickly, "Bendin, you're the most devoted person I know. There must have been another reason they didn't pick you."

"What?" Bendin pleaded.

"I don't know. I'm not you. I'll chat with you after class if you'd like. We really need to be paying attention. It's kind of important," She whispered harshly.

"Findall was right," Lyla chimed in quietly from behind them. "Your forms are sloppy and inconsistent. Not to mention you won't link with anyone ever."

Harmon's attention with the teacher was completely broken. "Ever?"

Bendin wanted to hide.

Lyla grinned. She knew she had executed a perfect humiliation. "Ever."

Harmon whispered harshly to Lyla, "Don't be mean to

Bendin. He's had a very rough day. You should be doing all you can to help him, not hurt him!"

Bendin beamed at Harmon as Lyla's grin of triumph turned to a shameful nod. Harmon smiled at Bendin before turning back to the teacher.

In addition to his regular studies, he was assigned to guard a set of halls and watch for suspicious activities. The word had gotten around that Bendin had discovered an intruder yesterday, and everyone was to be on the lookout. Bendin passed Lyla on one of his rounds who didn't see him, and he watched her till she rounded a corner.

"Why don't you just link with her and get on with it?" a voice said loudly in his ear.

Bendin jumped around yelping in surprise.

Ladak's voice had appeared out of nowhere.

"Whoa . . . you scared me." Bendin leaned on the wall in relief.

Ladak grinned and smiled at Bendin. He was holding a large mop. "It's the simple solution to your problem."

Bendin sighed. "I'm afraid of wasting it, Ladak. It's something so precious that I don't want to do it if it's not going to last."

"It is no different here for anyone else. I know you'll enjoy it and there are reason's this is the way it is. It'd help your studies, your concentration, help you relax, and most of all Lyla will be off your shoulders."

Bendin felt very irritated. "Ladak, there is a time when I will do it. I'm just not ready yet."

"Whatever you want. I'm just saying it would be best. Please think about it, okay?"

"I will. I got to get back to my duty. I'm a little behind tonight now that I've talked with you."

"Of course." Ladak waved as Bendin ran to catch up on his route.

Bendin moved back along his assigned route. Internally he was fuming. He felt like at any moment he was going to snap like a twig. Maybe he just needed to take a break and sit in his quarters for a while. He sent a message through a student that was near for his next class and went back to his quarters. He lied saying he needed health systems. Anything to get him away from Lyla and the other students for a few minutes. He was happy to see that Lyla was gone when he arrived. Bendin plumped himself down in his desk chair and grumbled to himself.

The day wasn't at all like he had imagined it. He had certainly imagined something far greater than being mere patrol for the department. He was worth more and he'd dreamed from the minute he had learned of Odge's beautiful plan for the order and structure of their kingdom eight years ago, that he was going to hold the highest and noblest of all the ranks. It was to be one of Odge's Vaelift. That was supposed to be today. *He* was supposed to be the one holding the blue staff and working with Master Findall. Not *Radu*! Thinking of Radu's wicked grin and the bruise on his shoulder, Lyla's annoying prodding and poking, and Master Findall's horrid crushing blow telling him he was not a faithful student to Odge flooded him with a force of grief so strong and overwhelming that he angrily slammed his hands down in a large clenched fist on his desk.

The desk responded to his fist with a loud crack. The center piece of the desk split down the middle revealing a space hidden inside the desk. Bendin, surprised, looked closer and saw a small notebook inside with writing on the front that read, "The quest for". Under this phrase there were several titles on the cover, listed vertically with every title crossed out except for the title at the bottom of the list. Bendin could read them all, so he started with the ones that were crossed out: "Interpretation, Understanding, Translation, and Vaelift." The word that was currently uncrossed out simply read, "Vanish". He flipped through the notebook and discovered that almost the entire book was full of writing, divided up into many different entries.

The first entry read, "It is 203yrs since the Great War and the triumph of the Vaelift, My name is Harvar and I am a student here at the upper temple. I've only been here two years, but I've been interested in the characters on the walls here in the building. I am going to write down all the characters, so that someone who comes after me may begin to make sense of them. They are written in a language I do not understand nor any of the other students here. I don't want to alert the teachers to my interest as they eliminate anyone who does." Harvar then listed off about thirty to forty characters. Bendin realized it was going to take longer than a class period to read the book so he put it back in the desk. Over the next week, with any alone time he had or that he created himself, he studied the words of the book.

The next entry said, "It is year 324. My name is Gilespie. I've discovered this notebook here in the desk. I am also curious about all the characters on the walls." Gilespie then wrote several sentences of what he thought the characters could mean.

Bendin had thought about it while doing his rounds. He thought that the characters they were talking about and writing about might be what he felt on the wall that other night. He quickly flipped through the initial entries, "370, Shawna; 594, Bowen; 600, Carl; 765, Myrando." All of them had entries, and all of them left their thoughts and work on the meanings of the characters and what they could be interpreted as. By the next entry though, they seemed to have figured out the characters. "It is 799, my name is Shaine. I have discovered some unique characters that I thought represented the Alcs of old. My understanding has changed and I've realized that this information may not be entirely correct. My only guess now at this point is that these specific characters represent the word 'Vaelift.'" Bendin felt his heart beat more intensely. He then checked her sketch of the characters and they were shapes, brackets, parallel lines, slants, and strokes that make up several letters. The characters on the walls Bendin had felt the other day were not etched in, but carved around the symbols as to make them stand out.

The next few entries began to be more interesting, and they began to take up several pages each. "1024, Clyden; 1121, Janice; 1202, Hawer; 1221, Astrid.' Clyden had finished the work on phonetics, while Janice and Hawer had recorded as many of the temple inscriptions as they could. Astrid finished writing down the inscriptions and had begun work on the translation. The next group of entries seemed dedicated to finishing Astrid's work: "1459, Jean; 1508, Campa; 1645, Pica." They each had written theories on what the inscriptions were describing, and they determined that it was a short history on the rise of the Vaelift. They noted that the current duties of the Vaelift that were described in the temple seemed to be accurate to the duties they had interpreted. There was a particular set of inscriptions that had caught Pica's interest and they dealt with something that she called the "Vaelift vanish". When Bendin read this phrase, he felt a deep sense of curiosity spring through him. Pica continued, "This is something they do, (I've seen master Yuant do it all the time when he spins his blue staff) but they don't teach us it in the temple. There seems to be a very detailed description on how this is to be done!" Pica must have graduated because her entry stopped. The next began, "It is 1689. My name is Hana. I've managed to finish Pica's work. The process seems to be to hold out your hands, fingers facing out, and rotate them in a clockwise fashion and shove hard outward saying the word, "vanish". I've tried it several times and several different ways, but it doesn't seem to work. I'm good friends with Sintiancus, the current leader of the Vaelift. I won't tell him about this notebook, but I will ask him what he thinks about the inscriptions on the walls."

"It is 1708. My name is Jenny." Bendin frowned. Something had happened to Hana as her entry had just abruptly stopped. He continued reading, "I didn't even notice that there were characters and inscriptions on the walls till I found this book. It turns out after checking myself, they have been painted and are kept painted. My only guess is that we are not allowed to know about the inscriptions. There are some unpainted sections though, and they are found in the south just past the control center to the right, then left, then right. There is some sort of inscription there not listed by anyone here, maybe I'm the first to know about it? I've tried the process and it hasn't worked. I wonder if I'm doing something wrong?"

Bendin would have to go there and check as soon as he had some time. He had never been to the place described. There were only a few entries left. "1719, Pearlendowe; 1720, Tora;" These only repeated the process noting that there might be something missing, but they couldn't find anything else to help them with it. The unknown inscriptions in that section of the temple were not any characters or sentences that were found in the book and the process seemed to be perfectly translated. The next guy called himself Peap said that maybe it needed to be done in the location mentioned earlier. He tried and noted that it didn't work. The last entry in the book was, "It is 1789. My name is Zyndale. I'm honored to find such a record in this place. I've also tried the process and have failed. I'm wondering if one might gain help from Odge, because I can't find any other thing that has revealed the correct procedure for this process. I'm not worthy to ask him as I am not as obedient as I ought to be."

Bendin finally finished reading the quaint notebook, sat back, and thought for a minute about all the information he had read. He felt a strange connection to them, like they were guiding him. It was like they all wanted him to succeed where they all had failed. And if he learned this vanishing power, he could finally have an edge on Radu. It was true that no one at the school taught them that ability. Bendin had always assumed you had to have the Vaelift staff to do it, but maybe there was another way. He grabbed the pencil that was sitting in the space inside the desk and wrote, "It is 1809. My name is Bendin. I seek this power and will try this and let you know what happens." Bendin closed the notebook and put it back in the desk. He opened the bottom drawer of the desk and pulled out some instant wood glue. He had always believed this glue was used for repairing the legs of the desk. He chuckled to himself as he glued the middle panel of the desk together and placed it back in its position in the center of the desk. Now he knew why the glue was there, and he had no idea how old the glue was.

Bendin felt empowered for the first time since the disappointments of the previous week.

Even Lyla's bantering, when she arrived in the quarters a few minutes later, didn't bother him as he now had a quest.

Chapter 4
Process of Vanish

Bendin woke up but didn't open his eyes or move a muscle. If this was like all the previous mornings, Lyla would be there on him. She was. He could tell that she didn't know he was awake yet so Bendin swiftly landed a kiss right on Lyla's cheek. Lyla tumbled backwards in surprise letting out a somber sound of shock; she rolled haphazardly off the bed into a crumpled heap on the floor.

"Hey . . ." Lyla managed to say before she moved over to one of her pink rugs and sat down.

Bendin considered the pink rugs covering almost the entire floor on her side of the room for a second before he asked, "How did you get them to give you all those anyway?"

"It's all in how you ask."

"It's usually not that simple," Bendin mumbled.

"It is for the girls."

"Oh." That definitely made sense. He couldn't count the amount of times they got special privillages. Bendin downloaded his schedule. He noted the vast amount of time he'd be patrolling and knew exactly when he'd be heading off on his quest. Right after breakfast looked the best because the morning patrol started him near the control center. Bendin was so excited that he couldn't help but smile at everyone, even Radu, at breakfast.

Breakfast, of pure wheat pancakes and orange juice to wash it down, seemed to be the most popular choice from the students when it came to breakfast. Bendin found Harmon and sat next to her. She looked tired. Harmon whispered to him, "I think they are going to move me."

"What? No. Why? You are doing a great job here. Why would they move you so early? Are you one hundred percent sure?"

Harmon smiled a little. He could tell she obviously remembered him saying that before. "Not that sure. But, that's just it. They think I'm doing so well they want me to move to a better science lab and improve my theories. They mentioned I might be expanding into other possible researching as well."

"And how do you feel about this?" Bendin took bites of his breakfast between his statements.

"I'm okay with the idea, but I was just getting used to this place and," Harmon grabbed his arm, "I really like the people here."

Bendin smiled at her. "Yeah, me too."

Harmon grinned back at him, "Can I at least spend some time that isn't in class with you today?"

"Yeah, you can meet me during my break at the frog pond in the middle of the day." He'd have just enough time to find the place this morning, finish up his route, and meet up at the frog pound.

"Sure." Harmon grinned excitedly and smiled nonstop for the rest of the meal.

Bendin felt a sense of peace knowing he had made her day a bit happier and more hopeful.

After breakfast, Bendin searched for the hallway or section that was mentioned in the notebook. He went past the control center and down the hallways, taking the turns that were mentioned. The halls were exactly the same width and height as the ones in the other parts of the temple. The further he went, however, the more they looked less and less used. It was quite far away from the normal hustle and bustle, so it wasn't surprising that it didn't look as clean. The section described in the book turned out to be a dusty, unlit hallway. The hallway intersected perpendicularly to another hallway at the end. The only light in the hallway came from the two other halls it intersected. It was indeed unpainted. Bendin slid his hands over the characters that were inscribed in the walls in awe. He wondered what was so important that they had all been painted except for here and why no one has ever mentioned it before. He then came across and instantly recognized the characters that had been recorded in the notebook as "unknown". They comprised a space of the wall about four meters high and four meters wide. From what Bendin could tell, the hallway was probably about thirty meters long. He listened and checked for anyone around; there wasn't anyone. He stood in front of the unknown characters and went through the process described in the notebook. He held out his hands, fingers facing out, rotated them in a clockwise fashion, and said shoving them hard outward, "Vanish."

Nothing happened.

Bendin tried it several more times, but nothing happened. He didn't know exactly what to expect, but he had been hoping for something. Anything. The whole hall stood there unfazed, secret, and he felt a bit cheated after putting so much effort in the research and attempt. Disappointed, he went back to his duties making his rounds.

As he was almost toward the end of his scheduled rounds, Bendin saw another glowing, floating, blue bubble. It was in one of the back halls of an outermost section of the living quarters in the DOOD. He drew his pistol and followed the blue light into one of the rooms. There was another one of the strange men inside. Strange because this wasn't common. This man was burly, shirtless, wore thick black pants, and carried a large broadsword. Bendin wondered why, in a world of guns, would you carry a broadsword. Bendin felt much more confident this time around because he had a gun.

"How did you get inside? Why are you carrying only a sword?" Bendin asked pointing his gun at the man.

The man doused the light by flicking something small and mechanical in his hand at it and spoke pleadingly in a deep voice, "Please, put your gun down. I mean you no harm." The man dropped his sword on the ground and held his hands up.

"Your temples are not impenetrable and we have some powerful contacts inside. I'm here to offer you freedom."

"Freedom from what?"

"From the queen."

"She loves us and has always protected us. Especially from people like you." Bendin wondered if that was true for everyone.

"It's an illusion. You are slaves. I offer you freedom."

"You have no proof."

"I do." The man pulled a device out of his pocket and a laser projected hologram appeared. The hologram displayed rows and rows of people working on machines. "See? Slaves, all of them and these are some of your recent graduates. See the clothing?"

"No." Bendin was done listening. "Please accompany me to the control center or I will be forced to shoot you." Bendin motioned with his pistol towards the door.

The man rapidly pocketed his projector and clicked a button on the mechanical device in his other hand. His sword lept to his hand and tripled in width so that it functioned as both a sword and a shield.

"Just as you have decided not to come with me, I will not come with you."

Bendin watched as the man tilted his sword down briefly

for a moment and a shot fired from the end of the sword. The bullet hit the wall above Bendin's head no more than an inch away. Bendin cleverly shot the man in the only exposed area of the man's body, his feet. The floor thudded as the large man fell, and while lying on the ground, he titled his sword towards Bendin again.

Bendin downed the man before he could fire another shot.

Not wasting another moment, Bendin went straight to Zist and reported the incident.

Zist looked very pleased. "Fine work, BD3. You have done a great service to the temple. I'll personally see to it so that a recommendation for promotion is immediately sent to Master Findall."

"Really?" Bendin said. He was surprised that something could be obtained so easily when it had seemed that he wasn't even close to his life's dream. Bendin's hope bubbled within him like water just before coming to a boil.

"I'm absolutely sure he'll be pleased to make an exception and offer you a position as one of Odge's Vaelift." Zist, however, frowned as he finished. "We are going to have to clean out the edges of the school. Two incidents in two weeks. We might have a rat, because this hasn't happened in years. Please be on the alert, BD3; Go tend to your regular duties. You are dismissed." Zist went over to several of the monitors and associates of the temple and barked commands of areas that needed to be searched immediately for possible breaches in security.

Bendin ran to the frog pond, because the recent event had kept him later than he planned. Harmon was already there playing with the frogs.

"I'm surprised you are still here," Bendin said as he sat down next to her.

"I thought you might have been held up or something. Besides, I was enjoying myself anyway."

Harmon handed a frog to Bendin. "Kind of neat, aren't they?"

"I think so." Bendin accepted the frog and watched Harmon for a minute before explaining.

"I ran into another intruder this morning."

"You did? Everyone was saying how you had ran into one before. I can't believe it! What's with you finding these people?"

"I have no idea. He was just there. I shot him though, right through the heart."

"You shot him?!" Harmon frowned. "At least he won't be going back to report to his leader on the workings of Odge."

Bendin frowned back. "He offered me freedom, but I've heard enough. I can't have them messing with my head. How's the science coming?"

Harmon hesitated and said, "I've managed to come up with some tests to prove not only the existence of Odge, but to prove how unlimited his power truly is."

"That sounds impossible," Bendin said unbelievingly. He scooped up a frog.

"That's what everyone has said. The only people interested in the tests so far have been Findall and some of the janitors. Those janitors are strange sometimes, aren't they?"

Bendin laughed. That they were.

"So what's one of your new 'tests'?"

"Well, one of them is getting a sure response from Odge. From the classes and books they have given us to read and the ones stored in the data sections of the school limiters, I've narrowed it down to a question you can ask. The way you ask it is the key to getting the answer from Odge."

"Isn't that just the prayers that we do?" Bendin responded, confused at her statement.

Harmon studied him seriously for a second and whispered to him, "I don't know what you get when you do your prayers, but I have never received so much as an *inkling* that Odge is communicating with me."

Bendin was startled for a minute and considered what she might not be doing right. Then he thought about his own prayers and recitations. Now that he thought of it, he hadn't really had an "inkling", as she called it, that Odge was communicating with him through the prayers. "What does that mean? I thought that the actions in our lives dictate the truth about Odge."

"It simply means that prayers are not a good way of classifying the power of Odge. If you are going to use those external incidents as prayers working, then I think you need a new system. This is what my tests are going to prove."

"Wow. That sounds brave, but isn't that against the codes and rules of Odge?" Bendin asked cautiously.

"There isn't anything in my tests that is against the current codes or rules. The only thing that it does is reinforce the greatness and glory of Odge and promote real communication with him."

Bendin beamed at her. "That's ingenious! So, what is this test in particular? Maybe I can try it."

Harmon slid her feet around nervously and explained, "You only need think of something you want to know, then ask under these circumstances: you really want to know, you're willing to act, and you believe Odge will tell you."

"That's it?" Bendin said surprised.

"Yes."

"But it sounds so simple. Does it work?"

"I don't know. I haven't tried it, and I'll explain why in a second. It's just that it's not that simple. If any of those conditions are not met, then there is no guarantee that my experiment will work."

"Why?"

"That's what I've been able to determine from the Book of Odge."

"Still, even if that is the case, it sounds easy. Why haven't you done it?"

Harmon looked sad, "I've never had any good questions that meet those conditions. The only thing I've considered asking about was the prayer system itself, but I'm still not sure I really want to know the answer to that question. Even if I don't get to it this year, I plan on including it in next year's experiments for Odge."

"So your system is limited by what questions you are going to ask Odge?" Bendin grinned. "I'm sure you'll come up with really good questions, and I think I'll give it a try tonight after my normal recitations. We'll see how it works for me. I think I have a good question that I'm going to ask."

"What is that?" Harmon's eyes lit up.

"I think I'll ask him about the ability of the Vaelift to vanish."

Harmon thought about it for a minute. "That's a good specific question, and it sounds promising. I don't think I'll ever have that kind of rank or position to do the "vanish" ability. Bendin, if you do try it, please let me know what your results are."

"Thanks, and thank you for meeting with me today. I enjoyed it."

"Yes, I enjoyed it, too." Harmon smiled as Bendin left to attend to his next round of classes after lunch.

Cycles class was particularly hard as he was teamed up with Radu and two of his buddies. From the start Radu hit him with his staff. He repeatedly did this whenever he was close enough to Bendin or Bendin wasn't looking. When they were midway through the cycle, a large ball of fire sailed toward them. Radu knocked Bendin down, spun, and vanished. Bendin sprang in front of the other two of Radu's friends, blocking the blast. The blow was so severe Bendin recalled nothing till the end of the cycle when he woke up being carried by Radu's friends. They had done their best and had bandaged up Bendin. He was both surprised and grateful. After a trip to health systems, they helped him recover immediately without any lingering injuries.

Bendin made it a game to try to stay awake in his class with Prof. John Goldbarm, and he would reward himself with a surprise hug for Harmon if he managed to stay awake the whole time. Prof. Goldbarm seemed to be pleased with his extra attention. Today they were talking about how complex and important some of the recitations were.

"How important are they overall?" a red haired boy asked in the back of the room.

Prof. Goldbarm answered, "The prayer recitation symbolizes our respect for Odge. If we do it, he responds with answers of actions in our lives. This is according to the Book of Odge page 13 paragraph 4. All the students looked at the board up front which also had the ability to display the many records when called forth. Sure enough there it was, and it was almost word for word what the Prof. had said.

Harmon spoke up next to Bendin, "What about what it says on page 15 paragraph 9?" The screen shifted in response to her section and the words were displayed so all the students could read them. "Prayer is the way by which Vaelift communicate with Odge," Harmon continued, "How can it truly be communication if we have to look for actions in our lives? Shouldn't it be something more real? Say, person to person transfer of information, whether it be verbal or thought?"

Prof. Goldbarm frowned and said firmly, "Because on page 18 paragraph 19 it says, and I quote, 'Only the head of the Vaelift has the right to commune personally with Odge and obtain his will for the Vaelift.' So you see that Master Findall is the only one who can actually communicate and receive the will of Odge. Remember, class, you are Vaelift's in training, not the head of the Vaelift."

Harmon scowled and mumbled angrily under her breath,

"translation . . . Goldfarm . . ."

"Harmon, if you have further questions, please see me after class." Prof. Goldbarm didn't look happy about this recent exchange. He described for the class the road of preservation and the perfection of the rules, laws, and codes of Odge by which they lived and the power by which it was evidenced in their lives.

Harmon whispered to Bendin, "*I do* have a problem with it, because the passage seems very clear to me. Communication itself means the two-way exchange of words."

Bendin nodded and whispered back, "I hope you're right." He then listened to Prof. Goldbarm explain the beauty and clarity of the current practices and rituals. Bendin felt undecided on who to believe.

That night Bendin decided Harmon's experiment was within reason, no matter what Goldbarm said. He had told Lyla that he was going to do his ritual prayers later, then she had gone to bed without noticing he had not done them. He felt himself cheer inside for being so sly. Saying that he was doing his evening rituals was going to be his backup plan in case she woke up and caught him trying out Harmon's test.

He sat in his usual cross-legged sitting position throwing off his boots and socks, and he did his recitations and prayers. He confirmed that they weren't meant for voice communication, only outward signs of his commitment as the Professor had described. They really weren't supposed to expect anything from Odge, except some actions later during the course of their day: good breakfasts, high scores on tests, and a decent rank.

Bendin then worked out Harmon's test. He decided to rest his hands on his legs and speak softly so that if Odge was going to respond, he'd hear him. He planned to do it exactly as Harmon had described.

Bendin said, "Great, powerful, and Holy Odge, I really want to know how to do the Vaelift vanish. I'm willing to do whatever it takes to learn this ability, and I believe you." Bendin pleaded with his mind and listened with his heart. After a while, nothing happened. The only sound was that of Lyla's rhythmic breathing. Disappointed, Bendin let go of all of his pleading, hope, and desires realizing that there was no way Odge was going to respond just because he wanted him to. Who has the right to command Odge to do anything? No one did. He had just hoped so much that Harmon's intellect and observations about prayer would shed some light on this whole vanish thing. Bendin placed the palms of his hands together and flipped his middle fingers up and down for a while. He cleared his mind and thought of what was really important to him. He hoped Odge would answer him not just because he asked, but because that's what Odge wanted to do. Lyla's rhythmic breathing comforted him because Lyla sleeping was Bendin's favorite state for her to be in. He thought of the goodness of Odge in keeping him safe. He was quiet, thoughtful, and thankful. But, Bendin noticed something, breaking into the room, from the ceiling. It was a shaft of light which widened and brightened the room till there was a flash of light just above Bendin. Instantly, there was a bright man in front of him. His white light filled the room. Bendin nervously scooted backwards till the man smiled, shook his head, and motioned for Bendin to stop.

The man spoke and his voice was aged, strong, pleasant, and soft, "Bendin, I am Jameus. Your prayer has been heard, and I come now in answer, a servant from Odge. Stand, I have a gift for you." Bendin stood, and he felt beyond the reality of physical objects in the room that this person was not an imitation or imagination. The man placed his bare feet on Bendin's bare feet and said again, "Bendin, I have a gift for you." Bendin was about to ask, "What gift is that?", when Jameus took Bendin's hands in his. The words were spoken so softly that Bendin couldn't understand them. Before he knew it, the man finished, Bendin felt a deep throb in his feet for a second, and Jameus simply disappeared. The room grew dark again, and Bendin collapsed on the floor completely exhausted. He wanted to stare at the place where the light had disappeared, but he was so tired he fell sound asleep.

Bendin woke to the heavy shaking of Lyla. Lyla was wrestling with his body trying to get Bendin to wake up. She then resorted to banging Bendin's head against the wall with a soft "thump" echoing through the room with each thump.

"What is it Lyla? Wha . . . " Bendin said sleepily.

"*Bendin.* I've been trying to wake you up for fifteen minutes straight! What did you do, stay up *all* night?" Lyla screamed at him.

"You must be tired from shaking me that long," Bendin mumbled, his eyes sagging.

Lyla responded by pacing back and forth looking for something.

Bendin knew that staying up late was okay, and you

could curve or bend the rules if you stayed up almost all night. However, you were never allowed to stay up all night with no sleep. Those who did were severely punished.

"I did not stay up all night. I only attended to my prayer recitation and fell asleep. It was a long day," Bendin explained knowing that the statement was true.

Lyla was like a shook-up bottle of carbonated soda that had its cap still on. She stopped pacing, glanced at her pink rugs, picked some up, and threw them at Bendin. She threw one rug with every emphasized word.

"I was *worried* you might have *died*, don't *scare* me like that *Bendin!*" After she threw the fourth rug, she threw herself into her bed and pounded her head on her pillow multiple times. "I will not go through it again!"

"What, what happened?" Bendin felt more awake now.

Lyla pulled her head up and glared at Bendin. "In my first year I had a roommate fail to wake up. She died in her sleep. From the analysis it turned out the strenuous training the previous day wore her out so bad her body failed to recover. It was all my fault, because I pushed her too hard." Lyla burst into tears, grabbed another rug, and threw it at Bendin. "So don't you die on me too! I can't take it."

"It's okay, Lyla. I'm not dead, nor am I going to die. At least I hope not anyway." Bendin went to Lyla and gripped her by the shoulders for a second before pulling her around into a large, comfortable hug.

Lyla was so surprised that she stopped crying and hugged Bendin back almost as soft as Bendin's hug.

"I'm sorry about your roommate. I didn't know," Bendin said gently, pulling himself away from her.

She sniffed and nodded.

Bendin went back to his desk and sat down. He felt slightly weird. Was Lyla getting to him? He was fine overall, it was just different for some reason, like what had happened last night had effectively bore a hole into his soul or something. It was really hard to explain, but incredibly serious in the deepness of the experience. He put his schedule from ADA on his watch and went off to breakfast eager that he could tell Harmon about the exciting results of her test.

The Feed Hall was packed as usual, but Bendin could not find Harmon anywhere. Bendin ate and anxiously waited for her. With news this good, and her not appearing, he was almost trembling. He asked several of the students that he knew roomed with her or near her.

"Haven't seen her at all this morning, and she wasn't in the room last night either," her roommate said.

"We were beginning to get worried about her, but I think she was transferred," said a girl next to her.

"You think? Does anyone know?" Bendin asked sitting down next to them.

"I don't know. Isn't that what happened to your friend Tyler?"

"No. They destroyed Tyler for heresy." Bendin was surprised they hadn't heard about that. Most things travel at the speed of sound around the various groups and departments.

"No way!" They responded, "They didn't do anything like that for Harmon. Maybe you should go and ask Commander Zist?" The girls giggled, and Bendin responded with a flat expression. He would definitely be doing that.

He asked Ladak, but Ladak didn't know anything about it. Ladak asked about him about Lyla again as usual. Bendin shrugged and told him things were going well, but he needed to go talk to Commander Zist.

Bendin stepped into the control center and asked Commander Zist about Harmon.

"HG9 was taken by the intruders yesterday after dinner. See this here." Commander Zist tapped a screen next to him and it showed Harmon in a similar hall to that where Tyler had been. One of the men with the floating blue lights came into the scene, approached her, and spoke several words to her. She shook her head furiously and turned to run. The man swiftly knocked her out and dragged her away. Bendin felt very intense heat surge within him. It couldn't be true. Not *again*, not here, not now.

"We are doing everything in our power to bring her back, and I'd like to congratulate you myself, BD3 on your promotion to be 'Odge's Vaelift'." Commander Zist grinned broadly reached out a hand and shook Bendin's hand firmly.

"Thank you, Commander, but I don't know what you are talking about. When did this happen?"

"At my recommendation, of course. Once Findall heard of your heroic, loyal efforts, he jumped at the opportunity to have you on." Commander Zist continued, "He and I signed the exception forms and everything. It's happening later today with a small crew to initiate you. We were not going to wait for a ceremony like 'the picking' to announce you. It's a bit tight with security issues coming up. We will do it at dinner."

"Sounds great. I'll be sure to be there." Bendin walked out of the room elated but also confused. Things were just happening so fast. He was going to realize his dream! Where in the world did Harmon get taken by the intruders? He felt strangely conflicted.

A few minutes later, when he was in the middle of his route, he noticed Harmon's roommate again.

"Yes?" She asked when Bendin pulled her gently aside and turned her around to look at his face.

"When was the last time you saw Harmon?" Bendin pleaded.

"I saw her in class yesterday, and she stayed after to ask more questions to Prof. Goldbarm." She thought for a bit then said, "But I did see her later after dinner running down the halls."

"Running?" Bendin eyed her suspiciously.

"Yes. Running."

"Why?"

"Wait," she clapped her hands together, "she was running from the Elect."

"Elect?" Bendin asked, confused at the mention of his rank. "Like me?" Harmon wouldn't need to run from the Vaelift. Odd.

"Yes, people like you. They were dressed just like all of us, but some had the Angel's gold insignia's while the others were like you."

"Vaelift Elect and Vaelift Angels."

"Yes, they caught her and took her away. I thought maybe they were practicing routines."

Bendin's eyebrows furrowed knowingly. "Yeah. I can see that. Thank you for telling me this. Why didn't you tell me this before?"

"You didn't ask about yesterday, just about this morning. Oh, by the way, congratulations on your promotion." She smiled very broadly for Bendin.

"What?"

"On your promotion, *everyone* has been talking about it since it was announced after you left the Feed Hall. They said there hasn't been two called into Odge's Vaelift in sixty years! We are all so proud of you for defending the ways of Odge and taking down an intruder yourself. You get to realize your dream!" She gave Bendin a huge hug and a kiss on the cheek. She whispered in his ear, "Harmon will be so proud of you."

~ 63 ~

"Y-y-y-yes. Okay, I need to go," Bendin stuttered, surprised at the high level of sudden displayed affection.

She waved goodbye to him as he walked down the corridor.

Two seemingly different stories, one truth. Why was Harmon running? Did her roommate misinterpret Harmon's reactions? He was hinging on believing Harmon's roommate, but where was she? Was she with the intruders from the Alcs? Was she perhaps somewhere within the temple itself? Maybe she got transferred? Bendin didn't know what to think, and that was his most primary concern. It was too important to rely on guesswork. What could he do? An idea hit him that maybe he didn't have to trust any source if he went for *the* source of information on one side of the equation. It would be risky, but he would know the truth. What about if he got caught? He'd never be allowed to get into Odge's Vaelift, and to risk giving up his dream sounded crazy. Bendin felt the words of Master Findall filter painfully through his mind, "You never will be faithful enough." He knew how honest Findall sounded then and realized that's truly how Findall felt about him. Bendin made the critical decision and the information about Harmon, he decided, was worth more to him than his life. He couldn't leave her in the hands of the Alcs, and if she was in the hands of the Vaelift, he would find her and personally ensure her safety.

He was going to attempt to lift information from the R-Limiter in the control center.

On the way to the control center, Bendin saw another floating blue light down a side corridor. He didn't have time to mess with the intruder, and he hoped it could be a useful distraction for the other Vaelift patrols. He had a much more important mission he was on now. As he approached the control room, he noticed that Commander Zist was not there and that the room was almost empty. He checked his watch and noticed that lunch for them had just begun. He thanked Odge in his mind as He crept into the control room staying low. He'd only have just enough time before they got back from lunch before they checked the recordings on the monitors. After this, he was going to be on his way to find Harmon whether she be in Alc or Vaelift hands.

The Limiters were kept in the back and access to the room was restricted to Findall, Zist, Odge's Vaelift, and the Elect. Now that Bendin was an Elect, he could simply walk back there. The scanner identified his markings and let him pass. When you opened any Limiter it would expand and rise revealing helixes of information that could be spun and rotated, read or retrieved, input or deleted. Bendin found his way to the fairly large R-Limiter and quickly activated its helixes. This one was special, however, because instead of a single helix of information it had a double helix of information that could be perused and read. It was faster and stored four to five times the amount of the other Limiters. Bendin found Harmon's record and to his delight discovered that she had indeed been transferred. It said that she had been moved to the Engineering Association. It was an upper temple located 4,023 kilometers away. Her exact position read, "3,035 Kilometers Rail 785:On time Vaelift Systems." His only route to Engineering Association was the same as hers, the lightning-rail subway system. Hope spread through him as well as confirmation of his doubt in his leaders. Harmon's roommate had been right.

He'd done it, he'd found her. Zist had lied to him. Harmon was going to be working in a temple all the way across the country, not in some Alc organization's clutches. Bendin heard the sound of tromping feet at the entrance to the control center. Bendin quickly spun the data values and helixes down and powered down the unit to its normal operating level, but it was too late. Bendin watched disappointedly as Radu entered the room and saw him finish powering the unit down. Radu was flanked by Vaelift Angels that Bendin had never seen before. Bendin strode up to Radu bravely as there was now only one way out.

"We've got you now, Bendin. I've already seen you on the monitor, and the alarm has been sounded. Tsk, tsk, tsk. Unauthorized use of the Defense of Odge Department's R-Limiter." Radu had never looked so happy in his life. "I've waited so long for an excuse to kill you Bendin. Till now, I've never honorably been able to justify it. The glory of Odge, how it smiles on me--"

Bendin didn't wait for him to finish He was angry, and he didn't want to know what he was going to say anyway. He had to get out; he had to get to the subway system. Bendin rushed Radu so fast that Radu barely had time to raise his staff in warding off Bendin's whole body assault. Bendin's fist smashed into Radu's staff sending it crashing into a nearby shelf. Glass splintered, shattered, and rose like dust. The Vaelift Angels raced to grab their pistols, but Bendin was quicker. He stopped both of their arms, and using their own weight and the force of them moving their arms downward, he pulled them down over his body. Both Angels flopped into nearby limiters. Bendin picked up Radu's staff and whipped it around to knock out Radu. Radu slyly ducked the swing and moved around Bendin. Bendin attempted to swing again, but a shot rang out. A bullet erupted from the gun of one of the Angels on the floor, sunk into Radu's staff, flung the staff out of Bendin's grip, and rammed itself and the staff into the R-Limiter.

"Don't shoot, you'll hit me!" Radu yelled as he kicked one of the Angels and dove for his staff. Bendin hopped over Radu, and bolted out the door drawing his pistol. He heard Radu and his Angels scuffle in hot pursuit.

Bendin saw the effects of the alarm that Radu had sounded. There were, coming from all directions, Vaelift Elect and Vaelift Angels. All of them were coming for just one purpose, to capture or destroy him. It didn't look good. Bendin knew that capture meant death, and didn't wait for them to start taking easy shots at a motionless target. He took immediate action and shot an Elect that was the closest between him and the nearest possible hallway. The Elect spun around and fell holding his shoulder. Two Angels catching up to the Elect were shot in exactly the same manner. Bendin frowned and traveled down the hallway next to the control center at breakneck speed. Shots rang out from the Vaelift coming into the area behind Bendin. The bullets hit, tore, and punctured the walls in front of him. One bullet luckily managed to tear right through his pistol sending it flying. They definitely needed to work on their aim. Bendin sprinted past the unlit hall and rounded the corner to find a whole new group coming in from the other side. He realized that this wasn't as dead end of an area as he had originally thought. He then backtracked to the unlit hall as the others were starting to catch up from the control center direction. They rounded the hall at the far end and let out a fresh volley of pistol fire. Some of the bullets hit the Angels and Elect rounding the opposite end from them, who shouted in protest and alarm. Both parties at each ends of the hall charged towards Bendin.

Bendin twitched uncertainly and raced down the unlit, unpainted hall. He could hear running feet echoing down the unlit hall as well and realized that people were coming from the other side of the unlit hall too; they just hadn't made it around the corner yet. He was trapped.

Once halfway down the hall, he knew it was going to be futile. Defeated, Bendin sat down in front of the unknown characters and crossed his legs. At least he would die with the words of the twenty from the notebook in his mind. He thought of Harmon and was sad. As the sound grew louder, which shook the very walls as the Vaelift Elect and Angels drew closer, he held out his hands, fingers facing out, rotated them in a clockwise fashion, and shoved hard outward saying the word, "vanish."

This time, it was different.

With the sound of a sonic boom, the 4 by 4 meter section of wall filled with the unknown characters in front of him lit up in vibrant colors. Instantly he felt his whole body pulled, sucked, twisted and turned into what felt like being split into two pieces. Bendin watched the whole room blur as he was uncontrollably thrown forward and thrust into the patch of brilliant white light that had appeared in front of him.

Bendin vanished.

Chapter 5
The House Under the Falls

  Bendin felt his body go into the white light and was immediately thrust with great force with a sound as loud as a thunderclap across a dirt floor. The sound echoed and bounced off the walls. He discovered he was lying in a rounded rocky room next to a small pool of water. There was a fine layer of dusty grit on the rocky floor. Bendin looked behind him slowly with great curiosity. There was nothing behind him really, except a dirt covered wall a good distance away. He could just make out, faintly, inscriptions in the wall where the dirt had piled up. There was a long mark on the floor from the wall to where his body had stopped sliding. Where he was, he did not know. His body and head hurt, and his vision was hazy. He stood up and instantly fainted.

  Bendin opened his eyes and rubbed them trying fruitlessly to figure out how much time had passed. He tried to get up, but unfortunately he found himself unable to move. He listened intently and could hear a soft roaring off in the distance, a light, rushing, pleasant sound. He noticed in the pool were several sizes and colors of frogs. *Frogs.* Bendin painfully and slowly lifted his body into a sitting position and slid himself over to the pool. He had a hard time seeing it due to his vision going grey and blurry every now and then. Bendin, after a few more minutes of trying to regain his lost strength, worked his muscles till he could move his hands and toes more steadily. He put his hands in the water hoping the water would help. He thought he could faintly hear the sound of whispering, but he couldn't figure out what the whispers might be saying. Frustrated, he picked up one of the tiny frogs and a violent electric shock coursed through his body. Bendin's body seized up, he dropped the frog into the water, and toppled over into the shallow pool.

  A female's laughing voice echoed off the walls. The sound came from a short distance away behind a ridge on one of the ledges inside what Bendin was guessing might be a cave.

  "Why did you do that? You should know better than to grab the electric frogs. Who are you?" She crept over the ridge and sat on the ledge, watching Bendin from the distance. The slim, pear-shaped girl appeared as normal as any he'd ever seen with auburn colored hair pulled back in a simple style that he had never seen. She was wearing an overcoat, shorts, and boots, but he was a little too far away to tell anything else clearly.

Bendin struggled to lift himself off the ground, so instead, managed to roll his body over out of the pond and rest his chin on his fists.

"My name is Bendin." At least it wasn't a problem to talk. "I'm from the upper temple, Defense of Odge Department. Who are you?"

"My name is Rachel." She sounded confused.

"Is this a cave?" Bendin asked.

"Yes?" Rachel responded as if it was a really dumb question, "Of course this is a cave."

"Okay. Thanks. I've never actually seen one in person, only in pictures. If you will excuse me, something must have gone wrong. I need to go back." Bendin rolled his body, rather tediously, to the space on the wall where his body had been so violently thrown from. The markings were the similar, but some were different and really faded. Bendin pulled himself painfully into a sitting position, his vision being hit with flashes of grey. Bendin put a hand on his head.

"Are you okay?" Rachel called from across the room, apparently still extremely cautious.

"Yeah, I'll be fine." Bendin, determined to not be held back by this strange setback, worked through the process. He held out his hands, fingers facing out, rotated them in a clockwise fashion, and shoved hard outward saying the word, "vanish".

Nothing happened. Bendin tried again. Nothing. One more time, and yet, nothing. Bendin turned his head slowly around and saw Rachel staring at him.

"What are you trying to do?"

"I'm trying to get back to where I came from, but apparently it's not working," Bendin said throwing his fist out angrily as his energy faded from him. He slumped over on the floor unconscious.

Bendin woke to water being dripped on him by Rachel.

"Well, hello there." Rachel smiled but acted as if she had awoken a bomb about to explode because she swiftly drew a couple of paces back from him. "You're from Toalt, aren't you?"

Bendin rubbed his eyes, trying to get a grip on things. He testily raised himself up on his arms. He'd never heard of that before. "Not that I know of. I'm from the upper temple number one. It focuses on Defense of Odge, Aviation, Agriculture, and Health. The upper temples really don't have names. We just call them by number or department. Surely, you must have heard of them."

Rachel frowned and shook her head. "I've never heard of them. Are you okay? You act as though you're hurt."

"I am, or I was at least." Bendin raised his arms in the air. He found he could do so much easier than before. "How long have I been lying here?"

"I went and finished checking on the Mangolas, which is what I came here to do in the first place, and when I came back you were still here. It took about thirty minutes."

"You left me lying here?" Bendin said pointing at the ground. "You are so skittish. Why?"

Rachel shyly looked away then back firmly and shrugged, "I don't know you, and I don't know what you do. You could be deadly, crazy, delusional, or who knows what else . . ."

Bendin raised one eyebrow. "Of course. Sure, right. Okay. Uh, Mmmm. Do you live around here?"

Rachel laughed.

"What's so funny?"

"This is my home. Just a part of it really. My family has been here for many generations."

"Family?" Bendin's head hurt, but his strength was definitely back in his arms and legs.

"Yes, my family," Rachel flicked her medium length pony-tail to the other side of her head. "Are you an orphan or something?"

"I do not know what that is."

Bendin didn't know what to make of Rachel and she apparently didn't know what to make of him. Rachel said insultingly, "You sound ignorant. It's hard to believe that you are a Vaelift. What's it like being a Vaelift?"

Bendin rubbed his head with his hand and said nothing.

"Don't try to hide it. The outfit that you are wearing gives you away. It's an exact replica out of my history books from the days of the Vaelift, and you came right through that wall like the stories say. I saw you."

Bendin smiled. "I'm glad you know about the Vaelift! I am one. Well, one in training or I was till this happened."

Rachel eyed him curiously. "Yes, I know about the Vaelift. You ran this place till Zadok got involved and blew them all up."

Bendin shook his head in confusion. "That can't be right; where am I? When am I? I'm starting to get very confused." Bendin shuddered at the thought that he might have jumped ahead in years.

"The Coils, year 904, about halfway through."

Bendin wanted to cry. "904?! I'm from 1809!" Bendin blacked out again due to shock.

Bendin awoke again to Rachel dripping water on him again. "You keep passing out. Take it slow."

Bendin groaned. "Easy for you to say. I don't feel very well, and I can hardly see."

"Nobody has seen anything like this since the old days," Rachel said very excitedly.

"What do you mean? There were plenty of Vaelift around in 904."

"No, haven't you been listening to me? There haven't been any Vaelift like I just said a couple of minutes ago," Rachel reminded him.

Bendin's expression on his face was grim. "So, you're saying that somehow, I've jumped into a different time? A time without the Vaelift?" This was getting really weird incredibly too fast. "What am I going to be? Some hot topic? I'm just Elect. I'm not one of Odge's Vaelift. I think you and anyone else would be disappointed if they knew about me." Bendin, confused, tired, and sore, laid himself on the ground. He pressed his hands gently against his head trying to push some sense into it. Bendin was delighted to find the pain in his head had lessened a bit.

"What do you want to do? I can send you to Hymingway if you want, or I could get you something to eat or drink. It is almost dinner time," Rachel offered helpfully.

Bendin felt like it was only time for lunch, not dinner, as that's what it was going to be before he left. He was already in such a state of shock that he had become increasingly numb. "Let's try a little water and see how that holds, and," Bendin paused, "no one can know where I'm from. Promise me you won't tell anyone. I don't want to become some sort of freak from the future."

Rachel sadly paused, brushed her fingers through her hair, and scuffed her feet on the floor. She then very hesitantly said, "Yes." She melted into the darkness of the passage without another word.

Bendin sat up again and breathed in the air. The air was fresh and sweet, even in this "cave" as she had confirmed. He had a lot to think about.

Rachel returned in a few minutes with a glass of water. "Here."

"Thank you." Bendin drank, and he felt the cool refreshing water soak through his system. His body was able to move much better than it had since his arrival here.

"Feeling better? Have you decided what you would like to do? Are you going to stay here? Head to Hymingway?"

"I have no idea. Let me try this one more time before I make a decision."

Bendin sat cross-legged and went through the vanish procedure as he had done before. As he completed his motions and finished with the word, he waited. Nothing. Everything was still here, from the low murmur bouncing off the walls to the silent gaze of Rachel. Bendin was nervous because he felt an overpowering feeling that he was trapped. He didn't know what to do, and he was afraid for Harmon and what possibly could happen to her. She was out of reach, and it hurt.

Bendin watched Rachel for a few seconds, which made her fidget uncomfortably.

"Bendin, please, it's almost dinner time and Dad hates it when we are late, not to mention Mom."

"Dad's a friend of yours?"

"Yes, of course." Rachel frowned and motioned for Bendin to follow her.

Bendin thought he'd have no other choice but to go and meet Dad, and He was getting a little hungry. "Okay. Let's go see Dad. I think I can move better now."

"You're filthy and your clothes give away that you are a Vaelift. You'll have to change."

Rachel eyed him over. "Come on."

Bendin slowly followed Rachel out a small opening in the rock and down a tunnel. The walls were smooth, and the low rumble he heard got louder. They passed several passages crisscrossing and going in all sorts of various directions till the rumble became a soft low pounding sound. They came to the end of the tunnel after it banked to the right. It opened up into a beautiful room. He could see a few other openings that led in and out. The ceiling was very high, and there were trees and grass. The rumble was definitely coming from the ceiling. The room was quite long but not as wide. It had a lofty diagonal ceiling that seemed the most elevated above him and it tapered down over the room. *Trees.* Bendin had never seen real trees.

He limped down the rocky incline and around down to the grass and trees. He approached it cautiously and touched the closest one.

"It's not going to bite you. This one's not an aggressive tree," Rachel said coming up from behind him with a hint of humor in her tone of voice.

"I've never actually seen one before. I mean, I've read about them, but never seen them," Bendin said admiring and feeling the bark.

"You are so weird. Whoever raised you must have kept you indoors and completely sheltered." Rachel shook her head in disapproval. "We certainly don't stay inside all the time. We call this the meditation room." Rachel spread her arms out displaying the room to Bendin. "See? There are several spots where you can kneel, pray, or meditate."

The thought of being able to meditate and pray in an environment such as this made Bendin feel very serene. He sat and felt the grass with his fingers. He really liked this room. "What's the noise from?"

"Look, and you tell me," Rachel said pointing up.

Bendin took a closer look at the ceiling, it was made of glass, and he could see water flowing down on the wall in front of him.

"Waterfall?"

Rachel nodded. "The sound is dampened. Otherwise," she grinned, "you wouldn't be able to hear anything at all!"

Bendin gawked at the different plants, the small cobble walkways, and the soft white light coming from lamps scattered around the room.

"You're lucky the big upper light isn't on. It gets really warm in here when it is," Rachel said. She beckoned with her hands, and Bendin followed her.

"Here. You'll need a pair of boots and a red pill." Rachel dug through a pile of shoes and found Bendin a pair of boots. She said quickly and apologetically, "I'm sorry Bendin. We don't have an extra pair of bladed boots. George doesn't have any either, but he'll get some soon. I just can't believe they aren't here yet. You'll have to use these till we can find you something better. I'm really sorry about that, but we just gave all our extras to our cousins. We had so many!" She then handed Bendin a red pill from the dispenser. "Chew it up and swallow it. It preserves your muscle mass and counteracts most of the effects. You'll need another one in about a month. Trust me you'll feel it when it wears off." Rachel's expression became disgusted and she tossed the boots at his feet.

Bendin wondered what effects she was talking about, but went ahead and ate the pill. He swapped his soft boots for the boots that she had tossed.

Rachel grinned at him. "We'll 'borrow' some of the clothes George is using."

Rachel went through the blue-lit rounded archway. Bendin followed Rachel into a small rounded hall that had padding on the sides. It was large enough so three or four people could walk comfortably next to each other. Rachel then proceeded up a passage to the right, her ponytail floating in the air. Bendin felt his weight disappear entirely, and his body didn't turn to the right like her; it kept going.

"Bendin!" Rachel called down from where she was.

Bendin couldn't stop his forward momentum at all till he had hit a wall that had been scribbled all over. Rachel grabbed his uniform and pulled him back. She then did something odd. She stooped to the ground and rubbed away a thick layer of dirt off of the bottom of the boots.

"Sorry. Not surprisingly, someone didn't clean these. You'll get real grip now."

Bendin raised his eyebrow, tested out his boots, and he felt them clinging to the ground a bit. It was the only thing that had any force on him whatever.

"Why don't I feel my weight? What happened to gravity? This is so odd."

"This part of the house isn't affected by gravity. It's normal." Rachel frowned. "You're going to have to really work hard to adjust then, since you apparently aren't acquainted with the environment. You can team up with George because he's new at it too. Now, come on before someone hits the water you're trailing in the house, not to mention seeing you wearing those clothes."

Bendin looked at the water drops that were floating around him slowly moving with the air currents. Even after forty minutes, his outer garment hadn't dried off. In the temples it was extremely rare for you to get them wet so it was never a problem there. A small girl walked in from the way they had just come. She was the smallest person Bendin had ever seen.

"What is that?" Bendin asked, his mouth dropping open in complete surprise.

"I've been looking for you. Dad says it's time for dinner,"

the girl said. The voice was so small and high pitched that Bendin was further surprised.

"Yes. I know, Starley. This is Bend n."

"You're like a tiny human and you talk?" Bendin sputtered. "How on Odge's world are you so small?"

Starley was dark haired and brown eyed, and was wearing black shorts and a green shirt. She giggled, "I'm my normal size! *Bendin*, nice to meet you. Gotta go!" Bendin put a hand on his head as she flashed up the passage his vision swimming for a second.

"Wow, she usually is all over a new person. You better watch out later!"

"Right. I'll try to remember," Bendin responded.

Rachel, this time, followed Bendin up the way she had gone before. She kept laughing as Bendin tried to walk, because he couldn't do it without flopping nto the walls of the curved shaped passageway.

"I can't effectively use any part of my upper body!" Bendin noted irritably.

Rachel nodded knowingly. "Sorry, we haven't got extra cuffs and I'm not giving up mine."

Bendin could definitely tell she was talking humorously. He didn't know what to make of that

Rachel showed Bendin wristbands on her wrists a little bigger than his watch that he hadn't noticed before. Small vertical parts within the band itself glowed with a dull faint light when she moved her arms.

"So they propel you?"

"No. It's more of a resistance."

They went past several openings, made a couple of turns, and Bendin was as good as lost. Some of the passageways had windows, letting in some light, and Bendin thought it might be sunlight. He wanted to stop and see, but Rachel kept urging him forward.

"We're almost there, just around that corner up there," Rachel told him, gently pushing him along.

"I'm going to beat you to dinner!" Someone shouted from around the corner. Bendin's body was plcwed into by two boys sailing at top speed. They all rolled in a big ball and smashed into the wall in a heap.

"Ew. You got me filthy!" said one of the boys.

"You got me filthy!" said the other. "Cool!" The boy then proceeded to wipe the dirt that had gotten on him onto the other boy.

"Stop!" the boy said laughing and trying to frown.

They noticed Bendin and Rachel.

"Rachel? Who and what is this?" They said at the same time. They flashed grins at each other before looking back to Rachel.

"This is Bendin. He's going to be staying with us for the night at least. Bendin, these are two of my brothers Pete and Ryan," Rachel bent and whispered in his ear. "Be cautious around them. They are something else."

Bendin didn't know anything about staying a night, but since he couldn't think of anything else he could do he didn't complain or argue.

Ryan was wearing similar clothes to what Starley was wearing. He was shorter than his brother but older looking. His voice sounded like a humorous mix of high and low pitches. Pete was wearing similar but his colors were a darker shade of green. They both had dark hair and green eyes.

"What are you wearing? Some sort of historical Vaelift outfit? Are you part of a Vaelift festival or something?" Ryan asked.

"If so, that's a really accurate outfit," Pete said fingering the clothes. "Can I have it? Wow, this feels authentic. Did you steal it from a museum?"

"He looks like a museum," Ryan said mockingly. "Did you leave your staff at the museum?"

"I was going to change," Bendin explained as he stepped back out of Pete's grip. Bendin flipped into the curved wall again.

"George is still in his room. Maybe he can hook you up with something he's got. See you at dinner. Better hurry though, we're already late!" Pete said laughingly shoving his brother down the passageway Bendin had come up. They seemed to have no difficulty moving considering the environment they lived in.

Since Pete and Ryan had come from the right, it wasn't surprising when Rachel led him left. The hall opened into a large open space. It was a circular dome-shaped room. At the top of the dome was a large circular area you could see through, and Bendin could see the sky for the first time in his life. It was a red color. There were several different kinds of openings into the room: doors, grates, holes, and an archway. The doors were on the floor, ceiling, and walls. There were tables and chairs feet down on all surfaces around the room either bolted down or shod with metal feet.

"This is the sleeping quarters for most of the kids. We call this room in particular the 'Kids' Lounge'. George's room is right here." She guided him to a hole in the wall that was closed off by an egg-shaped door. Rachel rapped on the door. "George!"

There was a rustle inside and a dark-skinned boy, roughly the same age as Pete and Ryan, opened the door.

"Hello Rachel and--" He blinked at Bendin in surprise. "Who are you? You look brilliant! Are you dating him, Rachel? He looks suspiciously artistic. hrm!" George's expression glowed as he felt Bendin's damp fabric.

Rachel gritted her teeth. "He just needs a shirt and shorts to tide him over till we can get him something else."

"Sure. I can give him some of the stuff your family lent me," George said.

"Please bring him to dinner. I can't believe you are not there already," Rachel said as she ran off, wrists glowing with each swing.

George frowned as Rachel left. "Here."

Bendin followed George into the room, and noticed that once through the doorway he felt his weight again. George tossed Bendin a shirt and shorts out of a couple drawers.

"You'll probably be sleeping in here tonight at least. It's not too bad unless you are a light sleeper. It can get pretty crazy with Pete and Ryan."

"What's up with the gravity? Or lack?"

George shrugged. "I don't know. I'm not used to it. But if you're asking that, I'm going to guess that means you probably are from the wilderness or part of the outcasts like me."

"How long have you been here?

"A couple of days." George sat on a bunk bed near the door.

Bendin saw another bed in the other corner of the room and asked, "Is that one open?"

"Feel free."

"Thanks." Bendin sighed.

George shrugged. "It'll be nicer tomorrow for me. It's been a real chore watching the rest of them flying around so easily. But, cuffs come in tomorrow and we'll be able to move easy like the rest of them. I also can't wait to have blades of my own. They're essential for this environment."

~ 77 ~

Bendin pulled off his outer layers of his uniform and put on the shirt and shorts. He felt uncomfortable with the outfit, too lose, open, and airy. But since George seemed so comfortable, maybe it would be okay.

"Ready? We are past time. I'm hopeful for tomorrow, Bendin. I'll show you their favorite way to travel in this funky environment. Bendin really didn't know what to make of that, but he grabbed George's offered hand and George pulled him out of the room. This turned out to be really tricky considering George didn't have the wristbands and both of them rolled out into the air, their weight gone entirely. They spun into the far wall.

George helped Bendin find his footing, and guided him to the passage out. He showed Bendin the loops on the walls next to the padding. "These are for people like us. They had to use these before they had the right gear. See how old these are? Some of the loops hardly are attached at all anymore."

"Right," Bendin said, overwhelmed. "Why didn't Rachel show me these?"

"Dunno. Maybe she was enjoying herself?"

"Maybe."

They used the loops to pull themselves down through the passages till George announced, pointing to some tiled floor ahead, "That's it!" The tile floor was empty as far as furniture went.

The passage opened into a large truncated octahedron-shaped room with windows in the walls. The others were there, in sturdy beat-up wooden chairs, upside down on the ceiling around an old wooden table with feet shod in metal. The walls had all sorts of things on them that Bendin had no idea what they were. Items, tools, and containers. The lower section seemed normal except that things went way up the wall so that, for Bendin, they'd be out of reach. The center was completely open space.

"We're here!" George shouted as he pushed off the floor, floated up, twisted around, and landed perfectly in his empty chair. Rachel gestured for Bendin to come up pointing to an empty chair next to her.

Bendin pushed off the floor with slight apprehension, but he rotated a bit too much. Luckily, Rachel caught his hand as he neared the empty chair and guided him into it. Gravity around the chair pulled him down so it felt just like sitting back in the feed hall as long as he was close to it.

Bendin counted fifteen people talking around the table.

There was a man and a woman, which looked the same age, at opposite ends of the table. Rachel, Ryan, Pete, George and Starley were present, but the rest of the faces he did not know. The ages varied, and Bendin was still puzzled by the smaller people.

"Rachel says your name is Bendin and that you are part of the smaller outcast group, the Bauyostens?" The older gentleman asked.

Rachel nodded her head very slightly.

"Yes . . . My name is Bendin Slight," Bendin said, following Rachel's guidance.

"That's perfectly normal for someone who is outside of our modern technology. I'm Tilmon Coil and this is my wife, Celeste," Tilmon said gesturing across the table to the other side. He then pointed to each of the people at the table and said their names: "Oldest to youngest, this is Mez, Josiah with his wife, Crystal, and their two kids, Jake and Joseph. Then there is Callapse, Rachel, Soladaque, George Chainlinker, Pete and Ryan, Jean, Charles, and Starley." Each person reacted differently, either smiling, waving, hiding, making goofy faces, or any of the combination. "I hope you enjoy it here and that you will find acceptance."

Bendin mouthed the word, "Bauyosten?"

Rachel whispered, "Later."

Bendin nodded.

Tilmon spoke, "My family, we are gathered here to show recognition for the great work that Celeste has done in preparing a fine meal for us to enjoy. Soladaque, please ask thanks."

"Odge, thanks for the food. Bless it this day. Amen," Soladaque said fervently.

Bendin was pleasantly surprised that they showed signs of belief in Odge. That was one of the reasons he had been uncomfortable with the intruders. The meal was passed around the table by Celeste on plates.

"Guess who turns nine tomorrow?" Pete said in a sing-song voice.

"Raaayyccchhheelll!" Ryan sang mockingly, his voice cracking at the end. Callapse threw a roll at Ryan, and it bounced off of Ryan's head. Pete retaliated instantly and chucked his drink. His drink, however, missed his target and sailed into the wall behind Callapse. It bounced sending water out into various sized drops. The water drops closest to the disk, in the bottom of the container, formed into a sphere around it.

"Pete!" Tilmon scolded. "Not at the table!"

"Callapse started it," Pete whined.

"What? You were being really annoying!" Callapse defended angrily.

Tilmon's majestic stare at both of the boys ended the argument.

"Are you ready for tomorrow's practice?" Celeste asked George.

"We don't have this kind of stuff at home." George turned to Bendin and slapped him on the shoulder. "Don't worry, my fears over, now that I'm not the only one doing it for the first time."

Bendin half smiled. He had no idea what George was talking about. How did he know if he'd be doing what they were doing tomorrow anyway?

"We hardly know anything about the Bauyostens. What made them change their mind about sending you here?" Tilmon asked Bendin.

"It's unofficial. They don't know I'm here. I went on my own," Bendin lied.

"Oh?" Tilmon blinked his eyes.

"Father don't bother him. He'd had a busy day and he's very tired," Rachel reasoned.

"It's okay, Rachel." Bendin closed his eyes for a second. "Sometimes things just happen that change what you expect."

"That's true. I guess," Tilmon murmured eating his roll thoughtfully.

A rumble shook the room and a pool of dark smoke slowly rolled into the room from seemingly everywhere. It coasted into the table forcing everyone to groan and cough. Bendin's eyes watered and blurred.

"Dad!" Jean cried out.

"I know--I know--I know," Tilmon said, a sharp bang going off as he left.

"What's going on?" Bendin asked Rachel.

"The recycler has broken something again," She coughed. The air whistled, and within a few minutes the sounds were gone and the smoke cleared.

"Dad really needs to get that permanently fixed. It breaks down all the time," Josiah said to Crystal who was feeding Jake some of her food.

"But he's not going to as long as it's working, what with him taking on the outsiders and such," Crystal said.

Bendin was trying to keep up wth the rapid pace of many conversations, but there was too much. Like he had thought it would be weird to be sitting in on the DOOD conversations, this was a very foreign conversation to listen to.

"I don't want to eat this! I want that!" Starley complained to Celeste.

"You'll eat what we all are eating," Celeste replied.

"What are you doing tonight?" Soladaque asked Callapse.

"I was going to study for my mental examinations."

"What about the DeSoto's? Think they will steal Dad's chair?" Pete asked Ryan.

"They were exchanging punishing insults with Dad. I think we should take his chair and see if it works," Ryan responded eagerly.

"Do you think they are going to go with powered again at the Airlarky match this year?" Pete grabbed his fork and jabbed it into the table.

"Of course, why wouldn't they? They can probably afford to buy the Heptahedron this year as well." Ryan pulled the fork out and tossed it back to Pete.

Pete made a honking sound with his mouth. "They could do that every year, but they still haven't gotten through to the secret. Haha!"

Ryan flipped his food purposefully up into the air and then grabbed it before it would float away. Once the food extended out a certain distance away, it wouldn't come back down.

"How's Sebastian?" Celeste asked Rachel.

"I think he'll be seeing me in a couple days. Thanks for asking."

Bendin turned toward George. "Who's Sebasti--"

"He fancies her," George explained.

Bendin looked at Soladaque. She would be more like what he thought guys would like. She was average size but well rounded. Her dark hair was up in two twisted hairstyles that Bendin was not familiar with.

Bendin finished his food, but everyone still seemed to be engaged in conversation, except Mez. He had only slightly inclined his head in Bendin's direction at his introduction. He seemed to be indifferent to any of the energy around him.

Bendin tapped on Rachel's shoulder and pointed to Soladaque's hairstyle. "What did she do to her hair?"

"She braided her hair. So what?" Rachel shrugged.

"Braided?"

"Yeah. It's a useful hairstyle. Here, I'll show you," Rachel explained and tapped Jean on the shoulder. "Jean, Bendin hasn't seen braids. Show him with my hair."

"Sure." Jean undid Rachel's ponytail and let it down like the women in the upper temples. Jean's fingers flickered rapidly with expert skill. It could have only taken a moment and Rachel's hair was braided.

"See?" Jean asked.

"Now I see. Well, maybe not. But, thank you." It was insanely fast and definitely too quick to see exactly what she did.

"It's no big deal." Rachel smiled and before continuing with her meal she asked, "George, can you take Bendin back with you? I need to check on the Mangolas again, one last time, before I go to bed."

"Yeah. Let's go, Bendin."

Bendin followed George's push off the ceiling and did much better in landing. Bendin was feeling much more tired now, even though he could think quite clearly.

They were almost back to the Kids' Lounge when Bendin heard a voice say, "*stop!*" Bendin stopped and looked around.

"What?" George asked.

"Someone said to stop," Bendin said cautiously.

"I didn't hear anything." George stepped forward but Bendin pulled George back as a solid hunk of metal slammed down where George would have been. The hunk of metal managed to trap George's foot to the floor.

"Pull!" George grabbed his foot as Bendin pulled on George's shoulders. The foot didn't move.

Bendin could hear someone coming. "Hey, help us!"

"Sure!" someone said.

Bendin had flickering greyish blurs obscuring his vision, but he did make out Pete and Ryan grabbing George and pulling him free.

"Thanks, guys," George said wiping his forehead.

"This is of custom make. I wonder where it came from." Pete pushed it with his hands and the whole column of metal hissed upwards, vibrated, turned red hot, and turned to smoke.

"And now it's gone. Phooey." Ryan frowned looking at where it had been. "You okay?" Ryan offered his hand to George.

"For now. Thank you, Bendin, for stopping me." George

let Ryan pull him on his feet, and George went into the Lounge. Bendin followed wondering just what was going on. Unfortunately, none of could come up with anything good.

Echoes of high pitched voices rebounded from the walls of the passages.

"Bendin, you better get out of here," Ryan warned. "They're coming, and you are new."

George rubbed his hands together excitedly. "He's right."

"I'll protect you, Bendin," Pete declared and stood directly in front of Bendin with his arm stretched out, hand raised, and palm outward.

"Sure you will," Ryan sarcastically said.

"I'm as stalwart as a war machine. I'm as tough as a Grandelegant. I will not be moved!" Pete announced.

Bendin stood confused. The echoes changed into a rumble of noise till there burst through the opening Jean, Charles, and Starley. He could hardly see what was going on, but he could make out that they plowed right through Pete, sending him flying. Slightly dizzy, Bendin felt their arms and legs wrap around him with questions being asked in rapid succession. So fast did they ask them that Bendin couldn't answer any of them.

"What's it like where you come from?" Starley mewed.

"How many people were there?" Charles asked curiously.

"Do you like red?" Jean wanted to know.

"What was the weather like?"

"Your hair is blond."

"Do you like your home?

"Do you have a girlfriend?"

"Do you live in a mountain?"

"Tell us. Tell us!" They cried out.

Bendin heard Rachel's voice, "Bed! Dad's orders."

Jean, Charles, and Starley moaned sadly and let go of Bendin's arms, legs, and torso.

Ryan eyed Pete and grinned. "Dad's orders."

"Must be like for real then huh, it's like he's here doing it himself; what, Dad? Too lazy to come and tuck me in bed?" Pete said imitating Rachel's voice with surprising accuracy.

"Maybe like a deputation or something," Ryan said nudging his brother.

"You know Dad's busy. Off to bed with you," Rachel said hotly. "Before Callapse comes and sees you two are still up."

~ 83 ~

"Right," Pete and Ryan said together.

"Because Callapse is Dad too," Ryan snickered.

Pete laughed and high fived his brother.

Rachel didn't need to say anything else to them. Bendin saw flickers of light through the flickering grey and the next thing he knew they were gone.

"Are you okay?" Rachel asked.

"I'll be fine, just need to sleep," Bendin partially lied. He somehow felt extremely nauseous.

Rachel pointed at George's room and gave him a slight nudge.

"Good night then."

"Night."

Bendin fell into bed without doing anything at all for his nightly routine and sunk into sleep.

Chapter 6
Airlarky

"Bendin, wake up!" George shouted.

Bendin stiffened, rolled out of bed, and stood up in a panic. "What? What's going on?" Bendin squinted trying to read his watch, but stopped when he saw George frowning. George pulled on his boots and said, "No need for that. We overslept. I can't believe I fell asleep after they told me to get up again."

"Don't they have something that makes us wake up?"

"Yes, we both slept right through it." George pointed at a funny shaped octagon on the drawers next to him. "We were very tired. Get your stuff on. Let's go."

"I have to look through this before we leave." Bendin peered out the circular window above the bed he slept in. He could see a lot of trees off in the distance, a cliff face, and birds flying around outside. Blips of grey and fuzzy images warped his view from time to time, but he could see just well enough to enjoy the view. He feared the vision damage might have been permanent.

George coughed. "Food?"

"Right," Bendin reluctantly said forcing himself to move away from the window.

They made it to breakfast, but there was no one there except some pancakes for them. George found a note that told them to catch class and be ready for Airlarky after that. They ate breakfast and Bendin followed George down several tunnels. George gave descriptions of where things went, but Bendin didn't know what the words he was using described.

"Where are the others?" Bendin asked.

"They have their own class rooms or jobs. Ours is right up here."

"Is up the sky?"

"Yup, up is always the sky and down is always the floor. That's what they tell me. I don't really see why that's important, but I'm new."

"Sure." Bendin knew what he meant.

"Here." George pointed to a room at the end of a narrow hallway off of the tunnel they were in. Bendin peeked inside from outside the doorway. The room wasn't too large. It was about the same size of the classrooms at the DOOD and there were desks here too. The desks were very lightweight and tiny compared to the ones at the DOOD. The room itself was an incredibly dull blackish grey color, and there was absolutely nothing else in the room at all.

"Welcome to the network," George explained as he studied the panel on the wall in front of the entrance. He typed in a seven digit code and hit a small green button. A loud hissing came out of the panel, and a small puff of smoke floated up out of the crack between the panel and the wall.

"Don't worry. I can fix it. Watch." George smiled as he worked.

Bendin watched closely as George carefully pulled the panel back and moved a few of the wires around. They heard a swishing sound as an engine started below the room.

"Don't mind that. They say it's an older engine that still makes the clunky rotating sound," George said as he moved his hands in a rotary motion and gracefully put the panel back.

They moved forward. As they walked into the classroom, Bendin was mystified as the entire room shifted, glowed, and pulsated. A teacher and about thirty students materialized out of thin air. The sound of the teacher, the students, and the reactions of them walking into the room came over him like a rushing wind. The whole room was alive with their sounds and the beautiful vibrant color of the things they wore. It was so real that Bendin found it very hard to doubt its veracity. At least gravity was normal here.

The teacher spoke welcoming, "Please take your seat, George. We just finished today's lesson. I'll be with you in just a moment. Who is this you have brought with you?"

"Forgive me for forgetting to introduce him, Proust. This is Bendin. He's new, from the Bauyostens and would like to sit in today. Sorry we're late."

A murmur broke out among the students in the class, and even the teacher hesitated, watching Bendin with interest, before moving on.

"Welcome, Bendin." Proust motioned with her hands before saying, "With that we are finished with the lesson on the greatness of Odge's book. Please write down your assignments before you leave." Two lines appeared on the board behind Proust near the bottom.

Bendin read the board for the first time. It read, "Odge is the book." He didn't know what that meant. Under it was some reading and reporting on the reading. The class dispersed.

"Odge is the book?" Bencin asked curiously. George was writing down the assignment quickly and didn't say anything.

"Yes. He is." Proust looked up from her post in the front of the room.

"May I see this book?" Bendin asked.

"Sure, it's in any of the desks."

Bendin lifted the lid on the desk closest to him and pulled out the largest volume of scripture he'd ever seen. It was even bigger than master Findall's book.

The title read simply, "Odge." Bendin flipped open the cover and discovered some writing that read, "translated from the holy language." Bendin wondered if t was the same one from back in the temple. There was an impressively long list of translators and Bendin put the book back in the desk.

"I didn't know the holy language had been translated," Bendin said nervously.

"Yep. They have been at it for many years now."

"Really." Bendin stood there transfixed. Not sure what to even ask. Maybe someone had translated the book a long time ago and they just lost the translation somehow by Bendin's time.

"Is there anything else you wanted to know, Bendin?" Proust asked coming over to him.

"Not really."

Proust extended a hand. "I look forward to having you in our class."

Bendin took it and gasped.

The hand was icy cold.

He pulled his hand back in surprise.

George chuckled next to him. "I know. It shocked me the first time too."

"Why . . . cold?" Bendin hissed clutching his hand to his body desperately trying to warm it up.

"She's not here."

Bendin saw a small grin creep onto Proust's face. "I couldn't resist. I enjoy new people. If you look closely enough we flicker sometimes."

Bendin studied closer, and this time he could see a slight flicker every now and then. It was very hard to notice because that was the only indication, besides the frigid touch, that she was not real. Bendin whispered, "What are you?"

Proust said, "We spin particles to replicate the people and things in the classrooms."

"It doesn't work outside the rooms yet though," George whispered as he placed his hand on his desk. When his hand contacted the desk, the surface flickered and a large chain began wrapping itself around George's hand.

"Help!" George said as the metal began to squeeze into his hand.

Proust grabbed the chain and pulled it while Bendin grabbed the other end of the chain and pulled it in the opposite direction. After struggling for a bit, they managed to open a space big enough for George to pull his hand free. Proust and Bendin let go of the chain and watched it coil shut with amazing force, spin in a rapid session, light up extremely hot, and turn into smoke.

George held his hand pensively.

"What was that?" Bendin asked nervously looking around.

"A trap," Proust spoke, obviously concerned. "Are you okay?"

George shook his head. "I'm fine. Thank you for helping me." He held up his hand and it was red, but working.

"I'll be sure to monitor your space to see what happened and also prepare for the future and prevent this from ever happening again," Proust said. "Take a break and get those assignments done."

"Yes, thank you, Proust." George led the way out of the room.

"Can I talk to Soladaque?" Bendin asked as they went on their way. "I want to know who she was talking about at dinner last night."

"Just relax. We'll go pick up some lunch, and she'll be outside with the rest of the family." George seemed to have gotten over the scare. "Today we get to practice Airlarky with the rest of the family."

"I guess I'll see her when I get there. What's after that?"

"Whatever you want. We'll probably be doing capture the flag with Pete and Ryan, but I don't know if we'll have enough time for that. We've got to get to lunch anyway before then."

George led the way and Bendin followed.

Pete and Ryan peeked around a corner up ahead. They laughed and purposefully followed slowly walking on the ground as Bendin and George clumsily made their way to the dining room.

"Guys, do you mind? We are trying to get to lunch,"

George whined.

"We just wanted to 'be' like you guys before you become fully integrated with cuffs, blades, and all! You'll never go back! Unless you want to tease someone." Ryan laughed gleefully as Bendin tripped and did a perfect flip in the air and landed on his feet.

They made it to the dining room with Pete and Ryan still laughing about how hard it was for George and Bendin to move around.

The only person there was plump Celeste. Lunch was simply a small pill.

Bendin gawked at it and said to Celeste, who was standing on the floor holding a small container of them, "What is this?"

"Aren't you funny. They had these in the Bauyostens group you were with," Celeste's smooth voice sounded like cool water poured into a glass, "Right, George?'

"Well, Bauyostens do live a little bit differently but I'm pretty sure they had the 'meal pills' there too," George stated. George rapped Bendin on the shoulders, "Stop teasing people, Bendin. He helped save me twice already in two days."

"Oh?" Celeste said raising her eyebrow.

"He did. He's a real hero," Ryan said grabbing and shaking Bendin's shoulders with his grip.

"Well, Bendin saved me from the metallic scary cylinder and the crazy self-wrapping chain. I've never seen anything like them before," George explained.

"I'm glad you weren't hurt, George." Celeste turned to Ryan and Pete with blazing fury in her eyes. "What did *you* do?"

"It wasn't us. Honest!" Ryan said backing away a step.

"Trust me, we don't *like* hurting other people," Pete assured her.

Celeste hardly acknowledged their replies.

"Why don't you eat these all the time instead of preparing large complicated meals?" Bendin asked curiously as well as trying to change the subject.

Celeste relaxed and explained, "Because these are actually very boring. They get really old after a while and you miss the good meals. Trust me, there are groups of people out there that this is all they eat. Works great for traveling." Celeste made a distasteful expression on her face and then smiled. "Time to move on boys."

Bendin's thoughts were still muddled over everything. He

was curious what had happened to the Vaelift and why the history had changed. He thought maybe he'd try Harmon's method of praying tonight. Still, Bendin thought he should ask someone as soon as they had time.

He didn't get his chance because the second he stepped outside the back door which led outside words failed him. Thoughts failed him. It was too fantastic to take it all in at once. His little bedroom window was nothing compared to *this*. He gazed out over the backyard of the Coils. There was a large area of grass, at least it looked like grass. Hulking trees off in the distance. A large lake stood off to his left, a distance out. A bluish sun was almost straight above him, it gave everything a slightly brighter bluish hue. There were birds and sounds flooding from all around suggesting that there was life in all places out here. To his right there was the rest of the house which was quite odd to look at from the outside with all the funky shapes and pieces everywhere. The highest thing besides the sun was a large cliff face off to the right which went up to lofty heights. Off of that, was a waterfall pouring off and crashing onto a section of the house that butted up against the cliff. He then realized he must have come into the house from there. The world was so open and vast that Bendin suddenly felt very insecure. It felt like there was nothing over his head and that he'd just fall out of the world. At the same time, the air was sweet and nothing like he had ever breathed before.

"Beautiful, isn't it?" George said from next to him.

"Yes."

Pete and Ryan didn't move past Bendin or George. They watched Bendin with great interest as he took in all the surroundings. Bendin realized that they were staring at him like a starving person stares at fresh cooked breakfast.

"What's up?" He could tell they were really excited about something. "Something behind me?"

"Oh nothing. Just this!" Pete screamed.

"No, Pete, No!" Came Celeste's voice from behind them.

She was too late.

Pete and Ryan had laughingly grabbed Bendin and George from both sides and before he could do anything they shoved them upward. Bendin felt the scariest thing he'd ever felt in his life; he was unable to do anything. He rose and wasn't going down.

"Relax, Bendin," George said calmly from next to him. "They did this to me yesterday. We'll come back down. Just enjoy the view."

Bendin felt himself slowly relax, and he watched the surface drift away as the rest of the family noticed, stopped what they were doing, and enjoyed what Pete and Ryan had done to him. Celeste scolded them, shooed them off of the porch, and they went out into the field. Bendin continued to rise weightless in the air. He could see the entire home and much of the forests that surrounded it. He could see past the edge of the cliff now and saw a mountain range curving off in the distance. The landscape was extremely breathtaking and he felt the joy of the view immensely. He rose higher and higher till he felt he'd never stop.

Just when Bendin started to notice the temperature dropping his weight returned and the familiar pull of gravity pulled him down again. George pointed at something off in the distance. "The edge of the range is the edge of the Coils property."

"Okay."

The pull didn't last very long because he was pulled right back down into the invisible weightless field. He guessed that this spot, way up here in the sky, was where the weightless field must stop. He traveled downward at about the same rate at which he rose. Most of the family had gathered a short distance away from the house in the field, minus Mez, Tilmon, and Josiah's little family. They laughed and smiled at Bendin as he landed on the grass just in front of the balcony. The balcony, he realized, was actually quite far up from the ground, probably six times higher than his height. Bendin noticed that there were lots of balconies and entrances to the family home in lots of different areas. Bendin was glad that his shoes had some adherence to the ground.

"Come on, Bendin, George!" It was Soladaque and she was calling them to come over to the place where all of the others had gathered.

Bendin saw that many of the kids were *landing* there followed by, from his distance, faint streaks of light. He was glad his vision was clear enough to see that he hadn't been imagining the yellow streaks earlier. They were huddled around a large pile of scrap metal. As Bendin got closer, he knew it wasn't scrap metal; it was supplies.

"Mom should you even be out here?" Ryan joked.

"You're *due* to go inside." Pete grinned poking Celeste's belly with his finger.

"Yes, Pete, it's good for me to be here with my kids," Celeste said as she swung Pete around with expert grace and hurled him up into the air. "You guys should already be wearing these things anyway, isn't that the latest rage nowadays?" She twiddled with her red belt, turned, grinned, and barked out orders quickly and efficiently, "Rachel set up the north goal. George help get Bendin fitted with these. He can use Tilmon's things till he gets back and Bendin gets his own." She pushed, through the air, Bendin a different pair of boots connected with drawstrings to put on. He studied the boots and saw that they were a little bit larger in the sole of the bottom of the boot than the ones he was wearing. They would probably fit.

"Ryan please grab Tilmon's staff. We don't have an extra one for Bendin yet. Soladaque the south goal. Callapse get the balls ready. George show Bendin what you've learned so far so he's not completely lost. Starley, Jean, Charles start your warm-ups."

Bendin watched in complete and utter amazement as Starley, the tiniest person he'd ever seen, *skated* up into the air followed by Jean and Charles. For the first time he watched and witnessed what he hadn't been able to see through glaze, blur, and smoke. In smooth expert skill they followed Starley around in the air skating in all directions. Bendin subconsciously let the boots he held go, opened his mouth, and gaped at the kids in awe.

"Pretty good aren't they?" Pete noted seeing Bendin's astonished expression. Bendin had been so engrossed in watching Starley that he didn't notice Pete had skated down next to him.

"It's unbelievable!" Bendin whispered.

"We are getting ready for the Heptahedron. Right now it's just us, but this weekend is the training with the rest of the official Coil team."

"There are more of you guys?" Bendin asked puzzled.

"We have a massive family with many cousins, uncles, and aunts. Do you have a big family?"

"No, I guess I'm not like most people." Bendin shrugged slightly confused about the mention of mysterious terms such as cousins, or uncles, or the insects. "When is this Heptahedron?"

"It's next month, and Dad got us seats for the whole family so we can go in person! It's only the biggest event of the tribunal besides the founding celebrations at the end of every year."

"Thanks." Bendin analyzed the boots again that were lent to him. They had a solid base, but there were no blades to be seen. In fact, Bendin wondered how he was going to get up there. Rachel was setting up a goal at one end and Soladaque at another spot, both high up in the air. When they were done, there were rectangular prism-shaped glowing outlines of goals. One was blue the other was red. George pushed his staff from one hand to the other. He had on his boots, his black staff (which Bendin noticed for the first time had bulky ends), his gold colored headband, gold belt with a silver box on it, and gold colored rings around his boot tops. Now that he noticed them on George, everyone seemed to be wearing similar attire in one way or another. All of the gear was well used, scuffed, tattered, and torn.

"What's going on?" Bendin asked. He looked like a little sad-eyed one-eared puppy that needed played with.

George tapped him gently on the shoulder with his staff. "This is Airlarky. It's the game that they play. Well, everyone but the Outcasts. It's not too hard to understand. It uses this staff and there are three small balls worth one point each, two medium sized balls worth two points each, and one large ball worth four points."

Bendin inspected all the balls sitting in the air above the supplies. The small one looked like the size of your fist. The medium one was double the size of the small one. The large one was double the size of the medium ball.

Pete explained, "Each team gets one set of balls. The Heptahedron gets shiny glowing balls, but we use regular ones instead. Officially there are 8 players per team, but I'm told they usually only practice on that scale for Heptahedron practice."

"Yeah, the biggest game ever organized had over ten thousand players," Celeste said overhearing them.

"Okay." Bendin could understand that. "What are these gold bands?"

"They are normal air gear." George shrugged. "I'm told they keep the balls from running into you. Some sort of high speed deflector."

"They're just high-kinetic repulsive bands," Ryan said as he skidded to a halt in front of Bendin spraying sparks all over, "they'll stop anything moving too fast and move it around you. If you're lucky. Trust me you don't want to get hit by those," Ryan said pointing at a ball. Ryan was already wearing his gear, and carrying, Tilmon's bands and staff.

"George, your cuffs came in!" Ryan said as he pushed George the cuffs and skated up into the air to join his brothers and sisters. The sound of the skating sounded like someone welding, at least that's what Bendin thought it sounded like.

George helped Bendin put on the air gear. The wrist cuffs were silver, like the silver box on the belt (which was large enough that it could be gripped in both hands), and Bendin noticed that the wrist cuffs also cut the air, but must have had smaller blades. He discovered that this gave the person more control in the air as they gave slight resistance in certain directions. He wanted to jump in and join the others, but George stopped him from moving forward by grabbing him with his hand.

"Bendin, you forgot your boots, and I don't know how to use the staff yet either."

Bendin pulled off and put on the other boots. They felt identical, except they were a tiny bit taller than the other pair. He had on everything now.

"Callapse, Soladaque! Please come down here," Celeste yelled.

Callapse was a tall, broad boy, with dark brown hair. He also sported brown eyes and a protruding chin.

"Watch Callapse closely to see how this works," Celeste instructed, pulled out a small gun-shaped device, and shot a medium sized ball towards Callapse. Both Callapse and Soladaque were just above the ground standing on their skates in the air. Callapse moved his staff into position and extended claws on the end. His catch was perfectly in the center of the end of the staff and there was an audible clicking sound as the ball lodged itself in the end.

"Watch. He only has a few seconds before it launches automatically." Celeste pointed.

Callapse twisted part of the other end of the staff while aiming carefully. He fired the ball with a loud concussion sound straight at Soladaque who waved her staff's clawed end up. She missed the ball catching end of the staff, but to George and Bendin's surprise the ball circled the end of the staff for a couple of seconds, it's revolutions getting tighter till it landed in the center of the end with an audible click.

"See, you only need to get close to catching it and it pulls the ball in, at the cost of precious seconds, but it's still better than missing entirely." Celeste smiled at Soladaque. "Shoot it back dear before you launch it straight up unintentionally."

Soladaque shot it back at Callapse, who instead of catching it, twisted his claws closed and batted it back to her.

"Can't you just carry it?" Bendin asked.

"If you want to travel with that kind of load, by all means do so," Celeste said. "The balls create tremendous drag when carried and not attached."

"Whoa!" George shouted as he skated up into the air, and as he did, the blades disconnected from his boots with a surprising ker-chunk.

"Callapse, you're closer!" Celeste hollered.

George sped uncontrollably toward the glass windows of the house.

"George!" Bendin yelled helpless to do anything.

"I'm coming!" Callapse shouted and sprinted in George's direction. He expertly caught him just before he crashed into it.

"You're lucky I made it to you. What happened to your boots?" Callapse questioned pulling him back over to where Bendin and Celeste were.

"I don't know," George mumbled helplessly and shrugging sadly.

Callapse helped George put together his boots so that the blades were where they should be. It took some special tools that Callapse had in a ground-adhering bag to get them fastened to the boots and cemented properly so that they wouldn't come out.

"Whoever put these pair together didn't lock the blades in properly. Junk service." Callapse frowned.

"What does the other end of the staff do?" Bendin pointed to the other end of the staff that was like the end of a gun barrel.

"It contains a blade that you can use for better maneuvering," Celeste said, "Who didn't lock in the blades?"

"Thanks, how do I get blades on my boots like you guys?" Bendin pointed at Callapse, who had finished fixing George's boots, and the others skating around everywhere. Celeste laughed and pointed at his boots, "Right there, Bendin. Just double tap your heels."

Bendin did so and the bottom of his shoes widened just a small amount and Bendin's feet slid right out from under him causing him to fall flat on his back. The air smelt of fresh lightning strike as the kids noticed his fall. Everyone that saw laughed, and those that didn't see soon joined in. Bendin leaned up and pulled his boot towards himself so he could get a better look. The bottom metal part of the boot had parted a small amount and there was a blade of dark metal. He pressed his foot against the air and found it to be perfectly solid against the blade and flawlessly slippery. "How do you stop?"

"Angles," Callapse said watching George lift a small amount over the ground. George was more cautious this time because of his mishap.

Rachel had completely finished and had come down to watch.

"Bendin, you okay?" Rachel asked. After Bendin nodded affirmatively, she explained, "You use the angle of the blade to adjust your speed, slow down, or stop completely. It works no matter what direction your facing, up, down, sideways, or diagonally." She grabbed Charles, "Charles, show him how to do the basics, Mom's calling for me."

Rachel skated off to help her mother with the ball box that was to be positioned in the air. Bendin thought that if anyone at the temple saw this they wouldn't know what to say either. It was amazing to see people move like this with no difficulty at all. Charles grabbed Bendin and pulled him up a couple of centimeters into the air, which was surprising considering he was smaller than Bendin. Bendin, no matter how hard he tried, could not even get that far.

After a few more tries, Charles exclaimed, "You forgot to turn on your GravBox!" Charles fiddled with Bendin's silver box for a minute, showing Bendin how to turn it on and off. Once the box was on, Bendin felt a small tug of gravity pulling him down towards his feet.

"There, now you can actually ride any plane and it will always cause you to go down towards your feet as long as it's on." Charles popped his blades in and Bendin watched him sink downwards. "See?"

Charles pulled Bendin up into the air, which this time seemed to be a little better.

Bendin heard popping sounds above him. Pete and Ryan were going really fast above them and then they stopped immediately. When they did this, they sent up a shower of sparks which exploded with a loud booming sound. They saw that Rachel had her back to them and they skated towards her at top speed only to stop suddenly and catch her in a shower of sooty dust and sparks complete with not only a loud booming noise, but surprisingly a large fireball. Rachel's face turned darker and sootier than the soot that covered her face. She screamed at them in frustration after they did it a couple more times.

"Bendin, over here." Charles waved his hand in front of Bendin's face. Bendin had been completely distracted by the boys antagonizing Rachel. "It's best if you start slow."

That he did. Bendin was too afraid to go very high, and he hardly moved more than a meter before his feet slid out from under him and he would again be upside down.

"Let's keep trying," Charles encouraged. Bendin noticed that George was moving better now and he was venturing higher off the ground.

Bendin took a deep breath and tried again. He doubled his distance this time by going two meters before sliding sideways and hovering over the ground. Charles skated around and took Bendin's hands.

"Here. I'll pull. You control with your feet. Don't think about anything or anyone else."

"Okay." Bendin wasn't sure what he was going to do.

Charles pulled on Bendin's arms and this time all Bendin did was focus on his feet. He did okay. He wasn't flailing, but he wasn't able to go very fast. He could hardly keep his legs straight under him as they kept going too far back, to the sides, and out from under him. It was quite sensational. He couldn't wait to be able to go faster.

"I want to master this form of travel. Like, Callapse! You will see," Bendin told Charles determined not to be disappointed by his apparent lack of ability. Callapse was skating around with no effort at all, and going all directions, stopping immediately, and leaving those air-welded trails that faded away into smoke after a second.

"Good luck with that one Bendin, Callapse has been skating since he was one," Charles cautioned Bendin's unrealistic enthusiastic desire.

"It's time to begin!" Celeste said skating up to the center of the playing field.

"Hi, Bendin, " Rachel said skating up beside Bendin as Bendin tried to get up to the center of the playing field which was high up off the ground. "How are you liking the air?"

"It's complete new and cool, but awkward."

"I like the freedom. I can go anywhere," Rachel said happily.

A powerful thought struck Bendin. *He* could go anywhere. Not just around the house, where the localized zero-gravity generator was. Anywhere, that is, if he could learn the footwork and keep his body stable. The staff was equally awkward. Right now all he was trying to do was to use the end that contained the tiny blade for support. Pete and Ryan saw him using the staff for support and laughed so hard they let go of their own staffs; they gave no thought to the force and direction they had let them go and by the time they recovered from laughing they discovered the staffs had went all the way to the ground.

"Pete! Ryan! Your staffs?" Celeste asked harshly.

"Sorry, mom, Bendin was just making us laugh," They said hurrying to collect their staffs. Ryan yelled up to Bendin, who was still awkwardly using the staff to move his whole body along, "Keep it up, Bendin! You'll be the best yet!"

Rachel stood aloof on the other side of the family while the rest were ready to start the game. Bendin finally made it where everyone else was in the center of the field.

Celeste then started the game with the words, "May the best team win!" With those words she clicked a button on her belt that no one else had, and the outlines of the ball box far above them lit up with a green color. All the balls for the teams floated downward at a slow rate. The kids collected the balls so fast and shot them off towards the goals that Bendin and George hardly knew what had happened. Only Celeste remained in the center, with Bendin, calling off shots. There was a scoreboard in the grass of the scores for the two teams. One was red, and the other was blue. He turned to see a ball sail right at his face, but it went around him mysteriously as if he wasn't even there, giving off a strange ebbing sound. It was like a hollow deep humming sound skipping through a familiar tune in a rhythmic low hum. It stopped a short distance from him in the air.

"That's why you need the staff, Bendin, to catch high speed balls," Celeste said to him. "Now go get it before someone else gets to it. Go. Shoo!" Celeste pushed Bendin towards the ball that had skipped past him through the air. Bendin gave it his best effort but just couldn't move in a straight line. He was constantly going either in a circle up to the right or back down again to the left. He continued his agonizingly slow pace with as much vigor as he could muster.

The rest of the kids were battling it up above him. They blocked shots, intercepted others, shot goals, and bumped around each other at times. George was moving well enough to intercept some of the slower moving shots or ones that deflected around randomly from people. Occasionally, someone would shoot one off in the wrong direction. But once it had traveled a certain distance from the box floating way above the field, it would flare brightly and the ball would reverse direction and come sailing back. When a score was made into the goal the ball disappeared.

Soon most of the balls had been collected and scored. Bendin was almost to the ball. He looked down and saw the two teams were tied. He didn't even know whose team he was on. Not that it mattered! What in the world was he doing up here playing a game he'd never heard of, wearing skates and gear he'd never seen, and chasing a ball that had stopped? He was almost to it, but why? Bendin didn't have time to think about it as he grabbed the ball. To his surprise he felt and understood immediately why the staffs were important. The ball was almost immovable when it was in his hands. Bendin wondered if when it was floating there, was it exerting a force in every direction? Bendin clicked the medium sized ball on the clawed end of his staff. The force the ball exerted was completely neutralized, and he could move the ball around with perfect ease while it was locked into the end of the staff. Bendin heard the massive amounts of welding above him getting louder for some reason. He turned to see both entire teams streaking towards him in a brilliant display of sparks, trails of hot yellow light turning to smoke after a second, and bright smiles.

He had the only ball left.

"Me! Bendin to Me!" Rachel shouted moving swiftly towards the sheer cliff face.

"No, me!" Pete shouted.

"You're not on his team!" Soladaque shouted back.

"I know!" Pete laughed at her grinning.

Bendin only had another second before Callapse was going to crash into him to fire the ball. With a fierce crack, he fired the ball at Starley.

Callapse came up next to him, tangled with Bendin, his legs temporarily wrapped around Bendins. Bendin's vision went blurry. Bendin's feet double tapped together and he felt himself pull free of Callapse's leg with alarming velocity.

Bendin found himself so out of control he was unable to push his feet back together. He sailed towards the jungle without any sign of slowing, Tilmon's staff and cuffs being the only thing that exerted any force over where he was going. He certainly didn't know how to use them properly as neither prevented him from flying into one of the taller trees. As he flew into the tree, the branches parted being redirected, but as he was redirected up the center of the tree, some of the branches whipped along him and wove around his feet, and wrapped Bendin around the branch. He then bumped his head and his boots gripped a large branch below him with decent pull.

Bendin watched the family as his vision swam and grew more blurry and dim. Grey shapes and outlines became more prominent as Starley caught another shot and fired it toward her goal. It was intercepted and caught by the staff of Ryan. Ryan wasn't holding his staff because he had chucked his staff down from above to which the ball had spiraled around and was caught. Pete caught the descending staff from below with his free hand and shot it into his team's goal. It was a perfect shot. Ryan's team cheered as the second the ball disappeared. It was the last ball, so all the balls redeployed from the ball box with green outlines above the space they were playing in. The balls fell at a faster rate than before, being caught and captured and shot by various family members. Bendin blacked out, his shoes luckily holding his body to the tree branch.

Chapter 7
Cleffs

The next thing Bendin knew he was shaken awake by a girl with a very pretty face. It was Soladaque.

"Are you ok?" Soladaque asked appearing very concerned.

"I think so." Bendin rubbed his sore and throbbing eyes. "I lost control and didn't see the tree."

"Come on. You're missing the third wave! It's just beginning."

"I missed the second?" Bendin was puzzled by the mention of a third.

"Callapse told us you had wanted some time to yourself, but when you didn't come back I was worried about you."

Soladaque extended her hand and pulled Bendin up off the branch. He felt his head and there was a sad lump on the back of his head where he had hit the tree. Bendin allowed Soladaque to pull him back to the rest of the family, but felt pretty useless as he couldn't move very far without flipping or doing the splits. During the rest of the game, he managed to catch a pass here and there. He was a pebble in the midst of a cyclone.

The game finished without any other oddity, and the kids discussed the events for the evening. Bendin decided he'd like to practice longer.

"Will someone please help me learn how to do this?" Bendin asked the family before they split.

"Who wants to help, Bendo, learn to skate?" Callapse asked sarcastically nodding his head and laughing.

"Have a heart, Callapse!" Soladaque swatted him on the shoulder. "I have some time. I'll help for a while, and I enjoy skating anyway."

Rachel let her air slowly escape before she said, "Thanks, Soladaque." Rachel skated towards the cliff.

"Going to work on her plantations." Ryan laughed.

Celeste smiled approvingly at Soladaque and cautioned, "Please be in time for dinner. You know your father. I'll be checking on you guys from the windows. I'll be here if you need anything."

"Yes, mother, I know," Soladaque replied.

The rest of the family members split off to their various activities. Pete and Ryan skated through the air in the direction of the jungle.

"Where are Pete and Ryan going?" Bendin asked.

"To quadruple check their set up for capture the flag that we are going to do in a couple of days. They've been so chatty about it the past week it's starting to wear on everyone. It had better be a knockout of pure, undiluted fun!" Soladaque spun around, the light in her eyes dancing excitedly.

"Why a couple of days? Why don't we just do it tonight or tomorrow?"

"Because we have things that we do Bendin!" Soladaque chuckled. "Not all of us get to get out of school every day like you Bauyostens; unless, of course, it's cleared by the parents. With mom and dad we're lucky if we get free time over the weekend!" She muttered, "Or we run away, take time out without them knowing, disappear, vanish away, or turn into a tree."

"Okay?" Bendin said, unsure how he felt about all of that.

"Okay, how do I do this? I would like to be as good as Callapse!" Bendin stated.

Soladaque grinned. "I like your enthusiasm, but let us simply go for skating in a straight line without going up, down, left, right, flipping, or turning. Perfectly straight. You need to learn simple control, balance for your body, and an awareness of how your feet line up. If you can do that it will make going in all the other directions much easier. It's just the simple practical truth that the blades only resist one direction." Soladaque put her hands up and in the form of quotes said, "'down'. Well, technically, they do have a slight counter resistance on the upward movement, but we'll not talk about that right now. For now, if you can glide straight comfortably enough then we will learn the basics of stopping."

Soladaque's voice had a nice deep rich sound to it. It was deep, open, and warm. Her blond hair was up in twin braids, and her tanned skin revealed she was outside much more than her sister Rachel.

"Let's begin then. Show me what you've got."

Bendin demonstrated by pushing forward on his skates.

"No, Bendin. Stop *'bendin'* your ankles. You need to *'bendin'* your legs more. You're as rigid as a staff. Loosen up." Soladaque smiled heartily. He looked at his feet and saw his body was straight as a board and was indeed bending his ankles inward.

"If you keep them straight up and down, you can let your weight rest on the lower section of your thighs and rear. Watch." With that, Soladaque blinked her green eyes in excitement and very slowly moved past Bendin. She overly emphasized her ankles being straight up and down by hardly bending anything at all. "See? Balance! Okay, no leaning, nothing. Just straight, only straight, straight, straight, straight!"

"Bendin peered down at her and grinned nervously. With her help this time he was successful in keeping his poor ankles straight.

"You did it!" Soladaque applauded proudly.

Bendin felt a glowing sensation of happiness hiding somewhere in this activity he hadn't recognized before. He excitedly pushed off on the other foot. Then the other surprisingly continually going in a straight line. He did this following Soladaque's lead, who had to grab him and stop him and turn him around every so often as not to stray too far from the homestead. They kept skating in straight lines till Soladaque deemed him ready to learn how to stop.

As hard as he tried, the only thing that Bendin could do was to stop and send himself into somersaults.

Soladaque went below him used her hands to simulate on a very slow scale just what they needed to do to be able to stop, two different methods.

On a micro scale Bendin duplicated her motions and to his surprise, he found himself stopping.

"There, you see? You have the ability to do it." Soladaque, smiling, clapped her hands enthusiastically and pushed Bendin forward. Bendin slid forward smoothly, his blades giving off the welding-sound and light-trail which turned to a smoky residue with every step.

"Excellent try, Bendin! This time try it again but a bit slower." Soladaque released his hands and motioned him to follow her. "Do what I do."

Bendin tried as hard as he could, following her motions perfectly. But as he pushed his blades forward to stop, he again tripped over his blades and flipped into Soladaque. She caught him, laughed, and dragged him back to the Balcony. "You look really tired."

"I feel tired," Bendin said as he suddenly realized every muscle in his body ached. He had been so in the moment that he didn't notice.

"Then you should take a break," Soladaque said looking up at two approaching figures in the air.

Pete and Ryan landed triumphantly next to them with a pair of loud thumps.

"We did it. Everything's ready!" They announced together and gave each other high fives.

"Soladaque, are you taking Bendin jumping tomorrow?" Ryan asked.

"That's a great idea! Bendin, would you like to go jumping tomorrow?" Soladaque asked pulling on his hand.

"Sure, um, if you think I can do it."

"You can if you are with me." Soladaque winked at him and smiled.

"It's a date!" Pete and Ryan laughed, nudged Soladaque, and skated into the house.

"Need anything else, Bendin?" Soladaque asked.

"No. I'm going to take the much needed break like you said."

"See you at dinner then." Soladaque followed her brothers into the house.

Bendin turned around and looked over the landscape. It was still so breathtaking and surreal he just couldn't fathom it. All his life he never knew he'd been so physically crammed, now it was wide open. Boxed in, now no walls. He felt something he hadn't felt before, and it felt very sweet: Physical Liberty.

He thought about the DOOD and thought he'd try to go back again. Bendin skated slowly through the house as he was extremely tired. He was so exhausted, halfway there he had to use the walls for leverage.

When he arrived in the waterfall room, he sheathed his blades, and felt the pull of gravity so surprising he collapsed on the floor. After a while, though, he recovered enough to be able to stand and walk around.

Bendin walked slowly through the waterfall room looking at the trees and grass with wonder, soaking in all the smells, the crunch of the gravel, the colors of the flowers, the smooth benches and sitting places, and the sound of the waterfall's humble rumble above him. After only a few moments, he hobbled through the cave and reached the scuffed, dirty, and worn wall through which he had made such a dramatic entrance. He leaned up against it and placed his hands on it. The dirt was soft, but the wall was solid. He sat and performed the vanish method.

As before, nothing happened.

Bendin sighed.

He was stuck.

"I thought there was a chance that I might find you here," Rachel's voice bounced off the ceiling.

Bendin turned in surprise and Rachel peeked her head over the same ridge that she had been behind when he was first here.

"Why? And why do I feel like we've been in this same position before?" Bendin smirked.

"It's definitely not a good idea for you to be here. People will wonder why and ask questions you don't want to answer," Rachel pronounced sternly as she came in the room. She appeared almost exactly the same thing she was when Bendin first saw her except that her coat was much dirtier.

"You're right of course, but I knew a girl there, and she needed my help." Bendin sighed. "She was becoming one of the best friends I ever had."

"I'm sorry, Bendin, but you shouldn't blame yourself for things out of your control. You gotta see my plants! Want to come see?" Rachel carefully extended her hand and pulled Bendin into a standing position, but his legs gave out and he crashed into the little pond of frogs.

"I do blame myself. I can't stand I'm too weak, and I think the strain of the skating has over exhausted my muscles." Bendin frowned.

"You think?" Rachel softly spoke. "Here, use my shoulder. You can lean on me, and I'll guide you there." She reached out and pulled him up with surprising strength. Bendin leaned on her.

"How was skating training?" Rachel asked without looking at Bendin.

"I think I can now skate in a straight line okay. She wants to take me jumping tomorrow, whatever that is."

Rachel raised her eyebrows curiously and laughed with a soft laugh that echoed lightly off the ceiling and cave walls. "I won't ruin the surprise. She's been wanting someone she likes to skate with, besides her family, for quite a while. You might be an Odge-send."

"You think she likes me?" Bendin asked in a monotone expression.

"It's possible. Let's not leave that option out, because I won't know till I ask her." She led him down a passage that went in the opposite direction from the waterfall room. The cave passages were narrow, and faded. The floors were well worn, and the walls smoothed. In fact, now that he looked at them, they were eerily familiar in their narrow width and some passages had high ceilings. This made Bendin feel very uncomfortable with the connections he was making in his mind to his old temple home.

Rachel paused and walked into a large atrium kind of room. There were plants everywhere, grass on the ground, and they were organized in rows. Some plants were even on special benches made of wood. Bendin noticed that it didn't have a ceiling that opened out to the outside, but it may as well have, because there was a light in the ceiling that was like the sun for its brightness.

"It's extremely bright." Bendin shielded his eyes from the intense light.

"It's nice, but it's a salad bar for the local wildlife. It's a horrible problem that needs solved as quickly as I can manage a reasonable solution. There are several passages here that lead in from the outside and several of the special animals have learned about my garden and have been eating my plants."

"This is bad?"

"It's horrible! I can't work with what doesn't exist, Bendin." Rachel made gestures that made it look like she was eating plants with her hands.

"Can you just kill the animals or block-up the entrances?" Bendin pondered aloud.

"Dad won't let me block up the entrances, he says, 'it promotes good air circulation in the caves', 'don't tamper with the natural crevices', and 'don't revive past mistakes' and such."

Bendin could tell by her voice she disagreed with her father's opinion of the situation. "I'm surprised he doesn't side with you."

She shrugged and continued, "These silly animals are protected by the tribunal's Special Animal Protection Privileges, SAPP, or 'S' 'A' 'P' 'P'. As long as they don't hurt us, we can't hurt them. If they break it, we get to have all the fun in the world taking them down. Understand?" Rachel asked.

"They understand?"

"Sure, they had representatives all over the world agree to it since the beginning when the whole world was organized."

That all seemed very odd to Bendin. He was taking in the smooth walls, green plants, and the occasional tree. All of them looked foreign to Bendin. He noticed something; there was something at the other side of the room near one of the openings to the room. He could just make out a small animal, a miniature possum. Bendin crept closer for a better look and he could hear a strange humming sound that seemed to be coming out of it. There was an occasional flicker of flame that licked off of the back of it.

"Is that a possum?" Bendin whispered to Rachel who had crept up next to him. They were both watching this small animal from behind a row of plants.

"Yes," Rachel noticed what it was doing, and she hissed angrily, "but it's taking the Mangolas!"

Bendin leaped up, charged forward, without even thinking why, and yelled at the tiny possum. The possum saw Bendin running and waving his arms at it and screeched. The humming stopped and Bendin heard a distinct, "No, don't!" from somewhere before he watched in disbelief as the tiny possum flashed red, spurted flames, and then a wave of fire shot out from it in every direction. The wave of flame knocked Bendin over backwards, his head just missing a row as he landed on the grass. Bendin struggled, got up, and saw the possum. There was a smoldering black carcass of the possum, its fists still clutching the smoking remains of the plants that it had been collecting. Bendin nervously saw other plants close by that had been singed.

"That didn't take long, did it?" Bendin shook his head sadly, "I've only known about SAPP for ten seconds and I've already broken it. He's beyond dead."

"No, it's okay, that's a flame possum. It's alive, it does that in self-defense. We better go though, as we are nearing Dad's arrival plus dinner time." Rachel observed the possum. "It's really spectacular that they can do that." She frowned at the damages. "It's going to take me weeks to salvage--" Rachel reached down and pulled tenderly at one of the plants still in the ground. "No, it's going to be fine." She breathed a sigh of relief.

Bendin looked at his watch and it read, "14:00." He was glad it still worked as he was afraid that the journey had damaged it. He hadn't changed it and had no plans to, because it was the only thing that he had from the temple. "Rachel."

Bendin imploringly looked at Rachel.

"What is it?" Rachel stopped short, struck by his sudden seriousness.

"What happened to the Vaelift? Why is it taught that they are all gone?"

Rachel gave a small kick to the ground, frowned slightly disappointed for a second, and then perked up watching Bendin curiously, "You really are serious aren't you? I'm surprised that you think differently from the rest of us. Here sit. Real fast." Rachel sat on the ground in a cross-legged position and Bendin emulated her perfectly.

"I'll tell you very quickly as Dad will ground me if I'm not there. About 750 years ago or so, there was an event so terrible, no one believed it would ever happen. It was beyond everyone's imagination. The Vaelift had their gathering convention for the initiation of new members, but this one was special as they were celebrating some sort of new technology breakthrough. There was an incident, a defection, and many betrayals. We know now that it had all been orchestrated by Zadok, the only person ever under permanent exile. They were all destroyed in a chain of simultaneous and large explosions. The entire temple area and grounds were obliterated. After that, there hasn't been another one since. Got it?"

"I understand parts of that. Only, what I have been taught is very different. I believe you and I possibly know about the same event. At least, history isn't that messed up for everyone. It happened much longer ago, and Zadok was the great hero who saved the Vaelift from destruction, and in preserving the ways of Odge for all of us. It's very odd that everyone seems to have a completely different take on it." Bendin felt hurt inside himself.

"I don't know what to say, Bendin, that's what happened. That's all I know. By the way, like I said yesterday, there hasn't been a single Vaelift till you since that great destruction." Rachel took his hand in hers. "Are you all right?"

Bendin looked as though he was going to cry. "I'm just trying to understand. I'll figure it out. I'll ask Odge, and he'll point me in the right direction."

"To dinner then," Rachel said doubtfully. She got up and rubbed her legs.

"Thanks for telling me about the Vaelift," Bendin said struggling to get up as well.

"No problem." She smiled and gestured for him to pull out his skates.

"Here? But . . . gravity. There's gravity!"

She kept on smiling and explained, "If you angle your blades you can ride the air, even with gravity, the bonds severed and created in the air are ridiculously strong as you have no doubt realized."

Bendin looked skeptical. Rachel tried again, "I'm not going to throw you over my shoulder and carry you to dinner, but I will pull you. Otherwise I'm tempted to leave you here. You pick."

Bendin immediately double tapped the heels of his boots together and tilted his blades up at an angle.

"Now we're talking. Hold on!" Rachel grabbed his arms and she towed him slowly at first. Bendin's blades cut the air with the welding sounds and the sparks and light as before. He was surprised that, just as she had said, the blades rode the air perfectly. He had to work really hard to keep them at the position though as he kept angling them wrong. This made him crash several times into the walls, and a couple of other times he angled too far down and smashed into the floor. Each time Rachel would sigh patiently, help him up, and start again. After only a few of these and half the distance to the dining room, he was able to maintain a constant angle in balance with her tug.

"I think you got it! Good job, Bendin!" Rachel rejoiced happily. "You should have seen Pete and Ryan when they used to tow each other around the house. It was really funny and really cute. They used to do it all the time, before they both got used to skating."

Bendin and Rachel approached the dining room. Rachel pulled Bendin, by the arms, right up to his chair. The rest of the family was already there preparing to eat.

Tilmon was sitting there in his chair looking proud.

"Glad to see you connecting with the Bauyosten. I hope you are sharing your unique cultures with each other." Tilmon turned and spoke to the rest of the family as they made their way to the seats.

"Once again I would like to congratulate everyone on their most excellent performances in practice today. I saw some of the practice from the Tribunal. Each member of the Tribunal shared small portions of their own family's practices. I am proud that the Outcast and the Bauyosten are in our group." Tilmon paused and wiped a tear that had formed in his eye. "The first ones that have stayed." It must have been Tilmon's dream or something because the rest of the family clapped enthusiastically. "Now, we thank dear Celeste for the charming meal and Charles, bless, so we can eat." Charles mumbled the fastest and shortest prayer Bendin had ever heard. He could hardly tell it had been a prayer it had been so fast. Everyone dived into dinner which consisted of strange bread covered in some sort of sugar. Bendin stopped thinking about what it looked like though as his lips touched the food.

It was absolutely delicious. Nothing in the temple had ever tasted like this. The entire table was quiet for a while as everyone munched on food.

Rachel swallowed her food and whispered to Bendin, "Notice how quiet it is?"

"Yes?" Bendin wondered where she was going with this.

"It's cause the food is so good."

Bendin smiled and continued eating.

After dinner, the family got together in a room next to the dining room. It was through a passageway that was up near the ceiling on the far wall. It led to a large oval shaped room with windows in every wall, floor, and ceiling. It was hard to tell where the floor or ceiling was due to everything looking very similar. Bendin decided the floor and ceiling might just have been called walls too. There were cushions to sit everywhere and irregularities in the walls allowing for people to sit in little crevices. Tilmon called it the "sitting room". All unnatural light came from spot lights that were embedded in the walls, floors, and ceiling. As everyone sat down in their usual spots, Bendin stood in the doorway failing at trying to not look out of place. Charles came to his rescue though, and before Bendin could feel any more awkward, he beckoned him to sit with him.

"Hi Bendin," Charles said to him as he sat down. Bendin realized this area behaved just as the kitchen table did, with small localized gravity just around the sitting spots. It was kind of weird to see the kids on the ceiling, on the walls, and on the floor, but things were beginning to be less strange after a day of seeing these kinds of things.

"Hi, Charles."

"Bendin, will you come with me tomorrow for mowing?"

"Okay?" Bendin didn't know what that was.

"It's just for the morning." Charles's eyes burned into Bendin as though he had been wanting to ask him the question since he had gotten here, but hadn't till now.

Tilmon put his hands up and revealed something for everyone to see. In his hands was a large black cloth bag with a bright yellow ribbon keeping the top closed.

"Loot!" Ryan shouted. Pete chuckled and slapped Ryan enthusiastically.

"Ha. Ha. Ryan," Tilmon sarcastically said staring at his son. "*This* is for our new friend, George. He pushed off the wall on the far end and floated over to where George was sitting. Bendin realized that he had all of Tilmon's things on and that must have been why Tilmon wasn't skating all over like everyone else. He hoped he wasn't in trouble.

Tilmon bent down and whispered something into George's ear before coming over to Bendin. He whispered pulling another bag from behind him, "Even the DeSoto's contributed to your gear, so be grateful. I apologize for it not being like George's gear, but this will make you feel at home. I'd like my stuff back now." Bendin couldn't remember where he had put Tilmon's staff, but he took off the boots, and the other pieces of equipment that was Tilmon's. Tilmon sat next to Bendin as Bendin removed the items. Tilmon put on his boots and put the rest of the things in a cupboard that was inset into the sitting area's wall next to them. It had the word "Tilmon" etched into it in shiny blue letters.

"Remember Bendin, I left my boots here for you today, just so you could use them." Tilmon smiled and skated to the middle of the room in the air.

"Everyone watch them." Tilmon pointed his fingers at Bendin and George.

George, suddenly embarrassed by the attention, nervously opened the bag. He pulled a pair of black boots with shiny chrome colored soles. He turned them around and found the letters "C-l-e-f-f-s" written once on each boot in cursive in gold on the upper part of the boot on the outside edge. The effect was instantaneous, and the entire family exploded in comments, praise, and wonderment.

Bendin reached in and pulled out a pair of dark blue boots with sliver trim. Unlike George, there was no reaction from the rest of the family. Bendin felt a surge of gratitude. These were his very own boots!

"How come--" Ryan started.

"He got *Cleffs,*" Pete finished.

"What are Cleffs?" Bendin wondered out loud.

"Only the best shoes available on the market," Callapse grumbled from the opposite side of the room, his eyes full of jealousy. He folded his arms in contempt. "You will probably never need to buy another shoe for as long as you live, considering you don't lose or outgrow them."

"Can I hold them?" Soladaque skated over to him. She

begged, her eyes large and teary.

"Sure." George handed over his new boots to Soladaque.

As the rest of the family was buzzing about the new boots, Bendin pulled out the rest of the items. His own wrist-cuffs, gold-colored headband, gold-colored belt, and silver box. He discovered a note in the bottom of the sack that said, "Welcome, Bendin. Your staff is on the rack." Bendin thought it was crazy. He'd get his own staff too? George pulled out a very fancy headband, cuffs, belt, and box too. His grin forced Bendin to smile. Bendin put on all of the gear and felt like he was part of the group.

"I'll trade you mine for them," Soladaque asked George quickly.

Bendin watched him about to say yes, but Tilmon cut in before he could even begin to answer.

"They are for him and him only. Tribunal orders," Tilmon authoritatively declared. All chance of argument was effectively silenced.

Soladaque's expression went from excited to ashen. Bendin felt snug and secure in his new boots. Although a little surprised and confused at the Tribunal's restriction. No one had ever given him anything that wasn't already granted him through the temple system. This type of giving without any prerequisite blew him away. Bendin flushed as warm emotions flooded him that he couldn't explain and wasn't prepared for. He watched George try on his new boots and sighed in contentment.

"They feel perfect," George announced. "Thank you."

"Rachel, please come to the middle." Tilmon smiled and motioned her to come to the center of the room. "It's that wonderful time to celebrate the yearly mark of the day she was born. She is nine!"

Rachel skated into the middle, and the whole family chanted, "Rachel" nine times before they sang together: "Today is the ninth year from the day you came, we are so happy as a family that you bear our name, and we hug you and bless you with the grand tidings of Odge just the same!" They chanted "Rachel" nine more times. Then everyone, except Bendin, in the room skated at her or pushed off the walls, ceiling, and floor into a pile around Rachel. Bendin watched open mouthed as Rachel laughed and pushed each family member away from her one by one till they had all been pushed away.

Tilmon took Celeste's hand and pulled her next to him,

and they whispered in Rachel's ear.

"Hey! So we all can hear!" Ryan shouted.

"We're family!" Pete chimed in. "Not fair!"

Tilmon hushed them, "Let her tell you."

Rachel screamed in excitement, turned to them, and said, "They're going to take me to Levathens."

"Nice choice!" Ryan approved.

"Good job," Pete chimed in.

"Outstanding," Soladaque agreed.

There was another applause from the entire group.

Bendin asked Charles, who had returned to his seat quicker than anyone else after being pushed out of the pile, "What's Levathens?"

Charles whispered, "It's the place with a lot of special plants."

"Okay then, that makes sense." Bendin nodded his understanding.

The family went back into the dining area for treats before breaking off and heading to their rooms. Ryan drug Bendin back to George's room and humorously bumped him into walls on purpose. Bendin sat in his room contemplating the events of the day and was surprised to realize that although he was incredibly tired, he was very happy. He didn't know why, or how, but something about the Coil's home and family really struck something inside of him. It felt right.

All George wanted to do was hold his Cleffs boots he'd received. He kept double tapping them with his hands and watching the blades be exposed and unexposed. They did so with a pleasantly addicting twang.

"You know, Bendin, the distinct sound is one of the most notible things about Cleffs. No one else's boots sounds like this," George explained. "I am very lucky to have them. I'm so surprised the Tribunal did this! I didn't know I'd get anything but a formal congratulations for agreeing to come and stay with the Coils."

"I am very happy for you, George. This is all so new to me."

"Congratulations for surviving your first real day here."

"Thanks."

Later, back in his room, Bendin sat down in his meditating position and pondered the day. He offered up his unspoken question about which Vaelift story was correct, if they were both wrong, or if they were both right. He followed the formula exactly as Harmon had given him and he pleaded for an answer. He received an answer, but it was different from the last time, as he saw no light. He simply heard a distant and distinct voice say softly, "Coil's version of their destruction is true." Then it was gone. A horrible shock rippled through his body that left Bendin both satisfied that he received an answer, but confused and perplexed as to its deeper meaning. The voice was right. Bendin wondered what else, in the history that he knew, had changed.

George put his boots down watched him closely. "What are you doing?"

"I was asking Odge about history. He said that the version that the Coil's teach is true. Which means, I have a lot of questions about what happened in my past, given that what happened in my past still exists. I don't know what's going on." Bendin sighed but was pleased that he had gotten an answer to a question that had been driving him crazy since Rachel mentioned it when he first got here.

George raised his eyebrows. "Does he like talk to you or something? You can't be from the Bauyostens if you are practicing this kind of nonsensical ritual. Everyone, even the Outcasts and Bauyostens, only give token devotions. No person has ever actually communicated with Odge."

"Have you tried talking to him?"

George narrowed his eyes. "No. It's a him now, is it? Conventional, rational teaching would lead me to say that you are tromping down a path of religious suicide. Odge has no form to bind him down! There is no 'he' or 'she' or 'it'. This is common knowledge. If he did, he wouldn't be able to be everywhere at the same time."

"Why do you say these things? Have you tried talking to Odge as you would to me?"

George sat next to Bendin. "Yes, but I really don't care where you came from, who you are, or what you are doing here. Really. But I do like you and am concerned. Please promise me you won't go spreading this around that you are some sort of Odge-speaker. Otherwise I'm going to have to believe you are simply insane."

"I won't as long as he doesn't tell me to," Bendin said carefully.

George turned around and knelt on his knees and pressed his hands firmly together. "This is how we pray in the Outcasts." He continued to demonstrate as he said several things very steadily and solidly.

When he was done, Bendin asked, "What's that from?"

George, half-amused, half-irritated said, "Book of Odge page 8763 section 5 part 2, the prayer. It's what we all say. Now go, get some sleep."

Bendin rolled into bed and wondered if the rest of the family would also have such negative reactions if they thought he was talking to Odge. Which, he didn't even know if it really was Odge, but he had no reason to doubt by the way he felt. What he knew seemed to be deeper and more meaningful than such a simple feeling, thought, or surface emotion. It was so peaceful to his soul. Bendin slowly fell asleep as he wondered what the next day could possibly hold.

Chapter 8
Fall Date

Bendin was woken by a light rapping on the door. Light barely seeped into his room from the window, so Bendin determined that the sun hadn't even risen yet. "What?" Bendin mumbled loudly from his bed.

"Go away!" George huffed.

"Bendin, you told me yesterday that you'd come with me. Please," Charles begged from behind the door.

Bendin got up and almost left before he realized he'd forgotten his new gear. He put them on and pulled open the egg-shaped door. Charles was ready and holding a black and chrome colored mechanical stick with a light at the top.

"Good, you got your gear on." Charles smirked, "Please, come with me." Charles double-tapped the soles of his boots and skated off.

Bendin found his strength revived enough to skate. His vision was less blurry, but he found following Charles impossible. Bendin kept running into the walls, clipping the hooks in the fabric, and bumping his head on the ceiling. He often got disoriented which way was up or down, but Charles pulled him while skating backwards and this got rid of the problem.

Charles led him to a different part of the house. They had to skirt around various things piled around the hall to get through the double gated doorway. The room was completely dark and, the echoes in the room gave the feeling of open space. Charles turned on the mechanical light in his hand. Charles's light reflected off of very tall objects next to them. Charles led them down a smaller walkway. Gravity was normal on the walkways but Bendin guessed that anywhere far away from it, it would be gone again. Charles flicked his light towards one of the objects at the end of the walkway and it sputtered to life. Lights glowed around a craft of some sort. Bendin could make out two tiny inline forward facing seats on a very large disk-shaped machine probably five to six times their size in both length and width. Charles jumped into the front seat and motioned for him to sit in the rear.

"Buckle yourself in. This is the mower." He waved his light at the endless blackness behind him. Sunlight crept through a widening crack as very heavy metal doors opened. As light flooded the room, Bendin realized they were in a docking area for the family's vehicles. When the crack was wide enough to fit their craft through, Charles raised the mower up. It responded to his control with a sweet sensational hum. Charles opened the throttle, the hum went deeper, and it purred wonderfully.

Bendin clicked his belt just in time because the rate at which they moved backwards became phenomenal. He hardly could breathe, the movement was so sudden and fast. The day dawn broke sending rays of sunshine rippling over the horizon bursting through the clouds. The morning exploded intensely showering the world with its bluish-red light

"Here we go!" Charles screamed as he carefully rotated the craft around and pushed it forward. Although Charles was completely calm, Bendin felt nervous about the now evident rust and condition of the mower disk. It was like a living repair. Charles directed the craft down to the ground with perfect accuracy and leveled out just above the ground. Here, Bendin noticed the abstract growths of grass. Even though they grew in whatever direction they wanted, they all grew upwards. Charles led them across the yard at a quick pace till he passed the point where gravity was in effect again. He would then turn around and continue. Bendin turned around and watched as the giant disk spewed tons of loose cut grass, and whatever else was down there, high into the air behind them. They left a fine cut trail in their wake. Bendin noticed that at the area where gravity was active the growth of the grass and plants were different and more aligned.

Charles made two more passes before Bendin heard a distinct voice say, "Oh yeah! Yes! That's great you're doing fine, keep it up." It wasn't Odge's voice or anything like it. It was a sharp high pitched voice. It would come and go. Each time the voice would say something different. "Yes! This is great. Breakfast!"

Bendin leaned forward and spoke in Charles ear, "Do you hear something?" Charles didn't even look back or up or anything from what he was doing. He simply pointed up. Bendin looked up and discovered a swarm of birds swooping down into the cut grass flying into the air in their wake. Bendin shook his head and cleared his mind. He watched mesmerized as the flocks of birds followed them around the entire yard. It sounded like they were cheering and cat-calling them as they mowed the grass. Finally Bendin understood, the birds were eating the bugs and insects that were being thrown into the air. The voices? He didn't know what to make of that. He was suspicious it might be the birds themselves. Bendin watched the birds for the rest of the time Charles mowed the yard. After they had parked again where all the vehicles were parked, Charles hugged Bendin. "Thanks for coming. I wanted you to see them. Let's shower and get breakfast!"

"Thanks, Charles. It really made my morning." Bendin smiled and knew Charles was right as they were both covered in dirt, grass clippings, and an occasional bug. Charles grinned back and led Bendin to the showers. Bendin showered and went down to breakfast. Only part of the people were there when Bendin and Charles arrived. There were Ryan, Pete, Celeste, and Soladaque. They just happened to be the ones that were going to go on the date.

"Bendin! We saw you out mowing with Charles. What did you think of the old mower?" Pete asked.

"It was beyond anything I've ever seen. Those birds were terrific," Bendin said in admiration.

"We were wondering if you were ever going to come back, let alone on time. We're almost late for our classes today!" Ryan grabbed a waffle from Pete without Pete noticing.

Soladaque spoke, her mouth full of waffles, "We were--mmmpf--waiting for you--mmmpf--up till the last minute to brief you--mmmpf--on the upcoming fall date."

"Don't speak when your mouth is full Soladaque!" Celeste scolded. She turned and smiled at Bendin. "It's nice to see you up so early and running the mower with Charles. I'm happy he shared it with you."

"We get to--mmmpf--go jump today after--mmmpf--class!" Soladaque said chomping away on her food.

Celeste's focus flickered for a moment in irritation, but she didn't say anything. Instead, she expertly grabbed a small utensil from the rack behind her with blazing speed and flicked it at Soladaque's plate. Soladaque's waffle pieces lifted off the plate in a dramatic change in direction right into Soladaque's face.

"Mom!" Soladaque moaned, "My face!"

Celeste waved the utensil again, and the waffles reversed direction returning back to the plate. Celeste grinned slyly to Bendin." Bendin, please have some breakfast before you go to class."

"But, George is not here. What am I going t--"

"You're going to class with Pete and Ryan today. They will take you after class to meet Soladaque for the date."

"Mom! *We* wanted to tell him he was coming with us," Pete and Ryan whined together, "You always ruin everything!"

"Moms have a tendency to do that," Celeste said mysteriously.

"Not always," Bendin heard Ryan mutter quietly under his breath.

"Is Dad home today?" Soladaque asked, her mouth now empty.

"He's home till the beginning of next week when the tribunal kicks in their preparations for the big Heptahedron event next month." Celeste threw eating utensils into a large slot in the wall. When they came out the other slot below, they were clean and slid into a large container. She put them away in cupboards, boxes, and bins, each in their respective place. Celeste cautioned Ryan without even looking in his direction, "Ryan, eat it all. You know I don't like it when you waste food." He had half a plate of food left and was already on his way to the disposal. He froze, turned to his brother, and slunk back to the table. Pete laughed.

Bendin asked Celeste, "If money is so hard, why not eat the one-meal-pills all the time?"

Celeste warmly wrapped an arm around Bendin, "My dear, Bendin, the food we have here is from our garden and storage. It's the maintenance, cost of specialized parts of specific machines, and fabric, which is so expensive. It's the principle of not wasting what we make that I'm emphasizing."

"Where is your garden?" Bendin couldn't recall having seen anything like a food garden anywhere outside, and Rachel's garden seemed to be too small and specialized for a group of people as large as this.

"It's in a very beautiful food growing chamber deep in the caves. One of our great-great-great grandfathers hollowed out the space just for growing, and it's provided food for us for generations. Anything else really fast? You guys need to go."

"No, but--" Bendin started.

Celeste placed a waffle in his mouth and pushed him tenderly over to the table. Bendin barely had enough time to swallow his second piece before he felt a tug on his arm.

"Let's go, let's go, let's go, let's go!" Ryan urged Bendin.

"Okay, But--" Bendin yelped as they yanked him from the table, "my waffle!" His plate still contained one piece left.

Celeste winked, grabbed it, and threw it down after him. It flew through the air with precision, and Bendin caught it before they pulled him on his blades down the hall.

Pete and Ryan pulled Bendin down to the floor where the various networked rooms were located. Theirs was at the far end. They didn't have any problems dialing and activating their room like it was for George. The engine fired to life purring and humming nicely. When they pulled him into the room, Bendin heard and felt the whooshing sound of air rushing past him, and the audio and visuals came up instantaneously.

"Good day to you," Pete and Ryan said to every single person they passed, "good day to you."

"Ryan! You brought a visitor. Who is he? Where is he from? Please introduce your friend," A male's voice commanded from the front of the room.

Ryan bowed till his nose touched the floor and made a wide gesture with his hands, between which displayed Bendin. Pete did the exact same thing only mirrored on the other side of Bendin.

"We introduce you to the great, Bendin!" Ryan proclaimed in a very formal voice that Bendin had never heard him use.

"Bendin is from the Bauyostens and seeks thy admittance into class unto thee this day!" Pete finished with the same formal tone as Ryan.

A murmur shot through the class.

"Welcome great Bendin from the Bauyostens, I am Nathan." Nathan was a man with a very large belly. How Bendin managed to miss him when he came into the room was beyond all belief. "Close your mouth, Bendin, that's rude." He paused, smiled, flexed his arm, and said, "I'm all muscle."

There were snickers all across the room.

"If you will all turn to chapter 3, we'll get started then. Prurenze's law. What does it entail?"

Before any student could answer, a loud rumble was heard in the room.

Pete and Ryan's expressions were grim and flat showing straight faces to the other students.

"Anyone?" The teacher continued, "Oh no. Not this ag--"

Pete, Ryan, and Bendin choked and coughed violently.

All the students turned to see what was happening. At first it was funny, but then dark colored smoke filled the whole room. The rest of the students seemed completely unaffected by the smoke and pushed it around with their hands.

"Sorry, Nathan. We'll have to get back to you again after it's fixed," Pete shouted.

"Right," The teacher responded.

Bendin could hardly see, much less hear, the teacher through his coughing. Pete and Ryan got up and Bendin had just enough warning to activate his blades as they pulled him from the room. Once out of the room Bendin noticed the smoke around them cleared almost instantly. They deactivated the room and before they yanked him off in another direction Ryan explained, "Sorry, Bendin, the air recycler doesn't usually break down so many times, especially in the middle of the day. It's usually about once a week. Let's go check on it, shall we?"

"We shall," Pete confirmed.

"Did the rest of the class breathe the smoke?" Bendin asked as he pulled his arms free of their grasp and showed them he was going to try to skate behind them unassisted.

"No, they just get to breathe colored air. It's hilarious!" Ryan explained over his shoulder. "It's some sort of check in the system."

Pete chuckled as Bendin carefully followed them.

They led him to another room, lower down. Bendin could hear many machines off in other places around this area. The room here was big enough to hold thirty people and had only one deep throbbing machine in it. It was taller than two men and as wide as seven with pipes and tubes going to and from it from like everywhere. Two pipes in particular were full of smoke while the rest seemed to be functioning properly.

"This, my friend, is the air recycler." Ryan patted it lovingly. "It has gotten us out of many classes without permission. Mom would kill us if she found out we were doing this!"

Pete grinned at his brother as he rapidly flicked three switches. The machine clunked five times before Bendin noticed that the smoky air was clean again.

"Wow, that seems so easy." Bendin observed Ryan's face cringe.

"It's not that easy, Bendin." Ryan described throwing his hands in the air, "We made it so it does this. It took, forever."

"You take the connector valves and string them through the main chamber around the hard nose pin. You shut off the system links, place three power jacks, and slice the resisters. Place the redirector and the communicator switch in that place.

~ 121 ~

Then you pull it around on the other side and yank out the--" Pete said swiftly.

"Yes, we get the point," Ryan cut him off. Bendin couldn't help grinning at their eagerness and methods to get what they wanted.

"This machine is extremely fundamental in a house like this though. See this?" Pete grabbed a bin and pulled it out. There were many pieces of junk and random items in the bin. "This is picked up by the air system and brought here."

"You don't want to be skating through the house without your gear on and hit flying pieces of junk all the time. Trust me." Ryan grinned.

"Over here," Pete walked over to another bin, "Is where all the dirt goes." He opened the bin inside was a pile of dusty brown colored dirt.

"What do you use the dirt for?"

"It goes in the garden. Where else?" Ryan explained.

"I can't believe it. How did this happen? Where are the people that stop you from doing this?" Bendin was genuinely surprised. He'd seen behavior like this in the temple, but you were shot on spot.

"Of course! This stuff is really easy. We do the studying on our own and pass all the examinations. This leaves us to spend most our time doing what we *want* to do. The teacher has mentioned to our parents that we frequently get smoked out of class, but they haven't figured it out yet!" Pete boasted excitedly.

"And if they have, they haven't cared enough to do anything about it," Ryan muttered to Bendin.

"Oh." Bendin had never really thought about it. He'd always wanted to do whatever was in the class, not what was outside of it. "I guess that makes sense, maybe."

"Come on. Let's catch up with Soladaque!" Ryan urged.

"Right. Come, Bendin, we are catching up with Soladaque!" Pete grabbed Bendin who shrugged off his hands and pointed at his skates.

Pete shrugged. "Okay, big guy, but you got to keep up with us!

Bendin was determined to keep up with them. He managed to keep them just in sight and only bumped his head a few times. They seemed happy he could move better, and they teased him about it a couple of times along the way. They led him to the waterfall room. There, they saw Soladaque. She was dressed in a very flattering green form-fitting shirt and shorts.

Most of their shorts had an outer layer that was free and an inner layer with elastic bands that made the inner layer tight around the thigh or leg. She had on all her gear, had her staff in her hand, and another Airlarky staff in the other hand. "It worked guys! She let me out right away, checked me off, and everything!"

"Plus one!" Ryan, Pete, and Soladaque all slapped their hands together at the same time.

"You did it to her room too?" Bendin said surprised again that they'd done it to more than just themselves.

"You didn't see back in the recycle room?" Pete said disbelievingly.

"Only those two rooms, Bendin. Give us more credit than that!" Ryan beamed pounding on his own chest with a closed fist.

"Yes, we all wanted to go early." Pete smiled.

"Okay, Soladaque, give Bendin his new staff!" Ryan said authoritatively.

Soladaque gave Bendin his new staff that had been given to him as a gift from the Tribunal. It was jet black and had a small inscription near the bottom written in silver, "For: Bendin. From: The Tribunal." He moved the staff around. It was slightly thinner and lighter than the other one he had used the day before and the blade on the end, like the others, had the option to be exposed or not. It also had the other gadgets and switches of Tilmon's. He smiled bashfully and said, "Thanks."

"Now for the best part." Ryan pulled out of his pocket a piece of cloth and tied it around Bendin's eyes so that he could not see. "There." Ryan chuckled.

"What? Why is this the best part? Do I have to? How can I . . . are I . . . am I supposed to know where or how or what we are doing or going?" Bendin sudden y felt very vulnerable.

Soladaque grabbed his hands and whispered sweetly, "I'll guide you, Bendin." Her hands felt very rough. She pulled him into almost a run in an effort to keep up with her excited brothers, who had run on ahead of her. Bendin could only guess where they were going. He smelled the trees go by, the walls of the caves, the drops of water, and the hum of the falls bouncing off the walls. He didn't have any idea how far they had gone, but she stopped and Bendin bumped into her.

"Hold on," She whispered. "There!" She pulled Bendin slightly towards her and pulled him into what he felt was a small room.

"Where's Ryan and Pete?" Bendin asked puzzled that they'd run on ahead of them.

"They took the other one. Wouldn't be much of a date if they were hanging around all the time you know."

Bendin, for the life of him, had no idea what a date was unless it was a date of the week or date of the month. He was too nervous to ask.

Soladaque pulled Bendin really close to her and he could hear her heartbeat. "What do you think? Should we go up right now?"

"Sure," Bendin said, not knowing why she was asking.

"You're sure?"

"Can I take this off yet?" Bendin pointed to his blindfold.

"Well, not anymore. I was going to let you take it off for a bit, but I guess not now. Not yet." She sounded a little sad, and Bendin felt the entire room shoot up with a lurch. He fell to the ground in surprise.

"I'm sorry. I didn't give you any warning." Soladaque picked him up and held his hands close to her. "I am really excited though that you are going to do this with me!"

"I'm glad that you are really excited," Bendin replied, trying to be nice. He still didn't know what was happening or what was supposed to have just happened.

The little room stopped and she pulled him out and he was hit by a breeze. "Don't turn on your box till I say to, Bendin," Soladaque counseled, pulling him across what felt like grass and rock. It was very bright, so for the moment Bendin didn't mind having on the blindfold. He could hear the sound of running water, *lots* of running water.

"How do I do that?" Bendin asked.

"You use your wrist cuffs. There is a button on them that turns yours on and off. It's off currently, obviously, as we feel our weight right now. There are many settings that can be adjusted. You can have more or less force down. You can even have no force at all if you want. All those adjustments are available to you." Soladaque pulled him further and she pulled him up. She quickly showed Bendin how to turn on and off his silver box by feeling. "It's better for you to be able to do it without looking at it. Trust me on that one," She explained. She had him do it several times before she was confident that he was able to do it at will. It was really strange to feel like you could adjust gravity's power and direction on and off at the click of a button. She pulled him a little further up a solid rocky surface.

"Great. You guys made it before we started!" Ryan's voice floated to him against the breeze.

"Why wouldn't we make it?" Bendin's voice shook uncertainly.

"You know . . ." Pete started.

Soladaque whispered in h s ear, "Sometimes it takes much longer for the lifts to make it."

Something about that should have made him cringe, but he didn't as he couldn't figure out what was going on. Did he do something wrong?

"Is it time yet?" Bendin shouted as the wind was beginning to be very distracting.

"Almost. Now, remember to do these things: do not let go of my hand, do not activate your blades till I give two squeezes, and remember to activate your box when I squeeze your hand once. If you don't you could rip your legs right off." That didn't make Bendin feel good at all. Soladaque finished and she said them again, "Don't let go of my hand, one squeeze activate box, two squeezes activate blades. Got it?"

Bendin shook his head n the affirmative, sounded simple enough.

Soladaque made him practice till she was sure he had it right.

"It's time," Soladaque whispered excitedly.

She removed his blindfold.

It wasn't simple anymore.

It was so bright and intense that he, at first, could see nothing but the occasional annoying grey blurs that obscured his vision from time to time. Then it hit him: they were on top of the cliff overlooking the Coil's home. It was beautiful.

They were on a small flat part of the rock at the top where they had a perfectly clear view and an extremely long drop. There was a wide, fast stream of water that cascaded over the edge next to them. He'd never been this close to this much running water and he stared at t. It was so tranquil it took Bendin's breath away. It appeared cool, crisp, alive, and fresh. He knelt and felt the water run over his hands. The water was indeed cool and fresh, everything he had imagined it would be.

"Pretty, isn't it?" Soladaque whispered from next to him.

"Yes."

They could see for miles. There was the home, the jungle, the lake, the forests, the plains way out, and the mountain range that this cliff was a part of.

"Hey, Bendin watch this!" Ryan shouted.

Pete and Ryan banged their wrists together and skated up into the air over the edge of the falls. They spaced themselves evenly in the direction the stream was flowing in.

"No, guys don't. Not again, Dad's going to. . ." Soladaque held out her hands helplessly.

"No, he likes it," Pete said.

"Can't you tell?" Ryan chipped in immediately.

Soladaque's expression on her face showed she obviously couldn't tell, she had heard this particular phrase before, and she was quite annoyed.

Bendin watched the impossible. The entire stream extended itself into the field that Pete and Ryan had created. The water, not effected by gravity anymore, freely floated through their fields. Once the water hit the gravity at the end of their fields, the water plummeted to the ground once more. It was as if they had extended the ledge and were pouring water out from the ledge meters outward from where it should have been. Some of the water lapped up into them, and Bendin realized they couldn't stay there very long unless they wanted to get absolutely soaked. They laughed as the water fell much further from the house. They skated back and returned to the edge, fields deactivated. The water returned to its normal course.

"And we are off. See you at the bottom," Pete announced.

"Don't die!" Pete and Ryan said together enthusiastically.

Bendin watched for a few more seconds as Pete and Ryan leaped off separately. He leaned over the edge and watched as their bodies fell to a certain speed. It was at this speed they activated their boxes, negating gravity, and maintained their speed the rest of the way down. Further down they activated their blades and maintained their descent. The activation made a terrifically bright streak and the trail of light took longer to fade than before.

Bendin gulped. So this is what jumping meant.

Before he could back away, which was what he quickly decided to do, Soladaque grabbed his hand. She leaped with him off the ledge and shouted for joy.

As Bendin began to think, "What did I just do?" a thought overrode everything, "We are going to plunge and die."

Soladaque surprised him. Before they had gained any real speed, she squeezed his hand, and he fumbled trying to activate the switch in the wrist cuff. He activated it a half a second after Soladaque. They now fell at a constant rate, but since Bendin was a little off on his activation, she slowly circled Bendin still holding onto his hand. She corrected them by using her free hand, and she pushed against the air till they leveled out. Now they traveled at a very reasonable speed, floating downwards. The fear Bendin experienced was replaced by wonderment and thrill. Bendin could feel the air rushing past his face, but it wasn't at some crazy speed. It was a very pleasant, slow, and beautiful drop.

Soladaque yelled with a short burst of sound, bouncing her voice off of the cliff face. She eagerly listened to the resounding echo and did this four more times. The water poured down the cliff next to them in a brilliant, glittering stream. They were out far enough so that they didn't get hit by the water or affect it with their fields. Pete and Ryan were nearing the bottom of their descent and they twisted their course and coasted over the grounds of the house.

"What are they doing?" Bendin asked.

"They are seeing how far they can coast."

It was obviously a game to them. After a bit longer, the house began to loom and the roof of the waterfall room was coming closer. Soladaque squeezed his hand twice. Bendin tapped his heels and brought out his skates at the same time Soladaque. She held out her staff and Bendin grabbed it with one hand. She then grabbed his staff with her other hand. She used her own blades to steer them into a horizontal plane over the house. Soladaque released Bendin's staff and hands and skated ahead of Bendin a few paces.

Bendin was able to stay moving this time and managed to skate smoother than his last attempts. Soladaque spun around and skated backwards, watching Bendin skate in the wake of her trail.

"Not bad, you're really starting to pick this up," She called out approvingly. She swung her staff around, painted the air with the light trail from the blade in the staff, and skated in a spiral. They skated over the jungle and noticed Pete and Ryan skating back towards them.

"We're going again! I'm not going to let Ryan beat me this time!" Pete shouted, skating a direct line up towards the top of the cliff face. Soladaque followed them at a distance with Bendin following her. They stopped above the jungle with a good enough view of the cliff and water face to see the whole thing. Pete and Ryan proceeded to repeat the earlier style of jump, only they went halfway down the cliff face before visibly maintaining a constant rate of drop speed. Bendin wondered how fast they were traveling. It had to have been fast because when they activated their blades, there was a very loud explosion and a huge fireball that erupted below both of them as they activated their blades and switched directions. The sound echoed across the landscape with report. Soladaque turned to Bendin and grinned.

"Follow me, this is really neat." Soladaque skated down into the jungle. Bendin followed her apprehensively down into the foliage. He was shocked at how much space there was below the trees. There were vines, huge trees with roots and branches that had spaces much bigger than he was. The mucky floor of the jungle was covered in moss, growths of plants, and bushes scattered everywhere. There were lots of bugs, insects, birds, and animals. Everything felt so, alive.

Soladaque whipped past vines so quickly that the vines didn't touch her, repulsed by her bands. Bendin on the other hand moved too slow and got wrapped and tangled in the vines. He hung there feeling helpless as Soladaque disappeared.

The Jungle sounds overtook and overwhelmed Bendin's senses. He'd never heard them before and all this new input was terrifying. It didn't sound like a place he'd want to be very long by himself.

"Bendin!" Soladaque's voice rang out over the treetops.

"I'm down here!" Bendin shouted.

Soladaque's face appeared through the leaves above him.

"Here you are, oh dear. You have to skate a tiny bit faster so that you don't get wrapped into predicaments like this!" Soladaque deactivated her silver box and skated next to Bendin. She pulled on the vines, and then at him, but neither wouldn't budge. She had a hard time even grabbing all of them. "Bendin, you have to deactivate your box so I can get rid of these vines, you are stuck tight."

Bendin forced his wrists together and clicked off the field. All his weight returned and he realized that Soladaque was now standing fully on her skates.

Soladaque studied the various twists and vines for a minute and said, "I got it!" She swung one of her skates out at an arch and sliced all the vines connected to the top with her blade.

Bendin fell instantly. He had almost no control over his skates at all and barely managed to spiral down to the muck down on the floor. Instead of smacking with the expectant plop, he was redirected without any feeling of change in direction. His skates provided a reduction in speed, and as he slowed, he felt himself dropped into the muck with a thud. The muck was surprisingly soft, but sticky and Bendin found himself completely covered in it.

Bendin slowly sunk into the muck, and there was nothing else in the area he could grab onto. Bendin could hardly believe it, but he was actually sinking. He cried, "Help!"

Soladaque skated down to him and grabbed Bendin's staff. He held on for dear life as she skated backwards pulling him out of the muck with a loud slurp. Soladaque looked him over and smiled with a wickedly enthusiastic grin, "You are absolutely filthy. I'm glad you are okay, because that was absolutely hilarious."

"Thank you," Bendin said sarcastically wiping off muck from his face. The muck floated out of the field and sensibly plopped back down to the jungle floor. He managed a wry grin.

"Come on, let's go back to the house, and we'll clean up." Soladaque took muck out of Bendin's hair and threw it out of the weightless field.

Bendin followed Soladaque back to the Coil home, above the jungle. She stopped in front of the area where the kids separated into the different shower places. She leaned over to Bendin and whispered, "Thank you so much for jumping with me today. I loved it!" She stole a kiss on his dirty cheek before withdrawing.

"Yeah." He watched her dance out of the room in a giddy sort of walking way so that she could shower too.

Chapter 9
Quip

The next day, Bendin ate breakfast quickly and went down to class. It was unbelievably confusing due to the science that was taught, all of it things he had never heard before. It went by quickly and Bendin found himself out practicing basic Airlarky with the youngest kids before the scheduled capture the flag match. They were patient and much better than Bendin at skating. They poked and prodded Bendin for fun from time to time. They thought it was very funny that someone as big as Bendin wouldn't be as good as the other's his size. Bendin couldn't believe someone as small as them were so agile and quick. George practiced too, and Bendin felt as though he was gaining ground much faster than George.

Pete and Ryan came out of the house bearing two flags. The poles of the flags glowed red and blue respectively. The fabric themselves glistened bright blue and a bright red. They were followed by the rest of the participants.

"What's capture the flag without some flags!" Pete declared as they got closer to the small group.

"Capture?" Bendin asked.

"Yes." Ryan replied grinning.

Besides Pete and Ryan, those that had wanted to play in their game were the following: Callapse, Rachel, Soladaque, George, Bendin, Charles, Jean, Starley, Tilmon, and Crystal.

"It's six on six, there is a center line, two sides, you're safe on your home side, a jail, a flag pole for the flags, and a dozen or so obstacles and 'excitements' we made ourselves," Ryan shouted out to the group. Bendin grinned and wondered what "excitements" were. He was feeling more confident today. He hoped to help his team be the victors of the game.

Everyone followed Pete and Ryan through the air in a great procession. Bendin was starting to really feel the freedom of the air. He wasn't tripping or out of control. He felt a unique feeling that was very warm and happy. He followed Soladaque, who kept shooting glances at him to see whether he was falling behind, or just to smile and nod in encouragement. Eventually, she slowed her pace enough to slide back to where he was.

"You're doing much better I see."

"Thanks, I didn't know if that muck was ever going to come off of me."

Soladaque smiled. "I'm sorry about the vines . . . most of the stuff in the jungle comes off. There are only a few things that don't that I'm aware of--death and paralysis."

It was Bendin who laughed this time. "I hope I'm on your team."

Pete and Ryan led them over the jungle till Bendin saw an area marked off with beams made of light. There were four really thick bright white beams marking the corners shining high into the air. Somehow there were beams of light traveling horizontal to the ground connecting all four large beams forming a walled in area. The horizontal beams went from the floor of the jungle to about twenty meters above the jungle tree tops. The area was vast, and it was thick enough that you couldn't see the ground at all in most parts. You could see that there were a lot of blue lights on one side in the jungle and red lights on the other through the foliage.

"There you go guys, this is the playing field. No going outside the walls marked with white beams. If you do you score an automatic 'plus one' for the other team for every minute you are outside of the walls," Ryan explained.

"There is no height limit, except the no oxygen level, and the current score is displayed here," Pete remarked giving everyone a small display that was black and had two sets of numbers. Right now it showed two zeros separated by a colon. Bendin watched how the other players clipped the little display to their wrist cuffs and he did the same. It fit so nicely Bendin was impressed with their work.

"Pete and Ryan certainly did their work in setting all this up haven't they?" Bendin wondered in awe to Soladaque.

"Yes! They take their games very seriously."

They separated out into teams: Ryan, Tilmon, Rachel, George, Charles, and Starley were on one team. They were against Pete, Callapse, Soladaque, Bendin, Jean, and Crystal.

Pete led his team deep into their territory clutching his blue flag like a prize. "Bendin, how about you guard the flag for now?"

"Okay?" Bendin said uncomfortably, "Where's that?"

Bendin spoke too soon because a few moments later they reached the place and it was so obvious where the flag went. The place was an area that had been hollowed out so that there was an even larger opening than normal in the jungle. The flag was going to be in a blue glowing pole in the middle of the area. The flagpole went up near the upper part of the trees, but not above the tree tops. Pete placed the flag in the pole and a bright blue beam of light shot up into the air. Pete then skated up following the light, to look across the playing field. The rest of his team followed him up.

Pete ordered, "Jean, Crystal, please help defend the mid-ground." They nodded their heads in approval. "Callapse, Soladaque, and I will attempt to capture their flag without getting tagged. Any questions? Comments? Criticisms? Praise? When he places his flag, there will be some intense action." Pete intensely watched the other side.

A bright red beam of light shot upwards through the air indicating the other team had placed their flag. Pete was right. The moment both flags were in place, the whole arena came alive. The entire Jungle wiggled and moved, indicating thousands of things were moving all at the same time. Rings floated up into the air, as well as large thick pieces of land, trees, boxes, and bins. The whole arena's airscape was filled thick with chunks of clutter, much of it from the jungle below. The whole arena became dense with loads of places to hide.

"Now, that's what I'm talking about!" Callapse shouted as he skated off weaving through the debris towards the red bolt of light. Everyone but Bendin followed him in pace and energy. Bendin watched Pete running on the rocks and floating earth bouncing and leaping from one to the other. Amazingly, the force from Pete's jumps didn't move the chunks and pieces from their positions.

"Good luck, Bendin!" Soladaque shouted as she disappeared around the first large chunk of floating earth. Bendin skated down towards the flag and listened for any sounds that sounded like welding noises. They had forgotten to tell him where the jail was, but after searching the area around he saw a walled in area not too far away from the flag lit up in pretty blue lights. It was far enough away that anyone who appeared in the hollow would be forced to choose what they wanted to go after.

It didn't take long for something to happen. Tilmon burst through the trees to Bendin's right with sickening speed. His skates flashed and sparks flew off with each motion. Soladaque appeared a second later in hot pursuit.

"Tag him, Bendin!" She shouted.

Bendin watched the charging beast of Tilmon Coil skate with all his might directly towards him. Bendin didn't know why

Tilmon was smiling so much and was completely taken off guard as Tilmon skidded to a halt in the fastest stop Bendin had ever seen. The effect of the stop lit Bendin's hair and face up in a blast of heat. The echo of the blast reached his ears as the concussion of the soundwave traveled around him.

Bendin wavered, and was completely stunned and unable to move for a few seconds. His ears rung and the heat of the fireball singed his face to soot. Tilmon expertly switched his box off and used natural gravity to his advantage pulling him down and skating at the same time, just in time to be out of Soladaque's reach. Tilmon flipped his staff around so that it increased his spinning velocity, and he reactivated his silver box climbing in a breathtaking spiral around Bendin. Bendin watched transfixed as Soladaque repeated his every motion, minus blasting Bendin, gaining a bit of ground with each motion. Tilmon made it to the Flag and pulled on it. It came out with the sound of a bang.

Pete's voice rang out of the display on everyone's wrists, "The blue flag has been stolen!"

Bendin felt the entire area around the pole fill with an upwards rushing wind. The wind was so powerful that it shoved Tilmon, Soladaque, and Bendin straight up. Soladaque used this momentary change of events to close the final distance between her and her father and she succeeded in tagging him. The second her fingers touched Tilmon, Tilmon was surrounded by a blue ring of light. Ryan's voice announced out of the display on everyone's wrist, "Tilmon, has been captured!"

"Good job, Soladaque. There is agility in youth, and you have gotten much more skilled. If it hadn't been for Pete and Ryan's surprise air-blast trigger I would have gotten away with the flag for sure!"

Soladaque grinned at her father as he went to the jail. "You wish father. The air-blast trigger, right!" She gave Bendin a high-five. "Thanks for not backing down. You see, you made him change his course. Most people would have dodged or ran the other way."

"It wasn't anything. You got him after all," Bendin stated, feeling like a barbequed piece of chicken.

Soladaque eyed him in an interesting way, which suggested that she wasn't as accepting of his comment as he was of saying it. "You are just fine, Bendin. I'm tired. You go and try to capture the flag. See if you can team up with Callapse or Pete. I'll guard Dad and the flag."

Pete's voice rang out of their displays in unison, "Jean, has been captured!"

Bendin wondered about the display. "How does this thing work anyway?"

Soladaque twirled her staff and smiled. "Not now, that's way over your head. Some other time. Go!"

Bendin skated in the direction of the red beam of light that was shining upwards off in the distance. The jungle was very thick, even more so with all of the clutter and debris at all levels of height, but Bendin skated a little faster than he had the last time. He breathed a sigh of relief when he succeeded in being able to brush aside the vines and growths with his repulsive bands. The feeling was tremendous and he realized that it was pushing everything away from him, bugs, animals, vines, and branches. If it didn't move then he was moved around it without feeling the change. This gave Bendin greater confidence as he skated. He tried to curve a little, but he realized instantly he wasn't ready for the turns that the others were capable of.

Bendin made his way to the center line, which divided the two sides of the area, low and as out of sight as possible. He found there was nothing really special about the center line. There were bright orange beams that ran horizontally across the arena at varying heights. It was also the place where the little bright lights that were scattered all over changed from blue to red. That also meant that he was able to be tagged.

"Pete's voice rang out of the display on his wrist, "The red flag has been stolen!" Bendin could see the beam of red light, and he watched expectantly as there would be people thrust up into the air. He watched, disappointed, as no one appeared. He saw motion off in the distance, to the right. It was George, Charles, and Rachel, they was chasing after Crystal. Crystal was nearing the line, but it didn't look like she was going to make it. He saw something red.

She had the flag.

Bendin saw Pete and Callapse above him to the right moving through the upper section, but they must not have seen Crystal. They were skating in the direction of where the red team's jail and flag should be.

Bendin thought he'd try to help, and he excitedly skated to intercept. Bendin found a cavity of a tree to hide in and waited for Crystal to come. Crystal came, breathing very hard, through the trees opposite him. He knew she was being pursued with vigor.

"Crystal, here!" Bendin shouted out of the cavity of the tree. Without any hesitation she threw the red flag, pole and all, into the cavity and Bendin caught it. The flag glowed and pulsed in Bendin's hands. Excitement raced through him. He quickly skated out and around the tree just as her three pursuers burst through the trees. Out of the corner of his eye, he saw them launch themselves forward.

Ryan's voice came out of everyone's wrists, "Crystal has been captured!"

Bendin didn't look back. He crossed over the orange center line, and Pete's voice rang out over the wrist display, "The red flag has been captured!" The counter on Bendin's display ticked and showed a "1" where there previously was a zero.

Bendin was as surprised as anyone else. He'd captured the flag. He felt exultant.

Rachel skated up to him. "Awesome job! We didn't see her pass it off to you!"

"You're not angry that we just scored?" Bendin asked confused.

"Ha! No way. I'm not that competitive." She laughed, grabbed the red flag, and disappeared into the jungle. A few moments later the red light activated, indicating the game was on again.

It was immediately followed up by Ryan's voice declaring, "The blue prisoners have been set free!"

Bendin watched sadly as Starley led her father through the air back to their side. Tilmon grinned the whole way as he let Starley pull him back to the red side. Bendin wondered what had happened to Soladaque.

Bendin still hadn't decided what he was going to do when he heard Ryan's voice declare, "The red prisoners have been set free!"

That would mean that both teams were free and roaming around. Bendin decided to take a higher path this time. He found, with joy, that not only could you hide behind the many objects, but many of them had crevices and holes directly through them. Unfortunately, Bendin realized it was impossible to completely hide the sound of your skates and the welding sound they made if you skated too fast.

Bendin crept towards the red light. He was determined this time to capture it all by himself without the aid of anyone else. This was his attitude when he noticed something strange going on with George below him. George was tangled up in a pile of vines. Bendin thought of his own plight yesterday and felt sorry for him. Bendin skated down to where George was, but didn't let him touch him as he was on the other team.

"George, what's this, what's going on?"

George was being pulled towards the ground, by vines Bendin could barely see and pulled upwards towards the treetops by vines Bendin could make out very clearly. He realized if nothing changed the vines were going to pull George apart. Bendin skated up and around to the vines that were being pulled tighter and tighter.

"Can I cut these?" Bendin pointed at the vines.

"Yes! But don't touch--severely adhesive," George managed to squeak out in great pain.

Bendin sliced the vines pulling George up and they snapped with a loud crack. The cut vines moved upwards so quickly Bendin had no time to move out of the way. The vines latched onto Bendin's leg for a moment and pulled Bendin upwards at incredible velocity. His boots double tapped, and the adhesive failed to hold him at the highest point of extension. With a lurch and a pop, Bendin flew at a ludicrously high speed over the jungle. He shot through the light gate and Bendin watched unhindered in horror as meters and meters of landscape rolled under him. He double tapped his feet in an effort to gain some control. But the moment he activated his boots and attempted to skate, he was immediately out of control and sent off course directly down into the jungle below.

Bendin continually struggled to gain control. His body was redirected around large trees, all momentum of collision redirected by the bands. His speed still hadn't slacked but a minute amount and trees flew past of all sizes. Bendin frantically tried to use his staff and his boots combined to slow his speed. This started to work. His speed began to slow. But in the process, he lost control entirely. Bendin spun towards the ground and instead of hitting the ground as he expected, he felt redirected and began to soar above the jungle floor unable to stop.

An idea struck him and he fiddled with the controls to the silver box. He turned it off and felt the pull of gravity. He propped his feet in a "T" shape and felt the drag of the skates finally slow him down at a satisfying rate. When his speed slowed past the point of the bands redirecting his downward movement, Bendin crashed into the mud floor.

Bendin had finally stopped.

He rubbed his arms and legs painfully and took gulps of air. Everything hurt for a moment. His mind and body was still racing, even though he had stopped

He was alive. His emotions were alive, but his confidence wasn't. He had no idea where he was. He listened to the world around him. His display was showing the other team's score moving up as he was way out of bounds. He was surprised it was still working this far away. There were bruises on his body from the impact, and he tossed aside a string of thorns that had lovingly attached itself to his face when he was facedown on the ground. At lease he could move. This mud was harder than the last time he plopped onto the jungle floor.

Ryan's voice cut through the noise of the jungle, "Starley has been captured!" Bendin sighed. He might as well try and skate back.

Something bone chillingly odd stopped him before he could even lift his feet. It was a strangled kind of yelping, and it came from up ahead. Bendin skated up into the air, his silver box field reactivated, and went to see what was making this strangled cry. Bendin's heart failed him when he rounded an outcropping of rocks and saw what was there. There was an open pocket in front of a very open looming cave. The creepy pitch-black cave spooked Bendin. The light in the grove was dim, but there were enough sunbeams breaking over head to make out a tiny form clearly struggling in the middle of the area.

"I'm sorry guys. Oh, it's all my fault. Why did I even *get* up this morning?" a voice moaned, floating over from the middle of the area.

"Hello?" Bendin said poking his head into the sunbeams in the open pocket of space.

"Shhhh!" the tiny form hissed, "the Onychophora is going to come back any minute!"

"But you were just talking?"

"Quiet. The Onychophora!"

"What now? The On-ee-koh-four-ah?" Bendin whispered, sounding it out. Bendin moved towards the form and it became quite clear that it was an animal trapped in a mysterious gooey substance. The small opening was littered with the remains and bones of animals. Bendin assumed it was the Onychophora's meals. Some of the remans were still smoking as if they were freshly caught and stewed.

"Yes. Go quickly before it returns!" The small animal hissed again. Bendin saw in disbelef as the small animal burst into flames and attempted to burn the substance, but it was not yielding to the heat or catching on fire. The sound of the grinding of pebbles echoed deep from inside the cave.

"*Go!*"

Bendin ignored the pleas. He moved close to the animal and finally identified the voice with a small red fox with white markings struggling to get free. It was probably about fifteen centimeters long and ten centimeters tall.

"I want to help," Bendin pleaded.

"Inconceivable," the little fox barked. "You're human. You people don't do things like that." It sniffed, stared, yelped, and screamed.

A very menacing beast emerged from the cave. It was enormous. It had antennae on its head and was a giant slug-like worm. It was half as big as a house. But before Bendin could study it anymore, it sprayed large globs of the stuff that was all over the fox at Bendin. Bendin skated defensively throwing himself on top of the fox.

"No! What are you doing?" The fox yelled. If it could show confusion, it did to Bendin.

Bendin watched the almost clear white substance move around them, redirected by the bands. Bendin smiled to himself. He was thankful for the bands. He used the blade on his skate to cut the fox free of the substance with a careful swipe. As he finished freeing the fox, the back of Bendin's hand got stuck to the substance on the fox. He could not pull his hand free from the fox's chest.

"Great, look what you've done now human. You should have just gone away like I said in the first place," the fox grumbled sarcastically.

"You'd have been lying there like a stupid animal and eaten if I hadn't done anything!"

"So, what's that to you?" The fox murmured eyeing Bendin with the concentration of a snake. The fox crossed its free arm over the top of its chest, above Bendin's stuck hand.

"So, what? Distract that thing while we skate away." Bendin skated up away from the giant worm, and to Bendin's disbelief, the giant worm actually jumped over him. The worm's body crashed down on top of them, but as the force of the land crushed downward, Bendin watched as his body shot off in a direction away from the worm like a ball being shot out of a cannon. The little fox couldn't have weighed more than a half a kilogram. The little fox shot a stream of fire at the Onychophora while under it. He instinctively decided to light his whole body on fire because Bendin felt an extremely uncomfortable burning feeling on his hand and arm.

"Stop! You're burning me!"

"Right!" The fox's body thankfully stopped burning and he focused instead on breathing fire from his mouth. "I've never been stuck to a human before."

Bendin wondered if that was supposed to be a joke as they shot away from the giant beast. Bendin relaxed as the beast didn't give chase.

Bendin did another "T" shape stop and skated down to the ground for a moment.

"How do we get you off of my hand, little fox?"

"I don't know!" The fox bantered, "Why don't we instead focus on getting you off of my chest!"

"Well, I can't. I may know someone who can." Bendin pushed off the ground and skated up into the air. He gripped the staff in one hand and the little fox was stuck riding on the other.

The fox watched transfixed as Bendin skated through the trees.

"Mr. Fox, I'm lost. You wouldn't happen to know how to get to the Coil's would you? The giant waterfall on the cliff that pours on a house?" Bendin's arm hurt and having a little fox stuck to the back of his hand didn't help it much either.

"No. I don't know where that is. What do I look like a Coilologist?"

Bendin didn't know what to make of that either, so he skated higher up into the air. Bendin thought that maybe they'd be able to see farther and see the lights.

"Help me look. Maybe you can see further than I can." Bendin scanned completely around and didn't see anything. "You see anything? Any ideas on how to get you un-stuck?"

"No, no, and let me see no." The fox frowned and completely relaxed onto his arm.

Bendin skated down and found a spot to sit on the top of one of the tallest trees. "My name is Bendin. Who are you?"

The little fox blinked several times obviously surprised to be asked, then slowly said, "I'm Quip. Thanks for saving me, although I'm still trying to decide whether I want to talk to you. Let me think about it for a few moments longer. Considering I'm stuck here to you, my choices aren't very complex."

"Can you pull yourself off?" Bendin suggested.

Quip tried feebly to pull his body off of Bendin's right

hand, but he couldn't break the adhesive. Quip was glued to Bendin's hand. "We'll just have to wait till the Coils arrive. Then we'll see about having you removed. I'm sure they can help. I really don't want to have you stuck on my hand for the rest of my life." Bendin knew it might fully be a possibility.

Quip smiled for the first time at Bendin, "Indeed."

Bendin scanned the area again and saw, in the distance, people skating in his direction. It was the Coil's.

Bendin felt relieved to see them.

Pete reached him first. "We were so worried about you! George told us that you got catapulted a billion meters per minute by a secret, sticky vine trap."

Ryan was next, followed by the rest of the group. "Good show, good show, sorry I missed it. George said you helped save his life."

George almost gave Bendin a hug before he realized that there was an animal attached to his arm.

"How in the--" George started to say. He then whispered in Bendin's ear, "Thanks for saving my life. They had to treat my back after you left it had pulled me so hard. Any longer and I'm not sure I'd have made it." Bendin could tell George was still very shaken up about it, regardless of the calmness in his voice.

"Bendin!" Soladaque screamed when she got close. When she saw that he had a fox on his arm she paled and fainted, floating unconscious in the air.

"Bendin," Tilmon clasped him on the shoulder, "Thank you, you have performed magnificently and have the honor of the Tribunal--my word, what is this thing?"

Starley exclaimed, "You've got a baby fox on your hand!"

"Yes, I need your help, Tilmon. Can you get this sticky stuff off so I can let him go?" Bendin explained and showed the adhesive attaching the fox to the back of his hand.

"This is serious. No one touch him or the fox till I get something on it. I need the chemicals from home. Bendin follow me."

The fox remained perfectly silent and unlit. This seemed odd to Bendin, since he had been very talkative before. Maybe it was all the people around him.

Bendin followed Tilmon all the way back to the homestead. He noticed that the capture the flag playing field had been turned off. That explained why he hadn't heard any more voices from his display on his wrist. Tilmon took Bendin to a spot in the house the kids called, "Tilmon's workshop." It was a room that had so many different kinds of tools and machinery, that Bendin didn't know what anything did. He was alarmed that you needed so many different machines.

"Got to have the right tool for the job," Tilmon explained, noticing Bendin's disbelief. "I've got most of the basics, and several of the good tools for rare circumstances.

Bendin did see something that he recognized. On one of the back shelves was an R-limiter. Shock of recognition rippled through his body. Even the fox noticed, raised his head, and gazed at Bendin for a minute before he set his head back down. Tilmon produced a bottle of something he simply called "slime-remover", and he poured it on the adhesive connecting the fox to him. The effect was almost instantaneous. The sticky coating melted away leaving both of them disconnected and both of them flexing their muscles respectively.

"Where did you get that?" Bendin asked pointing to the R-limiter.

Tilmon shrugged. "It's an antique from the golden era back in the 40's. I got it as a collector's item. They are pretty rare nowadays."

Bendin walked up to it, "Does it still work?"

"I don't know. Wouldn't know how to use it if it did. We have very different systems now with a billion times the dataspace. Like the ULR-Limitless. It holds so much information, you only need one per household."

Bendin noticed that the small fox hadn't moved from the table. It was just sitting there.

"You're free, Quip. Go!" Bendin shooed his hands and watched as the fox lit on fire and blasted its way out of the room in a brilliant fire streak.

"What on Odge's great planets? That was an elemental flame fox!" Tilmon exclaimed grabbing his table in shock, "Bendin, I don't know how you managed to get him stuck on you, but an elemental one at that? It's just incredible." Tilmon slapped his desk, "And you knew its name? I've never heard of this kind of thing happening!"

"May I play with this thing? Maybe I could get lucky and see how to get it to work," Bendin asked pointing at the R-limiter. He wanted to operate it so badly. It could hold untold secrets. Especially if it was as old as Tilmon said it was.

"Of course. Just be sure not to break it."

Bendin turned around and fiddled with the R-limiter. He feigned unfamiliarity with the device and slowly flipped switches, buttons, and sequence holes to see if it was still operational. He did so in a haphazard sort of way to make it look like he didn't know what he was doing. To his delight and Tilmon's surprise the device flared up and became operational.

"The core is still good," Bendin explained. "See here? I'll bet that indicates its power levels."

Tilmon eyed him suspiciously and said, "Yes, I see. What's in it?"

Bendin feigned pushing buttons, pulling things from the back, and lastly pushing the right set of switches that caused the double helix top to come up and display its contents.

"Hey, would you look at that," Tilmon murmured.

Bendin experimentally fanned the files with his fingers and showed fake delight in his discovering how to cycle the machine.

"It's an enormous list of people that are currently registered to be a part of the annual celebration at the end of the year, year 46. There is also a list of billions of current and past lineages. There are over 5 million initial name entries. Each has a complete description for the time and place the person lives. Some are in a place called Makarias, but most in a place called Toalt." The device was smaller than the one at the DOOD, but it seemed to function identically.

Tilmon watched incredulously. "You are incredibly lucky. Unlocking an ancient R-limiter. I have no idea how you figured out how to do that. Did you find one out in the Bauyostens to fiddle with? I will say, I am impressed. It's pronounced 'tolt' by the way."

Bendin became the talk of the evening as his experience with the vines trap, the Onychophora story, saving Quip, and figuring out how to use the R-Limiter from the golden age. They couldn't stop asking him before, during, and after dinner to keep retelling the experience about the giant monster in the cave and how he bravely saved a fox's life. After dinner, Pete and Ryan told him that the creature he found in the jungle was one of the Grandelegents, ancient creatures that have been there since the creation of the world. They explained that they were non-elemental, specific creatures made by Odge to give variation in the world. They were a hot topic in the Tribunal and among families all over the world. Some tried to hunt them, but only a very few had ever been successful at eliminating them. It wasn't till Bendin settled down for bed in his room with George did Bendin realize something odd. He felt a warm glow in his covers and jumped, yelling, out of his bed in alarm.

"What is it?" George said sleepily.

"There's something in my bed!"

"Quiet! It's just me," A soft light voice wafted out from under the covers.

Bendin threw off the covers.

Quip gazed up lazily at him lying there in his bed. "Come on, put the covers back over. I'm sleepy."

"What are you doing in my bed?" Bendin demanded.

"I tracked your scent to your lair. I think we'll make quite a pair. Just go to sleep you're letting in the cold air." With that, Bendin watched Quip motion Bendin to get into the bed with his paws.

Bendin slid into bed, and Quip nuzzled up next to his back and fell quickly asleep.

George frowned, "What is going on with you? I've never heard of this either. There is no collaborating interactions between humans and the animals of their kind. You are beyond weird, Bendin. I don't think I'll ever understand you." George rolled over and faced the other direction.

"What? Come on, George, give me a break. I have no idea what's normal or not. I just don't know, most of the time I'm just as surprised as you!"

George grunted and silently killed all conversation.

Defeated, Bendin dropped off to sleep. He was quite sure he'd dream of a large Onychophora that would try and snatch him up for supper.

Chapter 10
Worship

"Get them out of here, now!" Quip's voice woke Bendin from his sleepy dreamy state. Fire flashed from Quip's mouth as he shot flames off the bed and onto the floor. Bendin noticed that Quip was being very careful not to ignite his body on fire like he had the previous day. The entire floor was seething with tiny creatures.

Bendin grabbed one of the creatures from the ground and immediately dropped it.

There were thousands of *frogs* littering the floor. Bendin couldn't believe it. Somehow their room, during the night, was flooded with frogs. "George! Help us. Wake up! There are frogs in here."

George woke up and screamed louder than any girl he'd ever heard scream.

"I *hate* frogs! Pete and Ryan are going to pay for this one!" George shouted as loud as he could. He then screamed again.

Pete and Ryan arrived in time to hear George say their names as they pounded on the door a moment later. Ryan asked, "What? There's a frog crate out here. What did we do? We want to see the frogs. If anything is contributed to *our* name it *has* to be good. Share!"

Bendin waded through the frogs and Quip jumped onto Bendin's shoulders. Quip, even on Bendin's shoulders, barbequed frogs left and right with fire bursts. Bendin opened the egg-shaped door and saw Pete and Ryan standing on top of a crate the exact width of the door frame, half the height, and two door lengths long, in front of the door. The crate read, "Ten thousand frogs." Pete and Ryan almost pushed Bendin over in their excitement.

"What does it look like? And how is that thing still here?" Pete said, anxious to see inside the room but halted and pointed to the fox.

"Ten thousand?" Quip said in disbelief.

"Why did you do this guys? By the way, this is Quip." Bendin grabbed Ryan by the shoulder and shook him. Bendin turned and remarked to Quip, "Hey. You can read?"

"Sure? One of the many things I can do." Quip shrugged and went back to blasting frogs ten at a time.

"We didn't do this, but I wish we'd thought of it first!" Pete complained.

Ryan stared at Bendin and Quip in admiration and disbelief. "We'll need to talk to you about how wrong this is later."

George hadn't stopped screaming. At the end of his scream, he'd take a huge breathe of air and begin screaming again.

"I'll bet we can help you get rid of them though," Pete said grinning. He clapped his hands and somehow managed to shout louder than George could scream, "Callapse, Soladaque, Rachel, Starley, Charles, Jean!"

All the kids sleepily came into the room.

"We were already up. You didn't have to yell for us," Callapse angrily spat at Pete.

Pete recoiled defensively skating backwards a step. "I was just being nice."

"What?" Jean asked.

"What do you want?" Starley asked.

"Help us clean these frogs up! If we work together it will go much faster and we all can get back in bed and sleep for the next few hours," Ryan explained throwing his hands up innocently.

They all jumped in and helped move the frogs back in the box. The ones that had been barbequed were placed with the live ones. Even with the extra help, it still took thirty minutes to clean them up. Once they were halfway done, George stopped screaming, but refused to be removed from his bed.

Once the room was clean, everyone went back to bed.

George sat still simply staring out into the space that had been occupied by ten thousand frogs.

"George. It's okay. They are gone now," Bendin whispered, trying to comfort him.

George said nothing.

Bendin shrugged and got back into bed. "You're sure there is nothing I can do for you, George?"

George still said nothing.

Bendin asked Quip before he fell asleep, "Did you see or hear who put the frogs there?"

Quip responded yawning, "No, I can try to track whoever it was tomorrow if you'd like." Without another word, he fell asleep nuzzled up to Bendin's back. Quip felt warm and that made Bendin smile. This was really comfortable.

Bendin noticed that George was in the exact same place, still staring blankly at the floor when he woke up.

"George, are you okay? What's wrong?" Bendin asked as nicely as he could.

George spun his hands in front of him. "I'm thinking about going back to the Outcasts. I can't take this anymore."

"The frogs?"

George's eyes were as serious as Commander Zist in his disciplinary techniques. "Yes, and all the other horrible things that have happened to me here. I can't take it anymore. You must have come to realize I'm not the first person that has come here for this test, right?"

Bendin wasn't sure since there had only been one mention of other people on his first day.

"It's as bad as they described. They were right. This was a bad idea. The things that happened here were all true."

"George. Please stop. I'm going to find out who put the frogs there. Quip said he would track whoever did this down."

"I said I would *try*, Bendin. Get it right," Quip's voice came from under the covers in a muffled tone, and Quip's head popped up onto the pillow.

"Right, Quip would *try* to track whoever did this. Why don't we do that now?"

Quip gave a disgruntled expression that made Bendin laugh. It was really funny coming from a fox.

Bendin smiled at the little fox. "How old are you anyway? I don't know how old I would be here; but where I come from, I'm eight." Bendin got dressed and ready, his boots fitting snug.

"I'm two."

Quip leaped towards Bendin's shoulder. At the height of his jump, he shot fire out of his feet downwards to give him just the lift he needed to land squarely on Bendin's shoulder. The action of the fire made a small popping sound.

"I guess . . . if there is a chance these things might stop. I'll stay," George said grimly. He finally moved, dressed, and followed Bendin and Quip into the Kid's Lounge. Bendin watched with utmost interest as Quip sniffed the air around the place where the box used to be.

"I have more scents here than the people who came last night. I'm going to need more time to be able to separate out the scents here with the people. I don't know who is who yet."

Bendin said nothing as he was afraid George would

~ 146 ~

break like a sheet of fragile crystal. George showed neither happiness nor sadness. He was straight-faced, and he didn't talk or say anything.

"At least come to breakfast Geor--"

"Look at me, Bendin, look-look-look-look-look-look-look!" Starley interrupted with fast chatter and grabbed Bendin's hands pulling on them till Bendin looked down at Starley. She pulled him to the middle of the room and skated around the room waving an ordinary shaft of wood. To Bendin and George's surprise the ordinary shaft of wood, at its tip, left a trail of bright blue color for a short time before it faded away.

Rachel poked her head into the room from the lower passages, "Great, you are finally up You guys got enough sleep for the entire weekend. Off to breakfast with the both of you!" She disappeared back down the passageway.

Starley skated down around them, tapped her stick, and the color changed to red. She stopped in front of Bendin, drew the shape of a heart, pushed her head through the heart, kissed Bendin on the cheek, and shouted lovingly, "Come to breakfast silly!" She giggled nonstop all the way to breakfast. Even Quip laughed. It was a laugh that was higher in pitch and yet deep for something his size.

"I like Starley," Quip whispered to Bendin. "She's a winner."

"I'm happy to hear you say that considering you hated all humans yesterday," Bendin whispered back.

Quip eyed Bendin with an uninterested "give-me-a-break" expression. Quip stuck out his long tongue and put it back in his mouth again.

Bendin smirked.

Everyone in the whole family was at breakfast. Most were almost done eating when George, Starley, Bendin, and Quip came in. Bendin skated up and took one of the empty seats, Quip adjusted every motion with little fire pops from his paws to keep him sitting squarely on Bendin's shoulders the whole way to the chair. Everyone in the table stopped what they were doing and focused all attention on Bendin and Quip.

There was complete silence.

"What?" Bendin said feeling all of a sudden extremely self-conscious. "Do I have lipstick on my cheek?"

"You do," Rachel said watching him and rubbing off the colored mark on his cheek. "But that's not what it is."

"The fox?" Tilmon said carefully, "Why is it still here?"

"Is he supposed to be outside or something?" Bendin asked.

"It's . . . a special animal, Bendin . . ." Tilmon said slowly.

"I know what you are thinking, and thanks for helping me out yesterday. But, I need to stay here with Bendin," Quip stated lazily.

"Why?" Tilmon obviously didn't know what else to say. "It's supposed to be impossible for your kind to *want* to be here."

"That's not what's important to me at the moment," Quip said coolly. "The other animals do what they want. I can do what I want, if it's okay that you will allow me to be here with him."

"Yes, of course, but, it's just not happened before *willingly*," Tilmon tried to explain.

"I will it," Quip said simply.

Mez raised his eyebrows and went back to eating his food slowly deep in thought.

Tilmon stared at Quip, uncertain at what to do. All the other kids, except Mez, George, Ryan, Pete, and Starley, let their jaws fall open in surprise.

"I think it's lovely." Celeste admired Bendin and Quip.

Bendin saw Tilmon relax a bit and the rest of the family continued with breakfast as normal.

"What was that all about Quip?" Bendin whispered to him.

"The special animals fought for their right to be disassociated from humans a very long time ago. They fight to keep it that way. There has been misunderstandings and ill treatment in the past that lives today," Quip whispered in Bendin's ear as Bendin ate.

"What like beatings?"

"Slavery."

"Oh dear. Why stay then?"

"I like you."

"Well, thank you." Bendin blushed. He thought that was pretty funny to hear. He finished his breakfast faster than all the others, even though most of them were almost done.

"I know whose scent it was," Quip hissed in his ear.

"You do?" Bendin whispered excitedly.

"Yes, there is a distinct scent from a person who wasn't there last night, but his scent was. That man over there sitting next to the youngest one."

Bendin glanced at the direction he was indicating for a second and saw he was referring to Josiah.

"Thanks, Quip. I think I will pay him a visit today."

The family chatted about the practice today. The extended family was coming over to practice for the Heptahedron. Quip ate Rachel's food when she was distracted by Celeste.

"Who ate my food?" Rachel accusingly pointed a finger at Ryan who threw his arms up innocently.

"What? Not me, but that's a great idea."

"You guys are always saying that! Do something constructive with your time," Rachel said also throwing her arms up in the air. She skated over to get another helping. It wasn't till she got back did she see Quip grinning ear to ear.

"Quip!" Rachel whined.

Pete and Ryan went into fits of laughter. Even Tilmon thought it was funny.

Everyone finished breakfast and headed out to the Airlarky field.

"Of course, they come almost every weekend," Rachel answered politely when Bendin asked her about the upcoming practice.

Quip relaxed on Bendin's shoulders, and Rachel kept peeking towards the east.

The Airlarky field, this time, was set up to be much bigger than the field that Bendin had played on. He learned that the "official" team for the Coil family would be playing together against other members of the various families. Bendin didn't understand that very well because they used a lot of terms he'd never heard of to describe the various relations. Bendin couldn't hope to memorize all the individual names they kept talking about. The field had seven goals, each placed at various places: up, down, right, left, front, back, and diagonally up. There were ball boxes at each of the goals.

At length, the rest of the families showed up, and Bendin watched them arrive in their vehicles of all shapes and sizes. They drove on longer versions of the skates by which he stood on. All of them seemed to be wearing similar beat up types of gear and equipment, but occasionally he'd see someone with something new looking. Soladaque skated down next to them disgusted.

"Jerry doesn't want to date me." She sighed.

"You want to date everyone. Besides, he wasn't that cool anyway, Soladaque," Rachel accused.

"Is Sebastian here yet?" Soladaque retorted. Her

question was answered immediately in the form of Rachel skating off towards an energetic black haired boy that had just arrived and was getting out of a vehicle with the rest of his family.

"I'll bet you my fur coat that's him," Quip teased.

"Fur coat? *Quip!*" Soladaque scolded. "You have no respect for the past."

"It's in the past," Quip quipped.

Rachel returned a few minutes later incredibly more depressed than Soladaque had been and refused to say anything.

Soladaque tugged on Bendin's sleeve, "Bendin, will you sit next to me then during the game? If it's not you then I have to sit with George."

"You're not playing?"

Soladaque grabbed the bottom of her shirt and tugged at it absent minded. "They wouldn't let me."

"Why?"

"I'm not as good as the others."

"Can Quip be here? I'll have to ask him," Bendin asked. Quip rolled his eyes.

"Sure." Soladaque grinned.

"Quip do you mind if she sits with us?" Bendin asked Quip.

"Do what you want," Quip said and shrugged.

Bendin sat comfortably in one of the many chairs that had been set up in the air to watch the game. Hundreds of people arrived by the time the game started and many others turned up as it went on. Most sat in chairs and other forms of furniture all around the airfield. Some were even up on the walls of the cliff-face. Others were up on the cliff looking down. Most of the people, however, were around the main part of the playing field. He couldn't believe people were able to track what was going on when the starting bell went off.

Seven teams of eight players each, making fifty-six players total, swarmed the balls that shot out of the seven ball boxes. Each team was wearing a different color, but to Bendin it was all a blur as they went flying by. Bendin noticed that almost every person watching the game in the chairs had in their hands, their own Airlarky staffs. The only exception was some people who had really tiny people in their hands. He soon realized why this was so, as some shots would go astray and the people sitting around would catch them and fire them at their favorite players or towards their favorite goals. The air was livid with streaks and colors. Quip, unimpressed, hopped down to Bendin's lap and fell asleep. Rachel's expression remained stony.

The balls were quickly caught and the number of available balls dropped down to one and the entire mass of people were all going for one ball. Once it was scored, the balls redeployed and the chaos ensued again and the game continued. The abilities of the players were admirable. They were doing twists, turns, and things Bendin had never even thought you could do in the air. Soladaque tried to describe some of the moves they were doing like "the variel" and "the kloxem". Not surprisingly, the team that was put together for the Heptahedron won and scored the highest by almost a double margin to the next closest scoring team.

The game was over.

Bendin quickly asked Soladaque, "Where does Josiah live?" Quip stirred at the sound of the name.

"He and Celeste live on the side of the lake in a pod. I can show you."

"Can we go now?" Bendin wanted to help George as soon as possible since it seemed so important to him.

"Sure, follow me."

Quip eagerly leaped back up to Bendin's shoulder and placed his front paws on Bendin's head.

She got up and skated expertly through the crowd. Bendin did decently, but he kept bumping into people as they were moving back to their vehicles.

Every person that saw Quip would stop and stare as they went by. They'd whisper, point, and return perplexed to their vehicles.

Josiah's pod turned out to be a large and dirty white ball shaped structure next to the lake near the Coil's house.

"Pod? It should be called a good for nothing shack," Quip noted miserably. "It's ugly."

Bendin nodded smiling to himself at how true that was.

Soladaque led them to one of the doorways in the pod that opened up towards the sky.

Quip tapped Bendin's head with a paw and whispered, "The smell is stronger here. This place is more than it appears."

Bendin agreed with a nod of his head. It definitely seemed much bigger than it appeared on the outside.

When they went in further, they discovered several

different kinds of instruments and tools littered all over the floor. There were passages under the ground that branched out in different directions.

Collapse waved to them. "How'd the game go?"

"Great! Can't believe you'd do this and miss it!" Soladaque smiled.

Bendin checked around the edge of the room and he saw a set of monitors with Crystal frantically typing away things on a keyboard in front of her. She was wearing headphones and didn't hear them.

"Josiah!" Soladaque greeted Josiah with a clasp of her hands on his shoulders from behind. "What are you looking at?"

"New scanner tracks some powerful energy wavelengths. Want to look through it?" Josiah had a gruff voice, very scruffy chin, and appeared very tired. His speech was excited, yet slurred.

"Yes!" Soladaque waited a moment while Josiah moved to the side. She gazed through the lens and moved the instrument around the room on its post.

"Ooo! Bendin. You look so pretty, the colors coming off of him are beautiful!"

"Wait, *what*?" Josiah snapped, "Let me look through that!" Josiah shoved Soladaque off the scanner so hard she slid back into the wall.

"Josiah?" Soladaque appeared okay, but uncertain at his surprising reaction.

Josiah rammed his eyes to the eyepiece.

"Great grandfather Jameus! You're right. Collapse, you have got to see this. It's working!"

Collapse looked through the lens and gave a high five to his brother. "Nice work!"

Both Josiah and Collapse turned towards Bendin at the same time. Josiah pleaded, "Bendin, please let me test you. You are emitting a wavelength of energy that we've only just begun to understand. Will you please come by tomorrow for some testing?"

"I guess?" Bendin, for no reason other than he wanted to get another opinion, decided to ask Quip, "Quip?"

"You do what you want," Quip said, completely relaxed and seemingly not enthused.

Collapse and Josiah shuddered with excitement.

"Josiah, you didn't happen to be responsible for the frogs in George's room last night were you?" Bendin asked.

Josiah stopped moving immediately. "No, What? What are you talking about? Frogs? Were they special frogs?"

"No, just regular frogs," Soladaque clarified moving over to stand next to Bendin.

"Check with Crystal, she might know." Josiah shrugged.

Bendin turned around and found that Crystal's chair was empty.

Later that night Bendin found George in his room, all packed.

"Just in case," George patted his case. "Did you find anything?"

"Quip say's that Josiah's scent was mingled among the other kids last night. He is acting a little suspicious in the way he immediately denied the frogs, but nothing to be truly certain. I'm sorry. Are you still going to go?"

George rubbed his chin thoughtful y. "Well? That is true. He hasn't been around here too much. He only appears on the larger family gatherings because he's always over at his pod."

"So, dead end then?" Bendin asked.

"I don't know," George said frowning. "I'm very nervous. If things could change with certa nty it wouldn't be so scary here."

Bendin thought that sounded reasonable. "I will help the best I can."

"Thanks, Bendin, but I wil be going the morning after tomorrow if nothing turns up. I want to see what the worship service is like. Good night."

Bendin nodded and settled into his prayers to Odge.

Quip crept up to Bendin trying not to laugh out loud. "What's this sitting and pressing of your hands together. You look ridiculous."

"It's my nightly ritual."

"Who are you talking to? The dead?"

"Odge."

"Ah. You keep at that then Bendin-able." Quip satisfied himself by curling up in Bendin's lap. Bendin during his prayer for understanding and guidance heard a simple instruction, "Do not let them test you." Bendin thought that seemed simple enough.

The next day the whole family went to worship together. Bendin had never seen this and was more than a little excited to see how they worshiped Odge. They went to yet another part of the network floor of their home. The room was big enough to be a gym, but there were only enough chairs for everyone in the family. When they walked into the room Bendin heard the swooshing sounds and the sounds of hundreds of people filled his ears. The small gym room disappeared and was replaced by the largest gathering of people Bendin had ever seen. The gathering was in a room twenty to a hundred times bigger than the one he was in.

"We are part of the main followers of Odge group," Soladaque tried to explain to Bendin how the different groups had appeared over the years. "Unlike the school rooms, these have limitless walls."

"Limit-what?" Bendin said confused.

"Just be careful you don't walk into the real walls."

Bendin soon learned why this instruction was given because Quip, when seeing so many humans, went scurrying off to the side. He only went a very short distance before he slammed into an invisible wall. Quip yelped in pain feeling the part he had just smashed into. Others around him noticed and couldn't help a bit of mirth creeping onto their faces. Quip then returned swiftly to Bendin, rubbing his nose, and settled on Bendin's lap instead.

"Stupid fake room!" Quip grumbly remarked. Apparently Quip was not familiar with this technology.

Bendin caught Josiah on the sleeve and said firmly, "I'm not going to be tested."

Josiah's head drooped. "I'm very sorry to hear you say that."

Crystal watched Josiah and frowned.

Callapse cried, "Why?"

"Odge told me not to be tested."

"Odge?" Callapse laughed directly into Bendin's face. "Ludicrous! Odge only talks through the book, and that's only if you believe it."

Celeste slapped Callapse on the shoulder, "Callapse! We're in worship!"

Bendin didn't respond. He didn't have to because arguing just wasn't worth it.

The ceremony was simple. A man got up on a stage, which was twice the size as the one back in his temple, and they played very loud music. Most of the congregation got up and sang to the music, while some danced. Once the music was over, Bendin watched the man talk the entire time about the perfection of the Book of Odge and of the salvation of everyone. The people shouted, "Odge rules!" as loud as they could. They sang a final song and went back to their normal duties leaving the room in various different quadrants. Worship was over. For Bendin, it was quite a let down. There hadn't been a single firework launched the whole time.

"Do you guys do the same kind of thing every week?" Bendin asked Rachel.

For the first time since the family's Heptahedron practice, she spoke, "Yes, Bendin, it's been going on for centuries exactly like this."

"Is there a main room where this is hosted somewhere?" Bendin asked getting out of his chair and walking out of the room. Quip rode on his shoulders eyeing the room with disdain and everyone with concern and caution.

"There is the main one in Hymingway, and it's that center section over there. See how they are moving around in the larger area? The rest of us are from all over the place, but limited on how far we go due to the limitations on the size of this room. It's always funny to watch people go too far, which is very easy to do, and slam into the walls that you can't see."

"Thanks, Rachel. When are they taking you to the plant place?"

"You mean Levathens? That's not till next month. It'll be either before, during, or after the Heptahedron."

"How are you guys powering your place?" Bendin had been really wondering this.

"Wow, you haven't seen the fusion room yet. George?" Rachel rapped George on the shoulder. "Would you like to come down to the fusion room?"

"Sure." George's hair was messed up, and his eyes red. Bendin knew he hadn't slept well, constantly turning over in his bed speaking of the frogs.

Rachel led them down instead of up with the rest of the family. "These passages lead to the various machines that generate power to the place, recycle the air, check the environment for weather changes, run the networks, and produce the field that is around the home. This one leads to the heart of the source of power." Rachel pointed straight down the passage. The air in the passage seemed light and friendly. Quip smiled and breathed the air flowing past his face with exaggerated pleasure. He did it several times and after each one peeked at Bendin and slowly got closer to Bendin's ear.

"Quip!" Bendin laughed.

Bendin, Quip, and George heard, as they got closer, the

throbbing of a solid, heavy, bulky machine. It was much deeper and louder than the air recycler. The room they entered was very small by comparison to the gym, and the machine filled most of the room.

"Each family is given one," Rachel explained. "When the kids move away from their families they make or are given their own later. It's up to them whether to build it. This one has been going since the first original was designed. It is known as "C-Coil" the second one to become fully operational."

The silver machine emitted a bright green light through multiple square windows around the machine. There were pipes of all sizes running to it and away from it. There were also various wires and boxes scattered throughout the area surrounding it. Bendin thought that these wires and pipes must be what carries the power to the other machines.

There was no warning. Bendin watched Rachel and George collapse to the ground unconscious. Quip flew into the air for a moment before he crashed to the ground. Bendin was the last to fall, uncertain what had happened to any of them.

Bendin groggily opened his eyes to see Quip hanging by his tail from a large cable attached to the ceiling. He couldn't tell whether Quip was alive or dead. Rachel was tied to a chair next to him, and George was chained to the wall behind her. Bendin was chained to a large chair and had no idea where he was.

He knew the people the moment they entered the room. Broad shoulders, dark brown hair and a protruding chin matched the form of Callapse. He was followed by Josiah and Crystal.

Crystal spoke first authoritatively, "Get him down and going. I'll make sure the others stay under long enough for you to finish your procedures."

Josiah sighed. "I just wish we didn't have to take Rachel. She is my sister you know.

Callapse cringed.

Crystal frowned. "You know what's at stake."

Josiah and Callapse frowned, sternly strode over to Bendin, and tapped on several of the buttons that lined the walls. There were buttons all over the place. A large machine next to Bendin's chair buzzed to life.

"Let me go, I told you I wasn't to be tested!" Bendin tugged angrily at the chains and stared at them.

"So? Your pitiful squabbling won't prevent me from making one of the greatest discoveries of our day," Josiah said contemptuously.

"I'm telling you, Odge will be angry with y--" Bendin warned.

"Odge crodge bodge podge. Nonsense!" Josiah muttered. "I'm not scared of something that never shows itself. Nonsense. Odge is tethered in and to a book."

"What do you want from me?" Bendin shouted.

"To be quiet!" Josiah barked. He cradled Bendin's arm delicately for a moment and then shoved a large needle into it.

Bendin watched, horrified as blood from him flowed up a tube and out of the room. "I'm not to be tested . . ." He mumbled as he quickly fainted.

Bendin woke several times barely coming awake before Josiah's voice said close to him, "No, not ready yet. Here." After that, Bendin didn't remember anything.

When Bendin finally was able to wake fully, he was still chained in the same chair. The others were awake, but not moving. Bendin noticed that Quip was breathing very subtly. Bendin felt a slight sense of elation. At least Quip was breathing. Rachel was white as a ghost and wasn't moving. George's expression was mournful. There was no one in the immediate room, but Bendin could hear excited mumbles of chatter floating in from outside the room.

He picked up only pieces: "We . . . it . . . rays . . . machine."

Bendin studied the area for a way to get out of his predicament. There wasn't anything within reach because his arms were tied, his feet were tied, and he didn't have on any of his gear except his boots. He was surprised they hadn't taken them from him.

"Quip, are you okay?" Bendin whispered.

Quip grinned without opening his eyes and made a sound that sounded like a soft, "Shhh!"

Josiah, Callapse, and Crystal came back inside the room.

"Make sure they're still out,' Josiah ordered, "Check."

"Yeah, they are out," Callapse said lazily.

"Check them ya doof! I need to make sure these things are in place before we check this again."

Callapse grumbled and walked over to Bendin. Bendin tried to remain as still as he could.

"He will need put under again. I think he's actually awake this time," Callapse determined.

Bendin sighed internally. He had no idea how long he'd been there. He was nervous because of all the times he almost woke up. Surely someone would have noticed they were missing.

"We only need a few more tests, and we should be able to then turn them over to you and the WAAO," Josiah told Crystal. "Callapse put that on Bendin. Let's do this quickly. We've almost got it nailed."

Callapse put a small round disk on Bendin's head and Bendin fell asleep instantly.

Bendin felt like he woke again immediately, but after a quick check around, things were different. How much time had passed he could not tell, but he was still clamped and chained into his chair. His muscles hurt very much and he felt weak. Rachel and George were not here. He hoped they were all right. Quip was now in a ball on the floor.

"Quip?" Bendin said weakly.

Quip perked up his head and spoke clearly, "Yes, finally, you are awake. The time is now in which we make our escape." Quip showed his paws were free and that he was free of any bindings. He began working on the chair Bendin was sitting in.

"How did you . . ." Bendin started to say, but stopped when he saw Quip flip several switches on the chair. Quip blasted himself to the wall and flipped a few more. The latches on the chair snapped open, the chains clattered to the floor, and the chair vibrated lightly, as if it was glad that it was finally letting go of its captive.

"You are one foxy little fox. I can't believe you figured all that out."

"When you watch anyone long enough, you pick things up. We only have a few minutes in our window of opportunity. We have to make this work. Follow me."

Bendin staggered and fell to the floor. "I can't move hardly at all, Quip. I'm exhausted. I'm weak."

Quip trotted over to him and pressed his head up under Bendin's hand. "Use me."

With more force than Bendin thought Quip could do, Quip shot fire downward and pushed Bendin's hand upward. Bendin was astonished that such a small fox could put this much force into his hand. It worked. Using Quip as a counterbalance, Bendin staggered with a slow controlled gait out the door.

"Go right!" Quip commanded.

Bendin went right, walked down a short hallway, and, to

his surprise, through a doorway out into sunshine.

"Go straight, and don't stop till I say!" Quip shouted.

Bendin did his best and managed to travel quite a bit till they reached a small stream. The little fox exclaimed, "Okay. That's it. That's enough."

Quip fell to the ground as Bendin fell and they lay there for a moment looking at each other. Bendin drank from the stream as did Quip.

"What happened? Where are the rest of them?"

"They weren't taken far. They were taken to another room lower down."

"Why didn't we go get them? Quip? We need to go get them when we can!"

Quip sighed, then shrugged. "Whatever you want, Bendin."

"Thanks for getting us out, Quip. You were brilliant. Firery-ly." Bendin smiled at Quip and petted him admiringly.

Quip responded with a sigh of contentment and curled up next to Bendin. "Check your pocket if you hungry, I put some of those pills in there that they were using for their meals."

"You hungry?" Bendin raised one eyebrow.

"Haar haar, I already had one. It's how I have been able to keep most of my strength."

"You eat the pills too?" Bendin thought that sounded kind of funny.

"I eat everything that you do " Quip said with a wry smile.

"Oh hah." Bendin pulled out a pill and ate it. He felt his body kick inside himself and almost threw it up. Bendin made a disgusted face. "That went down hard."

Bendin only had to wait a few minutes before he felt strength seep back into his system It felt so good that Bendin leaned backwards, sighed, and gazed at the clouds flowing overhead. "Let's go help the others."

Quip shook his head affirmatively and blasted himself up on Bendin's shoulders.

They arrived back at the place they left coming from the other direction. It was then that Bendin saw a large lake in the distance and realized that the Coil household was on the other side of the lake.

"Quip, we've been here this close to the Coils this whole time? How long have we been here?"

"I'd say probably a week, Bendin."

"A week?" Bendin rubbed his eyes in complete shock.

They didn't see anyone going in or out, and they didn't hear anyone either.

"The scent trail is cold. They haven't been here for a couple of hours now. Let's go in."

Quip and Bendin went in and passed through other rooms that had machines automatically assembling parts and pieces. Whatever they were making was completely foreign to both Bendin and Quip because they looked at each other, shrugged, and went down a passage that led lower into the ground.

They passed room after room, and towards the end of the third floor down, they found Rachel and George conveniently by themselves. Rachel was locked to a table in one room and her clothes were tattered and torn. George was chained to the back wall of the other room. His body was bruised, thin, and sick.

"I'll bet they weren't expecting someone to try to come and break them out," Bendin said, happiness and hope surged through him.

Bendin found a switch for the first door, and Quip searched for the switches to release George's door and chains.

Bendin went into Rachel's room and shook Rachel lightly. She opened her eyes a little.

"Bendin?"

"Yes, it's me."

Rachel gave a weak smile and pointed to a switch on the far upper corner of the room. "That tiny one."

"Quip, please get that one up there. I can't reach it." Bendin pointed toward the switch she had pointed at.

Quip blasted himself up to the switch with his fire and flicked it with his paw. The braces that held her on the table released, and she rolled slowly into a sitting position.

"Eat." Bendin gave her a meal pill.

Rachel took the pill gingerly.

Bendin went to George and found he could not move or talk.

"What did they do to you?" Bendin asked.

Quip studied the switches for a bit before deciding on one. He flipped it and yipped happily as it unlocked George's braces. "That's it. Let's roll out of this dungeon of misery."

Rachel stumbled into the room trying to walk. Bendin carried George over his shoulder, even though George was not light and it took all of Bendin's concentration to keep moving forward.

"Quip, please guide us out of here." Bendin listened and was relieved to hear nothing but the machinery operating on the floor above them.

Quip led them up two floors easily, but, as he led them to go through the doorway to the first floor, it was filled immediately by the bulk of Callapse. Crystal, Josiah, and Callapse had returned from wherever they had been.

"They've escaped!" Callapse said astonished.

"How?" screamed Josiah.

"Stop them immediately!" Crystal commanded. "I still need them! They will ruin everything."

"Take them down that passage! Now!" Quip shouted to Bendin and pointed to a passage behind them. "I'll catch up!" Bendin, fearful for Quip, watched Quip in amazement as he backed down the passage. Quip filed the entire entrance and the room with very thick black smoke. Crystal, Callapse, and Josiah fell over in coughing fits.

Quip caught up with them down the tunnel.

"I didn't know you could do that, Quip," Bendin commented breathing very heavily.

"Neither did I! I just thought of it!" Quip announced proudly.

"Where does this tunnel go?"

"It smelled like it went back to the Coil's house. I trust my nose; it will."

It did.

It led directly into the fusion core of the house's back maintenance room. From there they went straight up to the passage that was connected to the dining room.

When Bendin walked into the dining room, he saw the rest of the family there eating lunch as if nothing had changed at all. He guessed they had been doing some Airlarky as they all had on their staffs with them.

Tilmon saw them first. "And here they come. Freshly back from the testing and trials!"

"Tilmon, look at them, they look horrible!" Celeste gasped grabbing the table with her hands.

Celeste quickly skated down to them and took George from Bendin.

The rest of the family skated down to see them.

"Bendin! What happened to you?! Rachel? Oh my!" Soladaque squeezed Bendin and Rachel's shoulders with her hands.

"Have you been on the wilderness survival challenge course?" Pete asked. "I've always heard it's really tough."

"Are you going to die?" Starley asked.

"No, let me guess, you've survived a tornado!" Ryan pitched.

"Bendin, what happened? How hard were the tests?" Jean pleaded.

The kids kept trying to grab Quip, so Quip jumped on Bendin's head to get out of their grasp. The small kids skated up to get him, and he blew a small flame in their direction if they got too close to keep them away.

"Hush," Celeste said calming the kids down.

"Charles, get some water. Starley, get some healing cream, and Jean, go grab me my towels."

"What kind of tests and trials did they do?" Tilmon asked.

Bendin described what he could. "I'm not sure exactly what happened. I was out of it for the most part. When I was conscious, which wasn't very often, maybe even only two times, they were doing blood tests. They had everyone chained. Crystal was managing them for the most part for something called 'W'-'A'-'A'-'O'".

"Awful!" Tilmon yelled. Bendin knew Tilmon wasn't just saying he believed that. He showed it. Tilmon's face tinged the color of red and he ordered, "Mez, Soladaque, Pete, if they're right, help me capture them in case they resist or try to get away."

"Yes, Dad," Pete and Soladaque said immediately.

Mez nodded his head and skated directly out the door.

Tilmon yelled as he bolted after Mez from the room in a rage so fierce he slammed the wall on his way out the door with his Airlarky staff. Chunks of the wall split open and dust filtered out into the air currents. Tilmon left a very visible outline of the staff end imprinted in the wall. Pete and Soladaque followed directly in the wake of his wrath.

"What's the WAAO?" Bendin asked puzzled.

"It stands for Wythan Anslaviate Authorities Organized." Ryan's face grew grim as he saw Bendin and Quip's confused expressions. "I think of it like this instead, We Are Against Outcasts," Ryan explained. "They are the largest group that oppose the work that Tilmon has been slaving over."

"I can't believe that Crystal would have taken such extremes. If so, I wonder how high up she is, but I really do hope she's . . . " Celeste wondered aloud. Celeste held Rachel close. "Found."

"I guess we'll have to wait till Dad gets back to find out," Ryan said grabbing some more food from the table.

They didn't wait long as Tilmon returned carrying an unconscious Crystal. He was followed by Josiah and Callapse muttering excuses.

"She resisted. They didn't," Tilmon said simply. "Josiah, please fill them in."

"She wanted to help us figure out how the new waves that we had discovered were associated with Bendin. Quip, Rachel, and George were for Crystal's personal studies," Josiah explained.

Crystal stirred, opened her eyes, and saw everyone around her watching her. Her eyes widened and she sputtered, "They made me do it!" She pleaded. "It was all my father's fault."

"Sure, whatever. I know your father. He's in no way what you are." Tilmon slammed his fist into his open palm. "What exactly did you do to them?"

"We tested Bendin to understand the new waves better and ran trials on the others. We've been teaching them and testing them. What we've been doing is revolutionary," Crystal enthusiastically explained with such conviction it was hard to believe that she wasn't telling them the truth.

Tilmon squashed her statement with deep clear distinct tone. "You told us specifically, 'you were taking good care of them, helping them expand their talents, taking them on trips, and watching over them like their own mother'. You lied. You've actually been working for the WAAO!"

Crystal twitched nervously but didn't change her expression, "So? What about it?"

"How do you fit into it?"

Crystal looked around the room at everyone staring at her. She started crying and didn't stop for minutes. Once she stopped, she gritted her teeth and glared at George.

"Of course I did it. I've done it to all of them. I've also been doing everything to you George. I'm proud of it! You disgust me. You are wretched, foul, slimy, dreadful, ugly, evil, sick, and full of grime! I *hate* you and your scum people. You do not belong in our society. You left us for your own righteous reasons originally, and you will not drag us down to your uncivilized, uncultured, sick and twisted level! I hate you!" Crystal got up and would have slapped George if Josiah hadn't grabbed

~ 163 ~

her and held her back firmly.

"Stop." Josiah stared into her eyes. "Crystal, how long have you felt this way?"

"I've always known them for what they are."

"Josiah and Callapse how long have *you* known about this?" Tilmon accused them.

Callapse shrugged, "I didn't think that it was wrong as long as we were pushing the boundaries of our knowledge."

Josiah held Crystal, "I've explained to Crystal many times during this whole test that I only needed Bendin. She threatened to cut off our extra resources if we didn't go along with what she wanted. The WAAO has actually been very useful as they have sent us quite a bit of expensive resources that I've been able to use in my experiments."

Tilmon eyed them carefully. "There will be no more association with the WAAO. We don't accept resources from corrupt organizations, no matter how lucrative. We don't accept this kind of testing in the pushing forward the boundaries of our knowledge. The only way is the right way."

Josiah frowned.

"We don't torture anyone in the name of anything. I'm going to send you through the court system. Are we clear?"

Callapse and Josiah, ashamed, sheepishly looked down and mumbled, "Yes, father," but Crystal remained silently defiant.

"You're going to the tribunal to stand trial," Tilmon said. "We leave tomorrow."

"No, don't make me go," Crystal pleaded.

"Then you agree to full restitution."

"I will never agree to that," Crystal said falling silent. She sat still, alert, and tense.

"Charles go and grab me three Static-Cuffs from my shop," Tilmon ordered.

Charles disappeared and came back with oversized handcuffs.

Tilmon put them on Crystal, Callapse, and Josiah and set them on the floor where they clamped down with an audible click. "No one release them. They are going to stand before the tribunal tomorrow."

Bendin could feel living tension in the room among every family member. Pete came over to Quip and nuzzled Quip's chin with his finger. "He's kind of cute, Bendin." Quip blew a perfect smoke ring around Pete's head causing Ryan to laugh.

The rest of the family came over and clapped Bendin and the others on their shoulders. Mez stood quiet, clad in black, and equipped with different items than the rest of the family. His face was very grim and sad. As his eyes lighted upon Quip, Bendin was sure he saw Mez stiffen ever so slightly. He was dark wonder with an air of mystery surrounding him.

The other kids helped them get back to their rooms for much needed sleep and recovery. Odge sadly didn't respond to Bendin's prayers at all.

Chapter 11
The Heptahedron

Over the next few days, Bendin spent time in class, learned to read, wrote some characters, learned to skate better with Soladaque, played capture the flag with Pete and Ryan, and helped Rachel with her plants. He taught Quip to pray, because Quip had wanted to learn this strange technique. Quip explained that after being tied up he began to take Bendin's funny ritual more seriously. So seriously that Bendin began to want Quip to go back to teasing him about praying. Even with that attitude, Bendin thought it was the funniest thing to watch Quip cross his legs and try to pray like he did.

Bendin ventured into Tilmon's shop to watch him work with the different machines every now and then. After Crystal's trial, she was locked up in the prison in Hymingway. She would be there for thirty years for holding captives. It was supposed to be forty years, but she had confessed true names and locations of a couple of other prominent leaders in the WAAO group. Josiah and Callapse had gotten heavy fines for assisting in keeping captives. They served no time due to Crystal's strong confession.

Rachel was much closer to Bendin now that he and Quip had helped her get out of Crystal and Josiah's lab. He had helped in her garden to come up with a system to keep the animals from converting her garden into a salad bar. He really didn't know anything about the plants, but he worked on the logical and defense strategies that he was familiar with in the DOOD department. Quip was growing a tiny bit bigger every day, and he claimed that he'd be full grown by the end of the year. Bendin had asked how big fully grown was. Quip had replied that he'd probably be a massive one kilogram fox sporting a thirty centimeters long and about twenty-one centimeters tall masculine body that the lady foxes would die for. Soladaque was as interested in Bendin as Rachel was. He was very uncertain about how to react to the extra attention. So, Bendin had decided to let it go wherever and see what would happen.

After Crystal had been sent away, George had been nursed to health and genuinely enjoyed himself. He had decided to give it another chance since she was gone, and the accidents and mishaps surrounding him vanished entirely. Quip showed a more positive side as well as time went on. Even after only a month, Quip was greatly loved by Tilmon's family.

The Heptahedron day finally arrived.

"Got everything? Quip asked as Bendin sorted through the last of the things he had managed to accumulate. Along with his gold colored belt, he now had little capsules that clipped to the belt that held the full meal pills. Another one of them had the once a month gravity pills. He also had found a nice water container to secure on his belt too, one that could be used in whatever environment you found yourself in. After his experience with Crystal, he didn't want it to happen again where he'd be without the option of having some extra food or water on hand.

"Which girl do you like Bendin?" Quip teased.

"I like them both, Quip."

"No, who do you like more?" Quip had adopted this habit of making it quite clear that Bendin was supposed to choose to like someone over someone else. Bendin didn't think it really mattered.

"I don't know yet. They both have admirable traits. So, I'd say right now it's about equal."

"You're impossible." Quip chuckled and rode on Bendin's shoulder out to the place where the family kept their vehicles. Bendin, so far, had only ridden a few times on the mower. He'd never been in one of their other vehicles.

Everyone was standing next to the vehicle in the light shining from the fully open docking door.

"This is the family bubble," Ryan declared making hand motions that were far to elaborate for just a vehicle.

"Please climb aboard mister Bendin and mister Quip," Pete announced making similar gestures as his brother and making it so Bendin and Quip would step in first.

Bendin noted they were wearing traditional green tinted Coil attire. Tilmon had managed to get seats in the Coil section of the Heptahedron, so this was the very first year that they were actually going to attend inside the Heptahedron. The rest of the families would be attending via the gym network room and use the limitless walls to see and hear the event as if they were there.

The family bubble was in the general shape of a soap bubble, but the only thing clear was a front cracked windshield and some portholes on the sides. The other parts of the bubble were made of a solid silver-colored material. The whole thing had blades on the bottom that sat in tracks that ran around the bubble. Bendin didn't know what the tracks were for, yet this didn't stop him from expressing incredible interest in its design. The bubble sat high above the ground next to the metal platforms.

"How do I look?" Soladaque's voice floated up from the back of the bubble.

"You look fine," Bendin said in a tone slightly higher than monotone.

Quip fell off his shoulder and landed on the floor of the bubble in a fit of laughter. "I'm sorry," he said after a few seconds. "I couldn't help it. You're so hopeless."

Bendin stared at Quip with a straight face and studied the inside of the vehicle. Simple red carpet, comfortable chairs, and soft benches.

"Get in get in get in! Tilmon pushed Pete and Ryan into the bubble. Tilmon got in and fired up the engine. It throbbed similar to all the other engines Bendin had heard so far.

"Bendin, sit back here!" Soladaque called out. On the back seat sat both Soladaque and Rachel. He sat in the middle between them and Quip sat on his lap listening to the pleasant throbbing of the engine that was just behind them.

"Where's Josiah and Mez?" Bendin asked. Mez had been off doing his job for the month and had only sent back one message to Tilmon that he had been closing in on one of the trails he'd been hoping to find. So far, no one had explained anything about him other than he had a special job.

"Josiah's staying with his kids, and Mez is doing his roaming job. Josiah didn't want to mess with the kids in public today," Celeste said from the front.

"I can't believe *you* are going out in public today," Pete pointed out sarcastically.

Bendin saw a smile creep up on the edges of Celeste's face before she turned around in her seat.

"Mom, can I have something sweet?" Starley asked. She was sitting next to Charles playing with a handheld device that Bendin had learned was used for entertainment. He hadn't ever seen anything like it in the temples.

"No, sweetie, not yet. Maybe later"

George settled down in the seat behind Starley and Charles as Jean fiddled with something she called "crafting".

"Is this bubble safe?" Quip asked.

"No, of course not." Pete laughed. "But it's lightning fast!"

As soon as Pete finished talking, the entire bubble moved backwards with a jerk. Tilmon apologized, flipped some different switches which sounded like chimes being swatted, and the bubble smoothly backed up. Bendin leaned over Rachel to look out the porthole. Bendin felt Rachel move slightly under him as he watched in elated awestruck enrapture as the landscape flew by them. Faster, faster, and faster went the bubble till the whole countryside was a blur. There were several pops and bangs that came from outside, and the bubble shaped vehicle was flying on its way.

"This thing isn't for sightseeing. That's for sure," Ryan noted seeing Bendin glued to the view at the porthole. Bendin relaxed a bit, leaned back to his middle seat, yet continued to watch the blurring landscape through the porthole. His mind mentally blown away at how fast they were traveling.

"I've never gone this fast before," Bendin remarked after a while.

"Bendin, check out my window. Look at this!" Soladaque called.

Bendin leaned across her and looked out her porthole. "What? What is it?" Bendin looked up at Soladaque and caught her grin and wink at Rachel. Bendin frowned and turned back to the window.

"All I see is a blur. But way out there at the horizon, there are forests and trees. Wait, you're right. What is that?"

"What?" Soladaque asked squeezing her face next to his. Quip squeezed his head next to Bendin's other side to see so that all three were side by side peering out the porthole.

"What is that forest out there? It's higher, taller, and bigger than anything else in the area," Bendin said describing the thick green mess he could see in the distance.

Soladaque pursed her lips together and let out a gust of air that fogged up the window. "That's Thibracketory. Massive area that is thick . . . unbridled. Full of Grandelegents."

"Yeah, the forest is so thick you can't get through it, and even if you could the animals are so dangerous there you wouldn't last a second," Pete said knowingly. "I might, but you . . ."

Ryan laughed and commented, "Anyone that has tried hasn't come back." He smiled. "Someday I'm going to be the one to navigate through and make it back."

"No, you are not!" Celeste scolded him. "The only thing you are going to be doing is not doing that."

"Mom, that's horribly vague and simple language. I need options!" Ryan whined.

"I am discordant with your desire and deny consent which I cognize obviously clashes with your ambitiousness!"

"Normal words aren't so bad," Pete whispered to Ryan who had widened his eyes in dismay.

Bendin studied the thick mass in the far distance with interest. It had to be thousands of miles away. "How many great creatures are in the world?"

"No one knows," Rachel said quietly. "It's a mystery."

"How about a secret?" Ryan wondered aloud.

"Yeah, the great secret," Pete agreed.

Bendin pulled himself back into his seat. Quip climbed up on his shoulder and watched the rear through a porthole above them near the ceiling.

"Thanks for letting me know about Thybracetary," Bendin said graciously to Soladaque.

"It's Th-ih-Braack-eh-tor-ee Bendin," Callapse argued from one of the front seats. He turned and glared at Bendin. "Let's go drop him off."

"Callapse!" Celeste scolded again from the front seat. She turned and slapped Callapse on the shoulder with her hand.

"Mom!" Callapse spread his arms out in innocence.

"No thanks, Callapse," Bendin said, and then mumbled more to himself than anyone else, "No thanks."

Bendin felt the mass of his body shift forward as the vehicle slowed down.

"We're entering the slower airspace," Tilmon explained from up front. "Sorry. I didn't warn anyone." Tilmon clicked a button and a beep came from the front. A woman's voice said clearly, "Prepare to decelerate."

"There, now you've been warned." He chuckled as Celeste threw him a look that was one quarter patience, one quarter love, one quarter squint, and one quarter grin with a hint of annoyance.

Most of the kids were asleep. Bendin wasn't as he was too excited, and everything was so new. Both of the girls had fallen asleep leaning their heads on his shoulders and Quip kept winking from his lap and pointing to the two girls. Quip's excitement and prodding only made him feel like being teased by Ladak back in the temple. Bendin found it a little annoying, but he was sure that if Ladak was here he'd have done exactly what

Quip was doing.

"We're here! Welcome to Hymingway's outer flying limits," Tilmon announced from the front. Anyone that wasn't already awake, woke and rubbed their eyes sleepily.

Out the front windows Bendin could see the city of Hymingway fast approaching. It had tall narrow buildings and he could see a large twisted bridge between two buildings on the south side. There were buildings in the air everywhere suspended by nothing that Bendin could see. The largest building in the middle towered over the other tall skyscrapers in the corners of the city. All the building work suggested expert craftsmanship. The air was clear with only a few clouds with the bluish sun shining softly down on the city.

"It's actually shaped like a Heptahedron!" Quip remarked pointing with his paw. Bendin didn't know how in the world Quip knew what a heptahedron was. The family apparently thought the same thing because they looked at Quip curiously for a moment before returning to the windows. The large airspace was full of traffic, and it was almost entirely random. There were no lines, and no large groups, just a massive seething pot of vehicles that rotated around the city in a counter-clockwise rotation. The sight was breathtaking.

Rachel tapped Bendin's shoulder and showed him a large glass building with a forest on the top of it. "It's Levathens!" Levathens put her tiny garden to shame, just by the raw size of the building. As they got closer and circled the city, Bendin noticed that there were lots and lots of people skating between places. Many people skated around in the city airspace, while the vehicles mostly occupied the upper space. There were almost double the amount of people skating around as there were vehicles flying in the air.

"Bendin see this!" Soladaque tapped Bendin's other shoulder, which caused Quip to snicker in his ear, and pointed at the Heptahedron. "There are two sections to the Heptahedron. They have an outer shell and the inner part where they actually play the game! I can't wait to actually be inside this time!" Their happy energy was very contagious.

"Quip, you are enjoying this way too much," Bendin whispered in Quip's ear.

"I can't help it. You are so funny." Quip laughed, batting Bendin's ear with his paw.

Tilmon brought the family bubble down to a place near the Heptahedron and Bendin watched in anticipation as Tilmon flew the bubble straight at the ground.

"What are you doing?" Bendin, Quip, and George shouted.

"Just watch," Tilmon said waving his hands nonchalantly. Just before they smashed into the ground, it split open revealing a very spacious tunnel. "See? Perfectly safe." Bendin, Quip, and George's faces visually weren't convinced.

"What if the gate fails?" Quip asked, clearly disturbed.

"The opening?" Pete smirked. "They have engineers that keep those working. Although, accidents do happen."

"Pete!" Celeste shot Pete a glance that made Bendin's skin creep. "Not here."

"Well it's true, mom." Pete shrugged.

Ryan whispered to them, "No one dies anymore. You'd just be redirected. No big deal."

Tilmon steered the craft below the city flying under the ground. There was an enormous cavern, and Bendin noticed the entire area was reinforced by the behemoth pillars, pipes, and beams. They flew down past layers and layers of vehicles till they found some open spaces.

Jean put her things away in a small bag that she wore around her waist. She turned around and explained, "It's down here that everyone parks their vehicles and skates up to the surface in whatever part of the city you would like to go."

"Thanks, Jean. I didn't know." Bendin smiled.

Once the vehicle was parked, Pete and Ryan were so excited that they plastered their bodies on one of the side doors for it to be open. Tilmon pulled it open with a yank and both of them tumbled out of the bubble into the air. Even Celeste smiled at the flipping forms of her boys.

"Bendin, George, you got to come see this!" Pete and Ryan shouted from outside.

Bendin had to wait behind everyone else before he could get outside to see what they were talking about. The air was moist but not too cold.

"Coil!" Ryan shouted. He listened eagerly as the sound bounced off of the walls and pillars several times.

"Hyde!" another person in the distance shouted back with the same effect.

Bendin realized that they had parked in the air, and there weren't any platforms or anything but various colors of light designations as to where you could park.

"Doesn't this need to be held down by something?"

Bendin asked fearful that it would move away in the air by the wind.

"It is. It's got these," Tilmon said as he rapped the front of the bubble with his finger and kicked up a flap that revealed a blade in the front of the vehicle. Bendin noticed there were blades in the front, back, top, and rear. They were all exposed, and he realized that the bubble wasn't going anywhere. Tilmon locked his bubble with a small mechanical stick that looked suspiciously like the one Charles had for the mower. Tilmon led them all across the air to a ring horizontal to the ground on the end of the row. Bendin followed Soladaque and Rachel followed him.

"What if they don't have skates?" Bendin wondered. They could be stuck here.

"Then they'd be in the Outcasts, Bendin," Tilmon said and shrugged. "Or even, the Bauyostens."

Callapse tapped his head, glared at Bendin, and mouthed the word, "duh" to him three or four times before he turned back around.

Bendin wondered what his deal was and watched Starley as she pointed to a column of people sailing up into the air through the ring. Bendin saw many of these areas where people would be in-line with each other or in an arc together traveling quickly.

"In you go," Tilmon directed. Don't lose each other.

Bendin watched as Callapse double clicked his heels while throwing himself into the air. He shot upwards rapidly. Ryan, instead of throwing himself in, put his head over the large ring and Starley laughed as his hair blew straight up. Ryan laughed intently at the people that shot upwards past them. Ryan bumped Bendin into the ring and Bendin frantically closed his blades. He felt a wonderful surge of speed and rose on the column of soft air.

Bendin peered down in time to see Pete push his brother in and the rest of the family followed quckly. In no time they were floating up above ground up into the city on the air. The family activated their skates and caught up to Bendin while still in the column of air.

"Off here. Off here!" Tilmon shouted. Everyone followed Tilmon off on to a ledge that stuck out from one of the buildings they had been rising next to. Bendin felt the soft localization of Gravity and his feet pulling down on the surface. He looked around and saw platforms for the buildings everywhere. There were more entrances and exits into buildings than he had ever seen before in any picture or in his imagination. There were people all over the place. All of them dressed differently; however, there were strong color themes representing untold last names and unity in the families they were a part of. Almost everyone had on the same kind of Airlarky gear that the Coil's had on, some new some old with all kinds of variety. Tilmon lead them to the end of the platform where there was a short lighted metallic post sticking out of the ledge at a diagonal. The person in front of Bendin jumped over the post and was blasted by a gush of air which sent the person at an arc across the gap between the buildings to another ledge. He noticed that these things were all over the place.

"Bendin, we'll show you the best one ever!" Pete called out behind him.

"No, Pete, not right now. We are going to the Heptahedron, not playing around with the air spurts." Tilmon grabbed him by the arm and drug Pete in front of the rest of the family.

"Dad, I wasn't actually going to do anything . . . dangerous," Pete whined.

Celeste smirked.

Rachel tapped him on the shoulder and showed him one of the plant and herb places. Then Soladaque would do the same thing, but on the other side and showing him various boot shops places.

They traveled a short distance passing through the crowds of people, keeping close to each other. The buildings were solidly built, even though many of them were simply and completely in the air on thick rails of blades.

Around the edge of the tall building towering next to them, coming into full view, was the impressive, black Heptahedron building. It was in the shape of a cube, but where there should have been an upper corner, it had been cut off with a giant slice. Each side had etched grids of squares. Inside each square, large shapes and characters lit up in colors. It reminded Bendin of the wall with the unknown characters. The side they were moving towards had a green outlines. The left side had blue outlines inside every cube. Bendin realized the side they were going to must be specifically for the Coils.

Thousands of people walked into the building on all sides, and he was one of them. Both Soladaque and Rachel eagerly kept his attention when they could, showing him things of their interest.

"You are the sun," Quip whispered in his ear. Quip had been clutching his head the entire journey and was watching the people around him warily.

"What?"

"You are the sun." Quip laughed. "They are the planets. They are kind of orbiting you."

Bendin couldn't help but smile. He could see that they were kind of doing that in the way they would tap his shoulder nicely and show him. He wasn't used to Quip's teasing yet even though his comments were mostly hilarious.

They walked inside the building and saw the long line of officers up against a tall impassable wall with grated openings scattered all across it. Bendin hadn't seen officers before and he thought they kind of looked like Mez's dress and equipment except not so dark. Tilmon passed the line and held out a small card up to a blue point of light in the wall. The card beeped with a loud chime, and the grate bars retracted with a loud hiss.

"Welcome to the Heptahedron," a lady's mechanical voice sounded out.

Tilmon waved the rest through ahead of him. "Quickly please."

Everyone passed the long wall and into a very deep, faintly lit tunnel. Bendin thought it must lead into the "inner" section that Soladaque had talked about. The echoes inside the shell were tremendous, and the shaking and pounding sounds were thunderous.

Once in the inner section, there were passages that opened all over the place: some going left, right, up, down, and diagonally. There were places to purchase items to eat, keep, drink, throw, and play with. Tilmon led them straight past all the passages and shops into the main arena--the core of the Heptahedron. Bendin thought it felt nice and open, but for the rest of the family, it was expressed best by Pete, who said, "This place is small!"

"It seemed so big from outside," Rachel agreed.

"It is very much bigger at home," Starley noted.

"That's because the limitless walls network makes it so you can see a lot of the people who are watching, not just the main room," Ryan explained.

There was seating on every single surface, although none were in the air like the Coil's Airlarky game outside. There was seating below him, above him on the ceiling, on the walls, and the upper walls. It was kind of like the gun range back in the temple, only you doubled it in size, flipped it over, plopped it down on top of itself, cut the upper corner off, and placed more seating there. He watched people come in from all sides and take their seats. Each sat as if they were on the ground and everyone else was above them. It was truly a grand sight to Bendin. It felt very intimate as the players were warming up and skating right past their seats. Every person in the arena would feel very close to the players and would feel like they were part of the event.

Each wall and goal, which was located in the center of its respective wall, were colored and lit to represent its family. Tilmon led them to their seats, which was part of a couple rows and Bendin found himself again sandwiched between Soladaque and Rachel. Each seat had a small scoreboard display, which read, "0 : 0 : 0 : 0 : 0 : 0 : 0". The scoreboard display and lights on the chairs for each wall of the arena were respectively, green, orange, yellow, red, blue, purple, and white. Bendin marveled at the engineering of the building. He could easily see a person sitting in their seats on the far end of the arena, and he couldn't have been more than twenty-four meters from the center of the building. The seven ball boxes around the arena were positioned just above all the goals each lit in their family's color.

"Bendin!" Soladaque tapped him on the shoulder and pointed eagerly at a skater that went whizzing by. "See Chamilin Hyde?"

"Who?"

"He's headed to the purple section across on the other wall. Look at the one leading the way."

He watched the short stubby man with light wispy hair skid to a halt. He could only have been a meter tall. "He's tiny! Is he like Starley?"

"No. He's always been that way. He is the best player in the whole world."

"In your opinion. Diggity Wight is the best!" Ryan pipped in.

"Not by an Airlarky staff's chance!" Soladaque retorted.

"Duh." Pete laughed. "He's the worst!"

Bendin watched as Chamilin skated up into the air. He was definitely as smooth as flowing water. Bendin eagerly moved forward in delight and almost fell out of his chair. Quip, however, did fall out of his lap and he put scorch marks on the spot where he landed.

"Watch it, Bendin!" Quip scolded, leaping back up to Bendin and settling himself into Bendin's lap. Quip watched the other people with mild interest.

"Is it supposed to be this dim?" Bendin asked Rachel.

"Don't worry. They turn up the lights when the game actually begins."

Pete tapped Bendin's shoulder, leaned up to Bendin's ear from the seat behind, and whispered excitedly in his ear, "I wonder what they are going to do this year."

Ryan leaned in and spoke in Bendin's other ear, "I think they are going to fill the entire arena full of laughing gas."

Bendin shrugged. "What are you guys talking about?"

"Each year the arena reserves the right to change one random thing. Last year they tripled the drag weight on every ball, both carried weight and not-carried weights. It threw the players off so bad, the air became a mosh pit of players bumping into each other." Ryan slapped his knees in good humor as if he just remembered the event.

"The players can modify things too to add a little more variety into the game as well, you are just not allowed to modify the blades, staffs, and use anything that would immobilize or effect the other player's movement." Pete grinned. "Last year the DeSoto's tried to add a little power to the movement of their players, but it was a disaster with all the players boosting in to the crowds, and slamming themselves into walls. They'll probably try that again this year."

"How loud are these?" Bendin asked tapping a pair speakers on his chair. Every chair had its own set.

"Plenty loud," Ryan said holding his ears in mock pain.

"Wait! How come they get to have Quintaulm candy?" Pete whined noticing Starley's bag.

"Because they are younger than you. They always get some first. If you are patient, I may be able to get you a bag." Celeste frowned.

Ryan folded his arms in contempt.

"Bendin, here try some." Quintaulm candy was passed to him by Tilmon. The green crystals popped and lit up inside his mouth and gave him the most wonderful sensation and flavor.

"It almost feels like it's alive!" Bend n said amazed.

"It's fun!" Pete laughed.

"It's Quintaulm candy," Ryan chipped in.

The preliminary warm-ups finished and it was time to start. An announcer's loud voice rang over the broadcast system,

"Welcome Airlarky fans today we celebrate the 390th Airlarky Heptahedron event!"

The crowd burst into applause.

"Pause, as we remember Peter Moyle and his family."

There was a great silence.

Bendin whispered to Soladaque, "Who is Peter Moyle?"

She whispered back, "He's one of the original eight Vaelift, his temple was the place of the betrayal. If you need to know more on history, I'll tell you later."

Once again Bendin felt a little out of place. He should know who that is right?

A few moments later the voice crackled again over the system, "Okay, we love you. We remember you, but now the game is on!"

Lights turned on all over the place, balls released from their boxes, and the teams scrambled to get them and score them. The three different types of balls were all sliver and clear, in a patchwork pattern. There were lights in each ball and the amount of lights in the ball was determined by its size. The smallest had the most lights, whereas the biggest ball only had about four lights. The glimmering lights changed to the color of the team of whoever was holding it.

Whenever Chamilin Hyde would catch a ball at all, Soladaque excitedly tap Bendin's shoulder, point it out with her fingers, and shout in glee. It was as if she wanted him to be his favorite too. Bendin kind of liked a couple of players, but they were mostly on the DeSoto team. They were just so cool to watch.

Rachel tapped Bendin's other shoulder, shouted, and pointed at an amazing shot made by one of the Wight's players. This continued with Soladaque tapping him one way and then moments later Rachel tapping him the other way. Quip had gone from hardly watching the game to completely watching the girls tap Bendin back and forth. He grabbed some Quintaulm candy that the kids were munching on. He stuffed his mouth, ate it, and watched with more amusement each time Bendin was tapped. This continued till Bendin was tapped at the same time, "Guys, take your turns please."

Rachel let out a soft, "Sorry."

Soladaque let her focus from the game pull to Bendin and Rachel and realized that she hadn't been at all noticing what she was doing, "Sorry, I was just excited." She grinned sheepishly and turned to the game with enthusiasm.

"It's okay. I just feel like everyone is trying to get my attention all at once." Bendin couldn't help but notice Quip's huge grin.

"Tilmon, why didn't they just shoot the balls from their goal right into their goal right off the start?" George asked Tilmon.

"Because that's one of the rules. You can't shoot your starting balls till another player from another team touches or shoots it first."

Bendin watched the wild dance in the air above him. Fifty-six players all skating around, leaving bright hot trails in the air, and leaving that curious welding sound where ever they skated.

Pete tapped him on the shoulder and then Ryan exaggeratedly tapped Bendin on the other shoulder. Quip laughed, his candy sparking brightly. Ryan laughed and Pete grinned. He knew he was being silly.

"Yes?" Bendin asked.

"Look at the yellow players."

"I have been," Bendin said.

"Right. The DeSoto's are really doing well this year. See the small machines on their backs? We've determined it's a smaller engine than last year, the one that gives them some extra speed if they want it, and they seem to really have worked out the kinks of last year's disaster." Pete's eyes glowed in admiration, "I'd love to have one."

Pete was right. The DeSoto team quickly took the lead as they were slightly faster than the other players. The Hyde team seemed to be fighting back and they were keeping close, but they just were not fast enough to intercept and shoot before a DeSoto player got there.

"What's the one thing that's different this year?" Bendin asked Rachel.

"I don't know, I've been watching for something, but I haven't noticed anything different. Pete? Ryan?"

"We've seen nothing so far," Ryan noted.

Bendin looked at the score counter. It read, "10 : 5 : 20 : 7 : 4 : 8 : 15." It looked as though the Finn team was lagging behind everyone else.

Things were crazier now that there were only two large balls left. One of the DeSoto's got the large ball and shot it towards their goal. Before the ball arrived, the goal changed to a blue color and the ball scored for the Finn team. A roar like a hurricane erupted from the yellow side of the room and a similar cheer exploded from the blue side of the room. A feeling of intense entertainment rippled through Bendin.

"What just happened?" Quip exclaimed temporarily distracted from the girl's tap war.

"Looks like we know what's changed," Ryan said smartly.

"Ha!" Pete roared. "The DeSoto's are going to go *insane!*"

The teams out in the air chased the remaining ball with gusto. Everyone's attention was now on the single ball and not knowing what was going to happen next. The goals kept changing places at random intervals. The large mob of people combating over the single ball was fierce, but the final ball was scored into a purple goal. With a roar of excitement from the crowd, all the balls were released again into the air.

The tactic was quickly adopted to get as close as you could to the goal before you shot it, in the hopes that it would be your color when your ball went through. Bendin even caught one of the stray shots on his staff and shot it towards the Coil goal. It was intercepted by the DeSoto's players, but Bendin didn't care because he'd actually caught and shot one. All the family reached over after he'd done it and clapped him on the shoulder. After a few more plays, Rachel and Soladaque began to be caught up in the moments again. Especially when one of the Finn players lost control, skated into wall, was redirected across it, and lost his staff in the crowd.

Rachel whispered excitedly in Bendin's ear, "That almost never happens!"

A few minutes later Soladaque also grabbed Bendin excitedly and pointed to Chamilin again as he spun around in a vibrant motion and made a large fireball at a DeSoto player that attempted to intercept his catch. This move was stunningly effective and Chamilin scored two shots in rapid succession.

Bendin watched the game again but became distracted when he saw Quip's tongue hanging out of his mouth for a second.

"Quip!" Bendin exclaimed, "Your tongue's green?"

"Quintaulm candy." Soladaque pointed at her tongue. It was also green.

"Oh."

"Yours is too." Soladaque giggled and Bendin heard Rachel snicker.

An enthusiastic cheer rolled across the DeSoto crowd. The DeSoto players were doing something different this time and it caught the attention of everyone. They were grouped up in a small ball of persons while everyone else was spread all around. Bendin watched intently as they began catching any and all balls that would fly past them. They began passing the caught balls in a loop between them. They did this till they had filled whole group, each passing a ball to each other in a simultaneous rhythmic interval.

"It's so coordinated," Rachel commented in awe.

"Chamilin will break it up," Soladaque said faithfully.

Chamilin did try, but only managed to snag a single ball before the entire group of DeSotos shot away from him.

Bendin watched in amazement as the group of DeSotos all skated in a bunch to one single yellow lt goal. They then shot every single ball they had been passing internally into the goal. Their coordination rooted Bendin in admiration.

The yellow side's cheers increased, and the skill displayed was certainly deserving. The score now read, "30 : 45 : 81 : 37 : 24 : 19 : 55".

Other teams attempted to do the same thing. This quickly revealed how difficult it was to hold a perfect ring of coordinated players. Their attempts failed in many broken rings.

Soladaque hit the chair in front of her with her fist and muttered, "Phooey."

At this moment in the game, all other teams began uniting against the DeSoto team. Even with this silent unification, the DeSoto team still managed to keep ahead of the competition.

"I think they've got this game this year," Pete grumbled.

"It's hopeless," Ryan tossed his staff from hand to hand.

"The Finn team hasn't scored a single goal since this round started!" Tilmon shouted.

With each cycle of balls, the DeSoto team stayed definitely in the lead.

"They might as well call it a mercy." Soladaque frowned in disgust.

"What's that?" Bendin asked.

"It's when the lead team is so far ahead that the remaining possible points cannot tie or pass them."

"How far away is that?"

"This is the fifth round, they only need to score ten more points ahead of the next closest team and the game will be determined a mercy. The game will then be over--"

A cry rang out from the Hyde's side. Something had happened. One of the DeSoto's players was being carried out of the arena by a fellow player.

"What. What happened?" Ryan asked earnestly.

"He was injured, by his own machinery," Rachel said as the word spread around the arena.

"You know, I don't want to have one of those machines," Pete slyly recanted.

"With a player down, we might have a chance!" Soladaque said pounding the table, and the game started again.

To everyone's surprise two more of the DeSoto player's equipment malfunctioned causing large yellow explosions and loud compression thumps to be heard throughout the arena. Each with the crowd gasping and roaring.

Soladaque's enthusiasm for change became insatiable. She shouted, "Get them all Chamilin! All the balls!"

Bendin watched the final ball for the fifth cycle get shot into the Hyde goal. It was now the final ball cycle.

The score read: "42 : 49 : 127 : 39 : 19 : 49 : 60".

As the balls for the final round were released, Rachel tapped his shoulder and said, "They are doing something different this time."

Bendin watched as the Hydes launched a new plan to counter the DeSoto cluster strategy. They positioned themselves separated around the arena at the various goals. Even though many of the players were getting fatigued, they were frantic to beat the DeSoto team. The loss of three players began to show as they couldn't get to all the balls as a group anymore. The Hyde's strategy began to be very successful as the crowds began catching stray balls and shooting them at the Hyde players as the goals switched around the arena. As the balls began to be depleted, Bendin knew, even with the advantages, it wasn't going to be enough.

Soladaque cheered as Chamilin smartly intercepted the final ball and blasted it into his goal for the final shot of the game.

It was over. With the final score being: "45 : 51 : 137 : 39 : 20 : 109 : 61", the DeSotos won and claimed the title for themselves. The entire yellow side of the arena immediately skated out into the open air to greet and congratulate their team. The rest of the crowd, that wanted to, skated out to their respective teams when the colors of all the sides of the arena turned white.

Soladaque screamed, "I'm getting Chamlin's autograph.

~ 182 ~

See you at the bubble!" She was gone in a brilliant yellow streak among thousands of streaks of people skating out and thronging the players.

"Bendin?" Rachel nudged him in the side as they got up and began to walk back. "Will you tell me about where you came from? What was it like?"

Quip perked his ears up and listened intently. "Yeah! What was it like?"

Bendin briefly mentioned his Odge class, and his cycles class. They were two of his favorite classes, so he didn't mind sharing his thoughts about them.

"Did you like them or were they fun? Why did you leave them and come here?" Rachel asked in wonderment.

"Were they hard? Did the people make fun of you? How was your family?" Quip asked a millisecond after her.

"Slow down. I liked them, for the most part. I certainly wasn't trying to come here," Bendin answered as he was trying to navigate the throng of people leaving.

"Then what were you trying to do?" Rachel asked.

"I was trying to find a girl that had been moved in a weird way to another location."

"Weird way? Was she prettier than me?" Rachel asked batting her eyes.

"Oh yeah, she was really pretty, with naturally rich red hair and beautiful blue eyes," Bendin said. Quip slapped his paw into his forehead.

"Foxpalm!" Ryan laughed seeing Quip slap his face. He gave a high five to his brother.

Rachel frowned, something obviously bothered her, but said curiously, "Bendin, there are no people with natural red hair."

"Like me?" Quip asked, "Do you think she'd like me?"

Bendin laughed. "Yeah. She'd probably like you."

Rachel asked more specific questions about his classes all the way back to the bubble. When they almost arrived at the spot where the vehicle was parked, she then asked softly in his ear, "When are you going to let me tell them you are a Vaelift?"

The word sparked an intense mental and physical reaction. Bendin's mind wandered and spun for a moment, blurs obscured his vision, and he remembered the unpleasant strange events of him coming here; all the painful events ran through his mind at a rapid pace. The pressure built up in his mind till he couldn't stand it anymore and fainted.

"Are you okay? Bendin? Bendin!" Rachel yelled as Bendin slowly spun lifeless in the air.

Chapter 12
Birth of Destiny

"Quip?" Bendin said as he blinked his eyes. He could make out the fox above him and could see he was lying in his bed.

Quip grinned ear to nose to ear. "Yes. It's me."

"Quip continually refused to leave your side this entire time. Frankly, I think he's going to shrivel up." Soladaque winked from a cushion in the corner.

"He's awake! He's awake!" Pete yelled as he peeked into the room and shot away.

"How are you doing?" Soladaque asked getting up and walking over.

Bendin sat all the way up and put a hand on his leg. "Better."

Quip was at his feet in a semi-praying position while George was in his bed listening to something as his ears were covered by fluffy speakers.

"Hi guys, how long have I been out?" Bendin said groggily.

"For a day at least. Are you okay?" Quip asked.

"I'm fine, just a little bit thirsty and hungry."

Rachel arrived a moment later with water and pills. "I had them ready, for when you would wake. Here, please take these."

Bendin took them.

"*If* he would wake," Pete joked coming in the room. He was followed by Ryan and Starley.

"We didn't think you'd make it." Ryan crossed his arms.

They gathered comfortably around Bendin and watched Bendin down the pills and drink the water, suspiciously. Bendin may not have felt as fine as he said he did, still very woozy, but mostly it was his vision. The way they were looking at him made him feel very uncomfortable. The blurs in his vision were becoming distinct grey outlines that would come into focus and go away again periodically and he found it to be quite taxing on his patience.

"What? Do I have something on my face?"

"Yes, actually," Quip said carefully.

"We weren't going to tell you till later, but it's awful," Ryan said stroking his face with his hand.

"You have a slight hue about your face," Rachel said, "Soladaque, go and get a mirror so he can see. He has to know eventually, so he might as well know now." Soladaque disappeared out the egg-shaped door.

"Did I always have it?" Bendin was afraid that maybe his time out ruined a feature of his face or maybe his trip here was catching up to him.

"No." Pete scrunched up his face in disgust.

"Yes, " Ryan countered.

Soladaque came back and gave Bendin the mirror. He searched his face quickly and saw his adoring self watching him.

Pete couldn't suppress the mirth building on his face and burst out laughing. The rest of the group did the same.

"Guys!" Bendin shouted with sudden realization. "I thought you were serious!" Bendin thumped the mirror down on the soft pillow, folded his arms, and faked a frown.

"Sorry, it was all Pete's idea," Quip said through laughter, "He made us promise to go through with it."

"It was great!" Soladaque said grabbing her cheeks. "You should have seen your expression."

"It's not funny," Bendin groaned, even though it was. "What else happened while I was out? Please, someone tell me."

Rachel said swiftly, "Soladaque helped you to the bubble and Dad figured you went into shock. Since it was going to be a temporary thing, Soladaque and Quip watched over you. Mom and Dad took me to Levathens.

"Okay." Bendin nodded. "What else?"

"We brought you here," Rachel continued. "And this is where you've been ever since."

"I thought you were dead," Starley added.

"I told you he wasn't!" Soladaque tapped Starley on the shoulder.

"Good to see you up, Bendin. We've got things to do! Come play our game again sometime," Pete said thumbing his finger at Bendin then at his brother. "Come on, Starley, we'll race you to the goal post." They left.

"Soladaque! Come here! Chamilin Hyde is here to talk to you!" Celeste's voice bounced up the passageway from below to them.

Soladaque looked at Bendin and then to Rachel. Bendin watched as the realization dawned on Soladaque as to just who was calling on her.

"Soladaque! This is your chance of a lifetime," Rachel said happily.

"Thanks, Rachel. But, Bendin, you know. I liked . . . wasn't su--" Soladaque responded flicking a finger towards Bendin.

"It's okay, Soladaque," Rachel interrupted, "It's not like I'm going to take him on a tour of Thibracketory when you are off playing Airlarky with Chamilin. Go. This is your opportunity. Your dream."

Soladaque squeaked in excitement and waved her hands in a circle, "How do I look?" She pulled on her braids nervously.

"You look fine Soladaque, just ravishing."

"Thanks!" She kissed Rachel, kissed wide-eyed Bendin, and sped from the room.

"You always have looked fine Soladaque," Rachel muttered after she left.

"How long have you felt like that, Rachel?" Bendin asked.

"Since she was seven. That's when she really started maturing. Even before that she's always been exquisite. A lot better than someone else I know."

Quip blinked his eyes and made moving motions with his paws to Bendin towards Rachel.

"I hope that person is okay with themselves. It's true, Soladaque really is very pretty," Bendin said absently.

Quip coughed and they stared at Bendin.

Quip slapped his paw into his forehead again.

Bendin asked, "Can you do something for me?"

"What's that Bendin?" Rachel asked, pained and still hurt from his last comment.

"Can you take me on an outing?"

Rachel was more surprised than Quip.

Quip said, "Are you feeling okay, Bendin?" Quip shot himself up into the air and flew around Bendin watching him carefully. Bendin hadn't done anything like this so far.

Bendin finally knew, after a month, that an outing or a date was time to spend with a special person. He felt proud that he at least understood that.

"What would you like to do?" Rachel asked watching him carefully.

"I don't know. Do you have any special place you like to

go? Anything neat you like to do? For Soladaque, it's leaping off of the cliff at incredible velocities. What would you like to share with me?" Bendin paused and turned to Quip. "May I have some time with Rachel? Is that is okay with you?"

"Do what you want," Quip said eagerly. "I'm glad you are alive and up again. I was worried about you sleeping forever. I'd have no choice but to return to the jungle with the other animals."

"Don't you miss the jungle?"

"No."

"The animals?"

"No." Quip stuck out his tongue.

"Why?"

"Because," Quip said, displaying frustration, anger, and teeth. "They don't like me. How do you think I got stuck there by the Onychophora in the first place?"

"It was an accident of course."

Quip shook his head. Rachel watched curiously.

"Honestly you couldn't have thought me to think it was any other thing. I had no idea that you were one of the special animals. That you were civil and cultured," Bendin said throwing his arms up and pulling Quip into his arms. Bendin snuggled up to Quip and put him down on the bed.

"Cultured, yes; civil, not everyone. Listen, it was no accident."

Quip began pacing back and forth on the bed watching Bendin, and then switching his gaze to Rachel.

"I was put there by fellow 'special' foxes. They then destroyed my father and mother in front of my eyes and killed my brothers and sisters with acid. They said that 'I should be alive to see them die. Lilly lilly gumdrop pie.' Then they left me there to die."

"Acid huh?" Bendin said. "That's terrible."

"It's completely appalling." Rachel shook her head miserably.

"There are many kinds of special animals, Bendin," Quip explained patiently.

Rachel nodded the affirmative and asked, "If you didn't like the animals, why didn't you join the humans earlier?"

Quip scoffed. "Humans are worse than that."

"What could be worse than losing your family?" Rachel's expression was one of complete concern.

Quip cried, his large fox tears dropping to the floor. He said in a low tone, "They don't just kill us. They enslave, torture, test and then kill us."

"But slavery is--" Rachel began to say.

"Isn't completely over!" Quip interrupted averting his gaze for a second. "Once Bendin saved me, I knew I had found a true friend, even though I was frustrated in general at first."

Quip smiled and warmed up, the end of his tail catching on fire in a nice warm red flame.

"Quip, do you think these terrible things will stop?" Bendin asked.

"Not without a strong outside force."

"Could we do anything?" Bendin thought of his own imprisonment and didn't want that for anyone.

"If you think we can take out those human strongholds, then sure. I'm going to say you don't stand a chance. You skate like a two year old, faint at something Rachel says to you, and you complain of grey blurs in your sleep all the time. So, no. Not till some things about you and I change."

Bendin was struck with the realization that Quip was right. Bendin wasn't ready to take on any sort of responsibilities like that. Still, he said what he could "Okay, so we'll take care of that when you and I don't have such problems."

Quips eyes blazed with a yellow flame in appreciation and satisfaction. "That's the nicest thing anyone's ever said to me!" Quip launched himself into the air and blasted himself around Bendin like a ball on a tether For Rachel, Bendin thought it was probably more like a comet orbiting him. Quip doused his flame and landed on the soft bed.

"Bendin, will you please come with me tomorrow morning before the sun comes up and see one of my most favorite places in the whole house?" Rachel asked calmly. She waited.

Bendin smiled and watched as Quip nodded slowly. "Okay, sounds good," Bendin answered. He stood up, placed a hand on hers, and pulled her out of a sitting position.

"I'll come get you." Rachel smiled.

Bendin held his other hand down to Quip, who ran up it enthusiastically.

"It feels good to be on your shoulder again," Quip noted in Bendin's ear.

Later that night Quip crept up to Bendin as he was praying and sat next to him on a small mat that Jean had made for Quip.

"You guys are so weird. How can you blindly pray every

night to a person that doesn't even exist?" George mocked from his bed.

"Shhhh. Don't be rude," Quip hushed him. "I know Odge now too." Bendin raised his eyebrows, but said nothing.

"How can you know him now too?" George sat up in his bed, curious that they were both claiming to have heard or known of Odge communicating to them. "You just got here like a month ago and you made fun of him then too! What's going on? What did Bendin do to you?"

"Bendin only taught me how to talk with Odge to where he would give an answer. I tried it many times over and over, and for some reason one day it worked. I was very surprised, but guess what? Odge said that if I am faithful, he will give me a great gift!"

"He told you that? What did he say he'd give you?" George said in disbelief.

"He said it was about the special animals. I was going to be an example for them in particular, something that not even Bendin could do or give me, but it had to come from him, Odge himself. I don't know anything more than that. We shall see," Quip said.

"Bunch of weirdoes," George said rolling over to face the other way, but the way he said it indicated he was slightly less harsh than he was before.

"Quip," Bendin whispered. "This is so great! You've discovered how to make it work."

Quip smiled.

Bendin was ecstatic at the thought that one of the things that brought him great joy, the warm fervor of the communication from Odge, was now happening with someone else. Someone, now, could relate to him. He thought of nothing more exciting that he would want to share with Quip and he had discovered it entirely on his own.

The morning rolled around and Bendin woke to Quip softly blowing in his ears. Bendin looked at Quip in the dark and he could see, through the flame that Quip was silently singing to him, "Wake up you sleepy head, haul your hiney out of bed. Motivate your sleepy head, and haul your hiney out of bed." He stopped, grinned, and said, "Your date is going to knock on the door in," Quip paused, "4 seconds." Quip counted down, "4 . . . 3 . . . 2 . . . 1 . . ."

Bendin jumped out of bed and true to his word, when Quip hit zero there was a soft tap at the door.

"Bendin?" Rachel's soft voice carried through the door.

"I'm coming," Bendin hissed. He pulled on his boots, bands, box, pants, long-sleeved shirt, and ran his fingers through his hair before opening the door. Quip waved with a puff of a fiery hand and respectfully went back to sleep.

Rachel had dressed in simple pants, a green lined dark jacket, and had her hair braided over her head down into a braided ponytail. She flashed a beautiful smile and took his hand excitedly, "Come on, we don't want to miss it!" Rachel had never shown this much enthusiasm. He wondered if she had been hiding this kind of energy on purpose.

She insisted on towing him through several passages, and now that Bendin was up to speed on skating, he found this very amusing. He used this as an opportunity to watch her skate and admire her simple skating style. Bendin shook his head for a second wondering why he might be thinking about skating styles. She took them higher up into some passages in the home that he hadn't been.

"Here, right here." Rachel rolled a small door out of the way. She guided Bending down the narrowing passage. She pulled Bendin close to her for a moment and guided him out through an opening. It was a little balcony on the pinnacle near the highest place in the house. The balcony had a small railing that ran around it and it was big enough to hold about three to four people standing side by side. The platform was positioned so that you were looking at everything upside down, to where the land was up, and the sky was down.

"There is only one thing higher than this and it's the balcony on the other side." She pointed across the passage where they had just come from. He could see another balcony on the other side similar to this one.

Bendin looked west upwards over the dark landscape. He could easily make out some trees and things in the distance, with the very dim outline of the sun's faintest light. The stars, millions of them, glimmered down below them in the heavens. They were very twinkly and there were several bright shapes he had learned were moons. They reflected the bluish light of the sun with exceptional radiance. Bendin had only seen the stars and moons from the windows of the house and vehicles. Now they seemed so much brighter and bigger.

Bendin put an arm around Rachel who took his free hand in hers and snuggled into his arms. Her body fit very cozily against his.

Rachel smiled contentedly, "Now watch."

Bendin enjoyed her warmth flooding his body and felt soft and peaceful. Bendin watched the west horizon turn a bright pink and slowly become more vibrant till they began to see the bluish sun peek out from the western most trees. The sun beams and clouds bounced the light with terrific color.

"It's beautiful. Thank you for sharing this with me," Bendin whispered.

"Thank you for being a friend to me and helping with my plants," Rachel said.

"Your welcome." Bendin nuzzled Rachel on her cheek with his nose and kissed her.

Rachel's eyes softened, appeared reflective, and she kissed him back too.

Bendin felt pleasant, a slight tingle of excitement mixed with something warm and good. It was very nice and refreshing.

"Can I pick the next outing?" Bendin asked bravely.

"Yes," Rachel said simply, smiling.

They watched the sun completely rise, holding each other and enjoying the moment together, before heading back to their rooms.

It was a new day, and Bendin felt absolutely fantastic.

Bendin followed Rachel around with Quip the rest of the morning and into the evening. At dinner, however, things took a turn from excellent to strange. Most of the family was there: Mez, Josiah, his two boys, Tilmon, Celeste, Soladaque, Rachel, Jean, Charles, Starley, Callapse, Pete and Ryan.

Soladaque was chatting about how much fun it had been for her date with Chamilin. Pete was trying to steal Ryan's chips. Callapse was talking endlessly about the machine he was working on with Josiah and their new discoveries. Rachel was blinking to Bendin in some sort of goofy eye twitch contest. Quip was laughing about them flirting while trying to eat, and the rest of the kids were complaining about how they didn't want to eat dinner but wanted to be doing more fun activities.

Celeste broke everyone's concentration when she suddenly turned to Mez and said, "Mez, get to the network and send for them. It's time. Tilmon, help me to my room! Soladaque, please entertain the youngest kids."

"But of course," Soladaque said.

Mez nodded his head and left immediately.

Bendin watched in wonder as the older kids rose from the table, helped Tilmon guide Celeste, and skate her to her room. Bendin followed not knowing what was happening at all; he could tell by the serious expressions on everyone's faces that it was important. The side of the room that Celeste slept in had been taken over with lots of blankets and like the other bedrooms, gravity was localized completely. The minute she entered the room Tilmon said, "Ok, Callapse, take off the belt."

Callapse carefully removed his mother's red belt, which was around her belly, and they set her on the bed. She refused to sit and started walking slowly around the room. She began singing softly. Mez came back and took up a position near the door watching quietly.

Bendin could take it no longer and spoke his thoughts aloud, "What's going on? What's wrong with her? Is she sick?" Everyone turned and looked at him completely shocked.

Bendin knew right then that he'd said something unbelievable.

After a couple of seconds for the shock to pass Callapse said sternly, "Nothing's wrong; she's going to have her baby, Bendin. Everyone knows that."

Callapse's words leaped out of his mouth like fire and drove horrible spikes of humiliation into Bendin.

Callapse folded his arms across his chest. "This is not the time for jokes."

"He wasn't joking," Ryan said.

"Trust us. We know jokes. He was being serious," Pete added.

"Mez?" Callapse asked. Mez nodded and folded his arms as well, the faintest smile appearing on his face.

Tilmon studied George curiously who was watching Bendin mouth agape.

"George. They have babies in the Outcasts right?" Tilmon asked George with a heavy hint of sarcasm.

"Yes, they do," George said seriously, "And they do in the Bauyostens as well."

"Bendin, where do you think you came from?" George asked him.

"I came from Odge," Bendin said.

"Yes, we know that part," Tilmon said forcing a smile, all sarcasm gone, "But physically, how did you come into the world?"

"I don't know," Bendin said nervously and shrugged sadly, "I guess I never thought about it. The first thing I remember is the temple patrons telling me that I was going to have to choose what I'd like to do with my life. So I did, and that's how everyone starts."

"Temple patrons?" Tilmon asked confused.

Bendin's heart filled with dread.

Callapse laughed. "The Bauyostens don't have a temple. The closest one is in the Outcasts, and even theirs is a rudimentary form of worship with only about twenty followers. But, even then, most of the Outcasts are non-Odge believers."

"That only proves then, that you are not part of their organization." Josiah's eyes narrowed suspiciously. "Who are you and who do you work for?"

"And where are you really from?" Tilmon asked him. "Bendin? Come with me right this instant. Mez, take over till I come back."

Bendin looked down. Celeste was still singing softly to herself when Tilmon led him out of the room, he was followed by Rachel. The rest stayed in the room.

"No, Rachel, go back and help your mother." Tilmon waved his hand dismissively.

"I need to be here father. Please."

Tilmon hesitated and watched as Rachel moved over and took Bendin's hand. Quip watched Tilmon apprehensively.

"Tell me the truth now, or I'm taking you straight to the tribunal and we'll have a chat with them about this. I'm a member and can do that you know." Tilmon's face was rock serious. Bendin thought Tilmon's face was going to freeze that way and if it did, that's definitely not how he'd want to look the rest of his life.

Quip watched Bendin curiously, bent down, and whispered in his ear, "Even I know about babies."

Bendin was at a loss for words and said nothing. He was totally blown away by this. He had no idea what anyone was talking about, and he certainly didn't know what a baby was.

Rachel tapped Bendin's hand softly, pulled Bendin's eyes in line with hers, and said pleadingly, "May I please tell him?"

Bendin knew it was useless to hide now. It was over. "Yes," Bendin said reluctantly, "you can tell him."

"He's a Vaelift," Rachel said beaming, finally being able to tell someone and Bendin heard her let out a lot of air like she was unloading a huge burden.

"Impossible," Tilmon stated firmly. "There haven't been

any Vaelift since their destruction and that was centuries ago."

"I know father," Rachel said patiently, "It's going to be very hard for you to believe this, but I was there and saw with my own eyes. He truly came right through the gate."

Bendin wondered what she meant.

Tilmon's expression changed from grim to surprise. He then turned and focused all his attention on Bendin. "Is this true?"

"I never made it to the highest ranks of the Vaelift, just a Vaelift in training. And yes, I did come through the wall."

Tilmon stared at him in disbelief, "Really. *Really*?"

Rachel shook her head up and down emphatically. "Yes, Father. It's happened. He had on Vaelift gear and everything."

"This hasn't ever happened. Okay then? What was Toalt like?"

Bendin rubbed his head. "Toalt? Rachel mentioned that before, and the R-Limiter in your storage listed it as well. What is it?"

"If you really are a Vaelift you would have come from there through the gate."

"Well I don't know what it is, and I came from the upper temple. Like I said before, I was training to be one of Odge's Vaelift which is the highest rank in the entire kingdom for DOOD members."

"It just can't be true that he came in through the waterfall gate," Tilmon said thoughtfully. "If true, the claim would make him the biggest news since the destruction of the Vaelift themselves. He focused back on Bendin, "I personally don't believe you are a Vaelift. The Vaelift could do many wonderful things that you haven't shown any ability to do at all."

"Like vanishing, and manipulating the Vurfenstaff," Rachel said eagerly. "Tearing the curtain, moving, flying, fading, stepping, and dancing!"

"Warriors of light. 'Move the light' they would say."

Bendin was confused. "Clearly we are understanding the Vaelift differently. They do vanish, and I had really wanted to learn that power. All it did when I tried it, was it sent me here to this time. They just call the staff's 'Vaelift Staffs', I don't know what a Vurfenstaff is."

"All guardians of the gates are under the instruction, that if any person were to come through their gate, they would be taken immediately to the tribunal. We then run tests on them to make sure for certain that they are indeed a Vaelift," Tilmon remarked. "So. . ."

Bendin thought about the tests that Josiah and Callapse had run on him and paled at the thought.

Rachel calmed him, "I know what you are thinking. They are not like Josiah's tests at all. It's a simple process they give anyone that claims to have come through a gate. The last test was given, what father, ten years ago?"

"Yes, when I was a kid, someone claimed they were from Toalt. Even though he failed the test, many still believed his wild hoax. Laws were passed that made it almost impossible to get tested because every person ever tested failed the test. It's not surprising because the Vaelift are extinct. You, Bendin? We'll see. We leave first thing in the morning as long as we've had the baby."

"What's a baby? Will someone explain this to me?" Bendin pleaded. He really wanted to know.

"A baby is what a person is first, before they are big," Rachel said simply.

"I've never seen one. I don't remember ever being that small."

Tilmon shrugged. "No one remembers being a baby, but you should remember being small say at two to three years old."

Bendin frowned. "I remember from the very start. We all start big. There are no small people at all where I come from."

"That sounds very weird, Bendin," Quip mused.

"Oh yeah? Well how do you get a baby?" Bendin asked.

"When a guy and a girl get together and get serious," Rachel interlocked her fingers together, "there is a chance that the girl might have a baby."

Bendin, for the first time understood what she was doing with her fingers. It just clicked.

"We call that linking, but nobody ever had a baby because of that."

Rachel, Quip, and Tilmon exchanged their simultaneous reaction of silence.

". . . I'm sorry, Bendin, we didn't know," Tilmon said, "If your ladies are not having babies, there might be some serious problems with wherever it is that you come from."

"You're past mystifies me," Quip inserted. "We are going to need a better inspection."

"Maybe." Bendin sighed. He wasn't sure what was going to happen now.

Celeste's singing grew louder and the word, "Tilmon!"

was shouted in one of the intervals.

"If the baby is here, we'll leave first thing tomorrow. See you then, Bendin, I suggest you get some sleep." Tilmon turned and went into the room.

Bendin held Rachel's hand for a bit longer before they went up to his room.

"Will you guys be coming with me?" Bendin asked Quip and Rachel once they arrived.

Rachel sighed. "I'll go as far as I can Bendin, but there will be a point where they will not let me pass. Tribunal stuff is pretty isolated to just the parties involved. Tilmon might get me to be able to be there, but I can't promise anything. I want to, though. Trust me, to be there."

"You?" Bendin asked Quip and scratched his ears.

"Do what you want. I'm with you to the end, Bendin. I don't want you getting into trouble without me to blame it on."

For the first time since his admission, Bendin felt reassurance sweep him. Bendin hugged Quip. "Thanks, you've become a good friend since we've met. I really like that."

Bendin smiled his gratitude to Rachel, but she seemed somewhat distant.

"I don't know what's going to happen," she said after a moment. "What if it's true that you are a Vaelift and this all pans out? What will happen to you?"

"I haven't the slightest clue in the world, but whatever happens I want you and Quip to be a part of it."

"Thanks. You two should get some sleep." Rachel smiled softly.

"We will, after our prayers," Bendin informed her.

Rachel watched as Bendin and Quip settled into their praying positions. Bendin, with his hands pressed together with his fingers extended, flipped his two middle fingers down in a flapping motion, "If I have enough faith, I can fly."

Rachel laughed, and Quip sneezed a fireball across Bendin's face.

Bendin frowned, laughed in surprise, and changed his hands back to the normal position: clasped together in front of him as he sat cross-legged.

"Sorry to interrupt, but do you really talk to Odge and he talks back?" Rachel said disbelievingly.

"Yes," Both Quip and Bendin stated at the same time.

Rachel sat, stared with a straight face, watched for a while, and left.

Bendin shared his fears, his hopes, and his dreams of having a life just like the Coils, with a family of his own to Odge. He finally, after the time he spent here, knew what he wanted. He expressed his anticipation of the upcoming tests and his fears in meeting the Tribunal. He hoped that everything would turn out all right. He prayed for his friends and the Coil's family.

Odge responded, "It's finally time. Be faithful as things are going to get much more intense."

"Time for what? Bendin said aloud.

Quip touched Bendin's arm with tears in his eyes, "Time for me to be just like you."

"What? You're going to become human?"

"No, don't be silly. Odge just told me that he is going to make me a Vaelift too. He says you are going to be a person of great importance, and I'm going to be there to help you."

"Did he say when you will be one?"

"No. That I just need to be patient."

"Right."

Bendin and Quip finished their prayers. He pondered on what the next day would possibly bring. He secretly hoped the day wouldn't bring anything, he could come back, settle down here, and enjoy the freedom he had enjoyed so far. Bendin was also silently glad that Odge was again talking with him, and that he had Quip to share it with. The grey blurs had now become shapes, and they seem to come and go at random. He still didn't know what to make of them except they were very annoying. Bendin turned over, snuggled next to Quip snoozing, and fell asleep.

Tilmon hammered on Bendin's door and shouted, "Rachel said you had a Vaelift uniform or something? You better wear it. It will help smooth things over with the council. I'm also bringing Rachel along as a witness. Her testimony will be of paramount importance for the veracity of your claim. We leave as soon as you're ready."

Bendin put his old Vaelift uniform on, which felt incredibly awkward and constricting. He frowned and said to Quip, "Once this test is over, I'm probably going to modify this outfit to better fit my needs."

Quip made no effort to move and didn't respond. Bendin put the bands on, silver box, his boots, and took the Airlarky staff too. He felt like a hybrid of their societies. Quip hadn't moved all morning, so Bendin shook him till he woke.

"Bendin," the little fox whispered.

"That's some greeting, Quip. Come on, we need to go!" Bendin lifted Quip and draped him over his shoulders. "Why are you so tired this morning?" Bendin noted. "Are you okay?"

Bendin heard Quip mumble, "Fine" before he fell asleep on Bendin's shoulders. Bendin wasn't so sure.

Bendin and Quip left following in the wake of the good news from Starley and Charles, who had already gotten up and were playing in the Kid's Lounge.

"Mommy had a girl! Destiny is our new sister!" They chanted to Bendin and Quip as they left their room. They went to the bubble to set out for the Tribunal. Tilmon was already there and never looked prouder. Rachel was sitting in the bubble waiting for them.

"Can't we just network with the Tribunal?" Bendin asked.

"Not for something as important as this. Everyone but Simon Wight will be flying out," Tilmon explained from the driving seat. "I told them all last night through the network and convinced them to meet."

"Why not Simon?"

"Because, Hymingway is his home. It's been the Wight's home since the beginning. Just so you know, the name was changed to Hymingway when it became the Capitol."

Quip sleepily tickled Bendin's ear with his nose. He whispered happily in his ear. "One of Odge's messengers visited me last night and gave me a gift. He said I proved faithful and he gave it to me in Odge's name."

"Gave you what?"

"The power to be a Vaelift now, under you."

"He never told me."

Quip shrugged. "Well, he said you'd believe me and said to watch out for you. He had a very nice warm smile."

"I had something similar happen to me before I came here. Do you see blurs in your vision from time to time now too?" Bendin asked.

"Not that I've seen, I was just really weak after he left. I still feel really tired." Quip yawned, got into Bendin's lap, and fell asleep again.

"Curious. Same thing happened to me."

Rachel held Bendin's hand the whole way to Hymingway. Bendin felt incredibly nervous and had butterflies in his stomach that refused to settle down.

They got to Hymingway and instead of parking down below, Tilmon flicked on special green flashing lights that lit up all round the bubble and flew straight to the oldest, tallest looking building in the middle of city. It was old-looking because the bottom of it looked like an ancient castle and the center of it was the tower, but as you went up it changed to new kinds of materials till you reached the top where it was made of glass and metal.

Tilmon parked on one of the ledges that was near the pinnacle. The only thing that came close in height was the enormous twisty bridge to the south.

The tile work was extravagant and detailed in style. It had a black background, but was intermixed with colors from all the families. There was also distinct patterns in the metalwork and woodwork, showing the symbols of the families. There was one circle for each family and in the circle was a symbol: the Coil's was green and black and had an axe emblem, the DeSoto's was yellow and black and it had a picture of a snow capped mountain with skyscrapers in front of it, the Wycliff's was red and black and had a picture of a pickaxe, the Sanga's was black and orange and had a picture of an oasis with a large metal structure next to it, the Hyde's was purple and black and showed the picture of a shepherd's staff, the Wight's was white and black and showed the picture of a non-octagonal eight-sided shape, the Finn's was blue and black and had a picture of a seagull in front of a castle, there was one more that Bendin didn't know who it belonged to, it was aqua and black and had a picture of a bushel of harvested wheat on it.

"Which family is this?" Bendin asked pointing at it.

"It was Peter Moyle's family. Remember him? He was the one that was betrayed and they all died," Tilmon said sadly, "It's time go in. Rachel, stay close."

Gravity was localized so the very few people they did see up here in this area were walking. The people who saw Quip riding on Bendin watched with strange expressions as they passed by. It was like they had seen a ghost. Quip was awake now and stuck out his tongue at them or shot flame into the air. This caused them to pale and in some cases even to drop things they were carrying. Tilmon led them down into a narrow entrance and up a few carpeted stairs that wrapped up one level. Once at the top there was only one place they could go, up to another small flat stair.

"Here." Tilmon led him up the stair through a very large silver door that had all eight symbols on it. He found the symbols again inside the room on the floor in front of eight chairs that sat in a semi-circle around a room that was higher than all the rooms in the city. The whole room had circular windows so if you walked over to them, you could look out over the entire city. The floor was impressively tiled with beautiful mosaics representing the symbols of all the families. Rachel stood by his side. There were eight chairs. The seventh and eighth chair were empty. Tilmon went and sat in the seventh chair, which was green and black. Bendin could tell who the occupants of the remaining six chairs were, both by the symbol and by the color of the chair. All of tribunal glared at him like he was a thorn in their side, but once they saw he was carrying an animal on his shoulder they all perked up with some interest.

"Is that a special animal?" One of the men to the left of center asked.

"Yes, but that's not why we are here," Quip said to the man. To prove his point that he was both special and they were not going to talk about it, Quip blew a large colorful burst of flame towards the man to show that he was indeed, special.

"By the great powers of Odge," another said in disbelief.

An old man on the far end introduced himself, "Tilmon, thank you for being on time. Bendin, my name is Simon Wight, welcome. We are the tribunal." Simon had white hair, a white beard that was braided, and his whole form was very old. He appeared to be by far the oldest member of the group.

"I am Carl Hyde. Welcome." Carl was blond, young, and had a slight quaver in his voice. He looked at Bendin with his green eyes and Bendin noticed that there was some sort of mirth there that matched Carl's really high boots.

"Pi Finn. Welcome." Pi looked to be about the same in age as Tilmon, but drastically thin in comparison. Pi sported dark hair and dark eyes. He seemed to be a little more unsettled than the rest of them, his eyes flicking from one person to the next in the highest frequency of the bunch. His clothes were so simple they seemed informal compared with everyone else, being shorts and a shirt.

"I am," a very large fat man said laughing, "Trudamanga Sanga, pleased to make your acquaintance." His tan balding head with grey hairs around the sides did nothing to damper the color on his rosy cheeks or stop the twinkle in his blue eyes. He had a grey mustache and glasses which he kept fiddling with.

"Aspertan DeSoto," was all a man with a large forehead, small chin, tiny hazel eyes, big ears and an auburn-colored mop for a haircut had to say. His attire was the sleekest and well pressed. He was fit and well kept.

"Aspertan DeSerious," Quip muttered to Bendin. Bendin had to work hard to not crack a smile.

"I'm Xenon Wycliff, welcome to the Tribunal," boomed a man that could only be compared with something as big as a bear and spoke with such power that it shook the walls of the building. His voice was so thick and penetrating, Bendin wouldn't be surprised if you could hear it while passing by the building outside. His hands and muscles looked as though he could crush Bendin's entire skull. They were very large and the vivid muscle showed that he used his hands a lot.

"Tilmon Coil." Tilmon smiled.

"Okay. Now to business. Tilmon. . ." Simon paused. "You believe he's really a Vaelift?"

"I do not."

The rest of the group said nothing.

Bendin felt both fear and hope well up inside him.

"But, we are here to see if he is as he claims to be. Please listen to my daughter who found him," Tilmon explained.

Rachel explained briefly the advent of his arrival of him coming through the waterfall gate.

Trudamanga Sanga laughed. "Of all the stories, this one is definitely the best! You say he grabbed one of the special frogs which turned out to be electric?" He roared in laughter.

Bendin forced a smile and Bendin felt Quip giggling.

"It wasn't that funny," Bendin whispered to Quip.

"Mmmhmmm," Quip mumbled to him.

Aspertan grumbled, "His outfit is superb. Best I've ever seen. Very authentic look to it. I vote test."

Carl glanced to Aspertan in surprise.

"Test?" Pi asked.

"Test," said Carl, "let's get this over with."

"Are we all in agreement?" Simon asked.

Every member nodded in agreement.

"Well, come my son, let us discover what you really are. You like the countless others before you find it so funny to play tricks like this on the tribunal," Simon said beckoning Bendin to go with him.

"Can I bring my friends?"

"Yes, come now."

Bendin felt some relief now that he wasn't going to be alone.

Simon turned and grinned knowingly to his fellow

associates. "We'll be back quickly." He led Bendin, Quip, and Rachel down to a lift which, Bendin discovered, took them to the courtyard of the castle that was far below.

"Here," Simon said pointing to a spot that was raised a couple feet off the courtyard floor. "This is where we are going to test you."

"Quip, do what I do please," Bendin commanded gently.

Bendin walked up the smal set of steps and sat down with Quip following suite sitting next to him.

"Oh how cute, the fox wants to be a Vaelift and deceive me too."

"I was called by Odge himself to be a Vaelift you old man," Quip said flatly.

Simon eyed him skeptically and said, "Right." He continued and described the test for them to do. It was a simple process of focusing your mind and pushing your hands together. Simon described that according to the ancients in times past, the ability for the Vaelift to vanish was performed until it was a reflex. Once learned it could be duplicated and done again until perfection.

"At least this is how they described it to us in tradition," Simon said clapping his hands. "Go ahead. Let's see if you really are."

Bendin at the same time as Quip crossed their legs and moved their arms in motion. They sat and focused on vanishing.

Nothing.

One hour passed.

Nothing.

Rachel sat down with Simon and began to talk to him and ask him questions. Bendin and Quip sat motionless for a total of two hours before Simon said, "Come on, I'm tired and you're not fooling anyone. Let's take you home."

Bendin and Quip were straining as hard as they could. Just as Bendin felt he could do it no more, a voice came to them. Only they could hear it and it said seriously and lovingly, "Not in the mind only or the heart only, it's deeper than that. It can be a reflex if you practice enough; it's muscle, spirit, mind, and heart; push your free hands into each other's hands, and push out with the other with your heart, spirit, mind, and body."

Bendin and Quip moved their free hands pressing against each other's hands and Bendin clasped his staff in the other. They looked down, closed their eyes shoved their free hands backwards as the voice had described. They emphasized the final motion.

Simon moved forwards to grab them shouting, "Stop it. You are not fooling anyone anym--"

"Behold!" A loud voice exclaimed out of nowhere with such firmness as it could not to be doubted and could be heard by everyone nearby.

The very air sounded as though it were being ripped apart, there was a crack as loud as the sound of thunder, a shockwave the size of the family bubble, and a light so bright you couldn't look at it, all together hovering in the place where Bendin and Quip were.

Once the sound and light had faded Bendin and Quip were gone.

They had vanished.

Chapter 13
Queen Vlasta

With a thunderous crash, light flashed from a point in the air. The air rippled with such powerful energy that every molecule of air around the point condensed into water. Bendin and Quip blasted downwards out of the light through the air and were redirected across the surface of a shallow pool of water. Water flew in every direction and Bendin reached out with his hands as they cruised. He gripped the edge of a low wall that ran around the shallow pool and stopped their motion with grunt. He wearily propped himself up against the wall. He pulled Quip onto his lap and Quip said with a faint grin, "That was *totally* wild." Bendin managed a smile before they each blacked out.

Bendin woke with what felt like a few hours later, still lying in the pool of water. Bendin saw that they were in an open, dimly lit, concrete, ornate room that had a very high ceiling. There were many thick round concrete pillars that went up out of sight into the darkness above. He peered over the edge of the tiny wall and saw that they had landed in a fountain in an indoor courtyard. It was exactly like a real castle courtyard, but you could tell that whoever designed the place had completely encased it. Bendin didn't know for sure, because he couldn't see if it had an open ceiling. There was soft light coming from a few inset square fixtures in the wall, the same engravings that were on his upper temple walls, and he began to be very suspicious as to where he might be.

Quip was still unconscious.

Bendin was surprised how much better he felt. The last time his body had been forced through the light he'd been a total wreck. He guessed that what had happened was exactly the same as being pulled through the wall before. He couldn't believe he had control over all his faculties, and he was annoyed that the grey blurs were still there. Maybe he could just shut them off.

Bendin closed his eyes and tapped his head with his fingers. This just made him more irritated. Bendin watched Quip breathe in and out in a comfortable easy pace. This made Bendin smile and he relaxed and focused on the experience that they had just been through. The trip here As he did so he used his heart, mind, and muscle. The images blurred and shifted into shapes, morphing perfectly till he could see in plain clear vision, exactly half opaque as his regular vision, the castle courtyard he had just come from in Hymingway.

Bendin gasped and held the wall for support. He could see Rachel, Simon, and the rest of the courtyard of people in Hymingway staring at him. Well, at the place where he had just been. It was a little blurry, maybe because he wasn't used to it, but he could tell by the expressions on their faces they all noticed he was not there. He saw that the courtyard was at exactly the same level as the one he was in. It was a fairly large courtyard, but both of the courtyards here and there seemed to be equal in size. Bendin realized he couldn't see through the walls in Hymingway, but that he was limited to where the light was hitting, just like as if he was still standing there. He focused again and found that he could literally "turn on" or "turn off" being able to see. He leaned back against the fountain and pondered this new exciting bit of information.

After a few minutes, he realized, that he must truly be a Vaelift, one of Odge's Vaelift. Just like Radu and Findall Quin or the other Vaelift leaders of the ages. He just needed to determine where he was now, or *when* he was. Poor Quip must have had it rough because he didn't move at all. Bendin felt sorry for the little fox. He'd already had an exhausting night. He still seemed to be breathing okay, and Bendin was glad that he had on all of his gear. He was extremely happy that he had thought of being more prepared in case of an emergency. It would make eating and drinking much easier now that he was in a strange place.

He carefully positioned Quip on his shoulders, said a prayer that wasn't answered, activated his blades, his silver box, and skated straight up into the air. He found the ceiling solid and impassable. Bendin skated back down and chose the right door of the two sets of doors at opposite ends. He guessed that they would head inward, but he really had no idea. Once through the doors, he was in a long, narrow hallway that had nothing but dim lighting and etchings on the walls. He didn't see anyone or hear anything for a moment, even though both of those senses were working just fine. He listened more intently.

He heard a low rumbling sound that he hadn't noticed before. It came from a small archway ahead that led out onto a small balcony. He walked out onto the balcony and almost fell over in shock. The tiny balcony was at the very top of the biggest room Bendin had ever seen. Yes it was bigger than many Heptahedrons. He saw millions and millions of large cylinders being moved all around. This is definitely where the sound had been coming from. Bendin saw several cylinders pass by him and inside each one was a person even smaller than Starley. The cylinders would come in one way and then move out the other side hung on tracks. Each was being processed, recorded and moved by people and machines. These were not students but people Bendin had never seen before. This made him extra cautious and slightly suspicious. He couldn't risk detection and ducked down behind the balcony rail.

The people were all wearing grey and he began to wonder where or when he was again. Bendin backtracked with sleeping Quip to the courtyard. He went the other direction this time, skating in the air. He rounded the corner and saw many doors and a long hall. The scuff marks on the floor made the area seem to have more traffic, but luckily the hall had high walls and a high ceiling. Bendin skated up and discovered that if he traveled slowly enough, he could move and not be heard or seen. That was even with the welding sound, light, and sparks that he made. It depended directly on how hard and fast he skated as to how bright and loud it was.

He skated near the ceiling down the hallway carefully till he couldn't go on anymore. This forced him down to the ground, so he deactivated his box and blades. He rounded the corner and the area widened into a very elegant walkway. The area was extremely worn, but the handiwork was incredible. Everything in this section of the hall got older the further you went in.

Bendin found carved ornate doors which read in silver etching, "Queen Vlasta's private quarters." Why would she be here in the middle of this place? The thought hit him and sunk in. He really was back. Queen Vlasta was the ruling monarch. Maybe he could ask her a few questions if she was here? But, would it be worth the risk of being detected? Why was there no guard? This was too good of an opportunity to pass up.

Bendin pushed open the ornate doors, and he found a room with bookcases on the left and boxes of chocolates on the right. Pictures lined the walls and at the other end of this section were modern reinforced doors. As Bendin crossed the room he noticed a date and clock on the wall. It read, "3:55, 2-15-1809". His watch, which he had kept from his temple, read the same minutes but different hours, "0:55". He was back in his own time, in his own place, but definitely not in his temple. This was probably the Center Section. If that was true it was the home of the queen, the headquarters of Vaelift, the Marshalls, and the other highest ranking people in the Kingdom. Bendin poked through the room nervously. What was strange was there was still no sign of any guards or official people at all.

He went through the doors at the far end and found himself in a small room with a small bed and one square inset light on the other side of the room.

"Findall? Is that you?" A voice said from the bed. Bendin recognized the queen instantly.

"No, sorry to interrupt you Queen," Bendin stated in the formal voice in which he had been trained to use when addressing royalty.

Lights flicked on from holes in the ceiling and Bendin could see the Queen rubbing her eyes, wearing a fancy nightgown.

It took a few minutes for it to register, but when she was awake enough to see him, she recognized him. Her eyes widened a little and she froze. "BD3, the betrayer and master escaper. We meet. What do you want besides me?" She pulled up the blankets to hide herself.

Bendin didn't say anything.

"You have thirty seconds to answer before I call the Vaelift and have you tossed into the lava pits."

"Why not just call them now?" Bendin asked with curiosity and apprehension.

"Because I was hoping you'd tell me how you escaped the hands of my finest Vaelift."

"I found a hole in the defenses," Bendin lied. He knew it wasn't a total lie.

"No one has escaped the temples alive, but you. Yes, sometimes the Alcs and bandits get in, but no one *ever* gets out. How did you do it?" Vlasta leaned forward eagerly.

"I already told you I found a hole in the wall and climbed through it," Bendin said. That was also kind of true.

Bendin saw her eyes flick from him to the sleeping fox on his shoulders, but she didn't ask about the fox. She just shook her head sadly. "BD3, Please. I offer peace and reconciliation. I'll give you whatever you want. Please tell me how you found this hole."

"I was just hoping you could tell me about the cylinders in the other room."

"Fair request. You first." Queen Vlasta's eyebrows raised

a bit and she twitched under the covers.

Bendin had hoped she would have just answered the question. She was smarter than that it appeared.

He sighed.

A shot rang out. Bendin flinched and watched the Queen fire more rounds from a drawn pistol, and then more from another one in her other hand. Quip twitched but continued to sleep. Each shot redirected around the bands and slammed into the reinforced doors behind Bendin. She was exceedingly expert and Bendin now knew why she had no guards. Without the bands, he'd have been completely shredded.

Queen Vlasta's eyes widened in disgust, she pulled the chain, and swapped out clips in her gun. She kept firing till the clip went dry. "*Spawn* of Pikuk indeed!"

There was a loud chime and a clicking sound. Bendin decided being here anymore wasn't the best idea and pushed on the doors behind him to get out. They were locked.

The Queen smiled wickedly but spoke with complete composure from hundreds of hours of practice, "BD3, you will not be escaping this completely enclosed and fiercely defended fortress. I may chat with you later. I haven't decided yet."

Findall Quin himself raced in through doors on the other side of the room that Bendin hadn't noticed before.

"Highness, are you ok? I heard gunfire!" He was so concerned that he didn't see Bendin standing at the foot of the bed. Three of Odge's Vaelift practically tripped over Findall in their rush into the room. They were flanked by, one Elect and one Angel. The Elect had a rocket launcher. Bendin recognized that one of the three of Odge's Vaelift was his old classmate, Radu Landus. It was Radu who spotted him first.

"Bendin!" Radu snarled. He got into some form or position that Bendin was not familiar with. Bendin realized Radu might have trained a bit since he was gone. "You're not getting away from me this time."

"Join the party. That's kind of what she just said." Bendin yawned lazily.

Findall glared at Bendin with sour eyes. He placed a hand on Radu's shoulder.

"Hold everything! Radu, he might just disappear again. Bendin, in Odge's glorious name, tell us *how* you managed to escape?" He raised his fist and waited. The Angel, Elect, and Queen were ready to fire.

"Ask the Queen. I've already told her."

"He *did*? What did he say?" Findall asked Queen Vlasta.

"He says he went through a hole."

"You don't say. Did he say there was light involved?" Findall turned on Bendin and shouted, "WAS THERE LIGHT INVOLVED?"

Bendin didn't expect this kind of thing at all and fumbled backwards awkwardly till his back was pressed up against the door. He thought it best not to answer that question.

Findall began to pace mumbling things under his breath. He then turned to the queen and exclaimed anxiously, "I think it's actually happened. Destroy him! *Now!*" The queen shook her head and before Bendin could do anything, everything in the room fired at him.

Bendin instinctively held Quip close so that Quip wouldn't be hanging out too far as everything blasted at him was redirected into the doors. They ruptured from the bullets but exploded outwards when the rocket smashed and exploded into it. Bendin laughed like a child.

"You missed." Bendin grinned, switched his box and boots on, and to the surprise of Radu and those who were there, Bendin skated through what was left of the doors, back the way he had come.

"Cut him off, seal every exit! Wake everyone up that is able to fight! Make sure he . . ." Findall's voice screamed in rage and faded away as Bendin sped swiftly away.

Bendin made it back in the courtyard and stopped, confused as to where to go next. He dripped some water from the fountain on Quip. Bendin was kind of mad he hadn't thought of doing it before.

Quip groggily woke. "Don't kill my family," he said whimpering.

"Quip! It's me, Bendin." Bendin gently stroked the fox's head.

"Bendin? Are you okay? I feel so tired," Quip managed to say.

"I know, that's why we need to get out of here," Bendin said hastily. "I've kind of stirred up a hive."

"What?" Quip muttered.

"I disturbed the Queen," Bendin explained.

"Great. Bother. Never touch the Queen of a hive, Bendin! Blech. I can't move, Bendin," Quip mumbled. "And I can hardly see you. Remember those grey shapes you were talking about?"

"Yes," Bendin said as patiently as he could.

"I see them now. They are really annoying." Quip struggled to lift his paw.

"Don't even try. I got you. We are going to find a way out of this place." They heard the rumbling of marching feet and Bendin knew they were just outside the doors.

Bendin held Quip tight and skated up behind a pillar close to the fountain. The doors clicked and whirred open just as Bendin rounded the pillar. Bendin peeked around the pillar and saw a thick bunch of Vaelift of all ranks march into the courtyard directly up to the fountain.

"What do you make of this?" One of them said pointing at the fountain.

"Wow, that's something you don't see every day," another said.

"What's wrong with it?"

"It's Pikuk's power for sure."

Bendin peered around the pillar to see what they were talking about. He gulped, and smiled to himself. The water spewing up out of the fountain snaked up into the field of negated gravity, reached the peak of the field, and reversed its course back down into it.

It was the perfect distraction, and he skated swiftly down towards the door. Shots rang out, missed, and bullets pierced the engravings on the walls as Bendin skated directly out into the huge cylinder room. He hoped that deeper would be a better place to hide. He skated carefully through the room moving behind objects of all sizes. It was a good thing too as the Vaelift group had emerged on the balcony and were taking careful shots across the room at him.

Bendin was hoping for a miracle as to where to exit. There were too many places he could go from this room.

"Which one do you think?" Bendin asked gently shaking the fox.

"I think we know where you come from," the fox said groggily waking and seeing the cylinders. Quip gave him a goofy smile.

"Right." Bendin didn't want to think of that abstract thought at the moment.

A shot punctured a cylinder and it fell down far below crashing to the ground with a large thunderous boom.

"That one. That one there is where the people go," Quip instructed. He pointed feebly with his paw to a passage that was near the very bottom of the room. Quip's paw fell limp immediately.

"It must be some sort of checking facility," Bendin noted. "If we can find the subway system we can go to whatever temple we want."

"I don't know what that smells like."

The passage was narrow and just high enough for him to skate over top of anyone he came across. Most of them were the grey cloaked people. Occasionally he'd pass someone who was dressed like a Vaelift. When Bendin would skate over top any one of them, they would gulp nervously and point in awe.

"I smell dank, musty air, metal, and fresh burnt oil fumes up ahead. Is that it?" Quip asked.

"Probably. We've got nothing else to go off of."

"Go left," Quip guided. "I mean, right!"

Bendin already chose left and switched directions.

"Sorry!" Quip hissed.

The error cost them, because when Bendin finished turning around, a huge gate thundered down and sealed everything in that direction. He listened and could hear the distant sound of the subway system. They had been so close!

"No!" Bendin shouted and swung his staff into the gate. The staff bounced off the gate leaving hardly a scratch.

"Took them long enough. We almost made it out that way. . . " Bendin said to Quip. "Any ideas?"

"Let's just get away from here!" Quip demanded.

Bendin skated up along the first passage they came to on the right. It led to a room that opened up with fat pillars that went all around the room. It was unfortunately filled with all ranks of Vaelift. Shots rang out all over the room and all areas around Bendin lit up in flakes, dust, chunks of the walls, and chips of the pillars flying all over the place. After a few more seconds of concentrated fire, Bendin felt an explosion rip apart the base of the pillar behind him.

The crowd cheered as it teetered and crashed down on top of Bendin. Bendin felt his body move like water being pushed aside as something falls into it. The room shook and quaked as the massive pillar smashed into pieces on the ground sending clouds of dust, chunks and chips of rock into the air. Their cries of joy were replaced by pain from the collateral damage.

Bendin quickly moved away from the pillar, skated into the air, and eagerly sought another way out of the room.

"Pikuk!" shouted many of the enraged Angels and Elect.

A group of them carried in and begun setting up a makeshift rope net. Bendin skated straight at it, closed his eyes, gritted his teeth, and performed his first successful double bladed stop in his life. It was just his luck as a fireball erupted from the stop and caught the whole net on fire.

Coming down that far cost him, however, as a Vaelift staff swung parallel to his movement and smashed into his hip. The force sent Bendin skidding sideways through the air on his skates and he hit the wall on the side of the room before he could correct his balance.

"Mortal!" Cried the Vaelift that had hit him. "He's mortal possessed by Pikuk!"

"An Incarnation!" Said another.

"It's a freak! A Hidiadion!"

"Bendin, that was too close. Please, don't do that again," Quip cautioned. "You have both of our lives in your hands."

"Sorry." Bendin checked again for a way out of this circular pillared room.

The Vaelift blocked up every single entrance, so Bendin realized there simply was no easy exit point. He frowned.

They were going to have to fight their way out one of the entrances.

A masked man entered the room wearing all black. Everyone in that area of the room parted nervously, shying away from him. Many of Odge's Vaelift simply spun their staffs and vanished, while their onlookers either stood their ground, or appeared jealous.

The man shook his fist and shouted, "Come down here and hit me, BD3, you worthless scumbag Hidiadion!"

"Careful, Bendin," Quip advised. "Wait, what's a Hidiadion?"

"Shhhh. Let me do this." Bendin skated directly at the man dressed in black. Bendin clutched his staff with accuracy and precision that he didn't really know he had. The man did nothing but stand there.

Ha! Idiot! This was going to be easy.

The man stiffened as Bendin made contact with the man's body. Bendin hit the man with the speed of a subway train and the noise of broken and twisted metal filled the air. Bendin spun and saw the staff fracture and disintegrate on impact with the man. All he had left was a broken jagged stub of a club. The man did slide backwards a few feet from the force of the blow before the ground beneath him cracked under his feet.

The man laughed wickedly.

This was the laugh of a man who simply didn't fear anything. Bendin landed with his feet on the ground and his back to the wall. All Vaelift spread out in a semi-circle around him and the man wearing black. Bendin taunted the man to come towards him with his fingers. The man let out an aggressive snarl and charged enthusiastically. Loud thumps echoed around the room and Bendin watched in awe as with each step the concrete under the man cracked and broke. Bendin was beginning to feel very nervous as he realized the full magnitude of what was running directly at him. Quip twitched. The moment the the man stepped into the negated gravity that surrounded Bendin, the force of his feet pushed him off the ground uncontrollably and sent him spinning upward wildly over Bendin. To Bendin's delight, the man impacted the wall with momentous force and caused the wall to buckle and explode outwards. Bendin skated up and saw that the man had plowed through many walls before imprints of his body arched downwards and disappeared.

"That guy is a tank, Bendin," Quip noted fearfully.

"I've never actually met one, but I think that was a D-man." It was Bendin's best guess. "Probably."

"Can we go the other way?"

The other Vaelift in the room shot at Bendin with their guns, and the ones wielding their staffs converged on Bendin. Using his movement to his advantage, Bendin skated around several of them. To their dismay, many of their shots landed on fellow Vaelift. A cry quickly rose up from among them, "Stop! Stop! Stop shooting! The power of Pikuk. It's the Hidiadion!"

After a few fancy loops and arcs, Bendin decided to go through the hole in the wall that was created by the man wearing black. Several walls later, he found where the man had landed-- nowhere to be found.

"Be careful, he makes me extremely nervous," Quip said. "Can't we find a way out of here?"

"Can we go out the way we came in?" Bendin voiced his thought.

"Can we?" Quip asked him.

"I don't know, I would assume so. We just need a place where they," Bendin jerked his thumb over his shoulder and down where the man had been, "won't get us for a few hours?"

Bendin felt the walls shake, and he skated away down the hallway.

Some of the halls went pretty high, but there was no

place here for them to sit. "Let's look around the temple as far as we can, and see if there are any of those paces that were in the upper temple that Franklin was in."

"Do what you want, Bendin."

Bendin skated up and dowr as many halls as he could find, staying high out of anyone's reach. He skated for an hour before he found a group of people below him in a dimly lit hallway he recognized. To his delight, Bendin found temple janitors like the ones from his temple near the end of the hall. The hall had engravings on every wall and they were painting the walls grey with vigor.

"What are you guys doing?" Bendin asked from above them in the air.

"Painting before BD3 can get here!' the janitor closest to him said without a thought. The janitor looked up into the face of Bendin, screamed, and threw his brush as Bendin moved around him. The brush went around Bendin and splattered the wall behind him.

"Why do you need these walls painted?" Bendin raised his broken staff as he asked the janitor.

The janitor bumped the wall with his arm, yelped, and moved backwards as quickly as he could sputtering, "BD3! Don't hurt us; we are just following Castle Marshall Storn's orders! He made us paint the walls grey."

Bendin could hear something from around the corner behind him down the hall, "Storn, are you sure?"

"Positively. Don't come inside the radius for any reason. Let this be an example for the rest of the men."

"Yessir!"

"I didn't do it . . . honestly."

A shot rang out and the scund of something hitting the ground could be heard. Bendin ducked looking around nervously.

"Please, don't judge us!" The janitor's hissed at Bendin.

"Yes, Castle Marshall Storn has a way of doing what is best for his country. Doesn't he, BD3? You betrayer. Or should I call you what the Vaelift call you? Plkuk incarnate? A Hidiadion?" A thick heavy voice huffed from behind them.

Bendin stiffened at this voice. He d heard it before, but had only seen Storn a couple of times. He remembered him being at the shooting competition.

"Janitors, leave!" Storn commanded.

The janitors fled in all directions. Bendin tried to think of what he could ask Storn. Maybe he could totally bluff it.

"Can you help me find a safe place to stay for a while? The people in this temple won't let me rest for a single minute," Bendin asked.

Storn's expression was a cold, hard set frown, one that showed years of experience. His bald head was slick, his dark foreboding diagonally shaped eyes were merciless, and his muscled arms were fit for his age. His beard was black and had bits of white laced throughout.

"BD3. You've caused a dark stir in the temple and in the kingdom. This cannot continue. However, I figured you would find your way here. I happen to have the perfect place you can stay and be safe. All you have to do is open the door," Storn said pointing down the hall. He walked slowly towards Bendin.

"What door?"

"The one that leads to Makarias."

Something stirred within him. Something about this situation spooked him. It was wrong. For some reason, there was a cold dark feeling that rushed over Bendin. He knew this was something not to do.

Even though Quip couldn't move, he still quivered and whispered warningly, "Skate away. This is a very sinister man. He reeks with blood. Don't trust him. Something's wrong!"

Bendin skated up into the air away from Storn, keeping his distance.

"Come down here, it's very simple," Storn said over to Bendin pointed towards the end of the hall. "There is absolutely nowhere for you to go. The fortress is completely sealed. No exits. No way out. It is simply up to you how you want this to end."

Bendin hesitated. It sounded unbelievable. But, then again, maybe not.

"Give me one reason why I should trust you. Everyone here wants to kill me."

"I'm not asking you to trust me. I'm demanding you do a simple task. If you are willing to do more, then I'd like to have more up to date intelligence about how you got to Makarias. I order you to come down!" Storn stamped his foot.

"No. What's Makarias?"

"Bendin, please don't say anything," Quip urged.

"I didn't expect BD3, the 'great obedient one', to be so disobedient. Did you not hear me? I order you to come down."

"You are not my leader." Bendin crossed his arms.

"Then consider this." Storm backed away swiftly down the hall, disappeared around the corner, and a moment later returned pulling a large box on wheels.

"I'm Castle Marshall Fredrick Storn. Although we have not formally met, I have watched your studies with extreme interest. You were going to be my personal trainee, that is, until your miraculous escape. Now it is time for you to be useful or perish."

Bendin began to work in his mind which way he was going to go after he left the room.

"Ppbbfftt. Personal trainee. You? Not likely," Quip whispered.

"Because, I have someone here, that you should know about."

Storn grinned and tapped the box with his hand. It collapsed and revealed a small huddled form with a blindfold over her eyes.

It was Harmon.

Bendin felt his body clench tight and felt like he was churning up inside. His spirit fought, his pulse accelerated, his face beaded in sweat, and his mind started to swim.

Quip could tell something was wrong, "Who is it?" Quip whispered.

"It's Harmon."

"Ouch, that's bad."

"Yes, thank you. Quip, always the obvious," Bendin whispered back.

Quip smiled. "You're welcome."

"Listen and work with me, or she dies," Storn said pulling out a pistol from his pocket and leveling it with her head.

"Storn!" Bendin exclaimed in astonishment, "You can't . . . No! Why would you do this?"

Storn slowly laughed. It wasn't high pitched, but a low slow methodical laugh. It was aged, rich and mysteriously sinister.

"Because we get what we want. Don't try my patience," he laughed again, "because I don't have any. Just do what I asked." Storn licked his lips and cocked back the lever that would release the hammer.

Quip noticed it and whispered harshly, "He didn't even have the weapon armed! The fiend!"

Bendin edged forward as close as he could, just out of Storn's range.

"What do you want me to do?" Bendin asked.

"Now that's the spirit." Storn smiled raising his gun into the air and backing up a few steps. "Good, with you helping I don't need her anymore."

The hesitation was all the time Bendin needed. He quickly skated down directly in front of Harmon and Storn's gun. Storn frowned as he fired directly at Harmon. The bullet went harmlessly around BD3 into the wall behind them.

Bendin stepped quickly forward and swung his broken pole at Storn's face. Storn laughed slowly as he easily ducked under the swing and countered with a short kick directly into Bendin's side. The kick sent Bendin sprawling backwards on the ground. Quip fell onto Harmon with a gasp.

"My, my, we all do have our little secrets don't we." Storn marched right up to Harmon and shoved the pistol directly against her head. "I *will* kill her this time. You are too far away to stop me!"

Bendin knew Quip wasn't strong enough to help and sighed. He knew if he could buy more time there was a chance he could save her. "I'll open this door . . ." Bendin began.

Storn smiled.

". . . If I can have her there alive next to me," Bendin finished.

"Done," Storn said lowering the weapon and picking up the girl, Quip managed to bite Harmon's shirt collar and hung on. Storn pointed his finger down the hall.

"Okay." Bendin skated down the hall. To Bendin's surprise, there was at the end of the room, the same markings on the wall of the unpainted hallway were right here etched into this wall. Storn's feet thumped behind Bendin while spinning his gun in his hands like a propeller. Storn tapped the wall with his gun.

"You want this open?" Bendin asked, "Set her here right in front of it and I'll open this, this. . ." Bendin thought of a word that sounded impressive, "gate . . . for you."

Storn dumped Harmon on the ground as Bendin scooped up Quip and wrapped him around his shoulders. Storn immediately nuzzled his gun up against Harmon's head. "Do it."

Bendin changed his vision to be able to see if he could see where the gate led. It led into another hall similar to the one he was in. He was impressed that the dimensions of the halls were the same on either side. There were a couple of people walking past, but nothing more. He wondered if he was looking at the active past, while living in the future. It was kind of a wild and strange concept to think about.

Storn frowned impatiently. "Do it, *now*."

Harmon was unconscious but seemed alright.

Bendin hoped this would work. He made the motions that he learned from the words of the twenty. At the last second, before he said the word, "vanish", he held Quip close. There was a brilliant flash of light, a thunderclap of sound, and a concussion wave that emitted from the place they occupied as Bendin and Quip were thrust into the white light that appeared out of the characters in the wall. This time, just after as Bendin went through, he watched Storn cry out in disgust, pound the floor with a fist, frown, grab Harmon, and drag her away. Only then did Bendin succumb to the darkness.

Chapter 14
Out of the dark

Bendin woke only an hour later to see Rachel, Tilmon, and the other members of the tribunal looking at him with more anticipation than any of them could bear. The well furnished room's windows revealed only the tops of neighboring buildings. His first thoughts were on Harmon but she had been taken away again from him. Something had went wrong. Why hadn't she been taken through the wall with him?

"Hi," Bendin said to all of them as he nudged Quip to see if he was awake yet.

Quip opened his eyes slowly and gave Bendin a sly smile. "That's quite a rush, isn't it?"

Bendin laughed. He felt fine, strangely, with no apparent weariness. At lease they were alive and okay. "So, where am I? What's going on?"

"You're in the area of the main tower sectioned off for visitors. We found you both unconscious by the Hymingway gate and brought you here. You've caused quite a stir among the people," Tilmon quickly explained.

"What happened to your staff?" Simon asked holding up Bendin's broken black staff.

"I hit a man with it."

Simon looked at the broken staff, then back at Bendin disbelievingly.

"We had been speculating on if you were really a Vaelift, but, now we have decided for certain," Tilmon declared.

Aspertan huffed, "Yes. But as for me, not so much. He doesn't act at all like the original Vaelift. He's no Desenzo DeSoto; I'll tell you that."

Simon frowned, as if his question apparently hadn't been answered to his satisfaction.

"Why are you here Mr. Vaelift?" Trudamanga asked with a smile.

"Because I didn't want to die or be captured by the people over there who wanted to kill me," Bendin answered.

"It's true," Quip agreed. "They were the nastiest people I've ever seen, even worse than here. They keep their babies in giant bottles and all wear the same thing that Bendin does."

Trudamanga laughed with such a deep rolling laughter that Bendin wondered what in the world could be so funny.

Bendin saw Rachel observing him, misty-eyed. Bendin mouthed the words, "What's goin--"

Simon gently tapped Bendin's arm and locked eyes with Bendin. "Bendin. We haven't had a Vaelift for over eight hundred and fifty years. Why Odge sent you to us is beyond us. Why? Why would he reinstate the old institution so many years after its destruction? We have all the works of the previous Vaelift and their teachings contained in the Book of Odge."

Quip coughed.

Simon eyed the fox distastefully and continued, "All the families lives are great, we have plenty of food, we have a small squabble going about the Outcasts, but it is negligible. Is something happening or going to happen that you haven't told us about?"

"I don't know. All I know is that Odge made me a Vaelift and that I was sent here to help." For the first time since all of this had happened, Bendin realized and accepted his position and authority. A sense of peace, but stern awakening flooded him.

Some of the tribunal groaned.

Simon crossed his arms and frowned.

"That's all you know?" Pi spun his hands around in a spiral.

Aspertan muttered in disdain, "No lights, or banding. He doesn't even have the staff. What's going on?"

"Surely Odge would have sent a real soothsayer like Jameus!" Carl complained brushing his face with his hand in discouragement.

"Can you imagine what is going to happen to the one true worship of Odge society when the word g--"

"Get a grip guys!" Rachel stood up and beamed over the tribunal with contempt. "Bendin has been sent to us by Odge himself and all you can do is question why he is here? Or that some great calamity is going to occur because of his arrival?"

"Why else would Odge bring the Vaelift back from the dead?" Pi asked.

"I don't know." Rachel shrugged helplessly. "He's definitely a Vaelift, and we must respect the will of Odge. If Bendin's here, there's surely a good reason for it!"

"It's decided then. I'll take the Vaelift. He can setup with me in the securest city on the planet," Aspertan announced sternly.

"No. If anyone gets him it's our people," Carl countered.

Aspertan declared triumphantly, "Clarendon *is* the safest. No outcast, or Grandelegant has ever penetrated the city or even came within a mile of our city without us being able to detect them."

The tribunal members continued to dispute as to who would get Bendin till Bendin himself spoke, breaking up the dispute. "Actually, there is a place I'm supposed to go."

Everyone in the room shut up instantly. They waited with baited breath.

"Don't say anyone," Simon said apprehensively, "I know what you're going to say, anywhere but there."

Bendin raised his eyebrows in confusion. "But I haven't even said anything yet."

"It's only going to cause grief if you stay at any one of the Families," Simon reasoned.

"No, you misunderstand. I'm going to be staying in Thibracketory." Bendin watched as every member of the council stared at him, as if he was going to explode at any moment.

Pi slapped his forehead, "No. That's suicide."

Tilmon whispered, "No."

"You're right I wasn't thinking that," Simon said dazed.

"No!" Aspertan thundered.

"Yes." Bendin frowned.

"Yes," Quip added.

"He's a goner," Carl muttered shaking his head.

"Definitely," said Pi.

"Why, do you have to go to, of all places," Xenon boomed shaking his head in despair, "Thibracketory?"

"Don't," Simon said. "We all agree on this: You're not going to go there."

"I have to. Odge has declared it," Bendin explained. "I don't know why exactly."

The entire Tribunal glared at Bendin.

"Wait, Odge just spoke to you just now?" Pi asked incredulously. "He told you that just now as we've all been standing here with you?"

"Yes?" Bendin replied slowly as if the question was a moot point.

Everyone, but Rachel, frowned even more.

"I don't believe you," Aspertan said stubbornly folding his arms across his chest. "Prove it."

Simon cut in, "We do know what he is."

"Still . . . unbelievable!" Xenon shouted.

"Believe what you want. It happened," Bendin looked honestly at each one of them.

"Why would he not speak directly to us?" Aspertan eyed him suspiciously.

"Probably because of something wrong with your book?" Bendin suggested. The second he said it, he wished he hadn't. Bendin felt as if he was about to become a smoking crater due to the amount of anger that appeared on the Tribunal's faces.

"Hmpf. Odge talks to us through the book, and in no other way," Trudamanga said defiantly.

"Where is your faith?" Rachel's voice rang off the walls. She raised herself off the ground. 'If he just went to Toalt and back, is that not proof enough that Odge knows what he's doing? Can he not bring Bendin to Thibracketory and back? Who cares if he can talk to Odge or not? What's the big deal? He's proven himself. We all just need to support him and give him the time of day to work. If not and he perishes, he's out of your hair!"

Bendin watched Tilmon smile and admire his girl with glowing pride.

The Tribunal members fidgeted but said nothing for a moment.

Aspertan broke the silence, "Thank you, Rachel, for your input. Please, sit down or get out. Listen to what I say very closely. Things will go forward as they have done since the destruction of the Vaelift. The fact that they are back doesn't change *our* authority or position. We will still rule as we have done."

Members shook their heads affirmatively.

"So it's settled. Bendin goes to Thibracketory, dies, and then we can get back to what we normally do," Simon declared. "All agree?"

Every Tribunal member shook their head yes, although some did it reluctantly. Pi and Carl were still grumbling and shaking their heads in disbelief.

"We almost had the Vaelift back," Pi muttered.

"Okay, now that things have been decided, let's let them recover from their journey. Even if it is true that they are just going to Thibracketory to die, that fox looks like he's going to fall over any second," Pi said leaving the room.

"Yeah," the rest of the members of the Tribunal murmured and left.

The fox did fall over, the second everyone went through the doors. Quip had no strength left to even hold his head up and fell fast asleep on Bendin's lap.

Rachel and Tilmon stayed.

"Where's Soladaque?" Bendin asked.

"She is with Chamilin I believe," Tilmon said. "We came as soon as we heard you were back."

"What is Toalt like?" Rachel asked smiling.

"I've never been told what Toalt is," Bendin said frowning.

"It's the place that you keep going." Rachel's eyes flicked to her father. "Right, Dad?"

Tilmon nodded. "Yes, according to history and the beginning of Makarias, Toalt is the old world. It's where we came from originally."

Bendin shook his head confused, "Wait. Hold on a second. What year is it here?"

"It's 905," Rachel said.

"I come from the year 1805. See? The time on my watch says, '6:23'. What time does it say on yours?"

Tilmon checked the clock on the wall that hung in between the windows, "It says, 16:33. Bendin, I don't think you understand how Makarias's time works. We don't run off of Toalt time. We run on Makarias time."

"There are two *different* times?" Bendin felt himself getting frustrated.

Rachel took his hand and calmly held his gaze, "Correct me if I get any of this wrong father, but from the record books and history of what Toalt was like back then our reckoning is half of theirs. We have 24 months in a year. They don't make calendars with Toalt anymore, because Toalt doesn't exist for us. It takes Makarias an entire Toalt year longer to get around our sun."

Tilmon figured out what Bendin's problem was, "1805 is the same as 905. We are reckoning the same time, just measured differently."

Bendin thought about that and it began made sense. "So I'm not traveling through time at all am I?"

Tilmon laughed, "No, the Vaelift could do a lot, but not that. You just go from one world to the other. It's simple. Come on, let's go home so you can pack and go to your death at Thibracketory."

"Father!" Rachel glared at her father.

Tilmon rolled his eyes. "Hey! No one has ever made it back after trekking into Thibracketory."

Bendin waved his arm and caught Tilmon's attention. "Tilmon?"

"What?"

"I need you to do something specia ."

Tilmon raised his eyebrows.

"I need you to make some repulsive bands for Quip."

"Okay?"

"Thanks."

"That will be thirty seven anc a half Crowlers."

Bendin raised his eyebrows.

"Father!" Rachel exclaimed slapping him on the back.

Tilmon laughed. "Just kidding. I'll see what I can do. Let's go, Rachel."

"No, I want to stay with them," Rachel said.

"Bring them, and they can sleep in the bubble."

"What about the Tribunal and them not wanting Bendin to go to any of th--"

"Bendin, bring Quip. We're leaving," Tilmon ordered and walked out of the room.

"It's okay. We'll figure it out " Bendin reassured Rachel. He actually felt perfectly fine; he leaped up, pulled Quip onto his shoulders, and followed them out.

The ride home was simple, fast, and Quip slept the entire way back. Once Bendin got back to his room, George expressed visual frustration. He had already confiscated the bed that Bendin had been using, so he reluctantly let Bendin take it back. Bendin didn't even get to say thanks because George grumbled and left immediately.

Bendin told Rachel of his adventures in Toalt: the cylinders, the queen, the man in black, and Storn.

"I wonder if that man you described in black was like my grandfather, a D-man," Rachel told him.

"You know about D-men?" Bendin asked bewildered.

"Of course! They've randomly popped up throughout the centuries."

"What are they?" Bendin asked, excited for a connecting topic and hungry for information on the people that the students in the temple rumored so much about.

"They are people that can make their bodies incredibly dense. It's rumored that they are completely indestructible." Rachel twirled her hair and watched Bendin with interest.

"Wow. Can I please meet your grandfather?"

"He's dead." Rachel scraped the floor with her boots sadly.

"What happened? If you don't mind me asking."

"He was old and died. He said that being a D-man was an interesting experience, but it does attract unwanted attention. The work, the hours, the demand, and the whole experience wore on his system. He was thirty years old when he died."

"How old are you supposed to live, you know, normally?" Bendin rubbed Quip's ears gently.

"Around forty your body can't support you, so you move on. He was very wise and fit, so he lived about five years longer than D-men normally live, which is about twenty-five years."

"Thanks, Rachel. Will you be going with me? To Thibracketory?"

"Me? Ha! No way. My research here is of far greater importance. Ask the older boys. Maybe you can get permission for them to risk their lives."

"I thought you cared about me enough, . . . you know, . . . that you'd support me."

Rachel held Bendin's hand in hers with fondness. "Bendin, you are the one that has been asked to do this, not me. I like you, but I'm *not* going."

Rachel left the room.

Bendin watched her leave not knowing what to say about that. Bendin put his pillow on the ground where he had been meditating before and got into his praying position.

Quip woke an hour later, "Bendin?"

"Yes, I'm here. How are you feeling?"

"Much better, I think I can actually move this time." Quip displayed this by getting up and moving around the room. "How did you get used to this, Bendin?"

Bendin laughed. "You don't, or at least that's what it's been like for me so far. I've noticed though, that my weariness from doing it has been much less than the first time. Maybe that's when it's the hardest?"

"I," Quip flicked his paws and belched a fireball into the air, "hope so. Remember those grey blurs I told you I could see?"

"Yes?"

"I don't see them anymore. Now I don't know what I'm seeing because my vision is messed up."

Bendin wondered if he had the same double vision that

he had. "Do you see that person right now? Down there?" Bendin pointed to a person he could see who was in his "other" vision. It was a girl who was walking along down below him in a regular passage in the upper temple that he'd been from. He recognized the hallway as one that he traveled down many times while on his way to classes.

"Yes, the one with the dark hair?" Quip said after a bit, "I can see her and the hallway at the same time as the room we are in now; it's kind of a fifty/fifty view. What is going on? What am I seeing?"

"You're looking at the place where I was before I came here. It is one of the upper temples for the instruction and training of Vaelift. I'm guessing we are seeing it in real-time."

"Why am I seeing it?"

"I don't know. I haven't figured out why it's important yet either," Bendin said. "I'm glad I'm not the only one who is experiencing it though. I thought there was something wrong with me for quite a while." Bendin stretched his hands up over his head thoughtfully, "I really like it here. I wish I could stay."

Quip nodded. "They are nice people, Bendin." Quip then hit himself in the head with a paw. "I can't believe I just said that. I can't believe it!"

Bendin laughed. "Let's go find something to eat."

The family gathered for dinner on the ceiling in the dining area. Tilmon stood proudly up from his chair, hushed the family, and spoke, "Dear family, we are gathered together again to celebrate the return of Bendin and Quip."

The family clapped as Quip crawled onto the table and bowed. Pete laughed and Starley giggled.

Tilmon waited till they finished clapping before he continued, "They have proven that they are indeed, Vaelift. They will perform a great work here in Makarias, and we welcome them. Thank you, Rachel for helping prepare the food tonight as Celeste is still in her room. Be sure to take her some dinner."

The family clapped and the prayer was offered.

"Did you really go to Toalt?" Ryan asked after the prayer finished.

"Yes," Bendin and Quip said together.

"What was it like?" Pete said, eagerly flipping his water glass up into the area without gravity. He spun it in the air and watched all the water remain inside the glass.

Quip eyed him mysteriously, "It was incredible. They ship babies in bottles, rooms easily the size of this whole house,

~ 227 ~

people made of stone, and doors made of *wood*." He emphasized the last word with such force that Pete pounded the table with his fist, and his face lit up with a smile.

"Want to go with us to Thibracketory?" Bendin asked Pete and Ryan quietly enough so that no one else could hear.

Pete choked on his food and Ryan spewed his food into the air, sending it flying out all over the floor above them.

Mez hit Pete on the back sending his food also flying out towards the floor. Rachel frowned at Ryan who went to clean up his mess. He grabbed a sucking machine off the wall and used it to clean the mess that didn't get immediately caught in the air currents.

"You're welcome, Pete," Ryan mumbled to Pete as Rachel left the room.

"You're going where?" Callapse asked.

"Thibracketory," Bendin said loud enough for all to hear.

"I'm coming," Callapse said immediately.

"What about your work?" Tilmon asked fingering his fork, "It's not reasonable that you should abandon your work for a flirt with death."

"Not reasonable? Father I'm old enough to do what I want. I'm going to marry Diane too, and you're not going to stop me."

Tilmon's eyes blazed and he slammed his hand onto the table in contempt. "Get out. Now!" He picked up his fork and flung it at Callapse.

Callapse skated from the room expertly avoiding Tilmon's flipping fork.

"Who's Diane?" Bendin asked Ryan.

"Diane is the stupidest girl on the entire planet," Ryan said disapprovingly. "We don't know why he likes her at all."

Bendin shrugged.

Charles watched Bendin with apprehension.

Mez caught Bendin's eyes for a moment, nodded his head up and down slightly, and went back to his meal.

Pete nudged Bendin on the shoulder. "Bendin, we can't go. We've got loads of stuff to do here before we can ever go to as crazy as a place as Thibracketory. Sorry man. Looks like you are on your own since Tilmon isn't going to let Callapse go anyway.

"Okay then. I'm sure we'll think of something." Bendin felt a little disappointed. Even though no one would be coming with them, it didn't change his resolve. Quip was his buddy, and they'd figure it out.

They were going to have to face the strangeness of Thibracketory alone.

The meal was finished with chatter about some of the Airlarky moves from the Heptahedron and their new little sister, Destiny.

After it was over, Bendin and Quip stopped by to see the tiny baby. It was a micro-sized girl, the smallest person Bendin had ever seen. She was bald and had green eyes like her sister, Soladaque.

He thought it was one of the most amazing things to see, but after a while he noticed something he had to bring up. "Why can't she do anything, and where's her hair?"

"All babies can only eat and sleep after they are born, Bendin. It's perfectly normal to start with no hair. It will grow in time." Celeste beamed with adoration over Destiny.

"That's awful."

"Bendin!" Celeste scolded alarmingly.

"Well," Bendin shrugged. "It's true."

Quip smiled knowingly at how true the statement actually was.

"Say that again after you've had your own. Now, Destiny needs some privacy," Celeste scolded him again pushing Bendin and Quip out of her room.

Bendin went to Tilmon's shop and picked up Quip's small bands that were going to go on his ankles and head. Tilmon had just finished them when they arrived.

"There shouldn't be anything wrong with them. Let's test them out." He set one up against the wall and fired a game ball directly at it. The ball was redirected around the band in the radius of repulsion that the band gave off. Quip put them on and said they would be okay once he got used to them. The first thing Quip did, when he had them on, was to burst completely into a flaming fireball.

"Quip!"

Quip stopped and showed Bendin the bands. "I just wanted to see if they would melt, bend, brake, or tarnish." Quip eyed the new hardware with affection. "I think they'll do nicely."

The bands only showed a small amount of wear, and that was because they had been beaten into that shape by Tilmon himself.

Bendin sighed and pulled at his Vaelift uniform. He decided to leave it unchanged. It wasn't really that restrictive now that he had gotten used to it and he knew it was an iconic image the way it was.

They went and finished preparations for themselves. Bendin had no staff. He had forgotten to ask the Tribunal for a replacement, and the Coils didn't have any extras.

They passed Pete and Ryan, they were carrying Airlarky stuff and some of the gear they used for their capture the flag game up to their room. They were chatting incessantly.

"What do you think they are up to?" Quip asked.

"Getting ready for another capture the flag game of course."

They refilled the pill vials and added some extra water containers to bring with them. Bendin planned on strapping them next to his other one on his gold colored belt. They calculated that they had enough food to last, the both of them, about four months. The water they'd need to refill at some time in the future. When they were done filling the pills and water in the waterfall room, they almost fell over Charles on their way out of the room.

"Sorry," he apologized.

They arrived in the kids' lounge and were about to go into their room when they were stopped by Rachel.

"Thought you were going to go to bed without seeing me? I see how it is." She smiled at them.

"I knew it," Quip declared, "You really do like me!"

Quip leaped onto her shoulders and licked her face continuously. Rachel somersaulted backwards from the force of his jump and they slowly revolved in the air.

"Ack, ack, ack. Stop it, Quip, stop it!" Rachel laughed.

Bendin laughed and pulled Quip off of Rachel, who laughed again.

"Thanks for that, Quip. I'm never going to wash this face again." She exaggeratedly stroked her face with her hands as if it was made of precious gold.

Quip smiled and went into the room.

"Thanks for sticking up for me, Rachel," Bendin said extremely grateful for her defence of him.

"You're welcome." Rachel skated over to Bendin and gave him a hug. "I'm busy early tomorrow morning and I didn't want you to leave without letting me say goodbye."

"It's been fun . . . thanks." He walked into his room, their hands being the last things to separate.

Bendin and Quip ran through their nightly prayers and snuggled into bed wondering what they were going to find tomorrow in Thibracketory.

"Bendin, wake up," Quip whispered to him in his ear. "I hear someone coming."

Bendin listened and didn't hear anything. He was amazed at what Quip could hear. "Are you sure?"

"Positive. If they are going to knock, it's going to be in a few seconds."

There was a soft rap on the door.

"Bendin, " Callapse's voice whispered through the door. "Mez and I, we're coming with you. It's been one of our dreams to go to Thibracketory. Let's get moving."

Bendin realized it was already early morning. He got up, dressed, and got all of his gear. Quip put on his bands and jumped up to Bendin's shoulder. They were excited, and they were ready.

Callapse wore black from head to toe and was wearing some sort of mechanical looking backpack. "Mez is waiting for us. Ready?"

"Yes, let's go," Bendin said. "Are you driving us there in the bubble?"

"Only Tilmon is allowed driving the bubble. We'll be taking my cargo scrapper."

"Cargo scrapper?" Bendin imagined a vehicle made entirely of cargo boxes.

"Yeah, I carry scrap in from all over so that I can help Josiah with his experiments. I also did it as a side job too. I'm really proud of my vehicle. I built it myself."

There was a bang and smoke filled the room. The kids appeared in their sleeping clothes coughing and hacking.

"I guess there are some things I will not be missing during our trip," Callapse grinned waving the smoke in front of him.

A few moments later, the air cleared and Bendin could see clearly again.

Their small group went out to the docking area and they heard a couple of bangs from somewhere in the dark. It was not yet sunrise.

"Does anyone else smell candy?" Quip said sniffing the air. There were more bangs from the walls of the bay.

"These noises are driving me crazy," Bendin said throwing his hands in the air, "and I can't see anything! Why is it so dark in the docking bay?"

Callapse chuckled. "When this place was built, the

~ 231 ~

docking bay anyway, they forgot to put lights in it."

"That sounds kind of important," Quip said sarcastically.

Bendin laughed.

"I know, it's funny. Dad says they've never been able to afford the size of lights this place requires. I think he's just lazy and doesn't want to install them. That's just the way it is. We can only really see in the room when we open the docking doors or turn on a vehicle," Callapse explained cheerfully and turned on his cargo scrapper.

Lights from the vehicle flooded the area, and Bendin gawked at the funkiest shaped vehicle in the bay. It was a conglomerate of miss-matched pieces thrown together giving it an irregular shape. It was welded and sealed together with shiny white paste.

Mez, leaning up against the side door, waved. He wore a full array of items and gear that Bendin was not familiar with.

"There she is, my scrapper." Callapse tapped his red, brown, and green rusted scrapper. He showed Bendin the compartments all over the vehicle. "This is where I store all of my stuff." He pounded on the closest cargo hatch and listened to the metallic report. "Ok, here is where you two are going to go. We'll park at a place I know of that is south of Hymingway and get this party into the air!"

They jumped inside. It was a small cockpit with only a few chairs. The craft roared to life and pulled out backwards on the scrapper's blades. Bendin noticed that it had a lot of the features the family bubble had, except that it was much smaller than the bubble.

"And I thought the bubble was beat up," Quip mockingly stated.

Callapse and Bendin laughed while a small grin appeared on Mez's face.

Chapter 15
Into Thibracketory

"It'll probably take an hour's journey to get to Thibracketory from here," Callapse remarked to Bendin and Quip after they had parked in a small makeshift shanty building with drums, boxes, and bags inside. "The angle of the sun, the sphildon-loaded trees and its proximity to Thibracketory make this the perfect place to hide things."

Callapse led them into the air and showed them the impressive, looming forest canopy off in the distance.

Mez pointed and held up 3 fingers.

Callapse interpreted, "He means it's about thirty kilometers from here."

"You measured?" Bendin asked.

Mez nodded.

"He's gone past many times on his visits with other Roam Keepers. I've been up to the rim many of times. I wasn't brave enough to go in before, but with you and Mez here, I'm ready to go in." Callapse tightened the straps on his backpack.

Quip coughed loudly.

Callapse turned around with an enormous grin on his face. "And Quip."

Bendin smiled, skated, and focused on keeping up with Mez. As Bendin skated, he felt small droplets of water hitting his cheek. He turned his face right into Quip's tongue. "Gaaa! Quip, other side please."

Quip chuckled and let his tongue hang out the other side of his mouth.

The landscape had beautiful, heavily forested, and rolling hills. The smell of the forest below them as they skated by was simply remarkable.

They had been skating for twenty minutes, crossed a ridge, and on the other side in the valley Bendin saw a procession of wide flat platform shaped structures below them. There were many people skating in the air above the platforms, and others riding on them. The structures had planks and large pieces of junk jutting out in all sorts of directions. Aside from people skating on and off of the platforms, the most unique thing was that everything moved at an agonizingly slow pace.

Callapse pointed down, Mez shrugged and mumbled a name under his breath, and they all skated down to see what it was.

Some of the people saw them coming and skated up to Bendin and Callapse.

"Friends?" One of the men asked wearing a large purple and blue striped hat.

"He's dressed like a Coil bro," another commented studying Callapse.

"He's obviously a Roam Keeper."

"You, my 'rend, appear to be like the ancient Vaeli't, but they've been dead 'or centuries," a lady mumbled wearing green and blue felt shorts with a lighter ruffled top of the same color.

"Imposter!" a younger child belted out, behind another lady.

"Don't worry. We're friends," Callapse declared.

"Oh, that's all right then," the one who started the conversation said throwing himself into Callapse in a big hug. Callapse awkwardly pulled the man's arms off of him and took a step backwards. Their attire was as if every color had been spun all over the place.

"Names?" The lady wearing green and blue asked.

"I'm Bendin, and this is Quip," Bendin said cheerily pointing to his friend. Quip puffed out his chest and attempted to look more sturdy than a simple red and white furry fox.

The lady smiled brightly.

"I'm Callapse Coil. This is Mez. How goes the traveling?"

"You know us, it's our life man," a different man wearing a multicolored floppy hat and long stretchy pants said lazily.

"Is Pikalop part of your group?" Callapse wondered.

"Part? He *is* the group. Feel my wave dudes?" another girl wearing white, blue, and red said waving at them.

"I feel your wave and return you double," Quip said waving both his paws in the air. He blasted his way over to her and clasped her waving hand in his two paws. His body now moved back and forth with the motion of her hand.

Bendin and Callapse laughed. Mez grinned.

The girl shrieked, giggled, and tossed Quip up in the air. Quip returned to Bendin with a huge grin on his face.

"Follow thou me," said the man who wore the multicolored floppy hat.

He led them to one of the smaller flying platforms. Up close Bendin could see that the metal was actually *woven*. Gravity was completely localized on the platforms, and the minute you left the close proximity of the floor, you floated again and lost your weight.

At the end of this platform, there was a decent sized make-shift canopy. The covered portion was as much a shanty as Callapse's shack, with hard planks for a roof and thick blankets for the doorways. A man, wearing a thick beige-colored robe, came out wearing a black top hat that had the colors, green, orange and blue in three horizontal evenly-spaced thin colored bands. He had sandals on his feet, and he clasped Callapse's hand tightly, "A Coil. Pleased to meet one of your specimens. I'm Pikalop Heptamon, the leader of the Nomadic Hermits. I am also the legend keeper. How are things over at the the lumberyards? Leafy?"

"They are all doing well. You know how everyone demands the finest Coil lumber."

"Do I ever. However, I do not share your love of the wood structures. I have a taste in colored metal for our structures. Stainless, Efethez, and Zath are some of my favorites." He turned to Bendin and whispered, "Performs much better in the rain." He chuckled. "Not that it can hit us. Ha!" He pulled his hand up to his chin. "It's the moisture."

"Just passing through?" Callapse asked, rubbing his ear.

"Always." Pikalop yawned. "Give your head Coil representative, Tilmon Coil, my regards. I have always appreciated the lands of the Coils. The Jungles are most magnificent this time of year, and the springs and falls found in some sections are most truly outstandingly marvelous."

"I will," Callapse said proudly.

"Roam Keepers are always welcome. I assure you all is well. No specials here."

Mez grinned slightly and nodded.

"Who are these two?" Pikalop asked acting as though he had just noticed Bendin and Quip for the first time. "And what *devilry* is this?" Pikalop pointed one of his long crooked fingers at Quip and shook it back and forth. "Did the great Zadok return and possess our poor fox here so that he is happy being this close to a human?"

"Say that again and I'll melt that hat to your head!" Quip lashed out at Pikalop with a breath of fire that came inches from his face.

"Fabulous flashing flames of fire! You are a special animal to boot. Charming. Very charming my young friend. May I have your name?" Pikalop asked almost unfazed by Quip's reaction.

"I'm Quip." Quip sniffed the air warningly.

"And I'm Bendin."

Mez allowed a small grin to appear on his face and he waved with one short wave.

Pikalop rolled his eyes. "Yes, Mez. No trouble down here as far as we can tell. Pesepohone has done a super job in this area. Excellent Roam Keeper." He winked. "So, what is it that you are doing down here so close to Thibracketory?"

Bendin was slightly hurt that Pikalop didn't seem to even notice him.

"We are going into Thibracketory . . . because of him. He's a Vaelift," Callapse said shoving his thumb at Bendin.

Pikalop eyed Bendin and grabbed a drink of water that he had in a bucket nearby. Bendin noticed in the bottom of the bucket was the same kind of disks that were in the glasses the Coil's had in their home. "There are better ways to die, Callapse. Much better. My advice, if you are looking for the best way to die, to skate straight up at night into the sky with your GravBox on and you'll never come back. You will pass out and later your body will cease to function and--" Pikalop paused and visibly shook, "Wait, you're a Vaelift? Don't be ridiculous. You may be dressed as one, but those guys glowed, flew, spun their staffs, danced in air, and disappeared. Yo, you ain't glowin'!"

Pikalop twirled his hands and laughed in Bendin's face.

"That's enough of that Pikalop. We are leaving now," Bendin announced. He had had enough of this strange man and his goofy friends. It looked like all they wanted to do was to lounge around, and this is exactly what the other people in the area were doing. They were lying on sofas, pillows, padding, and other assortments of soft material. They were either sleeping, reading, or watching the landscape very slowly roll by.

"Do you need anything? Besides a miracle from the great Odge?" Pikalop laughed as they skated upwards.

"No thanks!" Bendin shouted down to them.

"Well, that was pointless," Quip observed, "except for that one girl. She was fun!" Quip waved goodbye to the girl wearing blue, red, and white.

"I kind of liked him," Callapse said glancing back at him.

"It doesn't seem like they have a care in the world do they? Bunch of lazy bums," Bendin said to Quip.

"Yes, a bunch of useless nuts if you ask me." Quip frowned.

They arrived at Thibracketory. It was as big and as thick as anyone had described. The trees were twice as high as the Coil's jungle trees and that was saying something. It was four times as dense and from the looks of it Bendin didn't like the idea of going inside of it. Stretching above the entire border was a faint white mist.

"What are we doing here exactly?" Callapse asked.

"I don't know, he wouldn't say specifics. Odge only said we'd be able to see what it is that he wanted us to see when we went inside. Why didn't we just fly in there?"

A craft whizzed past all of them over Thibracketory at high speeds. Two other vehicles with brilliant lights blasted to a halt at the border. Four people got out quickly and pointed. In a few seconds the fleeing craft exploded.

"See? Yeah, that happens every time." Callapse shrugged.

The four people turned to them and saluted. Mez returned the salute and waved them away. They waved and drove back in the direction they had come.

"You know them?" Bendin asked.

"They're Keepers," Callapse explained leading them down into Thibracketory's thick growth. "Mez outranks the city Keepers. They were only recognizing his authority."

Their speed combined with their bands pushed back the thick foliage, and they skated down just above the ground searching for a clue.

"Over there!" Quip shouted excitedly. Mez noticed moments after Quip did.

Bendin looked once, twice, and it wasn't till he was right on top of it did he notice that it was the remains of an old beat up cobblestone road. Everything had grown over it and nature had almost completely reclaimed the old road. It was in such poor shape that unless you were searching for it, you would not have seen it.

Callapse whistled softly. "Good eyes, Quip. I am definitely impressed."

Mez nodded approvingly, and Quip smiled in reply.

They followed the road through the foliage, with much difficulty, till they reached a large thick archway. It separated two long walls that stretched as far as you could see in both directions.

It had the words "Thibracketory" etched in a large block above the arch, and the words, "Home of the Vaelift" etched into the arch.

"Home?" Bendin asked Quip, who shrugged.

Callapse felt the arch with his hands. "Looks a bit overgrown don't you think?"

Bendin nodded.

Callapse continued, "It was the Vaelift home? Maybe, I guess. No one talks about Thibracketory as a home, except to Grandelegants. People were never allowed to visit Thibracketory after the Vaelift died. Not that it didn't stop people from trying. Anyone that has really gone into Thibracketory never have been seen again. A nice hole in our knowledge."

"Real useful," Quip said sarcastically.

Bendin realized Callapse was right. There were broken parts of vehicles, metallic chunks, and other debris from failed attempts that nature had long absorbed, all around them.

The thick jungle was very alive and sounds of all kinds of creatures surrounded them. They continued onward, becoming immersed with fear and apprehension. The overgrown, broken-up road led straight down into a large pool of water and then up again on the other side.

"Who's this Diane Finn girl and why doesn't your Dad like her?" Bendin asked Callapse.

"She's a dream, Bendin, an absolute dream. Maybe you'll meet her soon. I'm planning on going to get her after I finish this project with Josiah. Dad thinks she is stupid." Callapse sighed then gasped. "What is that?" He pointed down at a small lit concrete obelisk on a small island just inside the outer rim of the pool. A loud rumble shook the earth and behind Callapse rose a gigantic fiery colored lizard with large red frills around its neck.

"What?" Callapse said and saw Bendin's eyes full of fear.

"A huge thingy-ma-thingy!" Bendin mumbled skating away from the creature. Callapse took one look at it and shouted, "Axolotl. Skaaaate!"

The Axolotl swiped down on Callapse. The arm redirected directly around Callapse's body and smashed into the water. The water erupted with the force of a geyser sending water up and around Callapse. The Axolotl grabbed again with both hands. They were redirected around and smacked into themselves on the other side of Callapse. It then was able to grip Callapse with its hands and tear into his legs.

"Help him!" Quip shouted. Quip blazed around it, shot

fire at the creature's inset eyes, and created a nice distraction. Mez pulled out a gun shaped tool and skated behind the creature. Bendin used his blades and skated around the Axolotl's large arm quickly three times cutting deeper each time till it fell, severed from the Axolotl's body. The creature let out a roar, and Bendin watched in horror as a new arm grew rapidly replacing the cut off arm.

"That's useful," Quip commented soaring up next to Bendin.

A large flash of light extended up from where Mez had been and the Axolotl roared again before letting go of Callapse and diving in pain back into the water.

"Quip! That way!" Bendin pointed at the other side of the large pond where the road continued.

"Right!" Quip shouted and streaked in a blaze of light in that direction. Mez pocketed his tool, pulled Callapse over to where Bendin was, and set him down.

Callapse held his legs in agony. "Mez . . . please." Mez quickly produced, from another pouch, a thin tube. He took the tip and gripped Callapse's torn legs holding them firmly in place. He carefully and smoothly streamed out a thick liquid from the bottom of the slice up to the top. Bendin watched as the seams cemented and blended with a thick patch of light. Mez quickly did the same thing to the long slice on the other leg. He replaced the tube and pulled out a small, thin, custard-colored rod with an obnoxiously large spinning dial in the center. He powered it up and scrolled down each leg with the device whining incessantly.

"Thank you." Callapse relaxed and his panting slowed till he was only breathing harshly. Mez watched him for a moment before he turned to the water.

After a few more seconds, the jungle felt surprisingly silent. All four of them stared down into the water in dismay.

Quip murmured, "How many more of those are there?"

Callapse turned to Quip and waved his arms. "You're a special animal! Why don't you know?"

Bendin noticed Callapse's legs were beginning to show no trace of the huge tears only moments ago. "Quip, you really don't know?"

Quip shrugged. "We stay out of their way. We don't communicate that much as one large animal kingdom you know."

Callapse continued, "Seriously how many? Dozens, hundreds? We don't know either. There is an uncounted number

Grandelegents. They're huge, horrible, hideous, and dangerous. Let's go, cautiously. I don't want to have to go through that pain or anything near it again."

The little group traveled cautiously onward, just high enough to see the road.

"Why haven't we seen anything besides the road?" Bendin asked Callapse.

"How should I know? I know just as much as you do Bendin!" Callapse retorted.

"I keep forgetting."

Quip smirked.

The road led to a very wide and deep canyon. They landed where the road stopped at the edge of the canyon. Mez guessed it was about 800 meters across the canyon, and they could see the road start again on the other side. There was no way down into the canyon and the walls were steep and the canyon spread for miles in both directions, as far as they could see.

"This would have stopped many a people back in the day," Callapse observed. "I'm beginning to think that these things are here on purpose. Just like the Axolotl."

"Pbbfftt!" Quip sputtered. "Like someone actually put a canyon here."

Bendin had an interesting thought and switched his vision to Toalt. He saw that in Toalt there was an equally lined up road in the middle of a quiet dark forest, and the moonlight reflected off the road through the trees.

"That's because the road is in Toalt," Bendin said smiling. "They may not have done this, but it certainly is interesting."

They skated over the deep canyon and went into the jungle following the road on the other side.

They came upon a clearing of grass with massive prong-shaped footprints all over it.

"Shhh. Thumps." Mez observed.

All the trees in the vicinity shook and throbbed with each resounding thump. It happened again and again, each thump getting louder.

"I think it's coming this way, whatever it is," said Bendin. More thumps echoed.

"Then let's move the other direction," Callapse warned pulling off to the left.

A giant Secretary Bird blasted through the trees and

thrashed it's feet stomping down on Bendin. His bands redirected the feet around his body and the feet pounded into the dirt floor. Bendin laughed and then screeched as the upcoming foot was slow enough to bump Bendin up slowly into the air.

The bird continually pounded down on Bendin with his feet. With each pound, Bendin noticed too late that he was rising closer and closer to the apex of the height of the raised foot. It was at this moment that the bird got a grip on Bendin's body and flung him at the ground on the bottom of its feet.

The strangest thing happened as the foot slammed on the ground. The foot redirected around like you would step on a marble causing the bird to come crashing down in a feather-flying crash. Bendin rolled across the ground uncontrollably and lay watching and waiting for his breath to come back.

"We've got to do something!" Callapse yelled skating up towards the Bird's face. The wings were unfurled and redirected around Callapse. He grabbed onto the bird's neck and before he knew it, he was flung away at high velocity out of sight.

Mez pointed towards the bird and said something to Quip.

Quip smiled and flew toward the bird in a bright glowing fireball. Pretty soon he was only a streak flying around the bird in all directions.

Mez had his gun aimed, but the bird moved so erratically, his shots kept going wild.

Bendin watched disbelievingly as Ryan and Pete appeared out of nowhere

Pete went down to the bottom of a nearby tree and fiddled around with his silver box. He then took a small tool from a bag on his belt and used it to effortlessly slice the trunk clean through.

Pete lifted the enormous tree with hardly any effort. He said something to his brother and pushed it as hard as he could in the direction of the large Secretary Bird. He skated close enough behind it and the tree carried on its course. To Bendin's surprise, the tree slammed into the bird's neck.

"You're in the wrong environment you stupid grassland's bird!" Pete yelled at the huge bird. As the tree hit the bird's neck, Pete fiddled with his box and the full weight of the tree plunged upon the bird's neck. The force pulled and pinned the fowl to the ground.

Bendin skated up as the bird was struggling to roll itself out from underneath the large tree.

"Come on, we need to outpace it," Bendin wheezed and said quickly, "Mez! Come on!"

Quip landed on Bendin's shoulder breathing hard. "That was some powerful wind."

"Yes! Now we need to move!" Bendin shouted to him.

"Come on, Callapse. We got to get out of here!" Pete yelled. Callapse had surfaced above the trees and was skating as fast as he could over to them.

"Over there! Do you see that?" Ryan said pointing.

"What?" Quip said and spun around to see what he was pointing to.

"That small outcropping of a building," Ryan noted.

"That must be where the road leads," Callapse said finally catching up with all of them.

"Guys go faster and dip into the jungle on your way there. The giant secretary bird is getting back up!" Bendin yelled at the group.

The bird was back and visibly not finished with them. His head popped up out of the trees born on his massive wings. The bird let out a scream that would have deafened them had they not been protected by the repulsive bands. The trees around them were partially uprooted by the sound wave alone.

Bendin, Quip, Callapse, Mez, Ryan, and Pete dipped into the Jungle, then back out skating with all their might. The bird plowed after them tearing up the forest like it was a bunch of dried weeds.

"I think it's working!" Pete said eagerly.

Bendin was trying to focus on skating and not on the bird. He stole a glance back really quick though and saw that the bird, even though it was knocking things over in a dramatic display of rage, was getting torn up from its efforts.

The small grey roof up ahead was barely visible through the thick jungle canopy. It seemed so far away, but at their pace they were going to be there soon.

Alas, nope.

The bird clamped its mighty jaws down forcefully on Pete. His bands redirected the bird's jaw around in a spiral, but they were still around Pete, upside down. The massive jaws then completely encased Pete.

Bendin gulped.

In that moment before the bird could swallow Pete, Quip appeared as bright as a descending comet of fury. Quip fired waves of hot liquid flames into the bird's nose and watched satisfied as the bird coughed Pete directly out of its mouth.

Relief flooded Bendin and Quip zipped off around the bird leaving a bright trail. The bird, enraged and in pain, followed Quip.

"Quip!" Bendin yelled. "No . . ."

It was too late. The bird let out a shriek and sank into the forest following the fireball, disappearing rather quickly in the trees.

With shrieks fading in the distance, they were gone.

Everyone skated down in front of an entrance to the building breathing heavily.

"We made it! We or I . . ." Pete declared. Then stopped short realizing something. "Hey! I almost died."

"Yes!" Ryan rejoiced. "But, you didn't!" He clasped his hands with his brother enthusiastically.

Bendin settled onto the ground and rubbed his muscles painfully. "Well, almost all of us."

Chapter 16
Ada and the Vaelift

"How did you do that?" Bendin asked Pete.

"What?"

"Move the tree?"

"Oh, that's simple, just tighten the screw in the hole for the adjuster and you can increase the range at which your field nullifies the gravity." Pete fiddled in his bag at his belt and pulled out some small screwdrivers. "I thought it would be something we might need. We use this stuff in logging all the time."

Bendin accepted the small odd shaped tool.

"Wish I had thought of it," Callapse said gingerly fiddling around with his mechanical backpack.

"What is that?" Ryan asked eyeing Callapse's backpack curiously.

"This? It's none of yours. I brought it here cause I thought I'd test it at a more appropriate place," Callapse snarled.

"That makes no sense to me. Let's move on." Ryan scratched his head and turned around.

Quip burst out of the trees, saw them, rocketed down towards them, and stopped instantly next to Bendin. Quip licked him happily, and settled down on Bendin's shoulder.

"I'm glad to see you!" Bendin said fondly rubbing Quip's head.

"I lost him." Quip grinned.

Bendin studied the wall in front of them. It was huge, made of fine sturdy brick with moss growing all over it. Strangely, there was no door. There was only a frame with an arch that read, "Welcome to Thibracketory, the home of the Vaelift. Only those who see, can open the door."

"Only those who see?" Pete mused. "What is that supposed to mean?"

"I guess we can't see the door?" Bendin said. "I'm a Vaelift, but I see nothing but brick."

They skated up over the wall and onto the roof and only saw tons of small openings. Some filled with vines, others with dirt. They were small enough that you could hardly fit your hand inside the hole. The entire roof was like that. They checked all over the building and found no visible entrance. There were many buildings connected together in a brilliant structure, but all they could find was solid walls and tons of tiny holes in the roof.

"For ruins, these do not look very ruined," Ryan noted.

"Who said they were ruins?" Pete asked.

"I did, just *now*."

"I guess they were very well built," Bendin reasoned.

They went back to the spot at the entrance where the road met up with the complex.

Bendin stared at the door trying to figure it out.

"We could bash it open if someone wants to try it." Pete shrugged.

Pete repeated the process he did with the bird and threw a giant tree at the stone doorway. The poor tree didn't stand a chance as it splintered and thudded against the ardent stonework.

Callapse laughed. "Nice guys."

Even Mez grinned.

"Anyone else got any bright ideas?" Pete said irritated. "This thing must be thick." Pete pounded on the hard stone surface with his fists.

"I got it!" Quip announced. He nudged Bendin. "See?" He pointed at the solid wall and said. "The door is right here."

"Dude this is solid rock. You need your eyes checked." Pete pointed and pounded the stone again.

Bendin eyed the door, thought about it for a second, and smashed his palm into his forehead.

"Duh! I'm so dumb. I just thought of that back at the ravine! Why did I forget now?" Bendin threw up his arms in frustration.

"I have no idea." Quip smiled.

"Idiot," Ryan whispered smiling.

Bendin changed his vision so he could see Toalt. He could just make out the shape of a door opening on the other side.

"Quip's right. The opening is in Toalt," Bendin said realizing how it was set up.

"Well what about us?" Pete grumbled.

"I got it!" Ryan exclaimed.

"What?" Pete said eagerly.

"We could dig under the place and come up from underneath!"

"Guys, maybe there is a way to open it on the other side. We don't need to be digging holes. The floor is probably as solid

~ 245 ~

as the walls," Bendin suggested. He turned to Quip. "Let's try the courtyard technique."

"The what now?" Ryan frowned watching with interest.

Quip and Bendin sat a few paces in front of the door and performed the courtyard technique that was shown to them by Simon Wight with the adjustments by Odge's voice. Once they finished, they vanished in a flash of light, a crack of thunder and a shockwave that forcefully ripped Callapse, Mez, Pete and Ryan off of their feet. All of them were stunned and groaning.

Bendin and Quip burst through the light and landed on the ground. This time, instead of fainting, Bendin only felt really dazed. It took him a few moments to focus, and he realized that he was starting to build up some sort of awareness to the effect, maybe even an immunity. It felt kind of nice, but Quip fainted right away. Bendin checked his watch and it read, "1:09". It was early morning. He surveyed the landscape around him and found himself outside in a dense tall forest. For the first time in his life he could see Toalt stars very high overhead, very spaced, sparse, and distinct. They were completely different than the riveting vivid display he had seen in the skies at the Coil's home. He then realized uncomfortably that Toalt's position in the universe wasn't where Makarias's was. He had been secretly hoping it was merely a different time in the same place. There was only one moon and it was off to the side. The rest of the sky was blocked by the leaves and trees above him. He turned a bit and peered down a different direction. He could make out, in the distance through the trees, a lower plain. There were endless lights flickering on and off. Bendin figured they marked the location of many sleepy towns and people.

The entrance here in Toalt was completely identical to the one in Makarias with the same brickwork and the same inscription in the archway over the doorway. The only real difference was that this doorway was completely open. When he switched his vision, he could see Pete, Callapse, Ryan, and Mez all sitting outside the solid brick talking together. He could see more clearly now, but he could make out nothing that they were saying. He could only guess what they were saying and it was probably pretty funny judging by the dramatic gestures from Ryan followed by laughter.

Bendin picked up Quip, who had fainted on the ground, and walked through the open doorway. It led into a square shaped area before he found himself stopped by another solid wall. The area was unused and cluttered with broken parts of machinery and other odds and ends. There appeared to be no way in, but by switching his vision, he saw clearly that the way through the wall was in Makarias. He marveled that they would design it this way. Then it clicked. It really was for only those who could see no matter which place you were in. Genius. Bendin nudged Quip and got him to wake up. "We need to go to Makarias, are you ready?"

Quip folded his arms tiredly, "Okay, but I am really going to need to rest when we get back. I'm so tired."

Quip sat next to him and performed the motions while Bendin tried them standing up.

Quip disappeared as before with all the light and sound. Bendin followed him a moment later.

Bendin was hardly dazed this time. "I think I'm getting better at it," Bendin said to Quip just as he fell asleep on the cobblestone floor. Bendin reached over and pulled a lever that was next to the wall between them and the others. Bendin watched as the large stone was pulled downward with a deep grating sound, revealing the surprised faces of Ryan, Pete, and the rest on the other side.

"You vanishing was one of the coolest things I've seen today!" Pete said feeling the wall with his hands.

"Eh, it's a toss-up, that Secretary Bird was pretty cool," Ryan countered.

"No, it was the Axolotl. He was literally the coolest," Callapse said straight faced.

Ryan and Pete slapped Callapse on his arms, "Good one, Callapse."

Mez rolled his eyes.

They all went through the door and Bendin slung Quip over his shoulder once again.

"What's wrong with him?" Callapse asked.

"You killed him!" Ryan moaned. "Quip, Quip, say my name."

Bendin smiled. "He's tired. When you move from one place to the other it seems to take some getting used to, or so I am learning anyway."

Bendin closed the outer stone door and moved to the inner section of the building. The place was completely dark and Ryan turned on a handheld light from his bag. It was bright enough to show that no one had been inside this building in an extremely long time. There was a thick coating of dust everywhere and with every step they took it threw up a small cloud. The only sign of life were small insects and bugs that had managed to squeeze through the micro cracks in the walls over time.

"Here." Ryan shined his light onto one of the walls that went off to the right, "There are more levers here."

As Ryan pulled the first lever he said, "It's says here on this brass plate 'front panel light'.

There was a loud creaking as something that hadn't been used in centuries was suddenly and rudely awakened. Bendin and the others watched as a section of the very high ceiling above them poured in light from the sky outside. There were a dozen holes that let in light, others were apparently broken, because they didn't let any light in at all.

"Now that's kind of ingenious," Pete said. "I wonder if it's simply bounced light from the outside."

"How do you fix them if they get broken or something gets trapped inside?" Ryan wondered aloud.

"That sounds about right. Look, you can see these are just mirrors," Callapse said skating up to one of the holes and looking in it.

Ryan flicked the rest of the levers and the whole room was flooded with light from the outside."

"I'm glad I didn't step another step," Bendin said simply. There was a huge pit in front of them, and normally it would have killed anyone that were to tread unknowingly.

"What's up with those?" Bendin asked. "They have doorways up there, but no way to get to them?"

"Maybe there is another way," Ryan said optimistically.

Bendin looked in Toalt and realized that there were no stairs over there either, but there was a solid surface over the pit. He smiled and skated over the gap. There would be no need of that. Then laughed to himself thinking how funny, or scary, it might have been if you absentmindedly forgot to go to Toalt and accidently fell down there.

They went through the next archway and came into a fairly long hall. Ryan found similar levers that pulled in the light from outside.

"See these torch mounts on the wall? I'll bet that they were for the light at night," Callapse noted.

I don't understand the design of the building. Why would they use natural lighting and torches when the technology was way more advanced when this was constructed?" Pete wondered.

"Cheaper?" Callapse shrugged.

"Hold up!" Pete said grabbing the torch from the wall. He yelled.

"What is it?" Bendin asked coming over.

The container holding the torch already had replaced a torch in place of the one Pete took.

"What . . . was that?" Pete asked. He looked at it. "This looks like a torch, but it's not made of torch materials!"

"Bendin! Check this out. What do you think it means?" Ryan dusted off a flat gold rimmed sign off on the wall. It read in block letters, "Remember the two fundamental rules: 1. Look before you leap. 2. Carry your head."

Below the message it showed a glyph of a man frowning, half of his body sticking out of the wall. There was another glyph below that one that had a body holding his smiling head under his arm.

"Creepy. I'm not sure what they mean." Bendin rubbed his chin.

"Hey! It works!" Pete exclaimed lighting the handheld torch. "It looks like a torch, lights like a torch, but it's not hot at all! Bummer, it doesn't light things on fire either. How do you make fake fire?"

They walked a couple feet further wondering about the rules when they discovered a model of the skeleton of a man. He had his arms outstretched, but only half of his skeleton was sticking through the wall into the room.

"Creepier," Callapse analyzed. "This is look before you leap."

"He must have come out inside the wall on this side when he made his jump, or at least that's what they are trying to show here," Bendin explained.

"This one is beyond creepy." Ryan said wincing.

"That's so cool!" Pete shouted happily.

Mez frowned.

The next few paces down revealed a skeleton on the floor holding a large iron pot. The upper body of the skeleton was intact, but the bottom part was strewn all over. The skull was in pieces in the pot.

"How about this oh great and wise Bendin?" Pete asked pointing at the skeleton, "Is this carry your head or not carrying you head?"

"Whatever it is, it's gross!" Ryan said making a sour face.

"Since he's dead, I'm going to go with not carrying your head. I don't get it. Let's move on." Bendin sighed. It really did look scary.

They came to another solid wall at the other end.

"Bendin?" Callapse said as he pointed at the wall.

Bendin knew before he even switched his vision that the answer was going to be in Toalt. "I'll go through and open the door. I'm guessing there is a switch like before somewhere on the other side that will open the door. Here." Bendin handed Quip to Mez and performed the motions much quicker than he did last time. With a blast, he was gone.

Once on the other side, Bendin noticed that the hallways were completely identical and the same glyphs were on the walls with the same descriptions. The displays here, however, had been torn off the walls. The ceiling destroyed. The parts and pieces of every display were scattered everywhere, and the only thing sticking out of the wall was just the stump of the skeleton. Toalt was so covered in pieces and debris it made Makarias's dusty rooms look clean. Bendin felt hardly dazed this time and he walked through the opening. More shattered, broken, and demolished items were lying everywhere. There were scrape marks on every wall. Whatever was here before was long gone. After a flash and a bang, he moved back over to Makarias. He found the lever for the door and pulled it open.

"At least it didn't take you as long as last time," Pete mumbled coming through the door.

"Here." Mez handed back Quip to Bendin.

"Thanks."

"Welcome back, Bendin," Quip said showing Bendin that he was awake, though not moving.

Ryan, not surprisingly, found the switches again and let the light come in through the holes in the ceiling. Bendin recognized the setup of the room instantly and was hit with a pang of nostalgia. Bendin sat down for a moment.

"What? What is it?" Quip asked. Everyone turned to him.

"This room is identical in setup to the control center where I grew up. It's much much bigger and longer, but all of this equipment is completely identical."

There also was a set of desks along the wall closest to the entrance, and a long line of staffs on the other. The staffs were thinner than the one's that the Coil's used for Airlarky. The staffs were grayish and rounded, and they had a fat spiral going from top to bottom. The old storage limiters, monitors, and crystal displays were all here. As he watched the staffs, Bendin noticed every now and then a glimmer of light would flicker from within the shaft. This room *felt* alive.

Bendin moved to the biggest desk. "These desks, let's see if they still work. Bendin punched several things on the desk closest to him. Everyone in the room watched him with the utmost curiosity. The crystal displays flared to life and the image of a woman appeared in front of him wearing the same uniform that he was wearing.

"See? It works. Haha!" Bendin smiled in recognition of the woman.

"Hello, I'm ADA. I don't recognize you, sir. What is your name?"

"I'm Bendin."

ADA seemed tense and concerned. "How did the celebration go?"

Bendin didn't know what to say so he decided to just roll with it, "It went fine."

ADA relaxed visibly, smiled, and clapped her hands together excitedly, "Good. Yes! Oh, excellent. I was hoping the celebration would go over well. Everyone was so energetic too! And to think that weapon actually destroyed Zadok. I told them it wasn't going to work, but you've proved me wrong!"

"Yeah, Zadok was destroyed over eight hundred years ago. Odge saw to that one," Bendin said, the information obviously being ancient.

"No." ADA frowned. "That can't be right. I would have been activated right away. Eight hundred toalt or Eight hundred Makarias?"

"Toalt."

ADA paused and said sternly, "We have concurrency issues. Let's sync. Is the following knowledge the same as yours?" She waited.

Bendin motioned for her to continue.

"It should be common knowledge that Zadok has been surviving since before the organization of Makarias, since before the organization of Toalt even. It's especially important now to get the details right." ADA began to quiver for a second. Then appeared concerned again and continued, "You know, right?"

Bendin shook his head no and motioned with his hands again for her to continue.

"At this desperate time with the sealing of the gates, the people of Zadok uprising, and the weakening strength of the

Vaelift in Makarias time 50." ADA put her hands on her hips and pointed a finger at Bendin, "And need I remind you of your basics as a Vaelift that we hold the true knowledge of Odge. Do not forget that."

"I'm sorry ADA. It's not the year 50 in Makarias. It's now the year 905 Makarias time. I've learned that the Vaelift were all killed. I'm afraid I'm the first Vaelift since that time."

The image flickered. It fizzled. ADA froze.

Fear, things Bendin thought must be pent-up hopes being dashed, frustration, and confusion appeared on her beautiful face.

"No! Nohhhh . . ."

Bendin wondered how that was possible since all the ones at school never showed any signs of emotion. She began to cry.

Bendin wondered dumbfounded. This definitely was new. ADA, crying?

Through her sobs she said, "Then . . . that simply means . . . Zadok won. They must . . . have failed . . . to stop him." The image of ADA put her elbows on her knees and buried her face into her hands.

"Why is she crying, Bendin?" Callapse whispered.

"*How* is she crying?" Ryan wondered.

"Sorry, Bendin, I can't help it. I have to ask," Pete jumped in front of Bendin and asked, "ADA, are you like a real person or something?" He gave a double thumbs up to Ryan who grinned.

"I'm a real copy of Alivia Daria Adius Sanga, wife of Byrd Sanga. Of course I'm not the actual person. I've been crafted and designed by the Vaelift for the monitoring and control of this facility as well as keeping track of things for people."

"The keeping track of things I'm familiar with, but monitor and control? Your later versions had much less personality and certainly more functionality," Bendin scratched his head knowingly.

"Whatever." ADA blinked the tears out of her eyes. "Everything I had access to in this facility is down, and everything that was networked between the temples of Makarias is down. The relays will need to be restored before I can access the information in the other temples. You seem to be very young, Bendin. What skill level are you?" She stood up importantly.

Pete and Ryan's faces lit up at her words and they roared in laughter and shouted. "Skill levels!"

"Skill level? I honestly don't know." Bendin shrugged.

"Then let's find out. Please all non-Vaelift visitors pay no attention as this doesn't concern you. How about you do the Byrd shift?

Bendin stared at her blankly before he mumbled a soft, "No."

"Okay then, let's start at the bottom and work our way up. Can you do the basic Vurfenstaf summon?"

"Summon?"

ADA sighed and clenched her fists. "You are not even at the most basic level." ADA screamed in agony. "Odge, why me?"

Pete and Ryan laughed again.

Pete pointed at Bendin accusingly, "I guess that explains why *you*, Bendin, are not of the 'glory' of the old days that Dad and the Tribunal keep complaining about."

ADA held up a hand and dismissed Pete's comment. "Oh, don't worry. You can train here and become a full-fledged Vaelift. Granted it may take a lot of time, but at least we can start. What is your lineage?"

"My what?" Bendin exclaimed. Bendin turned to Mez and Callapse for assistance. Callapse smugly shrugged while Mez shook his head no.

Pete and Ryan laughed again and got as close as they could so they could catch every word that Bendin didn't know.

Callapse and Mez backed off a bit and began to explore the room, only mildly listening. Callapse attempted to pull one of the staffs off the wall. He yelped in a cry of pain holding his hand. It hadn't budged a bit. "These things are completely fused to the wall," He noted.

"Your lineage, the person who gave you the ability to be a Vaelift," ADA grumbled impatiently. "Who was that person a descendent of?"

Bendin was very perplexed. "I - I'm sorry. I have absolutely no idea what you are talking about."

"Bendin, the only way to become a Vaelift is if Odge *makes* you one or if someone who *is* a Vaelift gives it to you under his direction. The latter always takes priority. Honestly! This is fundamental information. I will teach you these very basic of all basics before I pass you onto a real teacher."

"They have real teachers here?" Bendin wondered.

"Listen, *little* pupil. The masters have recorded so many teaching sessions for the Vaelift to learn from that they organized them into a smart automated reaction teaching system that has the ability to replicate what they would say, do, or teach in any situation. It is," she paused, frowned, and continued, "or was quite revolutionary. They couldn't always be here in person you know and the original eight expected their legacy to live on. So we have the eight styles of the Vaelift from them." ADA explained taking a deep breath. She continued, "You'll have to watch a display of the different styles to choose one, two, or any number of combinations. Whatever you find most comfortable to meet your needs. First, show me that you are definitely a Vaelift and not an impersonator."

"ADA, I already did the test to see that I'm a Vaelift. Please teach me to summon a Vurfenstaff."

ADA nodded. "Sure then, impersonator. Call your Vurfenstaff and it will come to you. Remember to use your heart and soul."

"Sure, of course, but what do I say?"

"Whatever you want."

Bendin put Quip on a desk next to the one that was activated. Quip woke and asked, "What's going on?"

"I'm doing the Vurfenstaff summon."

Everyone in the room watched as Bendin focused on the Vurfenstaffs on the far wall. He visualized just how he wanted to do it, reached out his hand, and called out loudly, "Come here!"

A pleasant humming sound filled the air as all the Vurfenstaffs on the far wall detached themselves at the same time, sailed with great speed and velocity at Bendin, spun around him like a top, and crashed into his body at the same time. The impact threw Bendin backwards to the ground with bruise marks appearing on his face, arms, and hand. The Vurfenstaffs scattered all over the floor around his body.

ADA, Pete, Ryan, Callapse, Quip and Mez could not contain their laughter.

"You should have seen your face!" Pete exclaimed.

"It was hilarious!" Ryan laughed.

"You were so shocked!" Callapse included.

"Good one, Bendin, good one," Quip said from the desk. "Thank you for putting me over here. Very fortunate for me."

ADA held her sides, "I haven't seen anything like that in a long time. That was some call. You have excellent strength, great power, but wretchedly horrible control. Try calling a little softer and only focus this time on one instead of them all."

They attempted to help Bendin put the various sized Vurfenstaffs back on the wall, but they immediately noticed that

Bendin was the only one that could pick up a Vurfenstaff. Callapse dropped the Vurfenstaff he was holding after a few seconds with another yelp. Ryan and Pete both gasped, grabbed a Vurfenstaff, got shocked, and dropped it. They kept doing it over and over again, after a while they began chucking them at each other.

"This is so cool, Bendin. You have got to bring one home for us so we can shock people!" Pete said grinning.

"We just have to figure out a way to handle them."

Once Bendin had placed all the Vurfenstaffs back in the racks, he returned to where he was and simply held his hand out and said, "Here."

A singular hum sounded throughout the room and one Vurfenstaff rose and coasted over to Bendin who clasped it in his hand. The Vurfenstaff he had called was just taller than Bendin was. With a shrill zip of sound the Vurfenstaff pulsed for a second and throbbed slightly. He analyzed the staff closer and saw a part at the bottom had been cut away leaving a flat part on the side with engravings.

"ADA, what do these engravings say?"

"They are the two rules of vifting."

"Vifting?"

"Vifting is switching from one world to the other. It's a sacred power. Rule number one, look before you leap. You don't want to vift into immovable solids. Rule number two, carry your head. You cannot vift with something larger than your head.

The others stopped what they were doing and focused on her.

"What happens when you do?" Callapse asked nervously.

"Your body instantly dies, unable to handle the carrying load. It's why the gates were created by the all-knowing Odge in the first place, to facilitate the passage of everyone and everything else. The gate's rules are a little different. For example you can't vift a house through a sealed gate, but you can do things like, animals, and objects, as long as they fit through the physical size of the gate."

Bendin held up the Vurfenstaff. "It feels alive."

"It is, in a way. It's because they are partially connected to the curtain that connects the two worlds. "ADA explained, starting to become agitated again.

"What's the curtain?" Bendin asked.

ADA frowned and said faster and with more intensity,

"The curtain is what the Vaelift draws on for all his energy, ability, and power. It is the very energy field that both separates the two worlds and holds them together, and it is not to be handled lightly," ADA said speeding up even more. "Being partially connected means that the Vurfenstaff can be of great aid to the Vaelift who wields it, giving greater energy and manipulation to both to and from the curtain itself."

"That's going to deep ADA, I'll take a rain check on that right? I like the Vurfenstaff though. It's pretty," Bendin said only understanding parts of what she had just said.

"What now?" Bendin asked Quip. "Is this all we were supposed to find here?"

"I don't think so, Bendin. Odge didn't mention a fancy pole," Callapse mocked.

"You also didn't mention that the headquarters and training center of the Vaelift was sitting in this Jungle nightmare of a place," Bendin said hotly.

"Stop it, Bendin." ADA reached out to him. "While your staff indicates you as the head, I don't believe it. Might I ask, to speak to the real head of the Vaelift?" Bendin's thoughts flashed back to Findall Quin over in Toalt and started to question the veracity of Findall's claim. If Findall had been able to vanish, why hadn't he or any of the other Vaelift in Toalt ever been seen in Makarias?

"It's him," Quip said to ADA. "He's the head Vaelift, called by Odge himself."

"But--" Bendin started to say, but he was interrupted by Pete and Ryan.

"Yeah! Bendin, congratulations! We didn't know you have been visited by Odge!"

"Don't tell me you're believers now too?" Callapse scolded them.

"Why not?" Pete pondered throwing his hands into a large "v" shape, "It sounds like fun."

"Stop stop stop . . . I wasn't visited by Odge."

"Oh," Ryan said becoming a bit disappointed.

"It was a servant of his called Jameus," Bendin said.

Callapse fell over from where he was standing and hit the floor with a thud.

"Jameus?" Mez said loud enough for Bendin to hear. "Thee Jameus?"

Bendin didn't believe it was possible that Pete and Ryan could have doubled the size of their smiles but, to his amazement, they did. They were like a pair of turbofans sucking as much air into their bodies at once as they could possibly get.

"That's even better!" They roared in excitement, "You met our ancient grandfather. He was one of the original Vaelift called by Odge himself!"

"Then you are of the lineage of Jameus Coil," ADA explained.

They clamored over to Bendin and took turns getting shocked by Bendin's Vurfenstaff. Bendin watched with amusement as they tried to pick their shocked bodies up off the ground.

"Bendin, now that we have your lineage in sure form and that you indeed have authority, why has Odge called you." ADA folded her arms. "I don't know what happened to Zadok, but I would think it's time for you to finish the former Vaelift's unfinished mission," ADA said. "You might as well sit down. It may take a little while to explain what was happening, as far as it has been recorded to me. I just don't have the most up to date details. For that, you will have to get that from someone else."

"Why should we take orders from you? You are a recording!" Callapse grumbled.

"Odge wills it," Bendin and Quip confirmed at the same time. They glanced at each other.

"You heard it too," Quip said to him.

Bendin shook his head affirmatively and Quip smiled. The others sat down around ADA, except for Callapse who stood near the wall. Quip moved himself, carefully, off the desk and into Bendin's lap. ADA's projected form moved onto the floor in full size. Bendin was surprised, as the one's at school never did that either.

"Just before the celebration, the Vaelift were hunting a man named Zadok. Zadok was banned from Makarias for trying to steal the plans for the weapon known as the S-Capacitator. It was theorized that it could annihilate or destroy the complete entity of a being from existence with a sort of transference or power. That included us. Zadok is not as we are; he escaped the punishments of former worlds and has brought his influence here to ours."

"ADA, you're making no sense again," Bendin whined. "Please speak in a way that I can understand: Simply."

"I will try. This is the basics, it's hard to explain any simpler." ADA grinned, and apparently suddenly thought it was funny that Bendin couldn't understand things that she thought should be common sense. "So, Zadok, because he is different, the Vaelift were making a weapon specifically designed just to fight and destroy him."

"Okay, so the Vaelift were making a weapon to destroy some guy that lived over 800 some odd years ago. What does that have to do with us? We were taught in Toalt that Zadok was the savior in preserving the Vaelift, so you can see how messed up things are in Toalt right now. If Odge hadn't told me you guys were right, I'd still believe it myself."

"How do we know that Zadok is even still alive?" Callapse asked.

"Odge told us to finish the unfinished mission just now. That's all I need." Bendin frowned.

ADA swirled her hands around in the air making motions that Bendin hadn't seen before. They were pretty and smooth. "The Vaelift failed. You just need to go find the weapon, find Zadok, and destroy him with it. That's what they had just finished making, were going to do, and gone to celebrate. That was the last thing I had been updated to. Zadok eliminated the Vaelift somehow."

"How can he still *be* alive?" Pete asked.

"Because he isn't from here, doesn't need to eat, sleep, and operates differently than you. He doesn't share your emotions." ADA winked. "I don't have any of those things at all either."

"She lies," Ryan nudged Pete smiling.

"Callapse, do they have network rooms here?" Bendin wondered.

"How should I know? No one ever talked about what they did here, and hello . . . Grandelegents. Don't forget the wild white mist and giant killing machines. I didn't know this was their headquarters. Sorry, their 'secret' headquarters. Their 'official' headquarters was at the Moyles." Callapse shrugged. "You can see how that turned out. They had the old relays to here, but nothing more."

Pete asked curiously, "Where is this S-Catapa gun?"

"It was more like a cannon in size than anything else. They were working on it at Master Peter Moyle's temple. The celebration was there," ADA said.

"So, this is what I think the plan should be. Bendin, you and Quip stay here and train your skills to be worthy of your Vaelift titles. The rest of us will go dig up the info on this S-Cata whatever gun and what happened at this celebration. We'll meet back here when we are done. It may take a while to dig up the information though," Callapse said taking charge.

"That sounds like that will work," Bendin agreed.

Quip shook his head. "Yes."

Callapse pushed off the wall. "Fine. We can take my scrapper because going out to that hole in the ground would take too long on blades alone. Mez?"

Mez nodded affirmatively.

"May we leave the doors open so we can get back inside? Pete asked as they prepared to leave.

"Sure, we'll close them at night though," Bendin said. "There are things out there we know we don't want to deal with."

"Great, I'll pull up the original eight for you, and you can then preview them to select one to begin your training. I suggest starting with, Byrd Sanga." She paused and smiled lovingly, "He was always one of the more enjoyable ones to start with. Be sure to leave Desenzo DeSoto for the last, because he was the strictest. You two," ADA gestured to Pete and Ryan before they left, "let me know what you find."

"Sure!" Pete rejoiced. "She talked to me!"

Pete, Ryan, Mez and Callapse left.

Chapter 17
Training

After cleaning up the central rooms of the place, they settled down. Bendin did a quick review of the introductions to each of the eight, and they went with ADA's advice to begin training with Byrd Sanga.

Byrd Sanga turned out to be a thinner version of Trudamanga Sanga. Both were smiling, funny people, but Byrd usually laughed before he showed them exactly how to hold a particular position. The lessons were performed in a room with mirrored walls and padded floors. Projections of the teacher would walk around and show them particular moves while correcting any mistakes he might see. They found out that the projections could interact with them physically as well as vocally.

Bendin set up a schedule for Quip to follow as well. They would train for a couple of hours, take an hour off, and then repeat. They spent the free hours exploring as much of the building as they could. There were hallways that went everywhere and nowhere. Some up, some down. There were many rooms that were up above on higher floors that had no conceivable way to get to them if you didn't have skates. There were doors that opened up into the tall hallways. Many of the rooms were designed so similarly to the upper temple he was raised in that he sometimes got confused thinking he was back there. Even the living quarters had the very same design that he was used to. A couple of bunks with one of the special desks. He turned a couple of them on just to see if they worked. Every single desk he tested and every ADA all asked the same haunting question, "How was the celebration?" He didn't tell any of them. The engravings on the walls were the same as the one's he found in the book written by the twenty.

Bendin found out also that there were eight main rooms that had been the offices of the eight leaders. The eight offices were set in a circular room with a pathway in the rear of every office that led to a connected space that had a large glyph engraved octagonal table in the center. Bendin determined this must have been the personal meeting room for the eight leaders. He couldn't make sense of what they were planning on as all the left over notes on the desks and tables didn't make sense to him.

They discovered that the ADA in the main control room was different from the others. She knew more and taught how Makarias had been created. She even shared a little bit of the calling of the eight. Odge himself had come down and given them all power to be Vaelift, protectors of him, keepers of the gates, and guardians of the people.

The first few training lessons, aside from the humor that Byrd gave them, were dreadfully taxing on Bendin. They consisted of strengthening exercises so his lower body would be strong and his upper body fluid. Byrd would say constantly, "Remember, lower, strong as a tree; but upper, fluid as the sea." Quip followed the lessons, and it was humorous to watch four legged Quip try to do the positions. He would squat on all fours so low that it seemed like he was lying on the floor. Byrd flicked a small stick under Quip, from time to time, to make sure he wasn't cheating. Each time he did it he'd laugh and then repeat it again. Even though he knew they were recordings, Bendin thought they had preserved their personalities very well. If it hadn't been for digital distortion every now and then, he wouldn't have known they were recordings at all. Byrd had Bendin and Quip practice vifting. They learned the more you do it, the better you get.

After a couple days of this, Bendin felt like his muscles were going to explode. Even with all the skating he had done every day prior, it hadn't prepared him for the workouts that Byrd Sanga was making them do.

"You need to arch your back less Bendin," Byrd instructed. "If it's not straight, you will be out of alignment."

Bendin couldn't understand why that was important. But maybe, with time, it would make sense to him. After all, these were the masters.

"Master Byrd, what is the end goal? What am I or we, supposed to be able to do with all these exercises?"

"My son, you will be able to defeat any foe you come up against! Except for maybe a bomb, which is what killed one of my friends. Still, that's not the point. Get in your stance."

Bendin and Quip stood in their stances and worked to perfect them. This they did till Byrd said they would be moving up to the next set of training.

Byrd advised, "In general you all need to work on evasion from Jameus Coil. Staff work will be for Bendin from Morgan Wycliff. Energy management for Quip from Stewart Hyde. Finally, you both need to practice meditation from Santiaga Flinn."

This was to happen before they embraced any one of the eight's particular style. Byrd explained that they were still brushing the basics. They should feel free to embrace anything new they learn with caution and excitement at the same time. He laughed and told them there were new things he was discovering still, even at the final day of the recordings.

These they did for a couple more days. They soon found out the wisdom in Byrd's selection of training and recommendations. The second Jameus Coil's projection was activated, Bendin knew at once it was the same man who had visited him back in the upper temple that night. It felt very surreal, but also refreshing at the same time. All of them enjoyed Jameus's instructions on how to be evasive and to not be where the enemy was thrusting or aiming. The trick was to find nothing but empty for every enemy strike. Jameus Coil had large and intimidating muscles, but he was kind. Bendin found he was excellent with the staff and Jameus praised him highly. Morgan Wycliff was witty and fast. He knew how to wield a weapon. He always kept Bendin running around and giving him swift hits on his butt.

Quip adapted fantastically and became very adept at focusing his energy. He began to be able to channel it so that he could keep flames going in different intensities and colors. He was getting good enough to make it so he was holding a tiny small ball of fire out in front of him. It pleased Stewart so much that he wished he'd been born a fox. Stewart was a younger recording, but he was just as confident and cheeky as the other masters. He was a master of controlling the release of your energy. He had abilities that Quip couldn't do or begin to do as he was still learning vifting.

Bendin and Quip threw in some time meditating and trying to learn to communicate with Odge. Santiaga Flinn was painfully patient with them and had absolutely no problem sitting for hours pondering, communicating every problem, and sending thought of gratitude you could think of.

Bendin and Quip were able to vift back and forth freely now, without any fatigue or fainting. The sound was very loud and the flashes were blindingly bright. This was frowned upon by every one of the teachers. Still, Bendin and Quip were happy with their progress after only a few days of work.

It was after those days that Mez, Pete, Ryan, and Callapse arrived at noon back from their journey.

"You would not *believe* the size of that hole!" Pete cried

out and interrupted their circular evasion lessons.

"Oh, I hope we are interrupting!" Ryan grinned pushing Bendin over.

"Look, Ryan, it's Jameus!" Pete exclaimed.

"Right." Bendin laughed. "ADA, go ahead and switch it off for now."

The recording of Jameus Coil waved at them as he faded away.

"It went so deep that at the bottom was a lake!" Ryan added. "We thought the weapon might be at the bottom of the lake. But when we got scanners to search, there was nothing there."

Mez simply shook his head yes in agreement.

"There isn't so much as a cust spec of what was once Pete Moyle's home," Callapse added. "Nature has filled in the rest. Whatever was once there, it's not there anymore."

"We then went and sought out some of the known historians of Makarias," Ryan said. "They all have different accounts of what happened."

Pete frowned. "I'm kind of getting tired of our past history, there are so many versions and interpretations." Pete kicked the floor with his foot. "It makes me angry!"

Ryan laughed, "Come on, that's nothing compared with every preacher replacing the Vaelift and Odge with the Book of Odge. I don't care how good they think the translations are. It still seems odd to me."

Bendin said, "That's all wel and good, but back to the history that we all care about right now, the Vaelift."

"One person said that they were celebrating the 50th anniversary only," Callapse explained. "Another said it was a member initiation gathering."

"When we asked about the S-weapon they all scoffed and laughed at us for believing such legends. They said there was no such thing and that's 'only a legend,'" Pete reported.

"When we pressed on them saying that there was one that was made, they would reason, 'Then it was destroyed in the explosion.'" Ryan grabbed Bendin's staff to see if it would still shock him. It did.

"So, we know nothing about what happened to the weapon," Callapse said. "This is what we do know. We know the Vaelift were all killed by Zadok. We also know about a third of the Vaelift turned on the organization and helped in its destruction. That part is the same among the historians."

"Why would they do that? Why would they all be at the same place?" Bendin said, "That seems very stupid."

Bendin heard Mez suck in a breath of air and whisper, "They never thought it could happen."

"My guess," Pete said, "Is that every single one wanted to be there when they pieced together the weapon and activated it for the first time. I know I wouldn't have wanted to stay away."

"Like you would know that? We don't even know which side they were all on!" Ryan argued."

"They might have escaped to Toalt," Callapse suggested.

It sounded good till ADA broke in, "No, they all died. Otherwise, survivors would have come back. You don't know the rules about betrayal. Vaelift can continue to use their abilities up till they turn against Odge and his rules. After that, they operate differently. If majority turned on the Vaelift that explains a lot. They *were* getting really prideful and arrogant. Be humble or it always leads to betrayal and alienation. You are going to need to do something to solve this problem. It's your duty; I certainly can't do your duty for you."

"So what now? We need the item from a legend, so who would believe in something as crazy as an S-weapon from a legend?" Callapse asked.

A minute of silence was broken by Quip. "That waste of space, Pikalop, would," Quip said grinning wildly. "Let's go ask him."

"That's a great idea, Quip. If anyone's silly enough, they are. We'll all go. I need a break from this. We'll be back, ADA, one way or another," Bendin said grabbing his Vurfenstaff and skating into the air.

All of them left following Quip's flame trail.

"I've definitely heard 'we'll be back ADA, one way or another' before. . ." ADA's voice trailed off as they left.

"I can't take you all in the scrapper without dumping people in the cargo pockets," Callapse grumbled.

"We can go on blade. They weren't too far ahead," Bendin reasoned.

Callapse shrugged.

They all skated to where they had last seen Pikalop and his group.

"They went that way," Quip said authoritatively pointing with his paws.

They followed Quip even though there was no indication

that Pikalop had gone this way.

"He doesn't leave much of a trail to follow, does he?" Callapse muttered to Ryan.

"At least he's clean!" Ryan said back.

After a while longer, they skated over the edge of a deep, jagged, and massive crater.

"This thing has got to be over three kilometers wide!" Quip gasped.

"What's this?" Bendin asked.

"A crater!" Pete and Ryan answered at the same time. You could tell they had both wanted to be the first person to say it, trying to pick up on the ridiculousness of Bendin's question. But since they had said it at the same time, they stuck out their tongues at each other.

Bendin sighed. "What *caused* this?"

"One large crater in the ground, a lost facility, and about thirty lives was the cost and payment for one mistake in discovering our source of power we have today. This was an advanced fusion research plant. They kind of miscalculated by a small percentage. By the time they realized their mistake, the entire place was inescapable," Callapse explained hastily. "We were lucky they transmitted their mistake before it went critical. That message saved the others working on advanced fusion, preserved millions of lives, and kept the future secure in power generation."

"I guess?" Bendin said to Quip. Quip was more energetic than he had been the entire trip, constantly buzzing around and hovering in the air with his fire.

Pete and Ryan made explosion noises with their mouths and popping sounds with their hands.

Quip landed on Bendin's shoulder and said, "Don't feel so bad. This area is quite pretty, see how nature has grown back and reclaimed it."

On the other side of the crater there stood a large lake. The explosion had blown away half of the lake and that side of the lake now poured over the edge of the crater. It made a very long and extremely wide waterfall. The water danced and raced itself down to the bottom of the crater, flowed southwards down under the ground out of sight.

"How has that lake not drained?" Bendin mused. "The amount of water going over the side is tremendous."

Callapse pointed to large flowing rivers and streams pouring into the far side of the lake. "There. There are also vast underground rivers that flow into this."

"Come on, let's go in for a closer look." Pete winked skating down into the crater.

"Do you think they came through here?" Ryan asked him.

"Only one way to find out," Callapse said skating ahead of him. "Race you all to the other side. Stay low or you're dq'd!"

Pete and Ryan weren't one to turn down a challenge and skated after Callapse at top speed.

To Bendin's surprise, Mez eagerly sped after Pete and Ryan.

Bendin loved the way the Vurfenstaff felt in his hands. It felt very much alive and tingly. The only thing he really missed was the little bit of extra control that you got when you were using an Airlarky staff. He was impressed that the others around him seemed to have mastered skating without one.

Pete, Ryan, Callapse, and Mez each skillfully cut around each other, nudged boulders down after them, and caused whatever setbacks they could invent to beat out the others. This continued in a wild dance through the rocks and canyon with Mez pulling ahead at the end near the waterfalls.

"There they are!" Pete shouted down from where he was. He pointed towards the rim of the crater. Indeed, there were the flying platforms of the Nomadic Hermits. They were jumping off of the platforms into the lake.

The waterfalls thundered and crashed in an initial beautiful singular cascade. Once they landed they split off into separate distributaries. The sound they made was simply breathtaking. The echoes created a beautiful rolling effect glancing off the walls of the canyon. The others were reveling in it. Pete and Ryan skated over the falls and did what they did to their own waterfall back home. They shouted in delight as the water floated through their fields and landed way beyond where the water had been falling only a moment before.

Bendin found Pikalop relaxing on the edge of his flying platform.

"Pikalop, I need to ask you something," Bendin said skating down and landing next to Pikalop.

"Bendin, the mighty Vaelift has returned from his stalwart journey of fortitude!" Pikalop said mockingly throwing his arms up. He didn't move from his lounging. "I'm perhaps, maybe, a little, slightly impressed to see you guys again."

Bendin checked his watch for Toalt, it said, "13:11". He

chuckled. It was almost the same time as here. He made a quick scan of Toalt and it was open air in the position where he was. There was an expansive network of towns and villages below and mountains were off in the distance. It would be plenty safe to vift. "Quip, let's vift there and back really quick for Pikalop."

Pikalop hardly moved his head and said lazily, "Yeah, whatever."

With a blazing blast of light, sound, and energy, Bendin and Quip vifted in front of Pikalop.

Bendin and Quip appeared in Toalt. They switched their vision and saw the surprise on Pikalop's face.

"Now that's funny," Quip said as they clapped their hands and paws together and vifted back. Bendin had started vifting without hardly moving his arms.

Pikalop watched, now with sudden interest, as Bendin and Quip returned from the other side. "Well done master Vaelift." He clapped his hands slowly together.

"I wouldn't say master, but I would say Vaelift. That I am," Bendin declared. "We need information that you might hold."

"Yes?" Pikalop wondered messing with the edge of his hat with his lips. His mouth curled slightly into a smile.

"We need to know the legend of the S-weapon."

"That is . . . yes . . . a very powerful legend and there are many who know it but almost no one who believes it. I will tell you for a Crowder."

"A Crowler?" Callapse whined. "Do we *look* like DeSoto's to you?"

"Crowder . . . can't even say the name right." Ryan mocked.

Pikalop grinned wider.

Mez shook his head no.

"We don't ha--" Pete started.

"Here." Bendin held out his hand with Quip watching him curiously. They heard a loud caw and the wild hum as an elegant coin landed in Bendin's hand.

Everyone stopped everything they were doing and stared.

Pikalop slowly clapped his hands and took the Crowler from his hand. "Outstanding. I have *never* seen that before. A real miracle. I can't believe what just happened. And people call *me* crazy."

"That or the bird?" Pete gawked watching the bird fly

away.

"A bargain is a bargain after all. I will tell you. The legend is that the Vaelift had created an eight part weapon that had the ability to destroy an entire being and give the being's immortality to the wielder of the weapon. It has been the dream of our people since we first set out to find the lost weapon that we would become the possessor. Mortals have always wanted immortality. It's a blessing of the gods! The reason this is a legend is that no credited historian wants to believe that the S-weapon exists and also because of its ability to grant immortality. However, contrary to historians, I believe it is real."

"I'm not surprised," Callapse said.

"Called it," Pete said winning a bet no one knew they had made. He slapped his brother on the shoulder.

"Hey!" Ryan whined.

Pikalop smiled. "I know you think me and my people are crazy. And maybe we are, but we are not crazy about this legend. Because . . . " Pikalop's smile blossomed into a huge grin and he tossed the highly valued currency into the air. "I have one of the pieces of the weapon here with me. Pikalop bowed and watched as Bendin, Quip, Ryan, Pete, Callapse, and even Mez's mouths all dropped open in disbelief. "I'm sorry, though, that we have failed to recover any of the other parts of the weapon. Whatever happened that day, one thing is for sure, the legend is true."

"May we see it?" Pete and Ryan asked at once. Bendin was going to ask, but they beat him to it.

"Sure." Pikalop went into the covered portion of his craft. "What good is a story without proof?" He pointed to Bendin and tossed the coin again into the air.

"Pikalop likes that coin," Quip mumbled.

Pikalop went to his bed and opened a very large compartment under it. He pulled out a large piece that was as big as he was. It shimmered in the light, gave off a faint glow, and was partially transparent. It was shaped like a massive barrel to a cannon, with a spot in the back that you could attach to something else.

"See? This is proof that the existence of the weapon is true and you can see how beastly this weapon must have been. This is only the front part. My ancestor found this among the dust at Peter Moyle's homestead, completely intact. Hit it. Throw it. It doesn't take any damage, wear, break, resists water, tarnish, or gather dust. Truly remarkable. Simply remarkable. A wonder."

Pikalop handed them the piece to hold and it hardly had any mass which was weird for such a large object.

"Wild!" Ryan said.

When Pete held it he acted as though he was going to hand it to Quip, "Now remember Quip, don't vift with this. It's a bit bigger than your head."

Quip laughed.

"What happened to the rest of it?" Callapse asked. "If it doesn't take any damage or wear, which is evidenced by surviving the Vapocolypse, we can reasonably deduce that the other pieces exist."

Pikalop eyed them grimly as he took back the piece and returned it back to its compartment under his bed. "Alas, we have searched everywhere. There hasn't even been one story, rumor, or tale of any mysterious materials showing up anywhere. My progenitors and I have all failed to find even one more of the lost pieces."

He said what everyone didn't want to hear, "They must be in Toalt."

"With Zadok?" Callapse asked.

Pikalo smiled. "Well, now that you guys have the ability to go there, you might want to think about finding the missing pieces and bringing them back over here. We assemble the pieces, you open the doors, and--bam--we blast Mr. Zadok to smithereens stealing his immortality."

Callapse clenched his hands into fists.

"The idea certainly has merit," Quip said.

"Keep this safe. I'm sure you will as you already have for generations," Bendin said, "We'll let you know when and if we find the other pieces."

"You're doing what he says?" Callapse asked bewildered.

"It's finishing the former Vaelift's work," Bendin reasoned.

Pikalo watched them all carefully. 'Promise me one thing . . . do not . . . tell . . . anyone . . . about this piece."

"I promise," Bendin said shaking Pikalo's hand. The rest of them promised the same thing. Pikalo held his hand, confused for a moment, before he grinned.

Quip whispered in Bendin's ear, "Like anyone would believe us if we did."

Bendin grinned at him.

"Let's get this over with then," Callapse grumbled.

"Sure thing. Good luck guys, take care. Till then, I will be enjoying life and continuing my search for the missing pieces." Pikalo waved to them grabbing his glass and sipping the fluids.

They all went back to Thibracketory and found some chairs in the center room with ADA and the Vurfenstaffs along the wall.

"Guys--," Bendin started.

"Hold it!" Mez hissed holding his hand up to cut him off. Every eye watched intently. Mez drew his weapon and slunk into the adjoining room. A loud bang rang out and Mez drug through their room a roped, very angry, and screaming ice-covered badger spitting ice shards out of its mouth. Before each attempt of spitting ice shards Mez flicked his wrists and rotated his arms. The tightly bound ice badger's spit attack went into the ground harmlessly each time. "Be back. Not the one." Mez marched directly around the next corner towards the entrance.

"Not the one?" Bendin asked once the sound faded.

"Ask him. It's his story to tell," Callapse said haltingly. Ryan and Pete simply looked at their shoes.

"Yeah . . . I definitely will," Bendin said as Mez came back, a grim frown on his face.

"As you were. Continue." Mez gestured with his hands.

The others turned to him. Quip's tongue hung out of his mouth.

"Right. I just wanted to tell you I have no idea who Zadok is. He simply could be anyone."

"He's not the ruler? Or a leader there?" Pete asked. "Isn't he like 100,000 years old?"

"Don't know. I just know he's not been mentioned except as a past historical figure."

Ryan fidgeted and asked, "Why are we all sitting around here? Bendin let's go to Toalt and find the missing pieces or see if they are there at all. If we do let's get them and be done with this. I want to get back to Airlarky sometime you know."

"What's stopping you?" Bendin said. "I don't know how to open the gates, and no one here can get to Toalt but myself and Quip. Not to mention this whole 'finding the s-weapon' thing is starting to sound very dangerous for everyone. Toalt isn't a safe place. If it weren't Odge telling me I had to do this, I'd certainly be living with you guys at your place."

"Correction," Callapse said grinning. "I can go too, right

now."

Bendin frowned. "How?"

"This!" Callapse demonstrated. He flicked the switch that was next to his right ear and the backpack activated with a deep throb. "Watch."

Bendin heard something lightly say, "Don't let him do it. It will only bring pain and sorrow."

"Did you say to stop him?" Bendin asked Quip.

Quip shook his head no.

Bendin checked with the others who merely shrugged at him.

"Callapse, don't do whatever you are going to do. It will only bring pain and sorrow," Bendin pleaded with Callapse. Bendin didn't know exactly why he was being told to say this, but this was the second strange cautionary attempt to stop Callapse. Even though Bendin liked the idea of his friends being able to do what he and Quip did.

"No? You're kidding, right? It's not your fault, Bendin. This is all me. It's time to make history!" Callapse announced proudly.

"This is not going to be good," Quip agreed. "I can't watch." Quip turned and watched Bendin instead.

"We certainly are watching." Pete and Ryan grinned at one another.

Ryan playfully pushed Pete and mocked, "Do you think he'll explode?"

Callapse pulled on a switch that was next to his other ear. Unlike Bendin and Quip's light, sound, and compression wave, Callapse's light, sound, and wave was ten times brighter, louder, and every member of the group were thrown backwards from the compression wave alone. Mez's body slammed into the wall knocking him out instantly. Quip and Bendin instinctively vifted to Toalt and back. Pete and Ryan both crashed into the wall of Vurfenstaffs before collapsing on the ground unconscious.

The sounds died down and the dust settled. Bendin wiped his eyes and noticed Callapse was not here. Quickly switching his vision he saw Callapse's body lying on the ground.

Callapse was in Toalt.

"I don't think that was how it was supposed to happen was it?" Quip said rubbing his ear in pain.

"I don't know, Quip. I don't know," Bendin said shaking his head. He checked the others in the room and after a few seconds they awoke.

"Sorry Bendin, but that was the coolest thing I have ever seen!" Pete exclaimed rubbing his ears too.

"You're crazy," Quip noted.

"Where is he?" Ryan asked.

"He's in Toalt, but he's lying on the floor and not moving. I hope he's asleep." Bendin feared that the mysterious warning might have been given to save Callapse's life.

Bendin and Quip vifted to the other side again and found Callapse asleep, just as Bendin had hoped. "I'm getting better at this Quip. My vifts are not as loud as I remember."

"That's because you *are* getting better at it. I'm not even close to feeling tired. In fact, I feel more energetic. Mine are still as loud as they were when I started," Quip replied. "Maybe your hearing is going bad."

Bendin turned and stared at Quip till Quip smiled back. He shook Callapse, but Callapse didn't move. He was completely out of it.

"What do we do with him?" Bendin wondered.

"Make sure he has water?" Quip said sarcastically.

"We just need to check on him from time to time in the hopes that he will wake. Otherwise he may have suffered permanent damage. We'll have to try something else then." Bendin decided that before he vifted back he was going to check so that he wouldn't vift into someone. It was the whole point of the first rule. It was almost habit to check, but he still had to remind himself.

Quip followed him instantly.

"How was he?" Mez asked. He had a nice red line across his arm where it had hit the wall, but Mez didn't seem concerned about his arm.

"He's alive," Quip said.

"Success!" Pete and Ryan said clasping their hands together.

"I guess," Bendin muttered, unsure of what exactly it meant. "I don't know what it means really. He might be seriously hurt." Bendin decided that they would do training exercises till he showed some signs of waking.

Callapse woke eight hours later.

"Guy's, he's awake!" Bendin shouted after another periodic check.

Bendin and Quip immediately vifted over.

"Are you okay?" Quip asked Callapse.

"I feel terrible. I don't think I was built for this." Callapse rubbed his head painfully.

"Do you feel up to trying to come back?" Bendin asked. "No one is in the way."

"No, but I will anyway. I didn't know it was going to be so exacting of your body to use something like this." He pointed at his pack and flipped the two switches. The pack activated and Callapse disappeared with exactly the same blast as the first time.

"I'm guessing that's how it's going to be," Bendin noted to Quip before vifting to Makarias.

Everyone gathered around Callapse holding him and his machine. Only his mouth was able to move. "It worked."

Pete came over to him. "You got to make me one, so that I can do it too!"

"Sure," Callapse mumbled before immediately falling asleep.

Over the next day, Bendin practiced with the others. He felt like he should be doing more. Callapse had planned on returning to the Coil's the next day.

Bendin found Quip in the main practice room. "Quip, we just need to find out more information. What do you think of trying to save Harmon and discover whether the pieces survived or not? I really want to help her and Odge hasn't given us any further instructions."

"You do what you want, Bendin. What about Pete, Ryan, and Mez?"

"They can go back too," Bendin said. He hailed the others and asked ADA to turn off the recordings of the teachers. "We're returning to the Coil's home with Callapse. He plans on making you guys machines like his while we scout for Harmon and find more information on the whereabouts of those missing pieces. We'll keep our eyes out for Zadok as well."

Pete exclaimed, "I'm with you Bendin. Let's go and win!"

"But you wouldn't be coming," Bendin reasoned.

"I don't care. I'm on the winning team!" Pete grinned and Ryan slapped himself on the forehead with his palm.

They all packed their things, shut down everything, and skated back to the scrapper with Pete and Ryan fitting into the compartments exactly the same way they came.

Chapter 18
A Voice of Warning

The reception at the Coil's house was more than scary. Tilmon had been stressed out for weeks and Celeste was tired. It wasn't until Bendin and Quip gave them a couple of vifting demonstrations did Tilmon and Celeste cool down. The Vurfenstaff was of particular interest as well until the younger kids interrupted his demonstrating. Even though Tilmon and Celeste were still angry at Pete and Ryan for running away, they agreed to help in what ways they could. So, the tension eased a bit. Bendin later learned that Tilmon and Celeste had feared the worst that they had all died in Thibracketory.

Bendin noticed Rachel staring at him oddly, so he mouthed the word, "What?"

Rachel blushed and left the room. Bendin would have followed her to ask why that was the case, but he was swamped with Jean and Starley hanging on his legs. They asked for more adventure stories of the great Axolotl and the giant Secretary Bird. They didn't stop asking till it was time for them to go to bed. Callapse went back to Josiah's to build more units while Bendin quickly grabbed a watch from Tilmon's shop to wear that would display Makarias time. He put this on his other wrist so his wrists now sported wrist cuffs and a watch on each hand. Finding himself finally free of obligations and others having gone off to do other things, Quip and Bendin sought out and found Rachel in her garden.

"Hi Rachel. How's Soladaque?"

Quip slapped his paw into his forehead. He then shook his head in disbelief.

"She's spending all her waking hours over at Chamilin's place. Thanks for asking, Bendin. How was your trip of tragedy? I am actually surprised you got back in one piece, not to mention the others. Mom was livid when she discovered Pete and Ryan had gone." Rachel watched Bendin warily. "I've never seen her that angry. If Tilmon hadn't stopped her, she'd have come after you."

"Oh, wow. I didn't know. I just didn't see Soladaque here, that's all. How are you?" Bendin asked.

Quip nodded his approval.

"You know," Rachel smirked as she flicked her eyes at him before resuming her planting, "Much better now that I don't have critters coming in and eating all my plants. I wanted to thank you again for that."

"Again? Well, it was nothing really. What do you mean?" Bendin shrugged.

Rachel paused as if considering what she was doing for a second; she then walked over to Bendin and kissed his cheek briefly. "That's what I mean. Thanks." She smiled and walked back over to her planting.

Bendin smiled in surprise. "You're welcome?"

Quip whined, "Hey? You missed me. It's my turn." Quip stuck his cheek out.

Rachel laughed, ran back over, and planted a kiss on Quip's cheek.

"You're funny, Quip," Rachel giggled, playfully tugging on his ear.

"I try."

"What is it that you are working on that is so important here anyway? Why these plants?" Bendin asked.

Rachel giggled again, jumped excitedly, and her speech came out in rapid chunks. "I'm so oh very very very close to finding a real cure to a horrid disease that has been plaguing the Wycliff people for a while now. I know I'm oh so very close because the solution we have staves it off for a while but Arrg! It doesn't cure it! Would you believe it uses Syan, Wascoth, Satulian, and even Berthoop!"

"What disease is that?" Quip asked.

"They have a strange strain of an old disease called Bulsion. Something happened to it where it mutated. The previous cures for fighting it actually made it worse! So, all that I need to do is combine it with some Seraphathorn in three separate tirathons. Once that's done, hopefully it will be right and the people will be saved. It's just this strain of the disease is odd. It tragically . . . " Rachel skillfully flipped her hair around.

Bendin and Quip watched her with interest waiting for her to land the critical hit.

"It blows people up," Rachel finished.

Quip laughed. "Seriously? Like this?" Quip demonstrated by bursting into flames and falling over.

"Yeah, pretty much, yes. It's horrible."

"They just die?" Bendin commented, not believing her.

"Exactly like Quip showed us. They catch fire

spontaneously and burn to death. All that is left of the person is usually a pile of ashes," Rachel explained sadly. "Me and the best seven others in this particular field are networked and working on a possible cure. I'm so close, but I don't know if I can finish the work. I've gotten the formula wrong so many times before." Rachel sighed kicking the floor of the cave with her boot.

"You'll figure it out," Bendin said confidently and walked over to her and put a hand on her shoulder. "I know you will."

"Thanks." Rachel smiled pleasantly returning to the plants.

"Do you think we'll find the missing pieces?" Bendin asked Quip.

Quip said jumping onto Bendin's head spinning around quickly, "I'm just going to say, 'yes'. Sure, Bendin. How should I know? If he found any of the pieces, I'll bet he'd have hidden them a long time ago. That's if he really does have them."

"Well, let's go and find out shall we?" Bendin announced raising his leg to skate out of the room.

"What are you guys talking about?" Rachel asked.

Bendin then realized she didn't know. It wasn't a strange thought that Rachel would want to know what they were doing. "Remember the death of the Vaelift?"

"Yes?"

"They had a gun there. We have been told to rebuild it. So, we are searching for the missing parts."

"Oh." Rachel frowned. "Good luck with that. That sounds much harder than the cure I'm working on."

"Maybe," Bendin mumbled. He wasn't so sure that was true.

"Yes," Quip said staring up into the light. "It'll take a real hero."

"Bye, Rachel." Bendin waved.

"Bye," She whispered back studying the next set of plants with intensity.

Bendin switched his vision to the other side to see where in the temple he was. He was over in the section that was behind the DOOD R-Limiter. He thought they would try the Limiter first to hopefully locate Harmon.

It was incredibly easy to get in this time. After checking the time of Toalt, which was, "21:57", Quip and Bendin vifted next to the DOOD R-Limiter.

"Quick, throw up a smokescreen," Bendin ordered. Quip blew thick black smoke around the corner and caused everyone in the control center, including those who were checking the disturbance, to fall over coughing and wheezing. Bendin activated the limiter and spun the helixes around till he found Harmon's current location.

"She's over at the Engineering Association in Upper Temple number two. Great good god of Odge! It's over 4023 kilometers away from here," Bendin yelled to Quip. He searched the list for any sign of s-weapon pieces or Zadok, but he couldn't find anything.

"Quip, that's enough. Let's go," Bendin yelled.

With that, Bendin and Quip vifted back and went to share the news with Tilmon. Bendin would need help getting to Harmon.

Tilmon offered to give him a ride to the Wycliff's temple. "It's dead on the distance you gave. It has to be it." Tilmon showed him a map and how far 4023 kilometers was. The other temples weren't even close to that distance.

"But, what about Bulsion?"

"Don't worry, that's only in a small area of their city. They have quarantined it. They're hoping to help the current victims and prevent anything like this from happening again." Tilmon grinned. "I'll be glad to drop you off there. Just be sure to get a ride to a tribunal meeting for the trip back, or if you can manage to find one from a person there, more greatness to you. We'll leave tomorrow morning."

Bendin felt excited. New places, new faces, and new adventures. They prepared by refilling their pills and water containers. After that, they even enjoyed a game of Planka's Fantastic Flying Darts in the Kid's Lounge with Charles. Bendin every now and then would pull a trick from Ryan's book and use his Vurfenstaff to shock one of the family members for fun.

The next morning, Bendin and Quip met Tilmon out by his bubble. Although the speed of the bubble was faster than Callapse's scrapper, it still took longer than Bendin wanted to traverse the distance. They were on their way back to Harmon and he wanted to see what had happened to her as soon as he could. What was she doing now?

"How are the Wycliffs?" Bendin asked Tilmon. Quip fell asleep in his lap. Bendin and Quip's prayers of late hadn't been very fruitful, and Quip was concerned that somehow he might have offended Odge.

"They are fine Bendin. Xenon Wycliff takes excellent

care of them. The are physically beasts. They can punch concrete with their fists and not be bruised. Impressive for not being D-men."

"Are there any D-men around right now?"

Tilmon sighed. "Unfortunately, no. The last D-man that we were pleased to witness was my father, Jameus Coil."

Bendin opened his mouth in confusion.

"Not the ancient Vaelift, Jameus Coil. My father was named after him."

Bendin closed his mouth and smiled. Tilmon tilted his head and continued.

"He was the most recent D-man. It was really neat to have a father that was a D-man. He told me that even if you have the ability to be one, it was only by accident that he activated his power. He said it was a confusing sense of emotions that were really random. He said that once you nailed it down though, you can turn it on and off as easily as you can walk."

"You believe that?"

"Of course. It fits the other D-men's descriptions. The exact set have all been different and it was some mismatched sense of emotions that trigger it. I've watched people try really hard to see if they are one. There is no real way to tell."

Bendin thought it sounded incredible. "Your father was a lucky guy."

Tilmon laughed. "He wouldn't have said so. He said it was a curse, because of all the attention. He lived with it well though and was respected as such."

Bendin imagined what it would have been like to have a father, to have a person raise you up one on one. It was something he had never thought about before and was very entertained at the idea. Tilmon's father was a D-man. It blew Bendin away. After a few more thoughts about the differences in his childhood versus someone here in Makarias, they arrived.

Or, at least that's what Tilmon said. Bendin couldn't see any form of civilization. All there was a small hill up ahead. He watched as they flew up to a hollowed out cave and down into it. Bendin watched, open mouthed, as they flew into the largest cavern he had ever seen or imagined. He was certainly getting very tired of seeing places bigger than anything he'd ever seen before. But, he just kept becoming more amazed with every large and eye-opening place he came across. The cavern was so open and roomy that it had an entire city lining the walls, floor, and ceiling of the cavern.

"Did I mention they're miners?" Tilmon smiled at Bendin's awed facial expression.

"No, you didn't. All of them?' Bendin asked not believing that everyone would want to be one.

"Of course not all of them. Only a large majority of them. Just like all the families, they have the majority in a single trade. They produce most of the metals and alloys that we use in our machines and products. Everyone produces small quantities, but nothing even close to this scale or quality. If it weren't for the different strains of Bulsion creeping up every few years, they'd probably all be miners. That and other strange diseases that are even rarer."

"I'll bet," Bendin said staring blankly as they drove towards the center of the enormous city-walled cavern. In the middle there was a round glass spherical building that Bendin could only guess was where they were going.

"Do they use pills a lot for food? You know, like the Nomadic Hermits?"

Tilmon laughed again, "No one is as crazy as the Nomadic Hermits and can go that long without getting incredibly bored of the pills. The Wycliffs have the biggest fusion lamp in the world in a cavern that way. You can see its light reflecting off of the walls back over there. You see, part of them grow most of the food underground, and distribute it at a fair trade. Everyone has their own small fusion lamps at their own homes to help supplement them. In fact there are caverns running off in every direction. This city spans for many kilometers in all directions except up."

"Do they have something against living on the surface?"

"Yes, they have always been too proud to live on the surface."

Bendin liked the cracks above them that let in light from the surface because great beams of light reflected off of the dust in the air.

They reached the center and Tilmon made sure that Bendin had been transferred to Xenon Wycliff's care before he left.

"Bendin!" Xenon boomed shaking Bendin's hand in his huge fist, rocking Bendin's whole body. Quip, sitting on Bendin's shoulder, had to grab hold of Bendin's head to not fall off.

"How can we help you here in our city and elegant mines?"

"I need to go to your old Vaelift temple," Bendin answered. "Or at least that's where I'm going to try first."

"That would be down a bit lower. We're a little backed up today, so--" Xenon turned and yelled down the hall vibrating the glass panes around them, "*XALA!* I'll cover for you! Guide Bendin and Quip down to the Vaelift Temple."

A tiny girl appeared. She was very muscular, despite her short height, and she had fair dusty skin, black hair, and brown eyes like her father. She spoke fast, promptly, and wasted no time.

"Come on, nice walking stick, let's go. What's your name again?" She asked when she had guided them to the bottom of the large glass bubble-shaped building. Her voice sounded deep like her father and her tiny size, huge muscles, and deep voice gave Bendin a very strange feeling that she more than made up for her height in strength.

"Bendin," Bendin said his name quickly and fell in behind Xala.

"I'm Quip!"

"Xala. But you knew that. Word has spread that the Vaelift have returned. I'm honored to take you to see Morgan's temple." She opened a hole in the bottom of the sphere shaped building and skated through it. Bendin and Quip followed her down. Quip rode on Bendin's shoulder till they were out of the localized gravity then hovered the rest of the way.

Xala led them down through the empty space that separated the central middle spherical glass bubble from the bottom of the cavern where the lower buildings were. Vehicles flew past them and honked when they were too close.

"Come on slow pokes!" Xala yelled far below them.

Bendin and Quip were distracted by everything; so obviously, they hadn't noticed that she had slipped ahead of them.

Xala landed on a roof below them. She waited for them impatiently stamping her foot. When they finally got to her she frowned, "Don't they teach you anything about skating as a Vaelift?"

"Nope," Quip said amusingly. That, at least, was true.

Bendin chuckled and batted Quip's fist amusingly.

She mumbled, "They didn't even need any."

Bendin noticed the partial form of a smile creep onto her face before she stomped down a flight of steps leading below. Gravity was localized in the buildings, outside of them it was negated.

The buildings were carved out of the stone and had many things inside that made them soft. Blankets, pillows, carpets and such. Bendin thought that was pretty good compensation since everything being natural stone. The buildings were very irregular and there was no space on the walls in which there was no building. It gave the whole area a random look to it. Any person they came across recognized Xala and peeled out of the way.

Xala led them through many passageways down through a chain of many different types of buildings. Some were shops, others homes, and finally she came to the rear end of an abandoned square shaped hut. Xala pulled open an unused elegant door with eight small symbols circled around the center. A staircase went directly into the earth in masterfully cut stone. "It's just a few more meters." Xala pulled at her hair and pointed at an opening around the corner. "Here."

Bendin couldn't believe his eyes. In the perfectly secluded cavern that they came out to, there was a single shaft of light far above that was almost as bright as the sun. It shined on a castle in the middle at an angle. This cavern was much smaller though when compared with the city above.

"Aren't you afraid the cavern ceiling will come down on top of the castle?" Bendin noticed pointing upwards to where the ceiling was supposed to be.

"Not anymore, everything pretty much stays intact all the time, as we have the generators that nullify gravity, things from above don't fall anymore."

Bendin felt kind of dumb. Of course they would have thought of that already.

"Nice one, Bendin." Quip laughed. "Next, you will ask if she has a boyfriend? Or maybe even something like Bulsion?"

Xala and Bendin didn't seem to think that was funny at all. There was a small winding path that led to the entrance, and that was the only path that Bendin could see in the cavern that led to the castle. Xala took to the air and Bendin realized that the Castle was sitting on a large chunk of sheer rock jutting up from the floor. There was a huge stream of water that fell just to the left of them in a free falling waterfall.

"If you have nullified gravity, why is that water falling?"

"Just the rocks, Bendin," Xala explained. "We don't worry about the airspace down here. After the Vapocolypse, no one dares come down here anymore." She shrugged. "Odge protects his stuff."

As they got closer, Bendin began to realize how vast the castle was and the more dense it seemed to appear. He felt like they were getting smaller and smaller. "It looks way bigger up close."

"Yeah, it takes some getting used to," Xala agreed. "You have to be realy careful! Perspectives in the mines always seemed to be off. We're here. Do you need anything else?"

"A key?" Bendin asked looking at the large gates.

She smiled, pushed the gate, and it opened. "Good luck, Master Vaelift. Now, excuse me I have very serious work to do." She swiftly skated back the way they had come.

"She was nice, Bendin, I think you should dump Rachel and date Xala," Quip reasoned watching Xala skate away with interest.

"Thanks, but I will only be doing that if she shows some crazy awesome thing I cannot live without."

"Okay Mr. Vague. Chime in again sometime when you come up with another great reasoning. Let's go inside!" Quip flew through the open door and the place was completely dark except for the light coming from his glowing fire.

Bendin switched his vision to Toalt. He saw hallways. They were similar to his upper temple in design, but he didn't see any people. At least the lights were on over there. Bendin switched his view back to normal. "Look and see if you can find anything that would turn on the lights here."

Quip flew up and around the entrance and checked the first couple of rooms before Bendin found a switch on the right inside of the entrance.

"Quip! Come over here, I need to see. Is this a switch?"

Quip flew back to Bendin and lit up the switch he had found. It had "lights" written on it in bulky white scrawl.

"Ah-ha! We've discovered the lights!" Bendin announced as he flicked the switch.

Instead of turning on the lights, they heard a rumbling sound and one of the entire towers to the right of them split apart and shattered sending bits of the tower in all directions. The larger pieces hit the walls with a resounding crash before falling to the ground far below in a thunderous roar.

Bendin grabbed Quip and pulled him close. "I don't know what just happened." He said staring blankly at Quip. "Let's just use you."

"Good idea." Quip grabbed onto the top of Bendin's

Vurfenstaff, and Bendin held it out in front of him with Quip hanging off of it. He flared up brightly before Bendin laughed at him.

"What?"

"I don't know. I felt like I was holding out a lantern or something."

Quip laughed and let go, flying out in front of Bendin.

Using Quip's flame, they scanned the rest of the halls of the temple and found near the bottom in a very large room, one of the gates. This gate was raised up slightly on a platform. Unlike the previous two gates Bendin had seen, this gate was in the center of the room and wasn't touching any walls at all. It was just a flawlessly connected solid stone gate with the same etchings as the ones on the other gates. Bendin thought it appeared to be more of a wall to him than a gate.

Bendin switched his vision and to his surprise he saw a dozen or so Vaelift students dressed in white lab-coats running machinery on the gate on the other side. The room was again identical to the shape, size, and dimensions of the room he was currently in. Even the gate was in the exact same space as the gate on their side raised up slightly off the floor of the room.

"Quip, what can you see? Anything useful?"

"I see Harmon," Quip announced. "What good fortune!"

"Really?" Bendin didn't know how he missed that. "Let's cause some disturbances then," Bendin said.

Bendin and Quip checked to make sure they were clear and vifted to the other side.

The effect of them appearing out of nowhere in shrieking light, blasting sound, and knocking everything down in a dual shockwave was creepy, freaky, and downright scary. Every person in the room shrieked, yelled, and stared in wonderment as the explosion, light, and concussion wave died down. Bendin and Quip stood there waving.

"Hello fellow Vaelift students. We're friends!" Bendin announced before they all scattered. They ran into each other, knocked machines over, broke cabinets, and bottles. Among the cries, were the yells of Harmon who screamed, "Stop, don't break that! Marshall Davis will kill you! No, Stop. Don't, please come back you have to stay and finish this!"

The room became alarmingly empty except for them and Harmon.

Harmon recognized Bendin so she stood still and pushed her red hair back away from her face. This revealed tears that began to slide down her cheeks. "Is it true? Bendin? All the things that they are saying about you?" Harmon sobbed, "And how in the world did you get here? You appeared out of nowhere!"

"What have 'they' been saying about me?" Bendin asked calmly.

"That you have slaughtered hundreds of thousands of innocent people in Center Section. That you are a murderer, a Hidiadion, even the incarnation of Pikuk himself. They say you have a demon dog that flies with you, you have declared war on the Vaelift, our country, and seek to overthrow the Queen!"

"Those are lies, Harmon," Quip barked. "I am not a dog!" Bendin thought Quip was being ironic on purpose.

"It talks?" Harmon squeaked out.

"Of course I talk, what do I look like? A normal, stupid, lazy, insidious fox to you?"

"I'm not even supposed to be talking with you right now, in fact," Harmon said nervously backing up a few steps.

"I'm not Pikuk. I didn't slaughter anyone at the Center Section, although I was there and saw how we," Bendin pointed at her and him, "are raised. Quip isn't a demon. He obviously isn't a dog, and he's my best friend. I did not declare war on the Vaelift, nor do I want to overthrow the Queen. Did I forget anything?"

"But why, Bendin, why? Why do you lie?" Harmon said taking a step backwards, "If what you are saying is true, which I don't think it is; why are these things said about you?"

"Because they're hiding the fact that their entire organization is false. I mean I don't know what happened to the Vaelift we were taught about, but I'm getting strong hints that the Vaelift here we know and love, might not actually be real Vaelift."

Quip spun around in the air and faced Bendin. "Fakes?"

"What other answer is there? How else can you describe how none of them have ever been seen in Makarias?"

Harmon's eyes lit up for the first time since they had been standing there. "You know about Makarias too? The Queen has been telling us all about Makarias and that we as a nation are striving to go to Makarias."

"What did she say exactly?" Bendin asked half out of disbelief, half out of pure surprise.

"She said that we were once blessed with a whole other world, and it was taken from us and sealed up against us by Pikuk and the evil forces of the Alcs. We are currently fighting the Alcs and we are fighting against the incarnation of Pikuk himself, which I am told is you. She studied them and focused on him closely. "I believe them."

Harmon took a step closer. "How could you betray us?" Harmon pulled a gun out of her holster and leveled it at Bendin. "I'm sorry, Bendin. I've been ordered to do this. Goodbye."

"You're really going to shoot me? But, I missed you and we came all this way for you."

"Then that makes this even more sad." She cried, closed her eyes, and pulled the trigger. Debris and chips of stone blew out of the wall harmlessly behind Bendin.

Harmon opened her eyes and was shocked to see Bendin still standing. She unloaded all the bullets at Bendin. Each one redirected harmlessly into the wall behind him. With each missed shot, Harmon grew increasingly more nervous. The wall splattered into more flak and flakes, and they bounced around Bendin and landed in his hair.

"Are you finished yet?" Quip said fairly annoyed.

"What are you?" Harmon demanded holstering her gun. "You have one chance to explain why I can't hit you because that's pretty convincing that you are indeed Pikuk."

"Wait!" Quip interjected. He turned Bendin. "I don't know who Pikuk is. Who's Pikuk?"

"He's *supposedly* the dark spirit of the world, opposite that of Odge. I don't know if he really exists," Bendin muttered quickly to Quip. He turned to Harmon who was backing away at a slightly faster pace. Her expression compressed into a mixture of confusion, hurt, and hatred.

"Don't worry about it. It's not magic. It's technology which, if I remember correctly, still interests you?" Bendin said quickly.

Harmon nodded, stopped, and waited.

"These," Bendin pointed to the bands that were on his head and arms and belt, "bend the path of things that travel fast around me. At least, that is how I understand it. It's never been fully explained to me. I don't even know how I can hear you if that's entirely true. I only know one thing, our history here is incorrect. What are you doing here?"

"Trying to open the gate. Marshall Davis keeps coming by and checking everything himself. He's invested in the greatest scientists in the kingdom to help me. In fact, there will be quite a bit of people here in just a minute to take you down. Marshall Davis assures me that if we can't get this gate to work, we'll keep trying all of them till we figure it out. The Queen is really determined."

"Harmon," Bendin intensely whispered taking a step forward. "You need to listen to me. You were right about Odge, and the method you showed me is true. Take this question to him and he can help you realize the truth, 'Is Bendin the true leader of the Vaelift?'" Harmon's expression was grim, but Bendin saw a faint flicker of recognition in her eyes. She knew what Bendin was referring to because she shook her head in the affirmative.

"Will you ask?"

"Yes," She whispered.

"Do it. I promise success. We will be watching," Bendin said as the entire room shook and hundreds of Vaelift Elect, Angels and Odge's Vaelift ran into the room. They surrounded Bendin and Quip but seemed to be waiting for something.

"Friends, fellow Vaelift, we don't need to fight." Bendin twirled his Vurfenstaff in a mock demonstration. "We just need to dance the dance."

Bendin and Quip waved to them and vifted in front of their disbelieving eyes.

Bendin immediately switched his vision and watched all of them get pummeled by the concussion waves.

"Now we follow Harmon around?" Quip asked, "She didn't seem all too interested in what we had to say."

"She's crushed. Why else would she say all those things and shoot at me? Something, maybe even . . . someone. Maybe Marshall Davis? I've heard he's a smooth talker. That's why I'm hoping she will go to Odge. Odge's influence is stronger than Zadok's, so Odge is going to be able to have greater sway on her than him. I hope."

"I really don't know what you just said, but I'm just going to say, 'sure'." Quip smiled.

They watched the group disband and a moderately tall gentleman with Castle Marshal ranks appear at the end of the line. He approached Harmon and placed an arm on her shoulder. He gazed at her tenderly before turning away from Bendin and Quip. He said some words to Harmon that Bendin couldn't see."

"I'll bet that's Marshall Davis." Bendin pointed to the gentleman.

"Bendin, sometimes I just can't figure out how you know these things," Quip rambled sarcastically.

~ 286 ~

Harmon confirmed it was Marshall Davis when she mouthed his name and left.

The second she did Bendin watched Marshall Davis scowl at the room full of trampled machinery. Davis pounded the wall in fury, recomposed himself, and marched off down the hall.

"I'll follow her. You stay on Davis," Bendin said quickly to Quip.

"Ok!" Quip said letting his voice trail off as he left, "the fox is a spy; the fox is a spy; the fox is a spy!"

Bendin caught up with Harmon who was walking in the halls. She was meditating or simply absent minded, because she kept bumping into people. Bendin was amazed, again, at how perfectly fit the halls in the temple in both Makarias and Toalt were designed. They were aligned, completely accurate in their measurements, and it was if his two separate visions were one. Sometimes he'd forget that he was looking at two different places and try to dodge people even though there was no one at his end. They certainly weren't the same n color or content as one side was completely lived in and the other entirely dark and deserted. Occasionally he'd see an opening that was in Toalt and not in Makarias, and sometimes the other way around. These entrances and exits could be where the Vaelift might be hiding things, but he'd have to check them out later. The real trick was that the lighting was in Toalt. He had to trust almost completely in the Toalt side. The only light he got in Makarias was from that shaft of light he had seen earlier.

Harmon entered a room, that Bendin determined to be hers, and she flopped herself down on the lower bunk of the bunk beds. Bendin saw that the room was exactly the same as the ones in his home temple without the least variation. After a while, she sat down and began to do the ritual motions of the prayers that Bendin used to do as a Vaelift in the upper temple. After a few minutes though she stopped, simply held her arms out, and cried. She calmed down and then prayed differently. She spoke her own words. Bendin could tell she was trying out her own experiment. About five minutes of her praying on her own she asked the question that Bendin had asked her to ask. She paused and listened for another five minutes. Bendin smiled as Harmon burst into a smile and cried even harder. This time it was for a different reason and as soon as she had done this she fell over asleep. Bendin vifted into the room. Surprisingly she didn't wake up.

Bendin placed one hand gently on her shoulder and

called her name, "Harmon."

Harmon opened her eyes. "How'd you get in here?" She paused and then said, "I tried my method and it worked! I feel so happy inside. I almost can't believe it but you really are the head of the Vaelift." Bendin held her in his arms to which she shifted her body around and clasped him in a hug. She smeared him with her tears and smothered his face with kisses of gratitude. She held him there for a minute more.

"I missed you so much," She said excitedly. "What now? What am I supposed to do?"

"I need your help. I need you to stay on the project you are dedicated to and try to keep them busy with the gates. If by some chance the gate project succeeds, you need to break it so that it doesn't work. The people of Makarias are counting on you to keep the Queen from trampling their world."

Harmon looked at him seriously, "Bendin, I don't know if I can do that. I mean, I can try. They are very determined to pry open the gates. The queen keeps announcing, 'It's time. We have to get over there.' So you can see that it's paramount that we get it open. I am going to give you a warning, be very careful what you bring here from Makarias. Queen Vlasta hoards technology."

"Hoards?" Bendin hadn't heard of this from anyone anywhere in anyway.

"Yes, for herself. Haven't you noticed that we haven't had any major advances in science or technology for over seventeen hundred years? Piku-- er, something stops anything that doesn't give the Monarchy power by either destroying it or keeping it for themselves."

"Well, now that you say it that way," Bendin marveled, "no, I haven't noticed. Where is Findall Quin and the other Vaelift?"

"They are almost always fighting the Alcs. They are the elite group of fighters. The troops really have their hands full and Odge's Vaelift are usually the ones that turn the tide of the battles. The group of outsiders have put up a real resistance. They don't tell trainees much of anything in the temples, only to those of us whom they trust. Is Makarias really another world?" Harmon asked eagerly.

Bendin showed her his black watch and his silver watch. The red colored Toalt display read, "14:56". The blue colored Makarias display read, "11:09".

"No way!" Harmon gawked at the differing times.

"See what time it is there right now? See how the clocks move at a different rate? I can only assume then, that they are coming from two completely different rotation speeds. Two different completely unique worlds."

"Wow. I hope you can take me there sometime." Harmon pulled at Bendin longingly, "I missed you, Bendin," she said again. Harmon pulled him closer. "They sent me away just as I was getting to know you. When they told me all the horrible things you had done, I thought you were truly gone forever."

Bendin felt slightly uncomfortable and didn't know exactly what to say about it. "Thanks, Harmon. Really. I can't believe you still have that." He pointed to her welder that hung around her waist and added, "There may be a way to get you to Makarias, but Odge hasn't shown me how. He has asked me to do some things before I can do anything else. Don't worry about me though. Please teach people to pray correctly with some good questions." Harmon nodded positively and sadly let Bendin go from her grasp. Bendin walked two or three paces away from Harmon, winked, spun his staff, and vifted back to Makarias.

Chapter 19
A Step in the Right Direction

Bendin felt his way back towards the gate muttering to himself about the need of a light. The gate area was full of people once again, he noticed that Marshall Davis was there issuing orders and things. Quip was lying on the ground watching him.

"Did I miss anything?" Bendin asked.

"Just a lot of smooth talking. If you hadn't come back just now, I would have fallen asleep." Quip flew up to Bendin's shoulder and licked him in greeting.

"I think we should check and see if there is a piece in this temple. That's just me, but it's a start I guess," Bendin suggested to Quip.

"We've got plenty of time. Let's look around," Quip responded enthusiastically.

They began at the top, in the halls and towers, and meticulously worked their way down. After feeling like a short time had passed, Bendin glanced at his watch, and to his surprise, they already had been searching for five hours. They hadn't seen anything but students and classrooms in Toalt. No sign of any pieces of the s-weapon.

As they worked their way down, they noticed the students beginning to thin out till they reached the level of the subway. The subway station was the lowest point in the temple both for Toalt and Makarias. The subway system in Toalt was alive and functioning with people going in and out at the scheduled times. The system on Makarias on the other hand was completely dead. The stations were there, but there was no activity. The train tunnels were overgrown and the tracks rusted, broken, and old. Bendin wondered if people could still use the tunnels. They continued searching making about eight hours total. He was about to declare it searched from top to bottom when Quip cried out, "What is that?"

Bendin saw what he was pointing at, there was off to the side past the entrances to the subway system, a small hole in the wall.

"How did you see this?" Bendin asked, paused, and held his arms up. "Never mind, don't answer that."

Quip laughed.

It was solid rock in Makarias, making the hole exclusive to Toalt.

Bendin knelt down and complained, "Well crutches and purple plazas. The only way we are going to be able to tell what's through that hole is if we are over there."

"Let's vift then."

Bendin and Quip vifted over and peeked through the hole in the wall.

"It goes down," Quip said squeezing through the small hole.

Bendin checked Makarias, and he knew instantly that they were not going to be able to vift out. It was completely dark which meant solid stone and death.

"Let's go slowpoke," Quip teased, "If I wanted to hide stuff from the Vaelift, this is what I would do." Bendin took his Vurfenstaff and jabbed the wall with it. The hole in the wall caved in revealing an opening wide enough for him to go through.

They went down a windy staircase that was crudely made. As there was yet again no light, Quip lit and led the way. The staircase ended at an arched doorway which revealed an open chamber. Quip's light reflected off a very large concrete wall.

"What in Odge's great world is this?" Bendin admired the massive wall.

"I have no idea. Let's check it out," Quip said excitedly. Quip blasted off and circled the entire thing in a bright red streak.

"It's a cube, Bendin."

They flew around the cube that filled almost the entire room. There was decent space on the sides and top to get around it. Bendin didn't see anything, but Quip discovered on one side, partway down there was an inscription. "I don't recognize the name so I'll call this person unknown. 'Unknown's Cube. You break it, I break you.'"

Bendin raised his eyebrows. "What is it, some sort of joke?"

"How enlightening." Quip rolled his eyes. "Let's break it, that piece may be inside."

"Yeah, why else would there be a concrete block in here?" Bendin mused.

Quip blew fire at the hewn cube but the fire bounced around harmlessly.

"Quip, I have no idea. Let's hurry so we can get back

and then out of here. I have no idea how to break this thing and I certainly don't want to be caught down here." Bendin hit the concrete block a few times with his staff. "It's definitely solid." His staff hardly dented it.

"I'll bet Harmon could help us," Quip suggested.

"Good call."

They climbed the stairs, vifted to Makarias, and were on their way.

Harmon was sleeping in her bed when they arrived. She woke when they vifted in, and she was happy and surprised to see them. After listening to their problem, she rubbed her eyes and said, "You just need some of the mining machines we use when we need another tunnel. But they are very heavy and awkward machines. It takes ten men to move one. So, moving them is going to be impossible. Arduous and clunky. Pwah!" She gave them the location of where the machines were, and Bendin recognized the description from their exploration of the temple.

"With faith, Harmon, all things are possible." Bendin winked, grinned, and vifted away from her as she suppressed a confused grin. Quip followed right behind him.

They found cute, cube-shaped machines. They were the size of half a tank, and weighed four times as much. Bendin lifted it with hardly any effort at all, thanks to the trick shown to him by Pete.

"Thank you, Pete, for showing us this trick." The next trick was getting it down to the right level without anyone really asking questions why. The majority of people would be sleeping at this hour so the halls should be empty.

Bendin was almost to the final staircase when a couple of students noticed the mining machine.

"How in the world are you moving that? You're going to hurt yourself!" Both moved forward to get a closer look, but as they entered the field their bodies sailed out of control right into the ceiling. Once the field left them, they fell, slammed onto the floor, moaned, and passed out. Bendin thought it was fortunate and funny, till Quip urged, "Bendin, go. They'll wake up soon."

They made it down to the hidden room, and on the top flat center of the room, placed the machine.

"Here we go," Bendin celebrated as he deactivated his field and flicked on the machine. The machine sputtered and whirred to life! BZZZZZZZ. It drilled for what felt like an eternity. To kill time, Bendin asked Quip to describe his childhood and his life in the jungle. Quip described the fun, free life they lived and the hardships of the politics surrounding his extended families. They had wanted to stay out of it, but some wanted them to be in. This eventually led to their destruction. The drilling machine made a groaning noise, threw sparks up out of the hole, sputtered, and died.

"You killed it, Quip!"

"Did not. I think it hit something!?" Quip said blasting himself to the hole.

"What?"

They peered into the smoking hole and Bendin activated his field. He skated down to the smoking machine and gripped the sides lifting it out. He placed the now broken smoking machine on the surface next to him. "Whatever it hit, it couldn't drill through it. Check out that drill!" The drill on the machine was now the equivalent of shredded paper.

Bendin cast his eyes over to the large bored hole. "What's down there? Blow some fire down into it and see."

Quip blew fire down into the hole, and Bendin saw with joy at the bottom a flicker of reflected light from a semi-transparent object.

"We got lucky!"

"Was it really luck though?" Quip eyed Bendin. "More and more I feel like we are on a track."

"Kinda."

Bendin skated down into the opening and found a small hollowed space inside the large hewn cube. They were lucky the hole that they had drilled was big enough to pull the piece out. Once they got it out, they studied it. It was sizeable, shaped like a "K", and had two ends that you could attach to something else.

"I can't believe we found one," Quip hooted. "We are not going to be able to vift that are we? It's huge!"

Bendin shook his head. "I have a bad feeling they all may be like that. What do we do with it?"

"Get it to Makarias."

Bendin stopped and pondered, then meditated for a minute thinking about what Quip just said. "Get it to Makarias, how?"

Quip copied Bendin's motions. "We are going to have to take it out the gate then." Quip stamped his paws down onto the block.

Bendin frowned. "I don't know. We know Marshall Davis was at the gate, and I don't know how to open it. We don't want to risk them finding out about our efforts. Who knows what they will do when they discover what we are up to."

"Wait, maybe you don't have to open it. Remember, you only have to touch it and vift with objects that will fit through! I say we sneak out of here."

"Perhaps . . . you are right. Maybe you could just smokescreen us out if we do run into something."

"But of course!"

Bendin carried the large awkward piece in one hand and held his staff in the other. They did their best to rebuild the broken entrance, but Bendin knew that it wasn't ever going to be the same. Even a semi-close inspection would reveal that someone had tampered with the opening and been inside.

The lights went out around them.

"Odd," Bendin whispered. "This thing kind of glows."

They traveled up one level with no problem except the lights going out as they continued. Quip asked, "Bendin?"

Bendin looked behind them and swung his Vurfenstaff to ward off a man-sized black snake.

"Snakes!" Quip observed.

One clean cut later, sparks flew out of it sending metal chunks everywhere.

"Mechanical snakes!" Quip shouted.

The broken snake pulled the sparks and metal in with a loud swoosh. Immediately the alarms sounded.

"Snooping mechanical snakes!" Quip roared. "Let's get out of here!"

"I've never seen that before in my life!" Bendin whined.

The snakes poured in from all lower halls and pursued after them. Bendin freaked out and skated as fast as he could towards the gate room. He knocked so many people over he lost count after a while. Quip kept up with him just fine filling the whole area with smoke and the lights going out as they went along actually proved useful. Bendin wished Makarias was lit so he could use that layout. Unfortunately, he was blind on both sides now. Quip counseled, "Hide it behind your back as best you can, and I'll distract them as you go through the gate. No one should notice because of my superior smokescreen."

They burst through the entrance to the gate room, the power going out in the room, and the people and snakes falling behind. Marshall Davis didn't have a chance to do hardly anything but draw his gun and shoot blindly into the large thick smoke that filled the entire room. All the scientists screamed, and fired rounds into the cloud as well. This worked until Quip zipped up to them individually and caught them on fire. They frantically toppled machinery, ran pell-mel into each other, the walls, and out of the room. Quip shot around Marshall Davis in a blazing fireball of light. Bendin skated straight at the gate, placed his hand up against the solid interior, and vifted with a loud crack. Quip vifted right in front of Marshall Davis with the same light, sound, and ripple.

"Do you think he saw the piece? Bendin asked Quip as they reunited on the other side.

"Look at him. I know he saw me! I don't think he saw the piece at all." Quip smiled happily. The thought made Bendin happy too. The less they knew what they were up to the better.

The power came back on in flickers. Bendin watched Marshall Davis rise, yell at the eng neers, and point at the gate again. Bendin rubbed his ear. "He sure has them up working very late into the morning. It's already four and they are still working."

"Or they are running shifts," Quip suggested.

"Still, it's not very Vaelift-like to have them up at awful hours. I don't like those snakes."

Quip shrugged, relaxed, and threw himself onto Bendin's shoulders. Bendin rubbed the top of Quip's head for a second before he asked, "What do we do with this thing?" Bendin realized not only was it semi-transparent, but it was slightly luminescent too.

"Take it somewhere where it will be safe, of course," Quip reasoned sticking his tongue far out of his mouth. "I'm sure Xenon knows of such a thing."

"I'm not so sure that we really should tell anyone about this, especially people in the tribunal." Bendin sighed. "They were really uptight about us already. We'l tell them once we've finished the work."

"Then let's not worry about it and take it back to the Coils."

They skated back to the center bubble and tried not to attract any attention to themselves. Aside from the power in any room they entered going out, it went rather well. They found Xala in one of the rooms dedicated to monitoring those who had been sectioned off; people that had caught the deadly Bulsion plague.

"How's it coming?" Bendin asked her, fearful to step into the room.

"There were thirty-five new episodes today." She hung her head down sadly, but she didn't turn around. "All complete disasters. We lost a whole group of families east of here. That one in particular is quite the catastrophe."

A screen popped up in front of her displaying a worried mother holding a child, "I think my husband has it. He's been suddenly feeling like he's floating on water."

"Tell him to get out of the house immediately!" Xala screamed, "He's about to explode!"

Bendin watched in horror as the woman screamed for her husband to get out of the house. A man appeared in the background and ran for the door. As he left the door, they saw his entire body erupt in a brilliant fireball of flames. The explosion blasted the door off its hinges leaving a gaping hole in the side of the house. After only a few seconds of intense heat, nothing remained but a small pile of ash. The monitor flickered off.

"That would make it thirty-six." Xala sighed. "I hope we can find a cure soon. If not a cure, then a better detection system."

"How do you know if you have the plague? How do you get it?" Bendin wondered.

"You don't know if you have it. You just have to hope you don't have it," Xala said irritably. "It's spread through person to person contact. We have to come to believe that it survives on organic surfaces. Which is why, all those who have been found to have it have been sectioned off and monitored. We've lost so many, and we are desperately trying to save the rest."

"Scary," Quip said, "I can't imagine burning unnaturally."

Bendin would have thought that to be funny coming from him, but the situation didn't allow him to smile. "We need a ride back to the Coils. Can you or someone else help us out?"

Xala turned around in her chair for the first time. "Well. Hmm. Are you coming in?"

"No."

Xala nodded, and proceeded to yell a lot of gibberish into a large panel on the desk in front of her. The desk was flat, angled, and had hundreds of buttons of all shapes and sizes on it. There were switches, levers, lights, sockets, bolts, touch sensors, keyboards, communicators that Bendin had no idea what they were, and several special variations of the crystal displays all over the room. The area was swimming in data.

"Seriously, Bendin, we need our own ride," Quip whispered in Bendin's ear.

"I'll take you there myself," Xala announced confidently after her gibberish ended. "Don't trust anyone, Bendin."

"Just like that?" Bendin asked. "What about your friends? What about all the infected pe--"

"Just like that." Xala smiled tapped his shoulder and spotted the luminescent piece.

"Oh, what's that?"

"It's part of my collection. Nothing big." Bendin shrugged.

Quip gave Bendin an immediate look of "I can't believe you just did that but I'll allow you to do that anyway" before shrugging as well.

"Come on. You don't expect me to stay at work all day right? My shift ended the moment you got here."

Bendin didn't know if that meant that her shift ended because he came here, or if it really was the end of her shift till a moment later.

Another girl that was probably the same age as Xala arrived and sat immediately in the chair Xala had been sitting in. She didn't even notice Bendin at all. Bendin took this lack of notice cheerfully and followed Xala down the hall.

"Thanks!" Xala said to the girl as they left.

"No problem, have a safe trip guys." The girl waved absently as they left, putting headphones on, typing frantically, pulling up displays, and operating communication links.

"We're going to take my father's cart."

"Cart?" Quip nudged Bendin in the shoulder with his paw.

Xala didn't say anything as she led them to a different part of the structure that had darker stained glass than the exterior.

"Here," She said when they arrived. She opened a dark, brown door, and inside a small room was a large cart that filled the entire space. It seated comfortably up to three people. It was identical in shape with a mining cart, but it had a driving cockpit attached to the front. "We use these in the mines. You have to move earth somehow, and this has been a method of transport for years. Recently we've begun to use pipes, so, it's kind of a mix."

Bendin noticed where there would have been wheels in Toalt, there were blades instead.

"Get in, get in, get in. Don't worry it's completely mechanical and organically powered. Completely safe. We don't have all night. This thing isn't as fast as some of the fancy models. *Dad*," She muttered shaking her head in frustration.

To Bendin's enjoyment, the cart rotated ninety-degrees,

so they were facing down, and it shot off with a blast. They traveled directly down out the bottom of the glass structure through an exit made of spiral retracting glass doors.

"We get special parking privileges." She beamed.

"That you do," Quip agreed.

Bendin noticed that most vehicles were parked out in front of houses in the air. He imagined there would be a similar parking area like in Hymingway, but he wasn't sure.

The trip to the Coil's home was mostly Xala talking about the problems of Bulsion and the efforts to cure it. He thought she sounded much like Rachel in her concern and intensity of focus on finding a solution to the problem. There were bits of interest in Airlarky thrown in and some small talk about the most recent news from the tribunal about what to do now that a Vaelift was in the world once again. The stars shown in the dark sky, and Bendin noticed that she tended to fly higher than the Coil's did. The moons felt much closer than the last time he saw them.

She dropped them off at the Coil's docking bay. Bendin and Quip gave her their thanks as she waved, fired up her cart, and flew back towards her home.

Bendin and Quip both went up to their room and fell asleep. It had been such a busy day, and they needed rest.

Quip woke Bendin and whispered cautiously, "They are out of their room. They sound like they are *up* to something."

"Who?" Bendin whispered back.

"Ryan and Pete, of course." Quip had his eyebrows raised, lit from a faint flame on top of Quip's hair.

"Let's go see what they are up to."

As Bendin left the room, he accidentally bumped right into Pete knocking him into a somersault in the air. Pete stifled his laugh with a clasped hand over his mouth.

"Shhh!" Ryan hushed him. They were fully dressed and ready for the day, headbands and all.

"Hi Bendin, Quip. Please be quiet. We have something we *have* to do," Pete whispered.

"We've been waiting for it for weeks now. She is finally tired enough and it's *raining*." Ryan grinned and giggled mischievously.

Bendin wondered what in the world that could mean and realized for the first time since he'd been here that it was raining hard outside.

"It's going to be so good. Come, see, but be very quiet,"

Pete said waving them to come. Pete and Ryan skated so slowly, that they only had a faint glow come off their skates as they skated up towards a room near the ceiling. Bendin took the opportunity to quickly grab his bands and boots, as he thought there might be a good reason that they were fully dressed. By the time he was dressed and ready, they were up to the door that was on the wall up near the ceiling. Bendin didn't skate at all, he just pushed off of the ground and floated up to them. Using the resistance from the wrist cuffs, he was able to swing himself around in the air to land softly on the ceiling above them next to the door.

"Nice," Pete whispered.

"Wish I had thought of that," Ryan muttered. "You're getting better, Bendin."

They carefully, silently pushed open the door. Even though the room was dark, Bendin could see a very nicely kept room. There was a nice long flat window on one side with a bed. The other side was semi-circular and it had shelves and a bed under them. He noticed that Starley was sleeping under the shelves and Rachel was on the other side of the room. Pete and Ryan moved stealthily. Before he knew exactly what was going to happen, they switched on their silver boxes, opened the window, picked up Rachel with hardly any effort, and pushed her body out the window. Rachel woke once the rain pelted her face, but by then it was too late.

"Help! I can't do anything! Pete! Ryan!" She screamed in fear. She drifted uncontrollably away at first from the force of their push but picked up speed quickly driven by a powerful wind.

Pete and Ryan were laughing so hard they fell to the floor holding their sides. Starley woke up and watched her brothers laughing on the floor.

"What's going on?" Starley asked seeing Quip laughing as well.

Bendin dropped his Vurfenstaff and threw himself out the open window and skated out to find Rachel. Quip followed keeping a constant light forward in a cone. Bendin was elated as the rain pelted down around him, but did not touch him because of the bands. It formed an ellipse of dry air around him. He skated further in the direction that Rachel had been moving searching for her. There was something in the distance. Could it be her? A flash of light snaked across the sky and they saw her flailing helplessly in the air over the jungle. She was rapidly approaching the edge of the gravity field; the place where the trees grew differently. He skated with all his might and caught her just after she began to fall to the jungle floor.

"Bendin . . . " Rachel managed to say, looking up at him. "Thanks."

Quip smiled at Rachel, then to Bendin, and remained close. Bendin skated towards the window holding her as close to him as he could. She was completely soaked and now that he was holding her, the water began to seep into his clothes. Her hair was thick with water, and she was shivering.

"Don't worry. I've got you now . . . you're icy cold. I'll get you inside." Bendin made it to the window and carefully set her in. "Quip, heat this place up."

Quip hovered in the air and burst into a full ball of controlled flame. Rachel, with a blanket over her, held her hands over Quip in an effort to warm them. Pete and Ryan had disappeared, and Starley was at the window with her hands still pressed up against them. She turned and watched them with her pretty eyes. "I knew you'd come back with her!"

"Thanks, guys. I got it from here. They are just pranksters," Rachel said after a minute.

"You're sure you're okay?" Bendin asked. "They just chucked you out a window in a storm in the cold in a careless act inconsiderate insensible in . . ."

"Seriously, this is nothing. I didn't get harmed in this one."

"You almost fell to your death!" Bendin pointed out frantically.

"Almost, but you saved me." Rachel threw her arms around Bendin, hugged him, and kissed his face. "Thank you."

"No problem. I just felt sorry for you. What they did would have been funny if it wasn't so dangerous."

"Unforgettable for sure. Yeah, I need to change out of these clothes. It's just they have injured others before . . . accidental of course." She waved Quip and Bendin out of her room.

"Hold on," Bendin said suddenly coming up with an idea and picking up his Vurfenstaff. "Starley, I need your help really quick."

Quip quizzically blinked his eyes before zipping to Bendin's shoulder.

"Yes?" Starley came over to the door and Bendin motioned for her to follow them.

They went down to their small room and Bendin handed

Starley the piece they had brought from Toalt.

"I want you to hide this. This thing is pretty much indestructible so put it in a place that no one will easily find it."

Starley smiled, nodded her head in a dramatic motion, took the piece, laughed and skated out of the room.

Bendin smiled as he heard the power go out and back on again from one room to the next as Starley went through the house.

"Are you sure that's a good idea, Bendin?" Quip asked.

"I don't want us to know where it is. We can say honestly we don't know where it is."

"Ah." Quip raised an eyebrow before letting his tongue roll out of his mouth in a yawn.

Bendin and Quip went further into their room.

"Quip?"

"Yes?"

"Thanks for being there."

"Sure."

"It means very much to me." Bendin smiled as he snuggled into his covers and fell asleep again. They were tired enough that they didn't even take any of their gear off.

There was a soft rap at the door of their comfortable room. "Bendin?"

"Yes?"

"I need you."

"It's Mez," Quip whispered.

"Sure. Sure. Let me get up." Bendin pulled open the door and saw, in the low light of pre-dawn, a fully dressed and geared up Mez. "You're talking to me? What . . . how can I help?"

Quip watched thoughtfully from Bendin's shoulder as Mez forced a one-sided grin.

"I don't like talking," he gruffly replied, "but I trust you and made this effort."

Bendin nodded.

"I've found the criminal. The special in Thibracketory led me to him. Will you help capture him?"

"Why do you need us?" Bendin asked.

"Time too short for others. You're talented. My effort produced nothing. I need you. I will pay."

"A percent?" Quip asked.

Mez's grin became more pronounced.

"Sixty forty of month's wage?"

"Sixty for us?" Bendin smiled.

Mez nodded affirmatively.

"I might be willing to help. Quip?" Bendin smiled.

"Sure, it might be fun. You do what you want."

Bendin and Quip quickly got ready and followed Mez out into the Jungle as the first bluish rays of light were breaking over the horizon. Mez communicated through hand motions and signals keeping low, fast, and moving skillfully through the shadows with precision. Bendin and Quip kept as close as they possibly could. Quip landed on Bendin's shoulder and whispered in his ear, "This area has had a lot of people traffic recently."

Mez kept changing directions, checking gadgets on his arm, and checking the trees from time to time. After a few more minutes Mez stopped and pointed ahead into the foliage.

"All sensors deactivated. Entrance there. Quiet or we might lose."

Bendin moved the foliage aside with his Vurfenstaff and his fingers touched something solid. Instantly a bright yellow flash of light filled the area. Bendin yelped, skated backwards, and flicked his hands as if trying to shake off something.

Mez chuckled and put a finger to his lips. He spoke quietly and quickly, "Only one entrance, and it's intricate. Took me forever to find. Observe." Mez approached the rock face behind the foliage and pulled out a small cylinder that seemed like a metal pencil. As he waved it over the face of the slab, the rock shifted and formed into a varied height grid of thousands of square shaped pillars replicating the surface. "A Hypasaptic lock. Over seven tredecillion combinations. Only one is right."

"Whoa," Bendin marveled.

"What can we do?" Quip twirled his tail fire streaming off with each rotation.

"Check from Toalt," Mez said grimly. "The shock barrier is embedded into the entire rock face."

Bendin rubbed his chin. "Sounds really handy if the whole place is surrounded by stone."

Mez nodded. "Please . . . help."

"Mez, we make a lot of noise when we vift. That isn't going to work if you don't want to alert everyone inside," Bendin reminded him.

"There has to be another way in," Quip gazed around, "for air." Quip shot upwards leaving behind a smoky outline of his grin and the shape of his body.

Bendin watched Mez raise his eyebrows and speedily

skate after him. Bendin trailed behind the two till Quip shifted off to the right and down behind a large outcropping of rocks in a small overhang in the rock face.

"Here," he whispered once Bendin had caught up.

Quip pointed at a rock. Bendin could see nothing special. Mez shook his head and frowned.

"Smells good. I can get in here. I'll open it up from the other side." Quip poked his head at the rock, crawled right into it, and with a flash of light he was gone.

"How is that an entrance?" Bendin wondered aloud.

"Vent. Rock projection deception," Mez huffed curtly. "Evil. Redemption. Gods mock me."

Before Bendin could ask what that meant, several slow beeps came from an item on Mez's gear.

"Confuddlepud. Stick with me." Mez motioned swiftly for Bendin to follow him. Bendin gripped his Vurfenstaff tightly and followed Mez. Mez skated swiftly downwards darting from tree to tree. Bendin mirrored his motions being careful not to make too much noise. Mez halted next to a tree so big it had to have a trunk as thick as a Josiah's pod. The beeps slowly quickened, till at once, they stopped entirely.

"Big group. Be fast. Use tree and Coilgun."

"Coilgun?"

Mez patted the gun at his belt that shot the cable.

"When is t--"

Mez stopped Bendin from saying anything else by holding up his arm in a fist. He started mumbling numbers and he motioned for Bendin to deactivate his silver box.

"70, 71, 70 . . . got to be perfect 71, now!"

Mez single-handedly sliced through the massive trunk while simultaneously deactivating his own silver box. Bendin watched the tree swing around as if it was orbiting a fixed point as a loud buzzing filled the air. A metallic vehicle burst through the trees at the exact same time the tree's rotation was just parallel to the vehicles speed and direction. Mez clicked another button and the tree imploded, wrapped its trunks through the vehicle, and exploded. Hot bits of tree, bark, leaves, wood, metal, and people flew in every direction.

Bendin slowed his breathing as the explosive energy died down. The silence only lasted for a few moments till the surviving people came back from every direction dressed similarly to Mez. Bendin crouched in the air in a defensive position while Mez curled around and pushed his back up against Bendin.

"All escaped criminals. Keep your stuff on. We got most of them," Mez whispered. "Nullify the rest."

"A Roam Keeper. And a V. . . whatever that is. Kill them!" One of the figures shouted.

Mez fired his gun immediately at the closest person to him. The gun shot a cable out at extreme velocity and the second it hit the area of being redirected it split into four cables and traveled in four directions around the person. The four cables clasped together when they met at the other side and the whole line constricted, binding the person. Mez yanked the person in and knocked him out.

Two others skated at Bendin carrying thick poles. Bendin knocked a pole out of their hands with a swift crack, while the other grabbed Bendin's Vurfenstaff. An electric shock blasted the other away while Mez spiraled around Bendin swinging a long crooked blade. One of the men shot and bound Mez with a Coilgun while Mez attempted to grab the tree cutter on his belt. The man yanked Mez toward him as Bendin swooped over and knocked the man out with a quick smack from his Vurfenstaff.

The next guy didn't even have a chance as Mez knocked him out in a blinding blur. Bendin could only see two left over, and both of them held out Coilguns. Before either of them could fire, the rock face behind them contorted, grew red hot, and erupted totally engulfing the two men in hot liquid stone fragments.

"Party!" Quip shouted standing defiantly in the outline of the newly created hole.

"Quip!" Bendin shouted skating up to him.

"Here I was sneaking safely around when *everything* went on alert. It's an acidic hornet's nest in there." Quip shuddered and launched himself onto Bendin's shoulder.

"After you, Mez," Quip ordered pointing down the hole. He then noticed the tremendous amounts of debris, wreckage, bodies, and tree chunks and scolded, "Dear me. What happened? You guys left quite a mess."

"All him." Mez pointed at Bendin and skated through the opening.

"But . . ." Bendin held up his hands in futility.

Quip laughed. "You should see what I did." Quip winked at Bendin.

The entire ground and rock face next to them shook vibrating the trees around them.

"What did you do?" Bendin asked skating down into Quip's hole.

"Wasn't me." Quip shrugged.

Bendin didn't have to say much else. The entrance opened into a complex weave of tunnels and rooms. They saw steam, smoke, holes, and smoking crevices splattered everywhere. It was more of a mess down here than up there. But, strangely, more so through the biggest tunnel that sloped downwards in front of them. "I'm guessing that is the way we need to go."

"Yup." Quip quivered.

Following Mez was easy. All they had to do was follow the trail of splatter and dents in the walls.

"These people. Who were they?" Bendin asked as they past more bodies of men and women strewn along the ground.

"Part of the mess we've stirred up. I'm not sure exactly. Most people I saw were already dead." Quip held more tightly to Bendin as they rounded the corner ahead.

Mez was struggling with a very large swarm of tiny hornets. The hornets would fly in taunting him and would back out of his range in time to shoot acid at him. Even though the acid would redirect around Mez, he visibly didn't take any chances. Mez skated over the swarm with expert speed and pulled a different flat metal rod from his belt. An electric cone rippled from the end of the rod and zapped the hornets in a chain. Quip relaxed and jumped into the air excitedly, his flame flickering. Mez saw them coming and waved them over. He was breathing hard, holding one of his legs, and his other arm had burn marks up the side.

"Acid Hornets. Finally caught them. Now, next room." Mez paused pocketing the rod. "He's still here. Stop him!" Before they could say anything else, Mez pulled out his Coilgun and skated at a decent pace around the corner. Bendin glanced at Quip for a second and smiled. Quip lit his arm on fire in response and pointed ahead.

They followed Mez into a cavernous room that held machines, power generators, all forms of limiters, and an elevated platform with people dressed like Mez on it. One of them wore a dark, tall, flat-topped hat that yelled orders to people around him. All of them were frantically grabbing things as fast as they could and shoving them into a tremendously sized rocket. The man with the tall hat noticed them and shouted indignantly, "Mezika Dogadon Coil. Congratulations on finding me. However, this is goodbye." He turned without another word, got into the rocket with everyone else, and the door slammed with a shocking thud.

"Siatcho!" Mez yelled. In a blur, He shot and used every item at his disposal at the rocket. The rocket stood stalwart as the entire section behind the rocket rumpled and fragmented.

The rocket shook and steam poured out of the large exhaust. Mez howled in frustration, pulled out a small stick that transformed into his crooked blade, and skated as fast as he could at the door to the rocket. Just as he got to it he felt his entire body redirect around the rocket in a spectacular failure. His own bands redirected his movement against the wall with such speed that Mez shot off uncontrollably back around to Bendin before he managed to regain control. Mez turned to Bendin and Quip and said passionately, "Please, please, help! Stop him!" Mez skated towards the large exhaust with a fierce look of determination outlining the features of his face.

"Follow my lead, Quip," Bendin quickly shouted as he skated forward. He checked Toalt really fast and was surprised when he saw a massive body of water stretching out in front of him. Bendin vifted with Quip following immediately after. Bendin and Quip blinked and heard the sounds of large booms over the body of water. Bendin checked in Makarias again, found the room with Siatcho, and positioned himself to vift near the ceiling of the room. He watched Quip emulate him and they both nodded.

Bendin vifted into the room and startled everyone in the rocket. Bendin quickly knocked out every strapped in passenger while Quip blasted the door with a steady stream of fire.

"Hurry, Quip, the rocket is about to launch," Bendin urged as the entire rocket began to beep and whistle.

Quip's flame stream increased, got brighter, the entire door buckled, and blasted outwards.

"Taaa Daaa!" Quip announced as a voice over the intercom announced the rocket's final initialization was complete.

Bendin frowned at the rocket's announcement. "It's launching now. Quick, Siatcho first, and then the rest!"

Quip burned the belts and Bendin barely got Siatcho out of the rocket before its main engine fired. Quip got clear just as the rocket lifted off and blasted its way out of the room.

Bendin heaved a sigh of relief. "At least we got Siatcho out. Where's Mez?"

They checked by the exhaust hole and there was Mez

lying on the charred floor pounding on the floor with his fists in rage.

"Mez, we got him," Bendin said clearly.

Mez looked up at them with a mixed expression as if the phrase hadn't sunk in. His expression switched from grim and defeated to one with a sense of victory showing on his face. Mez skated up to them with enthusiasm. He speedily disarmed Siatcho and shook him till he woke."

"Mez . . ." Siatcho mumbled.

"Us. Why them?" Mez hissed grumpily. "Betrayer! Murderer!"

"I had to. You ruined *everything* before. I was furious and it was the only way to hurt you. I wanted justice."

"You? . . . Wanted justice? That's what *I* want." Mez, enraged, pulled out his pistol, which shot the hot light, and shot just past Siatcho's ear. He pointed it at Siatcho. "Anything else?"

Siatcho said nothing. He didn't move. He resolutely stiffened his neck and squared his shoulders.

Mez hesitated.

"What did he do?" Bendin asked. "He's not resisting anymore. Why not take him to the tribunal?"

"He killed my family."

Quip perked his ears up.

"Well?" Bendin didn't know what to do or say.

Mez frowned.

Bendin could feel the pressure building in Mez, and he watched his hands twitch.

Mez gripped the pistol more resolutely and fired his pistol into the ground near Siatcho several times. "Justice, right. You're finished."

Mez pulled out of his small pouch the same kind of cuffs that Tilmon had used and bound Siatcho's hands. "Finished. Go." Mez elbowed Siatcho and the group left the room and went back to the Coils.

Chapter 20
Back in the DOOD

The moment they got back, Mez immediately sought out Tilmon and found him on a balcony. Tilmon beamed at his son's accomplishment.

"You've finally done it. Well done."

"No, I failed. They succeeded." Mez guestured to Bendin and Quip.

"Indeed." Tilmon winked at Bendin and nodded to Quip. "Let's go get this done then." He gripped Mez on the shoulder approvingly and moved past him.

"No. Two Keepers coming already, almost here."

"I understand, Mez."

"Thanks." Mez grinned to Bendin as he left with Siatcho.

Tilmon motioned for Bendin and Quip to come inside. "Come, have some breakfast. You've had a busy morning."

Bendin and Quip followed Tilmon to the table on the ceiling. Both were starving now and started eating as soon as Tilmon nodded his head in approval. He hadn't finished yet, but the others had.

"Thank you for helping Mez this morning. It meant a lot to him."

"Sure . . . No problem," Bendin mumbled through his bites.

"It's the least I could do, " Quip responded.

Tilmon's eyes focused seriously on them and he spoke quickly, "Bendin, you need to know that your reception among the tribunal leaders is fine, but there has been a lot of resistance among the various families of Makarias. Our extended family has been stiff in their messages to me. Most of them reject the idea of the Vaelift back in the world.

"They hate me?"

"No, not everyone. The Wycliffs were fine. The only Wycliffs that seemed to disagree with your appearance were those furthest out from their capitol city. The Hydes and Wights were around half. The Finns and Sangas seemed to be fine with the idea of Vaelift again, but as a whole they both reject accepting it as a legitimate organization." Tilmon paused and drank deeply from his glass and watched Bendin to see if he was getting it.

Bendin nodded this time. It was too much too fast for him to really get it all, but he didn't want Tilmon to stop.

Tilmon continued with a bit more concern in the tone of his voice. "For the DeSotos, however, only some of Aspertan's immediate family even believed him. They are entirely against the prospect that you even exist. They do not believe Odge would ever betray them like that."

"Okay." It just sounded a bit odd to Bendin. How was he going to convince people that he was actually here for them, but not of his own volition?

Tilmon continued, "Bendin, you may have to visit these families to convince them that you are indeed a Vaelift, and that you are here for their good. Aspertan is considering sending his son out to see you so he can see for himself. His own son didn't believe him." Tilmon shook his head sadly. "So, what I mean is that you need to be careful. There are people springing up all over that hate you. Some are even angry enough to kill you."

"Thanks for letting me know. That sounds like some very serious hate. What about the Outcasts?" Bendin asked. "And the specials?"

Quip spoke up, "Don't worry about the specials. They really don't care."

"The Outcasts don't care either way." Tilmon smiled. "By the way, they have contacted me though about George. They said they are going to send another person out after hearing about the progress George is making here. For some reason they liked the technology experiences George had described to them, but they didn't care for the book of Odge." Tilmon rubbed his hands together rapidly like someone warming his hands in the cold. "I'm very excited about that prospect."

"That's great!"

"That person should be here someday soon. What's your plan, Bendin? How can I help?" Tilmon asked. "How about the families? What can I tell them to help tame the fires?"

"Just tell them," Bendin cleared his throat instructed, "that if they do not accept the fact that the Vaelift are back and that Odge is serious about this, he's going to physically prove it to them."

"Physical proof is good right?" Tilmon asked.

"Physical proof *is* good, but faith is better as it leads to permanent proof inside you, your mind, and heart." Bendin tapped his chest and his head with his fingers.

"I don't understand that very well. Why is that the case?"

"I don't entirely know either." Bendin laughed. "I just know it's the case. It's like comparing something that is temporary on the outside that decays and falls apart with something that's already inside of you that lasts forever."

Tilmon shook his head, mystified. "I don't understand that either. Anything else?"

Bendin shrugged and focused on saying it as simple as possible, "It's like this. Tell them not to be angry, but to believe. Otherwise they will be forced to acknowledge his hand."

Quip affirmed enthusiastically with his head bobbing up and down and said, "Don't trifle with Odge. Don't force his hand. Got it."

"That was for Tilmon, Quip. Not you." Bendin chuckled.

Tilmon nodded his head in approval. "Now that, I understand."

Tilmon excused himself while Bendin and Quip decided what to do next. They decided to move on to the closest, most likely place they could find a piece, here in Toalt on the other side of the Coil's home.

They went to the waterfall room and Bendin asked, "Where do we start specifically?"

Quip smiled and said, "Let's say the Temples are very similarly designed, people are lazy, and that the secret piece would be at the lowest portion of the Temple again."

"That's an excellent idea, Quip! Wish I'd thought of that. Let's try it."

They had just passed the fork in the cave that split the paths from going to the gate or deeper into the tunnels when they heard a loud scream come from one of the tunnels.

Quip shot off ahead of Bendin in a bright trail of fire. Bendin blinked, coughed, and skated after Quip, trying to clear his throat.

Bendin used his nose to follow Quip's trail once he was completely out of sight. That's when he started to hear a loud beautiful voice of laughter, excitement, and talking. He rounded the corner of the one of the passages and it opened up into Rachel's garden from the far side of the entrance he had used the other times he'd been here.

Rachel was using Quip's fire to heat the bottom of a bowl in a ring she was holding.

"Quip! Rachel! What happened?" Bendin asked immediately.

"This, Bendin. This!" Rachel announced triumphantly; she gleamed as though she had found the most valuable treasure on the entire planet. "This is the cure we've been searching for! I know it!"

Bendin raised his eyebrows.

Rachel placed the bowl off to the side to cool, it was full of a lumpy mesh of plants in a thick sauce.

"It looks disgusting. You are sure about this?" Bendin noted.

"It doesn't matter what it locks like. The Wycliffs will be overjoyed. They are going to conquer one of the worst diseases in history." Rachel pounded the ground in excitement with her boots.

"That's great news," Bendin said calmly. "You're crying?" Rachel smiled as tears of joy slowly formed on her cheeks.

"I've waited for this since I began my research on this two years ago. It's actually done. I'm passing them the formula right now."

"You're passing it just now?" Bendin looked confused.

"Yes. Look behind you." Rachel giggled at the fact that Bendin hadn't noticed.

Bendin turned around and he saw others watching him absently, and knew instantly that the room was networked. He'd just been so worked up that he didn't realize that the sounds coming from the network were identical to the ones he was hearing normally in this room. Even the people that joined in on the network, hadn't said anything till she mentioned them. He didn't even know who had triggered the room to become a network. This one even had limitless walls because Bendin could not see the solid walls of the Coil's cave behind him anymore. Instead he saw the Wycliff's cavernous cliff face, and they were doing research on the edge of a cliff that dropped off. Bendin knew now from experience that he couldn't go and see over the edge. He sure wanted to though.

"What are you passing?" An elderly gentleman asked gently. He seemed just as surprised as Bendin. Bendin guessed that they also didn't know that they had been networked.

"Gas?" The gentleman smiled. "You really ought to give us a second to accept your signal rather than surprising us with a direct link."

"Sorry, but this is urgent. I have the cure!" Rachel explained quickly and displayed the bowl with what Bendin thought was an ugly soup.

At the word, "cure", everyone stopped and turned towards them.

"No way!" Another near the man exclaimed.

"Can't be possible, can it?" A lady said curiously.

"What is the formulation?" The elderly man asked suspiciously.

Rachel proudly gave him a very complicated combination of certain kinds of plants and liquids, that Bendin had never heard of, what proportions to combine them, and what temperature they should be fused together. "Trust me; this will work. You will know it works the moment the person eats and digests a small portion of it because it will flush the system immediately. Be sure no one is wearing any pants either. It creates quite a fireball on the way out. It cleans the system and gets rid of all the converting mechanisms that the disease creates. In essence, it converts, vents, and destroys the disease in one explosive punch."

Quip was smirking, covering his mouth with his paws, and laughing. When he saw Bendin watching him he pointed at a towel that was wrapped around her waist and winked. Quip jumped onto Bendin's shoulders and whispered, "Don't tell Ryan and Pete about the side effects, Bendin. She is going to get them back for the rain incident. It's going to knock their pants off!"

"Wouldn't miss it." Bendin smiled knowingly.

The scientists in the network smiled patiently at each other, "We will try it of course. We will let you know the results. We hope you are right. It shouldn't take long, Rachel. Thank you for your efforts."

The network link closed and the Wycliff portion of the network, their falls, plants, and scientists, and huge drop off faded away.

"We will know in a few hours. It worked here, it *will* work there," Rachel said determinedly. "I can relax now." She carefully spooned a couple morsels of her cure into a small vial. "I'll clip it on my belt when I put on some fresh pants." Rachel winked. "Thanks, Quip, for your help. You arrived at simply the most perfect time." She turned to Bendin and explained, "I was already so close and it was faster to use him than hauling that fat heater over here."

"No problem. Be well." Bendin peered up at Quip. "Quip, let's get back on our hunt." Bendin waved his hands dramatically in the air.

"But of course," Quip said launching himself back into

the air.

Rachel came over and stood directly in front of Bendin and Quip. "I'm worried you guys will perish in hot liquid magma."

Bendin and Quip glanced at each other for a second and laughed.

Rachel looked hurt, as if she considered it a real threat.

"You were being serious?" Bendin raised his eyebrows.

"Of course I was being serious. Why would I joke about that? Do I *look* like Ryan or Pete to you?" Rachel put her hands on her hips and moved them back and forth in a very feminine fashion.

Quip laughed again, thinking her action was funnier than her first statement.

"I don't really know, Rachel. You are welcome to follow us around, but I do have a question. This house, how long has it been here? So far, there seems to be a temple here in Makarias exactly where there is a temple in Toalt. Was there one here at one time? If so, what happened to it?"

Rachel sighed and rubbed her hand on her head for a second before replying, "There was a temple here, but all of it was torn down except the part in the caves. It was done by one of our ancestors who didn't believe the Vaelift would ever come back. He built this house instead, and our fathers have modified it as technology has increased. He has been the only one to dare tear down a temple. He caught an incurable illness right after and died. The perfect connection between his desecration and the illness along with all other desecrations and death made it so no one else has ever touched the other ones. In fact, most are abandoned."

"Where are all the temples exactly?" Quip asked.

Rachel rubbed some of the oils on her hands off on her towel. "Let's see. There was one here at one time, Hymingway, Wycliffs, Finns, Outcasts, . . . DeSotos have one near their city, probably a kilometer north, and you said there was one in Thibracketory.

"The Outcasts have one? Isn't that odd?"

Rachel laughed. "It would be if you didn't know the story behind how they obtained it. It used to be Hyde's temple and gate, but there was a huge volcano next to it."

"Let me guess," Quip said, "It erupted!"

"Yes." Rachel smiled. "It buried everything, and only a handful of survivors made it out alive. They determined that they didn't like living next to something so unpredictable and sought the herds and fields as their home. They've been moving around the plains ever since herding large groups of animals. It's pretty neat, Bendin. You'll have to go sometime and watch them tease their animals into the air and down again."

"But, what about the Outcast's temple now?" Bendin asked.

"Naturally. They dug it all out by hand. It took them *years*. The Bauyostens are a newer and younger group, and not as large as the Outcasts. They've only just recently started talking with anyone. Some people are angry for far too long."

"Thanks for the information, Rachel." Bendin spun to leave the room.

"Good luck, Bendin." Rachel turned to leave as well.

"And Quip?" Quip said, a hurt expression filtering over his face.

Rachel laughed. "Yes, and Quip. Take care of yourself guys. I wouldn't want anything bad to happen to you."

Bendin walked through the far doorway and passed out of Rachel's view. He silently wished her the blessing of Odge, and continued the search for the piece. They roamed around the caves and checked all the rooms. Bendin was surprised to see his likeness posted on every wall in almost every room he checked. It was going to be much harder to get around unnoticed. The high ceilings certainly offered space to skate, but they didn't go everywhere in the temple. Bendin found as they went further down into the caves that they truly were once part of the temple. He found the same inscriptions and characters on the cave walls in Makarias as in Toalt. The halls began to line up perfectly. But even after all this, there were still no sign of any rooms or hidden places on either side.

Bendin checked his watches and they read, "21:54" for Toalt and "16:20" for Makarias. That meant most students would be in bed at this time. After a few more minutes of searching, Bendin found something he had been desperately hoping to find at the lowest level: A solid metal gate in Toalt but the wall in Makarias was solid.

"Do you think this one is it?" Bendin asked.

"It's the best lead we've had so far," Quip answered. "There doesn't seem to be anyone else here either."

"Yeah."

Bendin figured they were again near the subway systems. Maybe it was for a quick exit if the piece ever came under jeopardy. Bendin and Quip vifted in and caused their usual blast of light and rush of sound. They heard a yell in the distance and footsteps echoed off the walls. Bendin skated upwards with Quip clinging to him. Lucky for them the ceiling was just high enough for them to be in the shadows.

A second later, two elect ran in from opposite entrances into the hall. They were wearing the traditional Vaelift uniforms, with the blue crests on their shoulders and both had their pistols drawn.

"Did you hear that?" The one asked the other when they found the room empty.

"Certainly."

"I'm glad you didn't shoot me!"

"I almost did!"

"Do you think it was him?"

"No. One of the Alcs?"

"I hope not. They've been everywhere these days. Sometimes I wish BD3 hadn't left."

"Me too. It's all his fault. Just thinking about all of the mysterious deaths keeps creeping me out."

"Did you see anyone?"

"Not my direction. You?"

"No."

The boys seemed young. They had to have been only in their second year. Yet, they were already an Elect? Strange. There must have been changes made since Bendin was here last.

"This is *so* odd." The student peeked around the corner.

"Still nothing?"

"Nothing. What was that?"

"Nothing. Usually there's a blue ball by now, or something from them. If you and I didn't see anything then no one should be here . . . unless." The boy shook nervously.

"Unless what?"

"Unless it's Pikuk himself."

"You actually believe that stuff?"

"Maybe. Either way, I don't see or hear anything." The boy threw up his arms in frustration. "Let's go check the other end."

They left and Bendin realized he had been holding his breath.

"That went decently," Quip whispered as he darted forward in the air, just enough to stay inside the radius of the negated gravity.

~ 315 ~

"Decently?" Bendin smiled.

Quip frowned and held his head up proudly. "Decently."

Bendin chuckled quietly and they skated down to the metal gate. Bendin tried to open it, but the gate didn't budge.

"Locked. Quip, please heat this lock till it's red hot and I'll hit it."

Quip heated the lock till it was red-hot and Bendin tapped on it with his Vurfenstaff. The gate responded to his tap with austerity.

Quip had other ideas. He intensified the heat till the entire lock disintegrated entirely. He thumped his chest proudly with his paws and beamed at his work.

Bendin smiled and pushed the metal gate open. "Melted the metal . . . unbelievable. You amaze me." Bendin walked down the dark unlit passage.

"Quip versus metal gate lock. Quip wins!" Quip gloated and happily flew up next to Bendin and lit the way. Bendin wasn't too surprised to see Makarias go black. He sighed; no vifting.

The passage curled down slightly to the left and opened into a room below similar in size to the one in the previous temple which held a piece. However, instead of the piece being hidden inside a giant block of concrete, it was shining and shimmering on a pedestal in the middle of the room.

"You don't say," Quip muttered.

Bendin couldn't believe his eyes. It was out in the open. Its shape appeared to be a shimmering section of a gun trigger.

"This is very suspicious. Malicious. Mal-content," Bendin whispered to Quip. It seemed way too easy. "It's really hot in here." Bendin felt sweaty and gripped his staff tighter.

"I feel nothing." Quip shrugged. "Unless you think of something better, I'm just going to go and get it."

Bendin skated behind Quip towards the piece, the only light source in the room. "Take it slow."

"I am," Quip whispered. But, as Quip got near the piece he yelped.

Bendin watched as the fire that normally pulsated around Quip's paw get sucked towards the piece like an invisible hand grabbed the flame and pulled it in. The piece glowed faint red and there was a burst of fire from the back end of Quip as he reacted in surprise. He began flipping in a forward spinning motion, his flames pulled towards the piece.

"Bendin! I can't stop!" Quip shouted in panic.

Bendin skated forward quickly to catch Quip,

uncontrollably somersaulting, but Bendin was too late. Quip smashed right into the piece and sent it flying off of the pedestal.

Immediately a pale, hollow, metallic pang shot out from the pedestal and the entire room echoed a deep thump far below the surface of the room. The piece flew out of the range of the nullified gravity and fell to the floor. It let out a deeper pale, hollow, metallic pang and increased in distance away from them. Quip lit on fire like normal, stopped, and simply sprinted after the piece. Quip caught the piece, sneered at it, and threw it at Bendin. Bendin stuck his Vurfenstaff out and caught the flying piece on the end of the pole. "Airlarky training just paid off!"

Quip gladly came and got on Bendin's shoulders muttering, "I don't like this piece."

The concrete of the room began to bubble.

"What is it now? Oh, you're right. It *is* hot in here." Quip frowned. "That's-"

Bendin turned and watched sadly as hot glowing red liquid flowed down the stairs they had come in. "We're not going to be able to get out that way."

"But, that's the only way out!'

"Figure it out."

"You figure it out."

"I can't think of anything!"

"But you're in charge!"

Bendin couldn't think of anything. The floor buckled and completely dissolved into rising hot magma from below. Bendin skated as far up as he could, but his hands were sweating and his staff fell along with the piece right into the swell of lava below them.

Disappointment surged through Bendin and he threw his arms up in disgust. He sighed, "So much for that idea. How are we going to get out of here Quip? Can you blast a hole in the roof here? Destroy it! Do something . . . Quip?"

Quip was staring below. "Look."

"Wha--" Bendin stopped and stared at what should have been solid rising magma. Instead of it being solid, a decently sized open space had formed. The lava couldn't get within a certain radius of the piece leaving a perfectly shaped circle of nothing but air. The piece glowed bright red and was pulling the light and heat towards it in a ring.

"What's it doing?" Bendin wondered aloud.

"Why complain? That is our ticket out of here." Quip grinned. "I like this piece."

Bendin skated down, picked up the Vurfenstaff and the piece.

"Gaa!" Bendin yelled dropping the piece in surprise.

"Hot?"

"No, Cold!" It was also surprisingly smooth. He grabbed it and began skating towards the stairs. The lava gave way to them and Bendin skated up the stairs back the way they had come in. Once clear of the impressive heat, both he and Quip paused, took several large gulps of air, and rested.

"I don't particularly care to do something like that again," Bendin muttered.

Quip nodded. "I usually like it hot, but not *that* hot."

They took a minute to calm and cool down.

"At least I know where to go." Bendin delicately pulled the piece in close as they both heard a large piercing tone echo to them from the passages.

"That can't be good. Hurry!" Bendin and Quip immediately skated up into the shadows.

Sounds of footsteps from all sides came bouncing to them and Vaelift students came tromping down the upward incline and down the stairs to the lower room. They were led by Commander Zist.

"Move it! Make it snappy. Groups three and five take the side passages. Now!"

There was a great split and various groups went in several directions.

Quip whispered quickly, "What do we do?"

"We sit tight and wait it out," Bendin mused. "After a while they should lose interest and we should be able to sneak through."

It all sounded good till one of the students passing by below pointed up to them shouting, "Up there!" Both Elect and Angels pulled out their pistols and volleyed shots up at them. Dust and fragments of the walls behind Bendin began to rain down on them.

"Oh *please,* ask anyone, no one *ever* looks up," Bendin whined.

"What do we do?" Quip asked again. "This thing eats my fire."

"Let's just go for it?"

"You know where to go, so, do what you want."

"You say that a lot, but, let's go!" Bendin turned off his silver box, used the additional pull of gravity to gain as much momentum as possible, and barreled through the first of the surprised Vaelift Angels. Bendin skated through all of them like water flowing around rocks in a creek. Quip waved as they skated by. Bendin skated up the incline and up the first set of passages that would lead up. He felt the thrill of success, only to have it crushed a minute later. The students had set up makeshift barriers in all directions and were prepared to meet him.

"We can't get this piece out without going through a barrier," Bendin said.

Quip nodded.

Bendin picked the closest group to him, knowing it was the fastest and shortest way up towards the gate.

As Bendin neared the barrier, he watched himself redirected across the front of it. He took advantage of the turn and slapped all the Vaelift with his Vurfenstaff.

Quip simply pulled out a distance away from Bendin and set everything around him on fire.

Students, discovering their firearms to be useless against Bendin, began to dive at him.

"Grab Pikuk!" The Vaelift students shouted.

"And his *dog*!"

"Who said that? I'll destroy you!" Quip yelled back and shot a blast of fire in the direction of the sound.

One grabbed Bendin's leg, but Bendin managed to slap him off with a stroke from his staff.

Bendin took one glance to make sure it was safe and yelled, "Vift!" Both Bendin and Quip vifted to Makarias leaving the piece behind. He watched carefully as the shock wave rippled through the crowd knocking most of them over

"Ooo. Fun!" Quip giggled.

Several of the students leaped forward and grabbed the piece cheering as if they had just been picked to be one of Odge's Vaelift. They hefted it in the air and cheered again. Their surprise was paramount to none as Bendin and Quip vifted back and the shockwave threw them all to the ground again. Bendin picked up the piece and moved forward till he was again thronged by the Vaelift students. They began vifting to Makarias and back to Toalt all the way down the hallway knocking all of the students flying. Bendin found that the less he focused on the actual vift, the louder the vift was and the shockwave more intense.

Now with each vift, Bendin started to see more and more

of the disjointedness and changes that the Coil homestead had made to the temple. He just narrowly avoided getting trampled by a fresh pack of Elect shooting like crazy by happening to vift right into the Coil's kitchen.

"Mmmm." Quip smiled, picked up a small piece of food, and vifted away leaving Bendin and Celeste's mouth open.

"Excuse us."

Bendin vifted right above a student who had the piece tucked under his arm. Quip climbed back up on Bendin's shoulder and urged, "Let's get to that gate. Hurry."

Bendin and Quip kept vifting away from the crazy, shooting, yelling, and madness, into the quiet lives of the Coils. Starley reading a graphical book, Jean doing skating exercises, and Pete and Ryan sneaking around holding some new toy they had created. They even vifted into Tilmon's conference and startled the networked tribunal. Tilmon shouted Bendin's name in surprise as several of the tribunal members' elbows fell off their chairs in shock. Simon didn't even get to ask Bendin why he had appeared in the room before Bendin and Quip vifted back again. Bendin was really glad he had searched both sides before this insanity, or this would have been extremely dangerous not knowing exactly where to go.

They were almost to the hall that would take them past the Control Center to the passages that led to the unpainted hall that held the gate. Once they rounded the corner to that particular hall, they saw Findall Quin, Castle Marshall Julian Harbreaker, Radu Landus, Commander Zist, and Mylin Samsove all standing in front of the Control Center. Each had their arms crossed over their chests and were frowning. Behind them, wall to wall, were Vaelift Elect and Vaelift Angels. On the Makarias side, Bendin noticed that he would be vifting into a safe passage inside the caves that had water pouring down from a jutting overhang above him. At least he would be able to vift. Quip remained smartly quiet. Bendin was glad that Quip was awake this time for all of this.

"Bendin. Hand over the sacred piece and we will let you go," Findall commanded, "or you will suffer the consequences." He tapped his blue ribbed Vaelift staff.

This surprised Bendin completely. He had no idea that this was all they wanted. He'd have thought he was a higher target than this piece. Something strange was going on.

"It's mine now. Step aside and I won't hurt anyone," Bendin warned waving his Vurfenstaff around. Students came up behind Bendin and Quip in a large mob and blocked their way back down. If they really needed to go that way, Bendin knew it wouldn't be too difficult. The students watched eagerly as Findall motioned for Radu and Mylin to take Bendin. This hall was almost as narrow as the other halls in the temple, but it's ceiling didn't go as high, so he wouldn't be able to skate up out of their reach. "Quip, fight or flight?"

Quip whispered in his ear, "The gate is close. Fight and vift."

"Okay." Bendin moved his Vurfenstaff into a defensive position.

Radu moved forward rapidly spinning his staff. Mylin was much more cautious and held her pistol professionally. She shot her pistol and one of the students behind them fell over wounded with a yell; she gasped in horror that Bendin couldn't be hit and threw her pistol on the ground diving for Bendin's feet. Bendin used his Vurfenstaff to block the wild spin of Radu, punch him in the face with his cuff, and clamp the Vurfenstaff down hard on Mylin's head before she could grab his feet. Quip hung onto the piece with his paws while attempting to hold onto Bendin at the same time. The shock of the Vurfenstaff knocked her out and Mylin's beautiful body when instantly as limp as a rag-doll.

Bendin tapped his Vurfenstaff on the ground signaling Quip to vift with him. They vifted to Makarias and back so quickly that the piece only hovered in the air for a moment. Two simultaneous shock waves radiated out at the same time catching Radu mid-swing, and he was thrown into the wall.

Bendin moved forward, and Findall clashed his staff against Bendin's Vurfenstaff. Surprisingly, It held, even though sparks flew off in all directions. Findall swung it around several times, each being blocked by the Bendin's Vurfenstaff. Radu joined in with his master and both of them took turns swinging their staffs with great speed.

"They've done this a lot before. They are pretty good." Quip whispered to Bendin as Bendin was forced backwards under their assault.

"Thanks for that, Quip. I'm trying to win a fight here," Bendin mumbled awkwardly keeping his feet firmly planted on the ground.

Bendin was not fast enough to take on two of them, and he failed to block one of Radu's swings. Radu took advantage of the failed block to swing swiftly at Bendin. His swing was redirected to the side by Bendin's field, and Radu stumbled forward, completely out of balance. Bendin saw the advantage and swiftly swatted Radu on the head with his Vurfenstaff. Radu became as Mylin Samsove, zapped on the floor.

"Okay, your turn," Bendin barked skating off to the side and pulling the piece out of Quips hands.

Quip floated for a second before sending an arc of fire directly at Findall.

There was an electric blast and Bendin watched in amazement as Findall spun his staff and vanished.

"Whelp, that was easy," Quip said flying back over to Bendin.

"It's not ov--"

Findall's staff expertly jabbed at controlled, yet steady speed, coming from behind and knocking Bendin forward into the wall. The piece bounced off the wall and Quip zoomed in and caught it.

"You've learned some staff work, but you are young," Findall noted, "and inexperienced."

"Well, you're an old fogey," Bendin retorted, spinning around. He smashed Findall's blue staff as hard as he could hoping to break it in two. It disappointingly held, sparked with a red mist, and Findall expertly positioned himself between Bendin and the gate.

Findall laughed and blocked another of Bendin's swings. But just before he spun it off, Findall twisted his staff, three prongs shot out the end, and it became a deadly trident. Using the new end, he finished locking and spun Bendin's Vurfenstaff onto the floor. Findall swung at a medium speed again, and Bendin knew it was going to connect. The swing painfully threw Bendin sideways onto Mylin.

Quip dropped the piece to Bendin and blasted his fire in response.

Mylin woke, shook her head, and saw Bendin's Vurfenstaff on the ground. She grabbed the Vurfenstaff and immediately dropped it. Shocked and surprised she rubbed her hands painfully as Bendin got back up behind her. He was glad he still had the piece in one hand.

Findall grinned and instead of disappearing he turned the staff directly at Bendin. An electric blast formed out of the end of it and a large blue ball slowly rippled towards Bendin with intensity. It was going to be too easy to vift out of the way, but then a distracted Quip, dodging Mylin's fist, slammed into the electric ball. With a loud electric pop, Quip's body flipped backwards into the wall, squeaked, and fainted. Bendin felt heat, frustration, and heartache fuel him.

"You can't possibly beat us all. Why not make it easier and end this now?" Findall mocked. It was then that Commander Zist, Castle Marshall Harbreaker, and Mylin came in swinging. Mylin's elegant fist closed the gap to his neck in a smooth pace. Bendin followed Jameus Coil's teachings by pivoting his body out of the way, moving his hands with grace, and getting around behind Mylin in time to shove her down behind him.

Marshall Harbreaker slid in with his feet first and knocked Bendin up into the air. Commander Zist was right behind him and used his full body to thrust and pin Bendin, while in the air, painfully into the wall. The air was completely knocked out of Bendin, his Vurfenstaff left his hands, and he could do nothing but try to catch his breath.

A cheer erupted from the students all around.

Maybe he could wriggle out of Zist's grasp. He tried.

Nope. It was over.

"I'm going to crush you!" Commander Zist yelled.

He gave a silent prayer to Odge in thanks for the adventure. Bendin felt the powerful grip tighten and incredible pain began to swell from his body. Bendin closed his eyes and thought of Quip, Rachel, Harmon, and before he could think of anything else there was a massively large and thunderous crash. The grip on him was losened immediately. Chunks of debris shot up, and the room was so dusty no one knew what was happening.

Bendin opened his eyes and began to feel his breath coming back to him. A very bulky black scaly figure blasted its way up through the floor, and it stopped the incoming figures with a couple of swings. A familiar voice spoke as if from the past, "Bendin. I'm 'ere to help! Get that thing 'n get out."

Tyler. It was Tyler!

Feelings of elation flooded Bendin and he grabbed the piece. Tyler shoved the four leaders backwards towards the Control Center as Bendin draped Quip around his shoulders and called his Vurfenstaff to him.

"Everyone shoot it!" Castle Marshall Harbreaker roared.

Quip groggily opened his eyes. "Ouch."

Bendin skated around Tyler and the leaders as all the Vaelift ripped off round after round into Tyler. Bendin could hardly believe that Tyler was back. Tyler threw off Findall's attacks and began edging his way towards the way that Bendin was already skating. "I'll ca'ch up," he shouted.

Bendin saw Ladak waving for him to come over to him and pointing to the wall next to him. Before he knew what to do about that he asked, "Can we help Tyler?" Bendin asked Quip.

"If we do, we lose."

Bendin found it hard to argue with that and he skated right to Ladak who jabbed a part of the wall with is fist and shouted, "Hit this wall three times!" Bendin hit it three times and it shot open. Ladak sped down it and Bendin followed him.

"Another passage?"

"Hello, I work here. Let's get you out of here."

"You know where I need to go?"

"Of course, the whole temple has been buzzing about it ever since you left."

Ladak pointed to the wall at the end. "Tap it three times. It leads to the hallway. I've got other things to tend to. Go!" Ladak raced back the way they had come while Bendin tapped it three times. The wall shot open and indeed, there was the unpainted hallway just in front of him. Bendin skated quickly to the gate. It was certainly a walk down memory lane as he placed his hand on it and vifted right through.

Chapter 21
Callapse's Folley

Bendin took a few breaths of air from the damp cave and checked out the piece in his hands. Now that he wasn't busy, he could look at it closer. The piece had the appearance of a triggering mechanism like he had thought before, but now he noticed the connections were the same as on the other pieces.

Quip groaned and peeked up at Bendin, "Although I shower it with love, please get rid of that thing."

"We will. How are you?"

Quip rolled off Bendin's shoulder to the floor and flicked his tail around letting it catch completely on fire. "Nope, we're good. Let's get on with this."

Bendin skated into the house and went straight to where he had seen Starley reading. To his surprise, she was still there.

"Whatcha doin'?" She asked pleasantly.

"I want you to take this and put it with the other." Bendin presented her the next piece.

"Okay!" Starley giggled and took the piece, which was much bigger than she was, out of the room.

Bendin found Celeste in the kitchen just like he had seen for just a glimpse on his vifting path. She was preparing dinner and humming a song that Bendin didn't recognize.

"Hi, Bendin. Hi, Quip. Back from your big adventure?" Destiny lay sleeping to Celeste's side in a fold out padded bin. She was curled up with a red band tucked around her body.

"Yes."

"What were you doing earlier? I saw you appear and disappear in the room. You were completely focused on something," Celeste said.

"I was. I'm fine now. Where's Rachel?"

"She went over to Josiah's Pod. In fact, I'm watching Josiah's two kids." Celeste jutted her hand in the direction of the sitting room. "They are in the other room just over there."

Bendin could indeed hear the sounds of kid's playing in the other room.

He didn't like the idea of Rachel being over at Josiah's pod again.

An explosion rocked the room from below.

"What was that?" Quip asked.

"I don't know, but who do you guess?" Celeste put down her cooking items, clicked a button that sealed the doors to the room the kids were in, and skated out of the room with Bendin close behind. The bluish sunshine streamed through the breaking clouds.

Thick smoke poured out from a lower section of the house while Pete and Ryan rolled out of it coughing.

"I think we used too much," Pete coughed again waving his hand across his face.

"Explain this," Celeste demanded as she pulled a small black mechanical object, that Bendin had never seen before, out of her pocket. "Tilmon, I'm going to need a repair grate for the lower section just outside of the assembly area of the house. You know, something to tide over till our two sons replace this section."

Bendin heard very clearly three beeps, then a low chime. Tilmon's voice sighed and said, "Yes. Of course dear."

"Why don't you guys have one of those?" Bendin asked Pete and Ryan.

"Those?" Ryan laughed. "Oh, sorry. You don't know. Those are w-a-a-a-y too expensive. Dad can only afford one for him and Celeste--"

A piece just above them fell and thudded on the ground only inches away from Ryan.

"The explosion wasn't big enough. You missed a piece." Quip grinned.

Ryan eyed the other parts of the area before he continued, "We built something similar, but they are way weak compared with those."

"But the ones you use during capture the flag seemed pretty strong," Bendin reasoned. They had gone all the way out to where he was when he found Quip. That wasn't anywhere near the Coil's home.

"Yes, those are weak and fail. We haven't gotten them to work very well around the settlements," Pete explained. "We'll figure it out, soon. I'm sure?"

"Explain this," Celeste repeated stomping her foot on the ground.

Ryan innocently rounded his eyes and said to his mom, "We were simply testing out the effects of the results of binding two distinctly separate noxious metals corroding at the high specific heat of the indexes of the right proportional angles triangulating the fifteenth flat insert of the third part of the section built for holding up the kitchen."

"You should not have done that my son, whatever it is that you just said, and you two will be shut out from all capture the flag games this week.

Ryan sank to the ground like he had his heart plucked out from him, and Pete shook visibly. "Sorry, Mom."

"Sorry isn't going to replace the hole in this wall." Celeste pointed at the hole. "But you will replace it with work." She let out a proud huff and skated back to the kitchen.

"What did you guys really do?" Bendin asked once Celeste was gone.

"It was his fault. He added too much to the composition and--boom--the whole recipe became an instant bomb," Pete accused pointing to Ryan.

"Says who? It was your idea to add it in the first place!" Ryan rejected throwing his brother on the ground.

"'It needed more zest' you said."

"It needed something!"

"Well not that!"

"Come on, we've had better results with fish than with that."

"Whatever," Ryan teased tickling Pete's side.

"It was supposed to be waxen candy!" Pete whined activating Ryan's box and pushing Ryan into the air. Pete activated his own and skated into his brother. Ryan retaliated shoving Pete backwards. Soon they were spiraling around in the air in a tangled mess.

"Guys! Stop, hey . . ." Bendin saw smoke rising out of Josiah's pod, "I'm going to Josiah's pod. See you later!" Bendin shouted turning away from them.

They stopped pushing each other around in the air. "Hey! Wait for us!" Ryan yelled.

"It's not like we are going to be able to play capture the flag anytime soon," Pete grumbled.

"It's a smoking egg," Pete mumbled skating up to Bendin and seeing the smoke much closer now.

"Poached," Ryan mumbled back. They all picked up the pace, Quip launched off Bendin and blasted off ahead of everyone.

Inside the pod, everything was trashed, broken, scattered and torn. The benches were broken in two, the monitors crushed, shattered glass everywhere, drawers opened and contents strewn around. There were blast and burn marks over the walls and machines. Bendin gasped.

Callapse's body was lying motionless in the corner.

"Callapse?" Bendin announced his presence carefully, tapping him on the cheek. Bendin felt sick. He couldn't believe so much stuff had been destroyed and that Callapse was knocked out. Callapse groaned and slowly opened his eyes. "Hello?"

"Yes, what happened?" Bendin asked.

Callapse tried to get up quickly, but fell down immediately.

Bendin moved forward, reached out, and held Callapse steady while he carefully got up. "What happened?"

Callapse pounded the ground with his bare hands. "I don't know! But I know they took her. Poor Jean. They took her. They took her and everything." Callapse burst into tears and pounded his fist on the floor for a few more seconds. He stopped, sniffed and looked gravely at Bendin, Quip, Pete, and Ryan.

"Who? Rachel took Jean?" Pete asked. "Have you been bathing in smoke, Callapse?"

Callapse composed himself holding his other arm painfully. "No. Not Rachel. A whole mess of thugs barged in here out of nowhere." Callapse began pacing around shaking his head as if trying to clear his mind. "They wouldn't listen to me. Men in dark clothes. They had Swyethe Blades. They attacked me. They took Josiah, Jean, and the backpacks. I had enough for everyone and everything was finally ready. They're probably ZF's. I need to get her and those backpacks back. I think Josiah did all this." Callapse clenched his fists repeatedly.

"Who?" Ryan repeated Pete's question again. "What family?"

"I don't know who exactly. I've never seen them before. They were here for Josiah, and they knew everything. What I was working on. What I planned to do. They made no offers. They immediately attacked me. Who does that? I mean, who just stands there and doesn't offer any type of compensation for all the hard work and labor I put into these! It's sick I tell you. Sick! Sorry." Callapse paused for a moment. Then resumed a bit more composed. "They attacked me, knocked me out, took Josiah, my sister, my work, and left. I think they might be DeSotos because they were as stern as any that I've ever met. I'll bet it was them."

"Where's Rachel?" Bendin asked.

"She was here, but snuck immediately out the back way

as soon as they showed up. I don't know what happened to her."

"That's what we are trying to find out now," Ryan said scratching his chin thoughtfully. "Before we were just curious what was going on but now..." His voice trailed off.

Callapse got up he gripped his left arm in pain.

"Your arm! It's cut!" Ryan said pointing at the long blood mark on Callapse's arm.

"Duh. I said that Jameus. We need to get those packs back before they do what I wanted to do with them." Callapse went over to a grate on the floor.

"Yes. Any ideas on how to find them?" Bendin asked.

"They were from the DeSoto's, right?" Pete reminded.

"That's what I think," Callapse spat cleaning his arm off with a shower of water from above them. He pulled out a tube from one of the drawers and sealed the cut. Bendin watched, again, in amazement as the area self-sealed shut and turned the same shade and color as the skin around it.

Callapse flexed his hurt arm. "Externally fixed. Internally healing. Mez's does both, but at least I can still use the arm. But it does hurt a lot."

"We can find them then! Pete burst out. "Follow me."

"Finally," Quip mumbled.

'You didn't have to wait you know," Bendin whispered back.

They all went outside and Pete turned to Quip. "Which way did they go, that's all we really need."

Callapse pointed. "DeSoto's are that way."

Quip sniffed around and said excitedly, "Rachel was here!" She went that way. Quip pointed in the direction that Callapse was pointing.

"See? Told ya." Callapse grinned. "Let's take the scrapper."

Ryan frowned but picked up the pace after his brother Pete.

"Shouldn't we ask for help?" Bendin asked.

"We'll do it on the way," Ryan grumbled.

"Sure we will," Bendin said sarcastically, skating down toward the kitchen. "Please pick me up."

Bendin skated to Celeste and quickly explained what he knew.

"I'll do everything I can. Do everything *you* can. Please get her back!" Celeste handed Bendin a long flat cylinder. Quip immediately took interest and flew really close to get a good look.

"This will open any non-Hypasaptic lock." Celeste made sure he clipped it to his belt and Callapse pulled up beside the door. "Go!"

"Squeeze in!" Callapse shouted from the driver seat.

Ryan waved from the passenger seat while Bendin and Quip got in the back with Pete. Callapse took off immediately up and out. They had only flown over four houses before they saw a large plume of smoke wafting into the air in the distance.

"Hello, fellow travelers in the back of the scrapper. This isn't your driver speaking: I think we may have found something," Ryan said in a monotone mechanically mocking tone.

"But is it what we are looking for?" Bendin said trying to see out the front window. Quip flew to the ceiling to try to see as well.

"I don't know. Let's go check it out." Callapse pulled the scrapper up next to the large fire burning in the middle of a clearing in the forest.

"Be quick about it, this could be nothing," Bendin warned.

"This fire was definitely caused by a vehicle, look at all the debris." Ryan pointed to the tiny parts scattered all over. "I just can't believe they did that."

"What happened here? Was this the vehicle?" Bendin exclaimed, "Something exploded into a million tiny pieces!"

"Yes. It was definitely a vehicle. All vehicles have a defensive trigger. It creates large protective bubbles around passengers in the event of a collision or failure. It actually doesn't happen very often; here it did. See the trails of the bubbles?" Callapse explained pointing to very large paths broken into the trees. The pathways were round and long.

Callapse set the scrapper down in the middle next to the fire. They got out and had a closer look at everything.

"It's definitely them. They haven't been here for very long. This fire is fresh and these trees are still wet from the rains," Quip said showing them the moisture on the leaves.

"That's RAIN, Quip, RAIN." Ryan smirked.

Quip eyed him out of the corner of his eye and shot a long thing stream of fire in front of Ryan's face.

Ryan froze. "It's whatever you want."

Bendin smiled as the slightest grin appeared on Quip's lips.

"It also means the fire isn't going to burn very long,"

Callapse observed. "Nice."

Bendin skated up higher so that he could get a clear view of everything. The trails of wreckage spread out, but there seemed to be no sign of people. Then he saw in the distance, a group of people skating northward.

"What about that group of people?" Bendin yelled to the others.

"We'll go cut them off and see. You stay and see if anyone else is here. We'll come back for you," Callapse ordered quickly, jumping back into the scrapper. Pete and Ryan jumped in with him, and they took off.

Quip followed Bendin as he skated around the forest seeking anything they might have not seen from above.

"Oh, no," Quip moaned pulling Bendin's ears with his paws. "Firebrand."

An ominous deep rumbling filled the air and from behind a sappy fat pine tree out flew a flaming brown bear. Bendin couldn't believe it was off the ground. It was smaller than you would expect a bear to be and it would have been cute if it had not been engulfed in flames. To his right came a fiery skunk, behind a fiery kangaroo, left a fiery ferret, up a bird and otter, and below a fiery wolf.

"DO NOT MOVE," the bear commanded stopping directly in front of Bendin with the others hovering all around them.

"Sure. What do you want?" Bendin moved his Vurfenstaff in an angle across himself.

"HIM." The bear pointed at Quip.

"Firebrand. Hello guys." Quip twitched nervously.

"Quip, why do they want you?" Bendin asked.

"I ditched their group when things went sour . . . and I'm probably wanted by them."

The wolf snarled, "We've got you surrounded."

Quip twitched again and all of Firebrand attacked at once. Fire shot from all angles and spun around Bendin and Quip in a swirling fiery mess. Bendin couldn't see anything but flames. None of the fire actually hit them, but the air that Bendin and Quip were breathing uncomfortably began to spike in heat and pressure. Hands shot in and gripped Quip by the legs and yanked him off Bendin out of the swirling flames. Just as fast as they attacked, they pulled away, and all flew south.

"Bendin!" Quip squeaked out before the bear clubbed him with his fist.

Bendin frowned, checked Toalt, gripped his staff, skated as fast as he could, and vifted to Toalt with a loud bang. He emerged above the air in a very smoky dusty storm and realized he couldn't see anything over here. His bands kept all the elements from smashing into him and he focused on the fleeing Firebrand group. The pure thrill of skating and the pursuit of Firebrand took over and Bendin felt an exhilarating feeling of freedom. But, then again, Quip wasn't moving. Bendin gritted his teeth and hoped for the best but feared the worst.

Bendin caught up with Firebrand, who had slowed their pace considerably since Bendin had disappeared, and they were all flying through the trees instead of above them. He made his choice of entrance at a most prodigious moment. The moment when the bear passed his position and was about to go under a fairly thick tree limb.

Bendin vifted, slammed the bear with his Vurfenstaff, and grabbed Quip from the grip of the bear as it smashed into the tree limb. The others, stunned, confused, and perplexed watched as Bendin skated off through the trees with their prize.

"ARISE YOU FOOLS! GIVE CHASE!" The bear boomed.

After seven rumbling booms, Bendin knew they were going to be on him extremely quickly.

"Quip, wake up! Wake!" Bendin urged Quip rubbing him gently while skating through the trees at odd angles to try to throw some kinks into their pursuit pattern.

Quip mumbled, but didn't wake.

The bird was first to reach him showering him with fire and shooting more up into the air. It let out a piercing wail and Bendin knew there was no hiding from the others that were sure to be on his heels. Then he had an idea. Bendin skated straight down through some trees and into some foliage out of sight from his pursuer. He spied some bushes that would serve his purpose and deposited Quip there. Bendin smiled, skating up at an angle so that the incoming bird would be sure to see him.

As Bendin thought, so it was.

The bird came through the foliage right next to Bendin and flew right into him. Bendin reflexively smacked the bird off with a crack from his Vurfenstaff. Stunned, the bird hit a tree and fell out of sight.

"That's enough." Bendin turned and saw the Wolf also cruising parallel to him. Bendin watched as the other six members of Firebrand collapsed their formation around Bendin.

Bendin did a double bladed stop causing a nice popping explosion. All Firebrand members turned and Bendin held up his hand. "We don't have to do this anymore. You are not going to be able to catch us. Just go back to where you came from and leave us alone."

The bear laughed then spat, "NON-NEGOTIABLE."

"Fine then, I'm not responsible for what happens to you." Bendin vifted, skated behind the wolf, and vifted back. One hit from the Vurfenstaff in connection with the resounding shockwave sent the stunned Wolf's body soaring into a tree and down below. The others reacted and fired jets of hot flames towards him. They were too slow because Bendin vifted again and shifted his focus on the ferret. Bendin angrily vifted behind the ferret and batted the ferret as hard as he could. Bendin didn't even see where the ferret went because he immediately focused on the otter.

"No, Zack! *Monster!*" the otter yelled launching himself with all his might at Bendin.

Bendin vifted just before the otter was able to be redirected and vifted back just as the otter was passing his current position. The otter flew directly into his staff stunning himself instantly.

"What are you? *Monster!*" The kangaroo shouted.

The bear, kangaroo, and skunk blasted him and rocketed towards him at the same time. They didn't rush all the way in, however, and when Bendin vifted to Toalt and back he had to get really close to take down the bear. The surprise was all Bendin needed to knock out the bear and it thumped to the ground, but the kangaroo slapped his tail in and pulled Bendin straight in towards the skunk.

Bendin felt the tail dig into his side and curl around him. Bendin gasped.

The tail completely caught on fire. He felt the hot sharp pain begin to burn into his sides.

A long and loud yell split the fire-filled air and Quip furiously beamed the kangaroo and skunk into the closest trees. The skunk fell out of the air and down to the ground, while the kangaroo only was briefly stunned.

"Bendin, finish him, we've got to keep moving," Quip urged.

"Quip!" Bendin rejoiced, vifted, skated over to the kangaroo, vifted back, and finished off the kangaroo with his Vurfenstaff. As it fell down below, Quip sailed over to Bendin and playfully tugged his ear.

"Thanks, Quip. Are you okay?" Bendin felt his side and winced. He felt the charred burns across his uniform.

"Yes. And I know where Rachel is. Let's go do this."

"But we almost died!"

"Well, we didn't."

Bendin waited till he saw Quip give a crooked grin before they vifted to Toalt and motioned Quip to fly on.

Bendin followed Quip to a cave in a cliff in the forest not too far from the explosion of the vehicle.

They vifted back and found Rachel lying on the floor of the cave. Her eyes were closed, face scratched, and her clothes had burn holes peppering them with dirt marks in various places. She stirred as they landed and opened her eyes.

"Bendin? Quip?" She sighed. "I'm happy to see you." She made an attempt at getting up, but cringed and leaned up instead.

"You're hurt!" Bendin twirled his Vurfenstaff nervously.

"Please, we've got to find Josiah and Jean."

"We will, but you need to heal."

"Can you skate or am I going to have to carry you?" Quip asked.

Rachel looked at Quip and smugly smiled. "I'm going to." Rachel held her stomach, used Bendin for leverage, and managed to get up.

"You guide us and fill us in on the way there." Bendin held her steady and Rachel skated out the entrance carefully. "What happened?"

"I went over to Josiah's place to check up on Jean, but after being there for a while, other people came in wearing Swyethe Blades. I immediately took a back way out and snuck around to their freighter. At first there were screams, then smoke started coming out of the pod. Then they all came out, threw all the stuff inside, including Jean, and fired it up.

Rachel winced and continued as they started to gain altitude, "I had to stop them, and I knew I wasn't going to be able to hold on when they accelerated past the sound barriers. I was losing grip and. . ."

Rachel scanned the distance for movement.

Quip interjected, "AND?"

"I used my skate to cut one of the main lines that leads to the core. The core's destruct sequence activated and everything blew up leaving everyone in the protective bubbles. I crashed into the cave there. Thanks for coming after me."

Bendin simply nodded. He wasn't really familiar with anything she was talking about. Still, something didn't click.

"If you were in a protective bubble, why were you hurt?"

"I was lucky to live. They have a fall-off distance of detection. I was on the edge and I was hit by part of the explosion before I was protected. It can't be too bad." She paused and lifted the side of her shirt a little so they could see the damage. There was a very large red mark where the heat had burned her skin going up her side.

"Way to go all hero on us," Bendin mumbled.

"Wow. Was it like this?" Quip flew in front of them and demonstrated the explosion by showing his paw close to the bottom of his body and exploding in a large burst of flames flinging his paw away on fire.

"That's actually really close. You don't fully understand, Quip. They are supposed to do that if there is external damage or external forces that would harm the structure or the core and in turn threaten the people's lives. The good thing is, I immediately stopped those crooks. They shouldn't be too far ahead, unless they've stolen someone's vehicle!" Rachel's voice was full of strength, even though her body didn't exactly show it.

"Maybe Callapse and your brothers were successful in capturing them. It will make things a lot easier that way," Bendin noted.

"Something's just happened. I see and smell smoke up ahead," Quip warned.

They heard it after Quip heard it. A clear, distinct, and loud explosion wave.

What had happened? People might be dead. Maybe the vehicles were all crushed. Bendin didn't think very long because a moment later Callapse flew his scrapper out of the smoke, up to them, and opened the doors.

"Get in! They're getting away. We've got to catch them. They have everything, and it looks to be all intact!" Callapse shouted excitedly to them. He was in the driver's seat and Pete and Ryan were somehow both squeezed into the passenger seat next to him.

"Help her first, then we go," Bendin insisted.

"Yes. Ryan you do it this time," Callapse commanded. "Quickly!"

Ryan skated swiftly to a compartment, opened it and pulled out a tube that was very similar to the one that Callapse had used earlier. Rachel applied it, carefully got in the back seat with Bendin, and Quip flew to Bendin's lap.

Callapse pushed the scrapper up to speed, sped past the smoke, and filled them in. "They broke down Jerry's door and, poor grandma, she was knocked over in the rush to her dock. They stole her older generation vehicle and crammed themselves and everything into it. I came back here to pick you guys up as soon as I determined that grandma was okay. The good news is that the vehicle is slower."

"See up there." Pete pointed. Way up in the distance Bendin could make out a small dot. "That's them."

"We'll hang back here and follow them all the way back to their home." Callapse smiled.

"Don't you think they know we're following them?" Bendin asked.

"No, they didn't see us," Ryan confirmed.

"Where's Jerry?" Bendin wondered.

"Jerry usually is trading with the Sanga's about right now. He married Astonia Sanga so he has some really nice connections," Rachel explained to Bendin. "I think she was a good find."

Callapse scoffed. He shook his head.

"Sorry, Callapse, not everyone can have someone like Diane Finn. What do you see in her anyway?" Rachel asked.

"You don't understand," Callapse muttered.

"What don't I and everyone understand?"

Callapse shook his head again and refused to say anything more.

"Do you think this is going to work?" Bendin asked. "Is anyone else going to help us?"

Callapse shook his head again.

Ryan turned to Bendin, "The officers said that we didn't have enough information for them to conduct an investigation. Mez is offline for a couple of days, Tilmon and the council are away, and we must help Jean."

"We could still use their help," Bendin said under his breath. He stroked his hands over Quip's ears thoughtfully and was surprised when Quip let out an affectionate sigh, rubbed his head up against Bendin, and curled up tightly in his lap.

Chapter 22
Disrupting the FZs

They followed the stolen vehicle to Clarendon, the DeSoto's capital. The city sat inside a flat valley in between a pair of mountain ranges. Unlike the Wycliff's irregular city structure, this one was a perfect grid. The terrain contrast and colors presented lush green trees against a flat rust-colored landscape. The majesty of the mountains were thrilling, and he found himself unable to pull his eyes away from the front window. The majority of the city itself was made up of large skyscrapers.

The vehicle they were following didn't stop at the city, instead, it went onwards past it to the north.

"Where are they going?" Bendin pointed to the vehicle. "I thought you said they were going to the DeSoto's."

"I said I *thought* they were DeSoto's. We are in the DeSoto's region, so you never know." Collapse frowned holding his arm carefully. "Almost all of their people live in that city, and they are very proud of it."

They went northward toward the tallest mountain that you could see from kilometers away. For Bendin, even though you could see it, it seemed to take a very long time to fly to it.

The vehicle ahead of them disappeared around the rocky, snow-covered mountain and when they rounded the other side of the mountain, all Bendin could see was an immense pine forest.

The vehicle was missing.

"Where did they go?" asked Bendin.

"They couldn't have gone too far," Pete reasoned. "There are not very many places to go up here."

"Except infinite, " Ryan spat back. "They could land anywhere!"

"I know where they went," Collapse announced after a moment dropping the craft's altitude.

"This thing is huge!" Bendin jutted his fingers at the large mountain next to them.

"*This* is Mount Desenzo," Pete muttered to Bendin. "The DeSoto's are almost as proud about their mountain as they are about their city and themselves. They *never* stop talking about it and selling mugs, plates, dishes, and other objects engraved with it. So annoying."

Ryan mocked putting his hands up and making quotes to emphasize his next words, "It's a 'monumental object' that inspires them when they look out their windows."

"Too bad the sun doesn't rise or fall from their angle of it or they'd be *set* for life," Pete joked.

"The sun is setting though," Quip mumbled.

"This is it." Collapse pointed down to a place in the trees that Bendin couldn't see because of a large cluster of clouds in the way. Bursting through the cluster of clouds revealed a beautiful, articulate, massive ornate building. As they got closer, Bendin realized he'd never seen a fancier building. "Who lives here?" Bendin asked.

"No one, supposedly. This, is the DeSoto's Vaelift temple, Bendin. It's my first time seeing it in person!" Pete leaned forward till his nose was pressed up against the window.

Ryan peered out gripping the dash excitedly.

The building was made of wood, cut stone, and carved brick. Even though it was made of many materials, the majority of it was made of stone. The roof was made of tiles, and the walls were of a composition to make Bendin think of dark amber. Bright yellow trim outlined the entire scope of every piece of every part of the building.

"The Desoto's spared no expense in making this place, did they?" Ryan observed.

"You can say that again," Pete said admiringly.

"The Desoto's spare--"

"It's just an expression!" Rachel interrupted nudging Ryan in the ribs.

"Hey!" Ryan whined uncontrollably jumping up and falling back down into his chair, "It's just an expression?"

Pete laughed and Quip smiled at Ryan's jump.

"Are you sure they went here?" Bendin wondered aloud.

"There isn't another building for kilometers. Why don't you go ask Odge? I'm guessing they are here. Do you have a better idea? Any kind of 'clairvoyance' would be really handy about now. But, since you haven't said anything, I'm guessing no. Let's go and find out." Callapse shrugged and parked the vehicle. Everyone got out and skated into the building. The walls were deeply detailed and revealed expert craftsmanship. The only problem was it hadn't been disturbed in a great many years.

"Spread out, we can cover more ground that way. If you

spot anything . . . yell really really loudly," Callapse ordered quietly. "Pete, Ryan come with me."

"Sure!" Pete said excitedly and skated past him down a dark tunnel.

Callapse grabbed Pete's hand and pressed his own finger to his lips. "Shhhhhh! Quiet! We don't want to alert them!"

"Right," Pete whispered as Callapse let go of Pete's hand slowly. Pete scampered off into the dark hallway.

"Wait up, Pete!" Ryan hissed, "I can hardly see!"

Callapse saluted Bendin and followed his brothers down the passageway.

Before Bendin went down a different passage, one that went down, he asked, "Quip you have this honor, will you please light the way?"

"Nice to know I'm at least valued as a candle." Quip smirked.

Quip flared up with enough fire to give a nice warm light to cover the area.

"Please don't leave me here "

"Don't worry, Rachel. We weren't. Just be careful not to be in the way of trouble if it so arises. You're hurt and I don't want anything to happen to you," Bendin said quietly.

"Thanks," Rachel murmured as she hobbled up to Bendin and Quip.

"Never fear, dear Rachel. I'll protect you!" Quip winked enthusiastically.

Bendin checked Toalt and, as he was beginning to expect now, the other side was very lively with students moving to and fro. They were carrying all kinds of equipment that were used in building structures. Many were comparing blueprints with each other. Bendin took Rachel in his arm to steady her and pulled her along on her skates.

"Rachel, you missed out on the fun of the last temple." Bendin frowned as they moved downward.

"Really? What did I miss?"

"Lava."

"Hot Lava." Quip blew out a fireball in disgust.

Rachel frowned. "What happened?'

Bendin gave a short terse description of their close call. When he described the piece absorbing the lava, Rachel gasped, "That's so strange!"

"Yeah, lucky. It saved our lives."

Rachel seemed to be moving along fine, but Bendin was

concerned if she had to move quickly that she might hurt herself.

"Why did you come along? Didn't you kind of already play the hero today by cutting into their vehicle and destroying it?"

Rachel looked at him with an expression that suppressed mirth. "I didn't even think of it like that. But, sure if you want to say it that way. I love my sister. I can't accept someone else doing something I should do myself. I really hope we can save Jean."

Bendin was also wondering if there was another piece here that he could collect while they were here hunting for those thieves. He kept his eyes open as he descended with Rachel. Bendin stared at the completely blank boring thick walls with nothing but the inscriptions on them.

Bendin stared down another hall for a minute and noticed Rachel watching him.

"What, are you doing?" Rachel pleaded imploringly. "You keep staring down the halls when there is nothing to see."

"I'm looking for signs that another piece is here in this temple. I'm beginning to think that a piece is in each one for some reason. Quip, keep your eyes open."

"You can see through the walls?" Rachel eyed him disbelievingly.

"No." Bendin laughed thinking of how ridiculous he must have looked to her. "But we can see Toalt. There is a temple on this exact spot in Toalt. I've been trying to decide which departments are being hosted there. So far I'm going to have to go with the District of Architecture and the District of Math. We don't get to go away from the upper temple of our choice till graduation, so I'm not familiar with the layout of these other temples at all."

"That would explain all the people with blueprints and counting machines," Quip reasoned from the front.

"You can see them too?"

"But of course, Rachel." Quip purred.

They kept going lower till they found a similar spot, as in the other temples where a passage dipped downwards out of sight. The problem was, this one was full of traffic. There were people all over the halls bustling in and out and up and down.

"What do you make of it?" Bendin asked.

"There might have been some changes?" Quip reasoned tersely, "or we may have the wrong room."

An explosion rocked the DeSoto temple from above

them and the three of them barely got out of the way as a large chunk of the ceiling tumbled down and crashed into the floor in front of them.

"What was that?" Rachel gasped waving the dust and dirt away with her hands.

"Let's go find out!" Quip whispered harshly scooting up ahead quickly in a bright orange streak.

Bendin and Rachel skated up through the newly formed hole and found, as Quip's light appeared over the edge, a dark gloomy room that had five men dressed in black kneeling on the floor in a circle. They chanted repeatedly one word: "Zadok . . . Zadok . . . Zadok . . . Zadok . . . Zadok".

Bendin saw one of them flinch when he came up out of the hole. He watched bewildered, finding himself in the very center of their circle. He checked Toalt and was shocked to see an entire room full of variously ranked people. Right next to him in the center of Toalt's room was Jean's body lying motionless.

Bendin vifted immediately with Quip following only a moment later. He reached down and knew she was alive. He flipped the switches to activate the backpack to send her back. The backpack sputtered and sparks flew out the backside of it. "Blast! Quip, protect her please!"

Quip snarled, "For the Vaelift!" and stood on her body with his head on fire while Bendin vifted back.

"Test successful!" A man shouted.

Bendin noticed that the other backpacks were next to the others in the circle. Jean had been the test.

"Go away, or suffer," hissed one of the hooded men in the circle. The voice sounded deep and sinister. Bendin thought the man might have a cold and he glared at the gold trimmed cloaked man defiantly.

"Jean." Bendin whispered. He felt a rush of pain, love, fear, and determination. He checked Toalt again and noticed the people in that room were recovering from Jean's entrance and getting up again. He was so glad Quip was there to protect her.

"If you will not go, then I'm going to have to *kill* you," the man hissed again. "Leave! Do not make the mistake--of staying."

Rachel moved back a bit, and Bendin frankly didn't know what to do.

The man moved, at least Bendin thought it was a move. It felt like a move, but it was much, much faster. The man instantly drew a long sword from a sheath on the ground behind him, hissed with great force, "Leave *now*!", and he lept forward swinging his sword quickly at Bendin.

Bendin didn't even think about it and defensively raised his Vurfenstaff. The man's blade swooshed through and with a loud clash, the man's blade connected for a moment with Bendin's Vurfenstaff. To the surprise of the man, a sharp electric current zapped through the momentary contact, down the blade, and shot through the man's body. The sword shot out of the man's hands with tremendous force embedding itself in the wall. The others, seeing the man's sword go flying, charged at Bendin with one accord.

Pete, Ryan, and Callapse opened a door on the far side of the room, light behind them in the hall gave them glistening outlines. Due to the darkness of the room and the brightness of the light on Bendin in contrast, Pete only saw Bendin.

"Hi, Bendin! This place is totally wired. Check it out!" Pete's voice boomed into the dark room. Lights flashed on from all sides of the room, ceiling, and floor. Every person in the room except Pete, Ryan, and Callapse groaned and shielded their eyes from the bright light. Pete had flipped one lever in a long line of levers on the side of the room.

"Oh, hello everybody! I didn't see you all there," Pete announced curiously.

"Great work guys! You found all of them!" Ryan said.

"No, Jean's missing," Callapse noted.

The man that had tried to hit Bendin grabbed his neighbor's sword. "You have friends, well, so do I." He joined his associates in the assault. Bendin raised his Vurfenstaff and with each block, a sword flew into the walls.

"I wonder what these do. Pete? Ha!" Ryan grinned wily to his brother.

"Cool!" Pete grabbed a switch in each hand and flipped the next one in the chain.

The man with the gold trimmed hood hissed wickedly, "No, don't!"

Slots opened in the walls and powerful fans of all different sizes activated and blew into the room. The air blasted Bendin so forcefully that he instinctively skated up and vifted out of the way. Quip had formed a firewall surrounding Jean that the others were trying to penetrate with guns and other weapons. "How much longer can you hold?"

"Forever."

Bendin knew that wasn't true. Bendin watched in Makarias as the jets of air slammed several of the men of the circle to the walls. Others were blown over, but managed to get under the air stream by flattening themselves on the floor. The man that had hissed so wickedly was plastered on the back of the wall and couldn't move. Pete, Ryan, and Callapse smiled. Rachel was blown backwards and the momentum caused her to skate uncontrollably down through the hole and hit the ground below.

The air in Toalt was hot, and filled with yelling of all kinds. Orders, frantic shouting, and loud thumping of feet. Bendin nodded to Quip who was sustaining the wall of flames, effectively keeping all others away from Jean. There was a loud crash and Bendin felt the fabric of the air in the room compress and vibrate before a thundering concussion wave erupted from the far side of the room. The wall closest to the blast crumpled instantly and chunks of the ceiling rained down on many of the people in that corner of the room. The rest were blown backwards into the wall.

Bendin skated over to the spot and saw a man from the circle clutching the place where there had been a foot. It had been completely removed by the wall he had crossed over into.

Bendin felt sorry for the man's pain and went over to him.

"Here, let me help you with that." Bendin flipped the switch on the backpack by the man's right ear and then flipped the switch by his left ear. The pack fired up and sent the man out of the room, back to Makarias. There was a rippling explosion of light and sound, far exceeding anything that Bendin had felt before. He shielded his eyes from the light, but was completely unaffected by the sound or compression waves. The floor groaned and splintered leaving very large cracks in the wake.

The man appeared dramatically in Makarias lying horizontally in the air, while the effects of the blast thrashed open the hole further sending more rubble in all directions. For only a moment the man seemed fine, but he flailed and fell through the hole as well.

Pete flipped some of the other switches. Things inside the room adjusted dramatically as he flipped them. Some of the sections of the floor shot up at great velocity while others sunk down. This sent many of the men into the air. Many of them were caught in the super powerful fans and shot them into the walls on either side, trapped by the air.

Another switch caused the whole floor to suddenly tilt at a hard angle. Bendin turned to help Quip and was stunned to find Quip's firewall gone, only a few bodies lying around, and

Jean missing. Bendin had no idea what was going on. He'd been the room the whole time. He checked the spot where Jean had been closer, and found, curled up on the floor, Quip.

Bendin carefully shook him. Quip moved and jumped off the floor flinching dramatically. "I . . . I . . . " Quip turned to Bendin. "What happened?"

"I have no idea. I was hoping you could tell me."

"Something came in, knocked me out, and picked up Jean so fast I couldn't even react." Quip frowned. "It had no scent and then she had no scent."

"What?" Bendin frowned. "How about, Jean?"

"Yes, but . . . I can't follow what I can't smell."

Bendin vifted to Makarias as a nasty stench filled the hot Toalt room.

Quip immediately followed, coughing. "Gas!"

Ryan and Pete were still altering the room and the men were still flying around the room in an uncontrollable redirection and eventually getting stuck to the walls. Bendin skillfully skated around the air currents, the jutting pieces popping out of the walls, and found Callapse pulling a backpack off one of the men from the circle. She yelled loudly, resisting, till Quip shot fire across her face and glared at her shouting, "Shut up or be ye barbequed!"

The woman rapidly changed her mind. Bendin and Quip checked that Rachel was okay and found she had bound and pulled the backpack off the unconscious man down with her already.

When Bendin came back up, the next switch caused all the fans to switch to reverse and new fans to blow in the opposite direction.

Everyone stuck to the walls on one side was immediately flung across the room and redirected around till they stuck to the opposite wall.

Pete looked mischievously at Ryan and grinned. "Are you thinking what I'm thinking?"

Callapse shook his head as Ryan smiled.

They alternately began switching the fans repeatedly from forward to reverse and back again. They'd wait till the people from the circle would be redirected around till they got stuck onto the wall, the pressure was enough to knock the air out of their bodies, before they switched the direction. They did this about eight times and were laughing so hard that they physically couldn't lift the switches anymore. Everyone yelled mercy but one.

The one who didn't protest was the man with the golden fringe around his hood.

During the course of the blowing air the man's golden fringed hood was blown back revealing a very old, scarred, and muscular face. Age didn't stop his resolve. He used his arm strength, gripped and pulled himself down the wall till he pulled free of the air and dropped to the ground.

His face contorted with rage and he shouted, "Curse you, and your wretched family!" With a final huff, he pulled himself backwards through a tall thin opening that no one had noticed was there and disappeared. Bendin and Quip chased him through the opening into a narrow passage behind the walls.

"Great, this is convenient," Bendin muttered to Quip riding on his shoulder.

"For him." Quip flew ahead and lit the way. The entire facility shook as an immensely large gust of hot air shot down the passage. Quip shielded Bendin from it in a brilliant arc. When the wave of air passed them, they finally crested the end of the passageway. A small craft shot upwards at incredulous speed into the sky rapidly shrinking in the distance.

"He got away," Bendin said slamming his fist into the wall next to him.

"You forget." Quip winked. "How fast I am. I will follow and let you know where he goes or if I can figure out some way to stop him."

"Oh, please, there's no way you can travel as fast as tha--" Bendin started to say skeptically. Bendin shielded his eyes and body just in time as Quip grinned, laughed, and let out a large shockwave of fire that blasted into the walls. Quip flashed upwards in the air in a bright, white-hot streak. He was gone in only a few seconds following the faded cut air trails of the other craft.

Bendin sighed rubbing his hot arms. The bands had repelled the fire, but they didn't stop the heat.

Curse him for making him feel like he was going to miss him.

Bendin returned quickly to the others and noticed on the way back lots of other tiny passages that linked up to the passage that led to where the craft had blasted its way out. Callapse, Pete, and Ryan, were all wearing Callapse's packs and were cleaning up all the now groaning men in hooded black outfits together.

"Did you catch him?" Callapse asked when Bendin came in the room. "What happened to your arms?"

"No. Regrettable. He flew away in a small craft with three fins. Quip went after him though," Bendin reported to them. Then he sighed." Quip's takeoff did this to my arms."

"Probably a TF-153," Ryan said dragging the last man in the black clothes to the middle of the room with the others, "They are small single person crafts. They may not have much space, but they can be very slow, or very fast. Very agile. We've been saving up for a pair of them for racing."

"How do you know that's the model he has?" Callapse asked.

"We've wanted a TF-153 for a while because they are the best model of that particular class of craft. How should I know if it is his exact model? I'm just giving it as an example of what it *probably* is." Ryan shrugged.

"What is this place used for?" Pete asked. "I love it!" Ryan smiled at his brother and Callapse shook his head again.

Bendin picked around the room hunting for clues. "I don't know let's check the entrance to the room." They found a small sign on the wall next to the doorway that read, "For building strength, durability, agility, and root."

"It's a training room for the Vaelift. What do we do with these guys now?" Bendin asked.

"We take them to be tried in the court system," Callapse stated. "We'll throw them all in the compartments in the scrapper, have them tried, questioned, and put away for their crimes. We were very lucky to catch them."

"You go. I need to find Jean and someone needs to be here for when Quip comes back."

"Right. We'll come back when the trials are done." Callapse clicked his fingers together absently. "They are high profile. Shouldn't take more than a day or two."

"Let me know what happens." Bendin skated down below to check on Rachel. She seemed fine and Bendin filled her in on everything that had happened above her.

"I would like to stay here with you."

"Are you going to be well enough?" Bendin said worried.
"Yes."

"Fine?" Bendin asked showing a small smile.

"Josiah? Why did you do this?" Bendin heard Callapse ask Josiah when Bendin skated back up to the room. He then realized Josiah was the real link to why all this had happened.

Josiah held his body in pain, "He will return."

"Who?" Ryan asked.

"Zadok will return. You can't stop it."

"You guys were FZ's?" Pete said disbelievingly.

"That's just lame," Ryan said disapprovingly.

"Disgusting."

"Dishonorable."

"Dirty."

"Da . . ." Ryan laughed being unable to think of a word.

"How many little groups are there that want to cause such harm as this?" Bendin said.

"Little one's here and there." Callapse shrugged, "but I had no idea that this whole science experimentation was to bring an ancient force back from the dead. Followers of Zadok. Who knew?"

"Callapse, how do you know he's dead?" Bendin challenged.

"Whatever. It is the only thing that makes sense?" Callapse shrugged his shoulders again.

"You expect me to believe you can bring an ancient force back from the dead?" Bendin pointed out sarcastically.

"No, I don't believe that. I was saying that because that's what *he* was just trying to do." Callapse frowned and glared at Josiah. "I didn't think you were capable of such, things. You and Crystal both. She must have known about this!"

Josiah said nothing for a moment. Then slowly he opened his mouth and spat, "Zadok is going to reward all his followers with power, glory, and immortaity. Only a fool would reject such a profound offer, and only we know of his true power and how to wield it."

"Power? Josiah, Zadok's not even here. You have been reading the wrong books, listening to the wrong people, and placing faith in things that don't exist!" Callapse reprimanded his brother. "I thought better of you. I really did." Callapse angrily paced around the room occasionally hitting things.

Bendin was dumbstruck with a feeling of emotional pain for Callapse. He was, in fact, right.

"Let's get them out of here before anything else happens. Dad will clear this up, and we can talk to him about it," Callapse said sternly. "The tribunal's authority will accelerate litigation."

Callapse, Bendin, Ryan, and Pete forced the men and woman into the air, out to the craft, and put them into the various compartments.

"Happy travels," Pete said kicking the compartment closed.

"Won't they just leave your compartments and get away?" Bendin asked.

"Bendin," Callapse said coming over and placing a hand on his shoulder. "You worry about your spiritual, mumbo-jumbo world, and I'll worry about my physical, scrappy, artistic world. I made it so they are not going to be able to get out. Trust me, this isn't going to be like our little stowaways who know my secrets. Mez should be here in a couple days. We'll be back as soon as we can. I wish you success in the meantime. And, please find my sister," Callapse said bowing to Bendin who couldn't tell if Callapse was mocking or respecting him.

"Can we get a coat or two?" Rachel asked. "It's getting a little clod."

"Clod?" Pete butted in.

"Clad!" Ryan said.

"No, Clud." Pete shot back.

"How about Clid?"

"Clyd."

"Cled!"

"Cl--"

"Of course I meant cold sillys," Rachel interrupted, cutting them off, shook her head, and looked to Bendin for support. Bendin smiled and shrugged. He didn't know what to do.

Callapse opened a compartment that wasn't already occupied by a black hooded person and pulled out a couple of coats for them.

"Heeeee!" Rachel exclaimed hugging one of the soft fluffy coats.

"We'll be back soon. See ya." Callapse waved and jumped inside.

Bendin and Rachel watched as the scrapper took off and sped towards Hymingway.

Bendin immediately skated back inside the temple in search of Jean. Surprisingly, he found Jean quickly in a containment unit lower down in the temple. He vifted over and discovered that there were no plans on moving her so almost all concern for her now was satisfied.

"I think she'll be okay. I'll want to wait for Quip before I make any more plans," Bendin described the situation with care

~ 348 ~

to Rachel. "Unless Odge dictates something better of course."

Rachel nodded kindly and suggested, "Let's skate to the top of the temple and wait up there for Quip, that is, if he's coming back."

"Pbbffttt. Of course. Sure. Ha! . . . I hope he makes it," Bendin said spinning his Vurfenstaff absently in his hands.

"But of course." Rachel winked.

Bendin and Rachel skated to a nice flat place on the roof and sat down together. Bendin placed the frantic thoughts of Jean's safey behind him for the moment. The skies were clear, and one of Makarias's moons rose. The only unnatural light came behind them off in the distance behind the mountain. Bendin switched his vision and locked at the Toalt sky. He was amazed again, as he viewed both at the same time, at how many more stars there were in Makarias.

"Do you have a favorite star?" Rachel asked.

"I don't know what any of them are. I grew up without stars. To us they were just something you looked forward to seeing after graduation. Why? Do you have a favorite?"

"That one over there," She stated immediately. "Do you see it? It has a greenish tint, but very bright."

Bendin moved closer to her so he could look down her arm to see exactly what star she was pointing at--there were that many. He saw a very bright, vivid, flickering, greenish colored star.

"I think I can see it."

"It's called Silfairalight. It's been my favorite star since I was young." Rachel gazed at the star w th a solemn expression on her face.

Bendin asked a question that had bothered him for a while, "What was that like? Being little? I remember nothing of being small at all."

Rachel took his hand and spoke with him seriously. "You really didn't miss much, Bendin. It is hard when you are small because you don't know as much as those who are bigger. You have annoying brothers who punch you, push you, and make fun of you. You have younger sisters who out skate you, out look you, and out date you. So no, you didn't miss much."

"I'm sorry . . . is it like that for everyone?"

"No . . ." Rachel sighed after a moment, "mostly just me I guess."

"I never had parents, or siblings. Our organization is the

~ 349 ~

closest thing I've had to a family. In some ways, I wish I had started here and experienced what you have because that's all I want anymore. If Odge wasn't encouraging me to get these pieces and clean up after the past Vaelift, that's all I'd be doing now. Your concept of families is against everything we were taught in the temples: Nothing ever lasts. Relationships are meant to be fleeting, if anything. If you aren't happy, then something is wrong with the system, and we have to force change so the system will accept you."

Bendin watched a shooting star streak across the sky and disappear. "Wow! I've never seen that before." He turned to Rachel. "That's why this place is so strange and foreign to me. I like it, don't get me wrong; it's just so different from how I was raised."

"I think I understand, although I'm slightly jealous of you skipping the negatives of childhood," Rachel said thoughtfully. "Not having a childhood? No family. Thanks for letting me know." A small, but very bright, light appeared on the horizon to the west; it was bright and it was moving fast. Towards them.

"Do you see that?" Rachel asked turning Bendin's face in the western direction. "It could be bad."

"*Now* I do. I hope it's Quip."

Bendin and Rachel watched the light get brighter at an extremely rapid pace. A few blinks later, Quip flashed to a halt in the air in front of them breathing hard, jets of fire shooting out of his paws holding him aloft. A sound and concussion wave ripped past them the instant after Quip stopped.

Quip watched the roof tiles break, tear, and spin into the air around him. "Sorry, forgot to slow down before I got here." He threw himself into Bendin's lap and slowly caught his breath.

Unbelievably, Quip had pieces of frost on his fur.

"Quip! What happened, and why is there ice on your whiskers?" Bendin said stroking Quip's face. "You were just totally on fire!"

"The upper atmosphere. Then on the way back, I was holding my breath in spurts," Quip managed to say after a few seconds. Quip lit just his whiskers and outer fur on fire, and the ice that was on them turned to vapor instantly.

Rachel asked, "I'm curious. Can you light any portion of your body on fire?"

"What like this?" Quip lit one ear on fire, followed by only his eye, and then his tail, then he showed his toenail and lit only his toenail on fire. Rachel clapped her hands and smiled enthusiastically.

"Wow, I had no idea you could do it that specifically," Bendin observed.

"Call me, Mr. Quiptionary, the language of surprise."

Rachel and Bendin laughed with Quip.

"What's up with breathing in spurts?" Bendin asked.

Quip raised an eyebrow, "It's kind of hard to explain. Once you get past the speed of sound you have no air, because these bands, at that point, push it all around you. So you end up going in bursts to catch a breath. It's kind of like swimming through the air. It's quite fun really since the bands also deflect all negative effects from going past the speed that sound goes!"

Quip let his tongue lull out of his mouth.

"What happened to the leader of the FZ's or whatever that guy or organization was?" Bendin asked.

"He's gone." Quip frowned. "He escaped out to a city in space above Makarias. I can only go so high before bad things start to happen to you: Cold, death disease, paralysis, implosion, explosion; you get the picture." He stopped catching his breath and ate one of the pills Bendin gave to him.

"Lavikuna." Rachel brushed her hair back. "That's where he's gone. They are part of the Wight's jurisdiction."

Bendin scrunched his eyes. "The Lavi-wha-now?"

"Lavikuna is a small space community. It's a fairly new group that wanted to live over Makarias. They passed ten thousand inhabitants the other day. Simon Wight was gloating about it and he believes they are the future of our society. I don't know. All they are right now is nothing more than a huge monitor for the weather patterns and a facility that manages many of the network capacities."

"Thanks."

"So, what do you guys say we go find some rooms in this temple to stay the night?" Rachel said winking at him.

Quip saw her wink and with a large smile on his face he flicked his nose expectantly over to Bendin. Bendin didn't seem to notice what Rachel had done so Quip frowned angrily, flew up, and playfully slapped Bendin on the face with his paw.

"Hey! What was that for?" Bendin whined, innocently pulling his hands up to shield his face from any more blows.

"For not paying attention. I'm thinking about making you my student!" Quip huffed grumpily.

"It's okay, let's go guys," Rachel said pulling Bendin up into the air.

They followed Quip around and found, after an hour of searching, rooms that they were able to settle down in. Bendin spied a nice seat and table near the bed and used Quip's body to dust off the wooden table.

"Hey! I'm not a feather duster. I'm a fire breather! You're going to pay for that one." Quip flared his nostrils and sucked in air till he couldn't hold it anymore. Bendin dove behind the bed in fear.

Just as Quip was about to unleash fury, he farted a large puff of smoke out of his rear.

Quip froze, completely embarrassed, while Rachel and Bendin fell over laughing. Quip belched a fireball into the air and relaxed into a loopy grin.

Once the dust and humor had cleared, Bendin sat down in a worship position and began doing his rituals. Rachel left whistling a tune Bendin didn't know. He focused and finished his peace-filled worship. Afterwards, they settled down on the bed.

Finally, sleep.

But as the light from Quip's fire died down, Bendin's eyes focused on the floor. He shrieked, jumped, hollered, and ran out of the room as fast as he could.

"What? What was it?" Quip asked flying up, confused.

"There's something creepy in there. I saw it."

"What's going on guys?" Rachel asked emerging from the room across the hall wrapped in a blanket she had found and cleaned. "I was just starting to doze off."

"Fast sleeper?"

"Maybe."

"Anyway, Bendin says he's seen something creepy." Quip rolled his eyes dramatically.

"Fine. Let's see what it is so we all can get to bed!" Rachel stomped past them. She flicked on the lights and to Bendin's dismay there was a single cockroach in the middle of the floor.

"That's it? Ha!"

Rachel smashed the cockroach flat and the floor was instantly flooded with insects of all kinds and sizes. Rachel screamed throwing her blanket on the bed in shock. "That's really creepy! How did we miss these guys?" Rachel danced around mashing as many as she could.

"I have no idea, maybe it was the darkness." Bendin peeked inside the room. "Blech. Creepy critters."

Quip stared at Bendin. "I'm a critter, do you hate me?"

"You're *not* creepy. You're like my hero or something," Bendin said, this time rolling his eyes.

"Quip, your hero to the rescue!" Quip shouted triumphantly, and he blazed into the room, did an elegant flip, and let out such a large fire blast that the whole floor burst into flames in a giant, sweeping, circular wave. All insects were instantly barbequed.

"The woodwork is on fire!" Rachel gasped.

Quip flew around the room so fast that the fire went out like you would blow out a match. Rachel went out, found a broom, and swept up the remains.

"Not anymore." Quip pranced proudly. "It's a good thing this floor is made out of stone, otherwise, there would have been no way I'd have been able to do that."

Rachel had to pry Bendin's hands clamped to the door frame off with force. "It's--all--right--Bendin." She drug him back into the room and playfully shoved him back into his bed.

"Rachel plus one," Quip saluted her and threw himself into Bendin and said, "glad I didn't have to pry him off the door. Ha! Your face though. You should have seen it."

Bendin didn't think it was all that funny.

"Good night guys, sweet dreams." Rachel yawned.

"Good night, thanks guys," Bendin said finally relaxing.

Chapter 23
Krawbus Hexalexus

Over the next day Quip, Bendin, and Rachel explored the Temple from top to bottom as fast as they could. It was then that Bendin and Quip noticed things changing very rapidly in Toalt. There was a huge influx of people, and this caused them to worry.

There was also another big problem. Castle Marshall Krawbus Hexalexus. Marshall Hexalexus was the embodiment of characters you hear about in tales and legends. A true giant and titan. So, naturally, Bendin and Quip wanted to avoid giving him a chance to ruin their plans.

The next morning came with decent weather which helped Bendin's mood perk up a bit.

"Rachel, we are going in today. We have a plan, and we are sure it's going to work," Bendin declared.

"Just like your recipe." Quip pointed at her with smoky claws, smiled, and thrust his nose proudly into the air.

"My recipe?" Rachel laughed. "Oh dear."

"We located a prime spot to find another piece!"

"Great! And guess what? I found the Makarias gate room before you guys got up this morning; come see!"

She took them down to it and displayed it proudly. "Not as beat up as ours at home. But definitely dusty!"

"They sure are busy," Quip noted.

Bendin saw, in Toalt, many scientists working again in front of the gate. This gate room was designed with the gate inset into a wall on a narrow ledge. In the middle of the room, bars and beams had been set up over a very deep hole on which they had placed walking planks and solid flooring for their equipment. The equipment and machines filled in most of the space in the middle.

"Who?" Rachel asked putting her hands on her hips. "You know I can't see over there."

"Right." Quip chuckled and caught his arms on fire. He then waved his arms in the air demonstrating what the people in Toalt were doing. "They are building here." He pointed at empty space. Then flew over the gaping hole. "They are working on this machine here, here, here, and here. I don't know exactly what they're doing but they are completely focused on it."

"Rachel," Bendin raised his hand to get her attention. "Before we go, we have an instruction we've received from Odge. Just in case we don't come back right away, you might have to deliver it."

Quip flew over and landed on Bendin's shoulder mimicking his arm movements before Quip added, "If you see anyone else, this is for them too."

"Ok." Rachel waited. "What is the instruction?"

"Don't come to Toalt."

"That's it?" Rachel waited for more.

"Yep!" Quip agreed. "And don't forget to brush your teeth!"

Bendin smiled. "What do you clean *your* teeth with? fire?"

"Yeah, watch this!" Quip displayed his hand and very forcefully formed the fire into the shape of a toothbrush. He shoved it into his mouth and "brushed" his teeth while smoke lulled out his ears.

Rachel grinned. She then grew serious being sure both were paying attention to her. "That shouldn't be a problem. But, please . . . promise to get Jean first."

"We promise." Bendin gave Rachel a hug and Quip danced across both of them ending up on Bendin's shoulder.

Bendin and Quip left the gate room and went to where they had found Jean.

"Oh, no," Bendin said once he got there.

"Where is she?" Quip observed.

Jean, was missing.

"Wait, they are moving her!" Berdin felt a surge of hope well up inside. "That way!" He pointed in the direction down out of the cell block.

"This is quite a number guarding her," Quip said.

"That's not what i'm worried about. It's what they are putting her in. Look."

Quip flew down the ramp in Makarias through the large line of Vaelift Elect, Angels and many of Odge's Vaelift.

The Odge's Vaelift were clamping Jean down inside a metal and glass cylinder, just like the cylinders in the central temple. "Let's stop them, break up the group, free Jean, and get her out the gate."

"We can take on thirty Vaelift?" Quip asked with a real expression of concern on his face.

"Let's vift."

Bendin and Quip lined up on either side of the group as they finished clamping Jean's other hand in place and vifted to Toalt.

Two thunderous compression waves blasted down half of the group instantly. The other half were stunned and dazed. Bendin quickly set to work bashing anyone that was around the cylinder.

"Bendin! Help me!" Jean screamed beating on the cylinder walls.

Her cry tore Bendin's heart. He beat away the two that were closest to him, but three more filled the space of the two fallen Vaelift, fresh and attacking. Quip got to the other side of the cylinder after blasting the whole line of Vaelift down, one falling into the other, and began to heat it up.

The two Vaelift on the ground pounded on the side of the cylinder and they heard it seal shut with a loud snap.

Bendin had to vift his way around till Quip shouted, "Ah-ha! I've got it!"

A lurching crack sounded and the floor split directly under the cylinder.

"Not the floor, Quip, the cylinder!"

"I didn't that!" Quip blasted another student who leaped up to grab him.

Bendin and Quip watched in horror as the cylinder fell through the growing opening into a chute that immediately began to close.

They quickly dove down after it into the chute. They heard a cheer erupt as the opening sealed shut. "Quip, go go go!"

"Heeeeeeeeeee!" Bendin heard Quip yell as he left Bendin far behind. The chute opened into a passage that tilted down steeply, and Bendin guessed they were moving below all of the rooms of the temple. Bendin heard an "ow!", and then an explosion. Three more "ow's" and three more explosions. As Bendin rounded the next bend in the passage, it leveled flat. He could just make out Quip's glow in the distance. Bendin passed a wall that had been violently blown apart.

"Quip!"

Quip turned and motioned for Bendin to come. "I can't blow through this one, Bendin. Or vift. She went through. I need you!"

Bendin skated to catch up and passed four more walls

with the same violent holes blown through them.

Bendin felt what Quip was pressing up against. It was a cold material Bendin was not familiar with and it was apparently unyielding to Quip.

"She went that way," Quip said again pointing through the material.

Bendin pulled the long flat cylinder Celeste had given him and pointed it at the material. A thin blue light beamed from the end and scanned the entire surface. A long thin metal rod extended from the device, split into four segments, inserted itself into four holes, and four loud audiable clicks were heard.

"Welcome, Castle Marshall Hexalexus," a voice announced, "access granted."

Suddenly, the wall slid upwards.

"I can't believe that just worked." Bendin stared in disbelief.

"Useful." Quip twirled in excitement.

Bendin knew the moment they walked in that they were not supposed to be in this small enclosed room. As red lights and sirens flashed across the walls, Bendin noticed for a moment a bright blue energy ball hovering above a complicated piece of machinery in the middle of the room, and a large display that encompassed the entire wall in the back. The display had a very detailed map with red dots and blue dots all across it with bright blue letters at the top that flashed, "The Balance".

"Intruder!" an electronic garbled voice spat at them. The display disolved into the wall, while the blue energy ball sparked and the entire apparatus, blue ball and all, shot down through the floor as if an invisible hand had reached up and pulled it under the floor. Quip reacted in the nick of time as the room compressed at incredible speed by grabbing Bendin and pulling him safetly back out the way. The room slammed shut with a terrific crash.

"The balance?" Quip eyed Bendin curiously.

Bendin shrugged. "Never heard of it. Look at this, Quip." Bendin pointed at every wall Quip had blown through and to the spot on the passage next to them.

"Doors?" Quip marveled at them.

"Yeah. You were in a hurry and missed them."

Quip didn't deny that. "Maybe we can find another way to her."

Bendin scanned the door and the device again unlocked it for them. "Did you see any of the Elect or Angels firing at us?"

"No."

"Odd. Me neither." Bendin skated down the new passage and it linked up with a hall that led to all the other doors they had passed. "Only one way to go." He was now very uncomfortable without being able to vift.

"I'll go first. Things smell really old down here, even though these passages are all new." Quip burst into flames and flew ahead of Bendin down the hall. It opened into a dome shaped room cut from solid stone.

"Now this stone is ancient. It's exactly like the other rooms with the pieces. They skated around the room cautiously looking for any sign of anything that might give an indication of a path out so they could find Jean.

"I found something! It's not Jean though," Quip yipped eagerly, pointing downwards.

He was right. It wasn't Jean.

There, in the middle of the room under a grate, was another piece. It shimmered and shined and Bendin sighed again. It was bigger than his head, again. "If they couldn't vift things bigger than their head, why make the pieces the size of a human?"

"Maybe someone made it that way as a safeguard?"

"Maybe." Bendin extended the range of the effect of his silver box and wondered if he could lift the grate off. To his surprise, at the slightest tug the grate floated up.

Bendin reached down and pulled out the piece. He checked around and gratefully saw nothing.

"At least we didn't have to dig that one out," Quip muttered. "Is there a way out?"

"There!" Bendin pointed at a staircase that wound up and out of sight.

Bendin and Quip headed for the exit. As they left, gravity was restored to the plate, and it clattered to the ground.

The entire ceiling exploded into millions of pieces, the path out sealed shut, as doors upon doors slammed closed. Hundreds of students fell on top of Bendin and Quip, everyone crashing to the ground in a living breathing human cocoon. For a moment all the bodies landing on Bendin were redirected around Bendin, but there were so many that they piled up around him like a wall and collapsed right down over on top of him. Thus, Bendin found the air knocked out of him and unable to move.

"I think we've got him this time," a voice filtered down through the bodies from somewhere above Bendin. "And his little demon dog."

The people milled around till they succeeded in stripping him of the piece, his Vurfenstaff in large rubber tube, his boots, his bands, and his belt. Once they had achieved this, the people slowly filtered out of the room and let him lie on the ground. Bendin found himself wearing nothing but his regular Vaelift outfit with Quip lying on the ground next to him also stripped of his bands.

A small circle of Odge's Vaelift, all faces Bendin had never seen, and two men in black wearing full faceless masks were all that remained of the people that had been piled on top of him. Quip shook himself on the ground after a bit and groaned. He sadly caught Bendin's gaze of concern. "I think they broke something important inside me . . . it . . . hurts a lot and I can't move." Bendin felt the first pangs of fear creep up his back.

The faces in the circle of people went from shock, to horror, and then to frowning.

The wall in the back split wide open revealing a secret, tall, narrow, dark, ominous hall. Castle Marshall Krawbus Hexalexus strolled into the light proudly. "It's finally over. You're defeated. You have lost, and you can't go to Makarias."

"Krawbus," Bendin grumbled angrily.

Krawbus turned and waved to all of the departing students and collaborators. "Beautiful job there. Beautiful job. That was quite the man-pile. By the will of Odge we've done it. You will be suspended permanently." He waved his hands and the two men in black seized Bendin, and metal handcuffs were slapped on him.

"Odge, help me, please!" Bendin pleaded aloud.

"Call *louder*, I don't think he can hear you," Hexalexus mocked.

"Maybe I will." Bendin glared at Krawbus.

The man placed the bindings on Bendin's hands and feet, and tiny ones were put on Quip's legs, binding all four together. Quip grunted painfully the entire time.

"I've got it from here guys, back to your posts. And be sure that gear gets to those labs. Don't steal from Odge!" Hexalexus commanded. The men in black and half of the group of Odge's Vaelift grabbed all the gear and left.

"Right this way! Make yourselves at home."

"What do you want with us, Hexalexus?" Bendin asked as he was pushed through the secret slit that hid the dark hall in the wall. The only visibility came from the lights carried by

Hexalexus and his henchmen.

He smiled at Bendin, "That's it exactly! You nailed it, Bendin. You're what we've always wanted once we figured out who you were." Hexalexus shouted incomprehensible orders to two of his closest attendants and they hurried away. Hexalexus turned back to Bendin, "You even have some new tricks and technology that we've been absolutely *dying* to obtain. Today is *that* day. So carefully planned, so craftily executed. We just needed you to bite. Just one small irresistable bite. And you did! Thank you for your delightful contribution."

They planned this? That seemed implausible. Then again, maybe not?

Quip eyed Hexalexus angrily.

"There is no way that's all you wanted," Bendin said disbelievingly.

"Yeah. Pretty much, yes. You've delivered me everything."

Bendin felt a long slow sense of sadness fill his heart. He wondered how Jean was doing. If only they'd have been able to break her out of that cylinder.

They continued moving down the dark hall into a white-bricked circular room that had chains lining the walls.

"Jean!" Bendin gasped seeing the small figure hanging on chains on the wall.

Motionless, she made no sound or effort to communicate.

There were two other people already in the room dressed in solid white, and they had large mirrored glasses over their eyes. Hexalexus motioned for them to link the handcuffs with the chains attached to the walls. There were even some janitors in the back that were cleaning orange goop up off the floor.

"Familiar with these, Bendin?" Hexalexus laughed and pulled the chains. "Only this time you will be stuck in here. No one knows about this place but myself and my closest attendants. You were the worst of all the students, Bendin."

Bendin felt a revived pang of hurt. He knew that wasn't true. He'd been an excellent student. One of the very best.

Marshall Hexalexus raised his hand and held it. "You were the hardest and most ardent student our system has *ever* seen in all the years of the temples. You had one flaw that ruined your entire future."

Quip tried to speak but coughed instead.

Bendin asked, "And what was that?"

"You figured out how to communicate with Odge."

Light dawned in Bendin's heart. He understood now why they hated him so much. "That's not a flaw! I'm surprised Odge isn't beating you up right now." Bendin pushed against the strong chains.

"Odge has no power here or there. He's so limited by his own self-righteousness, he'll let you rot in here for as long as I want you to." Hexalexus sneered.

"He stopped you before. It will be nothing for him to stop you again. You got what you wanted from us, so why don't you just kill us?" Bendin said.

"Because, this isn't only the beginning of your end, Bendin; it's the beginning of the end of every scrap of everything you stand for." Marshall Hexalexus twirled his fingers around each other. He grinned wickedly. "As long as you're alive, Odge can't call another. He would destroy himself if he did!"

"How do you know so much about Odge?" Bendin asked.

"You could say we have been instructed by one who knows him." Hexalexus frowned.

"Probably Zadok," Bendin mumbled. "Need anything else Krawbus?"

Hexalexus got within twenty-five centimeters of Bendin's face and said excitedly, "We got you. We got our people. We want your people. We want Makarias to be like Toalt. Completely under our control. There is no secret here." He smiled happily. "Enjoy your stay, bye-bye." He waved his hands and left the room. His cheerfulness stunk. And as it wafted away with Krawbus, the room fell into a dismal and eery silence.

Bendin felt extremely sorry for his faithful companion. "Quip is there anything I can do for you?"

Quip winced and spoke softly, the words coming out in-between breaths, "I can . . . hardly talk now . . . let alone . . . do anything. I . . . just need . . . some rest."

Bendin wasn't so sure that's all he needed, but he knew that being here wasn't going to be the best option. They needed to find a way out. But how? The attendants had taken his staff elsewhere, and even though it was gone, he could feel its location. Calling it would be pointless. They had him bound tightly so he couldn't wriggle out. Bendin really couldn't think of anything else he could do. He silently prayed for Odge to do something. The attendants in white left them, turned out the lights, and were gone.

"Bendin?" Jean's light voice asked.

"Yes?"

"What's going to happen? Are you ok?"

Bendin honestly didn't know. He had nothing. "Yes. Quip isn't. I don't know what will happen, but, Jean, we are going to be patient. Odge will save us."

Jean was quiet for a minute. Then she said softly, "I believe you."

The attendants only came back to bring small amounts of food and water. They would then immediately leave and shut down the lights. Hours upon hours went by. Bendin didn't have any of his gear, so time passage was only governed by the coming and going of food. The biggest problem was the sinking feeling of hopelessness and worrying about the completely quiet Quip. He'd said nothing this whole time.

Bendin was quite sure a couple of days had passed now. Hexalexus had only been in there one other time for a routine check before he quickly left.

Bendin felt the entire building foundation shake. Something had rocked the place. Then it stopped. Strangely, he felt hopeful. Maybe the Alcs were breaking into the building and he could get out of here.

A while later, the wall parted and the lights in the room were flicked on again. It was the attendants in white followed by people being carried in with faces that were immediately familiar. Hexalexus, grinning from ear to ear, revealed Rachel, Callapse, Ryan, Pete, and Mez all asleep being carried by students.

Bendin noticed that all of them were not wearing any gear. Callapse had a long bandaged gash across his face and he slumped down as he was chained to the semi-circular wall.

Hexalexus slapped each one awake as they were put on the wall.

"I'm sorry, Bendin," Rachel whispered as she sleepily opened her eyes and was chained near him. "They got us."

"Bendin, I'm going to assume you know these people. Would you mind introducing us?" Hexalexus gloated. "I'm very happy to have you come join us here in temple number three."

Bendin shrugged, his chains rattling. "Callapse, Rachel, Ryan, Pete, and Mez, meet Castle Marshall Krawbus Hexalexus."

Hexalexus bowed. "I'm in charge of this temple, and the

security which you, through serendipity, tripped. You shall stay here till I decide what exactly I am going to do with you."

"What do you want with them?" Bendin asked.

"Perhaps I'll enjoy playing with these descendants of despicableness. Or perhaps not." He turned and looked directly at Bendin. "Hmmm. People are no fun when they die, and you can't hear them whimper, whine, moan, complain, and break."

"You're a sad pathetic monster," Bendin griped indignantly not believing how anyone could have fun doing such a thing.

Hexalexus whispered many things into the ears of the prisoners that Bendin couldn't hear, each in their own turn. He started at the end and went down through the line only skipping Bendin and Quip. Ryan laughed outright and Pete grinned. Hexalexus smacked them both before moving onto Rachel. She burst into tears. Mez said nothing. Cal apse calmly watched Hexalexus the whole time, even as he left the room with his attendants in white. The slit and hall that led to the room slid closed leaving the room dark.

"Jean!" Rachel asked passionately. "How are you?"

"Okay," Jean mumbled.

"Bendin, what happened?' Ryan's voice sounded faint as if out of a dream.

"I was about to ask you the same thing," Bendin replied. "We did exactly as we had planned. We went to save Jean and she was used to lure us into his trap. He dropped a room full of people on us." Bendin sighed. "There was nothing we could do."

"Wow, I assume we were picked up and carried here. *Callapse* came up with a great plan. Rachel showed us where you guys vifted over and *He* said t--" Ryan explained weakly.

"I *know* what I said!" Callapse cut in with as much energy as he could muster. "I'm right here, please. I knew that would be a safe place to cross over."

"You knew coming over was a bad idea, but you wouldn't listen," Rachel accused.

"You came over," Callapse pointed out.

Rachel sighed. "I know. When you and Quip didn't come back after a few hours I began to get worried. But then after a couple of days, I was completely scared."

"What happened to the backpacks?" Bendin asked warily.

"They broke them all, destroyed with their blue rods," Callapse said sadly and sniffed.

"Apparently that wasn't what they were supposed to be doing, because that Hexalexus guy showed up and cried when he saw the pile of fragments of what was once our packs. He sent them off and I collapsed, unable to stay awake any longer," Ryan finished explaining.

"We are stuck here, aren't we?" Callapse muttered.

"Quip? Quip? What happened to Quip?" Rachel asked.

"Quip is sleeping. They landed on him and broke something. He is very weak and hasn't emitted so much as one flicker of light. I'm really concerned about him." Bendin wiggled his chains. "These chains are impossible."

"How are we going to get out of here then?" Rachel asked.

Her question was met by nothing but silence.

Hexalexus came back several hours later with several people. One of them was Harmon Greystead and Bendin felt a huge surge of excitement rush through his body. She was carrying one of the destroyed backpacks and was almost as excited as Hexalexus. She was buzzing in conversation with him. The others were scientists from the gate that Bendin and Quip had seen before. They must have moved the whole team over.

Hexalexus smiled. "It's time for a little fun." He had Rachel removed and laid on a table. The attendants brought utensils and tools.

"Krawbus, don't do anything to her," Bendin said defensively.

"What? Are you afraid I'll kill her?" Hexalexus mocked.

Mez and Callapse's faces paled whiter than the walls as he pulled out sharp objects. Ryan and Pete's eyes flicked all over the lighted room taking in all the tools and machinery. Hexalexus's aids launched into action taking samples from Rachel: Hair, nails, plasma, and blood. Hexalexus watched and made the men in white twist her ankles till Rachel began to scream in pain. They then rotated them around the other direction till she again screamed again.

Bendin felt his blood rush through his body and he called out several times, "Come here, now!" He held his hand out and his staff smashed through wall after wall till it burst through theirs. The staff smashed into one attendant before Krawbus pulled up a metal cage and got between it and Bendin. With a clang and a smash, Krawbus slammed the door closed and trapped the staff inside of it.

Bendin tried again, but the staff bounced around the

cage harmlessly. The cage was solid and his Vurfenstaff was locked up tight. Bendin could almost cry. Aside from Odge intervention, it was the only thing he had been able to think of that would have allowed him to escape.

"Thank you, cage," Hexalexus said looking at it. "We need some tears, please." He then had the men twist her arms around and tested the extensions of how far they would rotate. She again screamed in pain and did not stop. Tears of pain began to drip from her face. The drips were collected in a container Harmon held. She was straight faced and focused on the work.

Callapse screamed, "STOP! Dont do it. Stop hurting her!"

Hexalexus smiled softly. "And this," he said pointing to Callapse and showing the aids in the room, "is why you never have close relationships or anything of the sort. He is completely out of his mind."

Hexalexus walked over to Callapse who was red-faced, scared, angry, but uncertain of how to take a man who was responsible for having his sister tested and tortured walking up to him. He did the only natural thing that any person who is chained to the wall would do. He swung out at Hexalexus's face baring his teeth. Hexalexus had one of his attendants in white knock Callapse out at the snap of his fingers. Bendin noticed Jean flinch, sigh, and look at the floor.

They finished working on Rachel and put her back on the wall in chains. She stopped screaming, but she didn't stop tearing up and crying.

Hexalexus proceeded to do this set of experiments with Pete, Ryan, Callapse, Jean, and Mez. All of them cried and tears streamed from their faces. Harmon continued to be straight faced the entire time. Bendin didn't know why they were doing all of this, and he hated every second of it.

Hexalexus observed the tests and the final results, packed up everyone, all the collected assets, and left. Hexalexus returned every single day for three more days and got more samples and did more tests and more 'torture' on his visitors. Each day, all of them were getting more emotional, louder, and more depressed. At the end of the third, which was another long grueling day of testing and torture, Bendin felt tired and guessed everyone else must be too. Quip remained motionless the entire time and was the only one not tested. He would only blink his eyes to show he was still alive. Bendin didn't have much hope for his friend or anyone else for that matter. Pete and Ryan were saddened and only passed the time asking each other questions on different topics. Callapse voiced the most regret at first, then he hadn't spoken to any of them in the three days after his initial outburst. Mez was typically quiet.

"How much longer do you think we'll be chained here?" Rachel asked.

"As long as we live," Ryan said sadly tugging on the chains. "I've given up hoping to get out of here."

"I don't think that will be long at the rate he is going," Pete said hopefully. "How about you, Bendin? What do you think? Any help from Odge?"

"What?" Rachel asked. "You are asking what?"

"I was asking Bendin. I think if there's even the remotest chance of his existence, I'd like his help."

"Oh."

Bendin answered, "Odge has said nothing. I don't know what to make of it."

They heard the walls slide open, the dark hallway flickered in a soft light, and Harmon walked in carrying a torch.

Hope and relief washed over Bendin. Finally, they could get out of here.

"Harmon!" Bendin whispered admiring Harmon in the faint light. "What took you so long?"

"Bendin. I finally got some time to come back here. It took me *forever* to find a little free time. Hexalexus has had us so busy tearing into the new technology he stole from you guys, I haven't had time till now. Most tech is impossible to duplicate, others, we will get fairly close. I came to talk to you, Bendin," Harmon said cautiously coming closer to Bendin.

"Talk? . . . But . . . What do you mean? Help us out of these please!" Bendin rattled the chains desperately.

"I can't do that, you see, Bendin," she showed him the shoulder of her Vaelift uniform. In the faint light Bendin could see a symbol he had only seen in one place before--on the cover of the great book of Odge. It was in the shape of a square spiral. It was very similar to the circular symbols that the Elect, Angels, and Odge's Vaelift wore in the school system on their Vaelift uniforms. "This is the sign of Odge, the truth. After our little experience, I had the opportunity to talk with Findall about my experience. He gave me some really good advice and he said that I really hadn't given the Vaelift system and Odge a real chance. He said that I needed to study that first and not trust in my feelings because you can be easily deceived. Bendin, I didn't want to be deceived so I did what he said and studied the great book of Odge much closer."

Bendin didn't know how to react to what she was saying and just stared at her, his heart beginning to sink to the pit of his stomach.

"I found that it's true and that you believe in a false Odge. It's actually Pikuk in disguise. You've been deceived Bendin . . . please, come back to the truth," Harmon said this softly and firmly. She was completely serious.

"I can't believe you'd throw your experience, which you know is true, away for his imitation of Odge!" Bendin said to her.

"So what? It's a deception! I know I felt something, but it's not Odge's power! Can't you see you are being played?" She implored. "Don't trust the false Odge, Bendin. Odge doesn't work like that. He doesn't talk to you through your feelings or your heart. There are entire sections in the book that talk about this. I don't know how we missed them before. Tell me you will cast away this horrible lie and come with me to the truth! If you will do this, I will unlock you now and we can go and work on the gate to Makarias together!"

Bendin sighed. "Harmon, you're right that you can't trust feelings alone. I know what has happened to me is true, and it's much deeper than a simple feeling or impression. If it had happened only one time, that's something. But it's a daily thing. These experiences are my whole soul and my life now. It's knowledge, and it's deeper than the book that you are talking about describes."

Harmon's resolute expression on her face flickered for a moment.

Bendin explained further, "I'm not coming with you, and I'm not leaving my friends. Come with us, Harmon. What Findall told you isn't true. You don't want to be deceived, right? That's exactly what has happened to you!"

Harmon looked at him sadly. 'I'm sorry to hear that, Bendin. Findall was right, you are a Hidiadion. Everything he said is exactly what he'd said you'd say. He can't know that unless he's right. I can't believe it, but you truly either are the servant of the dark lord, Pikuk or you are Pikuk himself." Harmon, crying, left as quickly as she could.

Bendin was speechless. He had no idea what to even think, except it hurt.

"Idiot!" Callapse roared, for the first time in days, once

she was gone. "Bendin, you are now officially the stupidest person on the face of the planet."

It was so dark, Bendin couldn't see him, but it didn't matter. Bendin's heart had been ripped out of him and thrown on the floor and trampled by someone he cared about. By Harmon. Bendin felt all his frustration, feeling, and pain thrust into a vocal yell of anguish.

So loud was his yell and the energy of his feeling that the Vurfenstaff lunged forward with ridiculous force. The force ripped the cage off the wall, where it had been placed, and the cage slid across the floor till it stopped at Bendin's feet. A semi-translucent, partially-luminous white mist appeared around Bendin shoving hard on the chains and the walls around him causing them to rattle and shake. Several wall tiles shattered and rained down over Bendin. There wasn't anything he could do about freeing the Vurfenstaff though.

"A girl comes and offers to unlock you and you say no?" Callapse roared again smashing the wall with his hands. "Idiot, idiot, idiot, idiot!"

"Stop, Callapse. No more," Mez huffed. "Leave Bendin alone."

Bendin felt a touch of appreciation for Mez. "Thanks, Mez." He gripped the chains sadly.

Ryan coughed, followed by Pete.

"What's *your* problem?" Callapse said exasperated.

"You have no idea what just happened here," Pete explained and coughed again. "Ug, I think I'm coming down with something. Did you give it to me Ryan?"

"No," Ryan coughed. "Not *me*."

"I can't believe she would do that," Bendin said sadly. "She knew. Why would she believe Findall after that?" Bendin let his betrayed sense of trust and love continue to turn into tears of sadness dripping down his face to land softly on the floor.

Chapter 24
Hexagasp

Three more days went by and the tests continued. Bendin could hardly believe what Hexalexus was doing. He would do the exact same experiments and tests, day to day. Unfortunately, everyone continued to become more irritated and depressed. Callapse especially became more angry and discouraged. Bendin really didn't know what to think, but he hoped that they would be able to get out of here soon. Quip was speaking softly now from time to time, but when he did it was usually that he was going to die. Bendin hoped Quip wasn't seriously injured, but that seemed very slim.

The wall opened again and Hexalexus waltzed in. He was flanked by Harmon, some of his students, and his attendants in white.

"Hello my prisoners; my favorite prisoners in the whole entire world. Today we are going to try a different tactic along with the normal routines. We will see how long it will take before your body actually breaks down and dies. People here don't take much before they die. Your tests have shown excellent stamina. Except you, my young native Toltian, you don't count obviously.

"But you said you don't have as much fun if you kill them," Bendin mocked.

"I know, and I know you much better than you think I do!" Hexalexus frowned.

Bendin spoke softly, "Hexalexus, we are going to leave this day. You've had us long enough."

"Bendin? What are you saying?" Rachel whispered to him. Pete and Ryan both shot him a glance and Callapse frowned. Mez actually looked hopeful.

Hexalexus laughed. "Whatever. Did Pikuk tell you to say that to me? Odge wouldn't help losers like you. I have absolutely nothing to fear. Go, grab her."

His assistants grabbed Rachel harshly and pulled her off her chains and put her on the main testing table. They continued with their regular routines but instead of twisting the muscles in her feet, they strained them. They poked, prodded, extracted, tested and observed. Rachel grimaced and yelled in agony. Harmon was stone-faced the whole time.

Rachel's anguish tore at Bendin's heartstrings. Jean's face shriveled up like the end of a hot pepper and turned ripe red.

Hexalexus watched and enjoyed every moment. "You are making a very effective contribution to my Queen's society. Here, I will make it all the more interesting. Take our young friend here who looks as though her face will be permanently deformed if she keeps it like this." Hexalexus pointed at Jean. "You are so weak. You *infant*. You all look so sad. We must do something about this." Hexalexus grabbed a feather off of the table and handed it to one of his attendants in white. He let go of Rachel's foot and walked over to the kids grinning almost as wickedly as Hexalexus.

Bendin knew any minute Odge was going to give him the power to escape. He just had to be patient. They were going to be free.

"This will change your minds, faces, hearts, and attitudes." Hexalexus smiled and waved his hands in the air at everyone. "It will make all of you happy!"

The man in white tickled them by putting the feather under the nose of each one in turn, even Bendin.

"For once, I don't want to laugh," Pete managed to say in between a tickle.

"I know!" Ryan chimed in, agreeing.

The rest of the scientists continued on finishing their work on Rachel.

"How much longer before we are ready for the final test?" Hexalexus asked one of the aids.

"We are ready, sir."

"Good, bring out the end, THE HEXAGASP!"

Harmon clasped her hands excitedly at the word.

"Odge, please. I'm ready," Bendin whispered under his breath.

"I heard that," Hexalexus barked at Bendin. "Ha!"

"We have it," the aid reported.

The walls rolled back, exposed the hall, and several attendants wheeled in a black, metal, red-trimmed machine. They shoved four cables into into four operating outlets in the wall. It whirred to life and a door opened on the front of the black metal casing revealing a spiral shaped razor end sparking and whirling in red light.

"Yes, perfect. Tested on animals successfully. Time to test it on humans! One blast to the chest ought to do it."

The red-trimmed, black, metal machine pointed directly at Rachel and accelerated its motors.

No one moved as no one could. Bendin knew now was the time for action. He focused on his Vurfenstaff. Bendin he knew if he had that he could stop this. He gathered what energy he could and felt the reassuring presence of the love of Odge. It was surprisingly strong.

The hum reached its apex and the machine fired a large red pulse of light and it struck Rachel in the chest. Rachel gasped catching Bendin's gaze in horror. All movement from Rachel ceased immediately.

All focus shattered instantly as sadness, anguish, pain, and frustration filled Bendin.

"Success!" The attendant in white next to the machine announced. Harmon nodded the affirmative. They clapped enthusiastically and Hexalexus bowed.

Callapse, Mez, Pete, and Ryan yelled and tore at the chains. They stopped as Hexalexus drew his pistol and aimed it at each one.

"Excellent. Let's grab the infant n--"

He was interrupted by a loud gargle from Jean. She then fell silent.

"And down she goes . . . goodbye." Hexalexus waved his hand.

Jean's body began to shake and the vibrations rattled the chains incessantly.

Even Callapse tore his eyes from Rachel's lifeless body and turned to see what was going on.

Bendin watched terrified as Jean's face drained of all color.

"Get her, now! We need to be sure she didn't just faint." The attendants in white pulled Rachel off the table and placed her on the floor. They then went over to grab Jean.

"Stop! That's enough; you've already killed one!" Callapse cried out.

"No . . ." Pete started.

". . . Way," Ryan finished.

Quip was hardly conscious, but even Bendin could tell he knew something was wrong.

Jean's neutral colored body was immediately filled with a thick black pigment. Then thick scaly skin ripped throughout her entire body. The floor on which she was standing cracked under her feet.

The attendants in white stepped back in surprise.

"What's wrong with her?" Bendin asked, "Did she just die?"

"Shoot her!" Hexalexus roared angrily. "*NOW!*"

"No . . ." Pete started again.

". . . Way. She's as grandfather was," Ryan finished staring disbelievingly at Jean.

Jean open her bright, green eyes, which pulsed, smiled for the first time in days, and ripped the metal cuffs off her hands and legs like they were made of paper. She roared and charged at the operating table in a mad furry. The attendant in white closest to her was trampled immediately, and Hexalexus fired a couple shots before he turned around and raced to the wall. He quickly grabbed a cube-shaped device from off the wall and jammed his hand into it. With a blinding flash of blue light, he vanished. Jean's body smashed through the place he had been standing only a moment ago and bored a hole right into the wall on the opposite side.

Harmon and all of the other assistants fled out the dark hall in a frantic free-for-all. Jean pulled herself out of the wall and broke everyone's chains and bindings.

"Unbelievable, Jean," Bendin said rubbing his hands painfully. He felt weak and refused to be happy. He'd lost so much but maybe Rachel was . . . Bendin rushed to Rachel's body to check to see if she was truly gone.

Mez was already there holding her limp hand and said simply, "Gone."

Callapse pounded his fist repeatedly into the ground gritting his teeth and yelling louder with each repeated word, "No no no no no no no *no*! I did this. It's all my fault and now she's gone."

Pete and Ryan stood by saying simply nothing. But, by the looks on their faces Bendin could tell they were grieved.

Bendin felt devastated, twisted, and destroyed inside.

"She deserves to rest in Makarias. What's worse is Hexalexus is going to have this place swarming with people if we don't move," Callapse argued. "I will carry her."

Jean broke the cage open and Bendin happily retrieved his pulsating and lively Vurfenstaff. It was as if it was happy to see him too.

"How are we going to get out of here?" Jean asked.

"The only way we can get out. The gate!" Bendin said.

"Well, that's comforting," Ryan said. "I've been waiting

forever to get my hands on this." He picked up one of the tools that the aids used to shock them. It was shaped like a small pistol.

"It's payback time," Pete grumbled grabbing one as well. "For Rachel."

Bendin was glad they seemed in a better mood.

"We may be beat, but we are not broken," Ryan said limping to the middle of the room.

"Flip around that statement and you've got it," Pete corrected.

Ryan eyed him with a neutral expression on his face.

"Jean," Bendin said. "Will you take the front and lead us out of here?"

Jean shot back what Bendin guessed was a smile as it was pretty hard to tell. The only feature that really stood out was her green pulsing eyes, which were luminescent against her black scales.

Bendin picked up Quip and heard him groan. "I'm not going make it, Bendin. Leave me here to die," Quip mumbled.

"You've got to. What do you think is broken?"

"I don't know. It's got to be something important though, because I can't move."

"Guy's wait, I have to check him really quick to see what's broken," Bendin said.

Callapse, carrying Rachel's body on his back, Mez, and Jean limped down the passage back to the room that had held the piece.

Bendin set Quip down gingerly on the table and felt along Quips back. Near his shoulder, his hand felt something tiny jammed into it. Bendin pulled it out and Quip yelped so loud that Bendin thought for sure he killed him.

Quip erupted in flames in all directions, scorched the table, and singed Bendin. Pete and Ryan efficiently ducked under the table.

"Thanks," Bendin muttered sarcastically teetering on his feet.

Quip let out a sigh of relief, yipped in joy, jumped up, and flexed his muscles. "That feels so much better. I almost feel like a new fox!" Quip jumped on the ground, shouted, and shot around the room bouncing off the walls in joy. After a second or two he collapsed on the ground. "I feel woozy."

"Because, we've been in here for days. But it is good to see you up and around again," Bendin explained holding his hands out to Quip. Quip ran happily up Bendin's arms and licked Bendin in the face. "That's so much better, may I see what was so devastating to me?"

Bendin held up a tiny metal sliver.

Pete and Ryan laughed. Pete said, "That's all it was?"

"Hey, it was a killer sliver, you pair of twigs!" Quip shot back.

"Catch up guys. Come on!" Collapse yelled from the end of the dark hall.

"Let's get out of here." Bendin tested his legs to see if he could run. He came up with a half-run and hobbled down the passage after the others.

"Where do you think they put our gear?" Collapse asked once Bendin caught up.

"In pieces. I'm trying to think? We will do our best to find stuff," Bendin said moving into the room that held the piece a few days before. They were all barefoot and vulnerable. Quip flew over and checked to see if the piece was there.

"There is no piece here. Let us get out of this room as fast as we can," Quip urged.

Without another word they hobbled up the stairs and out into a room full of students working on models and projects on the floor. The floor trembled and shook and Bendin knew the temple was moving a lot of big objects. The students saw the group stumble into the room and scattered running in every direction throwing blueprints and calculators into the air as they ran.

"Let's get set up. I imagine the Elect and Angels will be here soon." Bendin ordered.

Pete and Ryan threw themselves in the far ends of the room, near the entrances. Mez joined them hiding in the shadow of the ramp.

"Just give us a few moments and we'll take them all down!" Ryan called out to them.

Bendin wondered just what they had in mind.

Two masked men in black followed by Hexalexus and a group of Elect, Angels, and Odge's Vaelift marched down the ramp a minute later. There were only three other entrances into the room: the path down which they had come, the path up, and the hall that went off in a flat direction away from them.

"Jean, you are going to have to take the bullets," Bendin instructed.

"I know," Jean said bravely. "I will."

"Good, wait for Pete and Ryan." Bendin looked at Rachel's lifeless body and felt pain and furry fill him.

Hexalexus crossed his arms and said unhappily, "Don't think you are just going to walk away. There is no escaping this fortress no matter what advantage you think you may have." He waved his arms and every Vaelift in the room aimed at the group.

"Three are missing. They are not above. Find them!" Hexalexus ordered. The two that ran in the direction of the hallway didn't even have a chance. Ryan lept from his place and zapped both of them. Pete rolled from his position behind the group and nailed two more elect from behind. Mez silently took down two more with swift kicks and armed himself. He quickly dispatched the next closest pair to him before retreating down the hall.

More shots rang out and Callapse went down holding his leg in pain.

Jean took two steps in front of Callapse as Bendin and Quip vifted out of the room. The two masked men in black charged Jean and shoved her into the concrete wall with a loud and deafening crash. Their body language showed excitement like a child that had just discovered a new toy.

"Cuff him!" Hexalexus ordered. "Leave the dead girl."

Two elect stopped firing down the hall and went over to Callapse. Callapse waited till the two Elect were directly next to him, and in his anger, he rose from the ground swiftly, grabbed their heads, and bashed them together.

The temple in Makarias was so spookily quiet and contrasted so starkly with Toalt it took Bendin by surprise.

Pete and Ryan used the stolen pistols and wounded any of the other gun wielding Vaelift as they backed separately away; Pete ran up the ramp. Ryan took off down the hall. Hexalexus split those who were able to fight from those who were not. He kept the Odge's Vaelift with him and sent the rest in two groups one up the ramp and the other down the Hall. He stood transfixed as Bendin and Quip vifted in to fight with the ones that were left around Hexalexus.

Bendin slammed the Vaelift in the face with his Vurfenstaff while Quip dodged the swing from another. Each of them vifted out of the way of any swing that got too close knocking the person backwards.

"You try my pat--" Hexalexus was yelling. Vifting cut off the sound in Toalt so Bendin only got bits and pieces as he was fighting.

Two of Odge's Vaelift attempted to hit Quip from behind, but Quip vifted, turned around in Makarias, vifted back facing them, and set their clothes on fire. The pair of them panicked, spun their blue staffs, and vanished with sparks of electricity shooting everywhere.

"We have the upper--"

Bendin vifted, spun around, vifted back, and did a sweep under the legs of one of the last two while Quip buzzed over his head.

"Your inconceivable breakout--"

Bendin vifted to avoid a deadly swing, vifted back, and clocked the last Odge's Vaelift in the shoulder, held it, and shocked him till he fell over into a heap on the floor.

He ran towards Hexalexus but instinctively vifted as Hexalexus unloaded his pistol.

Bendin was stuck with a brilliant idea. If he could get close enough and capture Hexalexus, he could secure safe passage through the gate. Quip followed Bendin as they vifted right on top of Hexalexus.

Bendin swiftly swung his Vurfenstaff down on top of Hexalexus as Quip blasted him with fire. To their surprise, an electric blast erupted from Hexalexus as he shoved his hand into the same kind of device he had down in the semicircular room. With a flash of blue light, he was gone.

"Please!" Bendin shouted, slammed his Vurfenstaff directly into the floor, and it responded with a resounding crack.

The far side of the wall was almost completely demolished and giant holes revealed the room below that had contained the piece. The battle between Jean and the men in black was tremendous. Jean climbed out enthusiastically and tried attacking them again. The men in black would eagerly throw her back into the wall again.

Bendin knew he had to get all of them to the gate, the piece probably being long gone, but the way was getting hampered up. Callapse was wounded and the group was breaking up. He'd have to gather them quickly.

"Quip, Follow me!" Bendin shouted and vifted to Makarias. Quip followed him instantly.

"Do you have a plan?" Quip asked hopping on Bendin's shoulder.

"Don't die."

"Mmhmm."

"Let's catch up to Mez and Ryan. They are going the wrong way," Bendin said urgently hurrying after them.

Bendin caught up with them at the end of the hall down a large curved staircase that hugged the arcing wall. Fat pillars, evenly spaced around the room, jutted up to the ceiling and, from Makarias, Bendin observed what was happening.

Ryan hunkered down in the middle of the room behind one of the columns. He shot around the corner at several Vaelift Angels that fired with continuous fire. Ryan was trapped.

Mez shot from the bottom of the staircase in an attempt to provide some cover for Ryan. There seemed to be too many Angels for him to escape.

"Quip talk to Mez. Let him know he can use the stairs up here to provide better cover fire. None of these passages lead to the gate room! We're going to have to go back the way we came and up and out to the gate room. You vift in first, get Mez moving, and then I'll create a distraction."

"Then can I set the Angels ablaze with my enlightened fire?" Quip asked.

"But of course. Do what you want." Bendin chuckled.

Quip laughed and flew away.

Bendin ran over to the opposite side of the room behind one of the groups of Angels and held his Vurfenstaff ready.

Quip vifted next to Mez and relayed the message, and Mez quickly ran up the stairs.

Bendin vifted in and knocked over three Angels while zapping the three with three swift strikes from his Vurfenstaff. The fourth grabbed the back of Bendin's uniform and wrapped his arm strongly around Bendin's neck.

Bendin couldn't vift, move, or breathe.

As Bendin was about to pass out, a shot rang out from across the room and Bendin felt the grip loosen allowing him to breathe again.

Bendin looked gratefully across the room and saw Mez dip his head in his direction. The other groups turned from each of their columns and shot at Bendin as he vifted.

Quip vifted behind the various pillars blasting down Vaelift angels one at a time. If they shot at Quip, he vifted away. That worked till one of the Vaelift smacked Quip down out of the air. The three left over Angels all turned to fire on Quip's stunned frame.

But, before they could fire they were thwarted by three swift shots from above. All three collapsed and Bendin turned in surprise to see Mez nod in Quip's direction. He then pointed at his gun and motioned for Quip to bring more. Quip quickly grabbed three of the fallen Vaelift pistols and flew them up to Mez. Bendin watched Ryan back towards the wall next to the stairs.

It was working. He was pretty sure Ryan would be able to make it up the stairs now unhindered. But, the wall behind Ryan exploded outward showering the room with rubble. The explosion knocked Ryan through the air perilously towards the wall on the far side.

Quip vifted, raced in front of Ryan's flight path, vifted back, and caught him using his fire to slow Ryan's descent to the floor.

It was a tank.

Bendin's mind didn't even stop to think of anything rational. He raced to the tank, vifted next to it, and crawled to the top, while Ryan found a pillar to hide behind. Bendin beat on the hatch with his Vurfenstaff till the hatch began to bulge inwards. The tank shot and the wall on the far side exploded in chunks. More Angels began to appear at the three lower entrances into the room.

Bendin was almost through the hatch before being forced to vift to avoid being shot by the newcomers. Ryan sprinted towards the stairs as Quip blew fire into each of the entrances. Mez shot anyone that tried to cross through Quip's fire.

The tank turned its turret towards the stairs and that's when Bendin saw Mez tactically retreat. Ryan closed the last of the distance as the tank shot again. The explosion ripped the wall to pieces and knocked Ryan's body through the upper entrance. Bendin quickly ran up the stairs in Makarias and caught up to were Ryan should have been. The hall was filled with chunks of rubble and rock.

Bendin vifted back to Toalt. He hoped Ryan was still alive. Quip arrived there a moment later.

"Can I help?"

"Yeah, smell Ryan out. Hurry!"

Quip immediately shot off in the direction of a large rock and Bendin could see Ryan lying on his side behind it.

Ryan coughed and held his side. He had a wound in his side and bruises on his face, but he appeared to be in good spirits. "I've never seen one of those before. Quite the jolt, aye?"

"Can you walk? We need to move before it decides to

break down all the halls in the building looking for us. I've never heard of them using tanks in the halls before," Bendin said quickly.

"Yeah, I think so," Ryan grunted as Mez helped him off the ground. "I'll live. Mez, thanks for your help."

"Yeah, thanks, Mez. You saved me." Bendin threw Mez an appreciative smile.

"Yeah, thanks, Mez. You saved me." Quip said mimicking Bendin's voice perfectly.

Bendin saw a happy grin appear on Mez's face. He gave a short nod.

"Let's go find the others and get out of here," Ryan shouted as Quip jumped on Bendin's shoulder. They all hobbled back to the room where Jean had been.

A massive blast shattered the hall floor ahead of them in block sized chunks. They all fell snaking to the ground. Bendin looked behind them and realized the tank had rammed itself into the opening to the hall, allowing its cannon to open fire.

"How in the world did it get up the stairs?" Bendin wondered aloud.

"Get *up* the ramp and out of this whole room, *move!*" Quip yipped.

"It's tearing this place apart!" Bendin said disgustedly.

The floor rumbled and shook.

The men in black burst through the almost completely demolished wall and lunged towards them. Jean slid in behind them and pulled them back by grabbing their ankles. The force was great enough to make both of the men in black miss their targets and go crashing into the opposite walls.

"You're getting better," Bendin noted. "Thanks, Jean."

"Thanks, Bendin!" Jean giggled. "Go guys, get on ahead. I'll catch up." Mez was already carrying Rachel's body up the incline.

"By yourself?" Quip and Bendin said together.

"Yes?" Jean said focusing again on the two men in black.

"You're so small!" One of them shouted. "I'm going to tear you apart."

Ryan followed Bendin and Quip to catch up with Mez and Callapse.

Everything had been changed. There were rails down the hallways going everywhere transporting minecarts full of supplies, gear, and students.

~ 379 ~

"What is going on?" Bendin wondered out loud. "What is happening to this place?"

"Industry," Ryan observed. "Old industry."

They ran to the end of the hall where it split in two main directions forming a small room that had carts zipping by every now and then. It was here that Callapse sat on the floor next to Rachel's body and placed his head in his hand. The other hand carefully held the place where he'd been shot.

They could see through the main opening that a large part of the center of the temple had been renovated into an enormous plant making machines by the thousands. There were thunderous engines with thick steam pouring into huge pipes connected to the ceiling. Students filled the room doing tasks that Bendin didn't have the slightest idea what they were.

"They're building out of metal," Ryan whispered.

"Is there a way around?" Bendin asked.

"I'll check," Quip vifted knocking Ryan and Mez over.

"You guys need to warn us before you do that," Ryan complained rubbing his side and ears painfully.

They watched all the students working and noticed Vaelift Angels and Elect milling around the room as well.

"I wonder where the Odge's Vaelift are?" Bendin asked.

Quip vifted back a bit later and reported that this newly created foundry had plenty of exits and entrances, but the gate room was only connected to one entrance on the opposite side of this one.

"And, there's a bit of a problem," Quip continued. "Hexalexus is in the way with an army of Vaelift and strange machines."

"He thinks he's got us for sure, doesn't he," Bendin said sighing.

"Ideas?" Callapse asked looking up and frowning. "I can't believe I did this to you all. I'm so sor--" He cut short as his leg twitched in pain."

Everyone, even Ryan, shrugged.

Mez studied the room but didn't offer any advice.

"I'm hurting all over," Ryan said. "But I'm sure we'll think of something."

"You're always coming up with ideas," Bendin said nudging him with his foot.

"Look out!" Quip shouted as a minecart flew around the corner, missing Bendin by a small margin.

Bendin, perplexed said, "Those are more dangerous

than I thought."

Another cart sped around the corner carrying a student but instead of flying past them, it stopped.

Ryan and Mez immediately pulled out two pistols each and aimed at the student. Bendin held his Vurfenstaff ready.

"Guys, it's me," the student said holding his hands up.

Bendin couldn't believe what he was hearing.

It was Pete, but completely different. His hair had been altered in color, clothes changed, and face so smudged by dirt that no one recognized him.

"What?" Bendin asked puzzled.

"Perfectly brilliant!" Ryan patted his brother on the shoulders.

"Tell me . . . that you have not, been riding in minecarts all over the temple this whole time," Callapse said as he grit his teeth and rose from the ground.

"Well, not the *whole* temple. There are some really nice spots where you can go nice and fast though. Really fun!"

"You know what we're going to do, right?" Ryan asked eagerly.

"First I'm going to *rip you to pieces!*" Callapse shouted and ran towards Pete.

"Enough!" Mez stiffly spat and grabbed Callapse pulling him back.

"No? Well . . . What then?" Callapse crossed his arms, still angry.

"We all do what he is doing, but stay in this general area. Where did you get your outfit?" Ryan asked.

"I stole it, how else? We can get more!"

Quip added, "Bendin and I can clear the gate room and come back for you."

"Quip, we can't take on Hexalexus, an army of Vaelift, and a bunch of tanks."

"No, not by ourselves we can't. We have Odge." Quip smiled.

Bendin raised his eyebrow.

"I'm sure we'll come up with something." Ryan eagerly rubbed his hands together.

Bendin wasn't so sure. "Okay, Odge has shown me one thing though, and that is how to get you guys through the gate. All of us have to make it that far, and we shouldn't have a problem. Mez, please get Jean to come up here. I'm sure if we can have her tussle with those guys in that foundry thing there,"

Bendin pointed at the large industrial room. "It would be very handy. Meet back here if you see Quip burning bright blue at the top of that large foundry machine in the middle of the room. Got it?" Everyone shook their heads affirmatively as Bendin turned to Quip. "Quip, ready?"

"Yes!" Quip and Bendin walked away a few steps from the others before they vifted to Makarias.

"I hope they will be alright," Bendin muttered as they navigated through the halls under the light of the fox.

"What do you think we should do? Any insight?" Quip asked as they turned a corner.

"Odge says the key to getting everyone out is to check the gate room first."

"Sure. Then what?" Quip said.

"We'll see what the key is."

Bendin checked Toalt as they went, and saw for the first time, Hexalexus and all the missing Odge's Vaelift. They were all in the far side of the foundry room. There were tanks lining the walls as well as Elect and Angels. Hexalexus moved around chatting with all of the Vaelift, probably giving them instruction but Bendin could only guess. The cart tracks ran all over all the rooms buzzing with activity and Bendin noticed with elation that one of the tracks led to the room that they were headed towards. Bendin ran directly into a Makarias wall and exclaimed painfully, "Tarnish!"

"There's a wall there," Quip mocked. "Is the wall okay?"

"Not. The time," Bendin said grinning slightly in Quip's soft orange light. "Ow!"

"It's just like the limitless walls in Makarias." Quip laughed. "Only it was you this time and not me."

Bendin smirked. "Ha-ha. Very funny."

"You know it is."

They went to the doorway at the top of the ramp and carefully observed the gate room. The cart track led past them, down the stone ramp, turned left on the ledge, and ran up to the gate. From what Bendin could guess, it stopped right in front of the gate itself. Harmon was there dressed in her usual white coat with her hair tucked back with a headband, ordering around several other people. The space in the middle of the room was even more filled in with bolted tables, equipment of all kinds, wires, lights, meters, and an exotic variance of testing tools. Every few moments a large engine, in the corner opposite the ledge, would flash and pop sending sparks through wires that went to the gate. Bendin realized he wasn't going to be able to check around the room from Makarias due to the very deep hole in the middle of the room.

"Quip, please fly over there and see if they have anything of our gear at all?" Bendin asked.

Quip flew over and checked around. "I see some fragmented remains of what once was everything that we had. It's useless."

Bendin frowned, disappointed What were they supposed to find then? What was the key? Then it dawned on him in a warm simple word. "Harmon," Bendin said with certainty. "Something about Harmon."

Bendin vifted directly into the room on the ramp timed perfectly with the engine's sparks with Quip vifting onto his shoulder immediately after him. They slid down the ramp and startled many of the students that were working on instruments.

"Stop right there!" Harmon ordered brandishing a pistol, a large sneer crossing her face. "You're not supposed to be here at all. Leave immediately or I will shoot you."

Bendin rolled into the students working on the mysterious equipment. He dodged, rolled, swung, and zapped each student in turn with quick thumps from his Vurfenstaff.

Quip sped directly at Harmon in a bright flash catching her direct attention. Harmon shot repeatedly at Quip but was disappointed when Quip vifted to Makarias and back just before each shot and every time Quip appeared in a different spot. Finally Quip vifted in from Makarias on top of Harmon's gun and heated the piece of metal red-hot. Harmon threw Quip and the hot pistol into the gaping hole that was next to the gate's ledge in shock, holding her hand painfully.

"You vile dog pal of Pikuk spawn!" She spat.

Quip flew up out of the hole screaming, "*I am not a dog!*" and angrily blasted fire all over Harmon. To Quip's surprise, the flame went around her.

"These bands are useful. I just wish we knew how to make them!" Harmon laughed revealing the bands tucked in her uniform and under her headband.

Bendin stepped up and offered her his hand. "Harmon, please reconsider. We know what we are doing and you have to realize you've been deceived by Findall. Now he's only using you to get what he wants!"

"Whatever. The Castle Marshalls, Findall, the Queen, and the true Odge have a dream. Only through them will

Makarias be realized! Your words mean nothing to me, Hidiadion, or should I call you incarnate Pikuk?"

Bendin cried, tears flooding his face. "But . . . I love you!"

Harmon stared at Bendin, paused, flushed slightly, but the hardness slowly returned. "You . . . can't. Your evil . . . I mean I used to, Bendin. Used to, before . . . I learned the truth." She displayed the simple symbol on her shoulder again, the squared spiral. "This is the real truth. . . . Thank you for the new technology."

Bendin knew what he had to do, even though he didn't want to do it. "I'm sorry, Harmon."

"For what?"

Bendin skillfully spun his Vurfenstaff at a slow speed, connected with Harmon's head which knocked her unconscious, and she fell clattering onto the boards.

Bendin pulled off her bands one by one. "But, I still love you. Why can't you see?"

"I'm proud of you, Bendin. I didn't think you could do it," Quip commented landing on his shoulder.

"Do what?"

"Hit her."

"Ah . . . right. I thought you were going to say, 'love her'"

"Ah . . . right." Quip grinned.

"Ah . . . right. Anyway, we have Odge's key. Let's go and get the group back together. Now that we have these, I think we can blast our way out of here." Bendin winked pointing at the bands in his hands. "Please go and vift in at the top of the room and signal the others."

Quip saluted humorously with a lopsided grin with his tongue hanging out of his mouth.

They vifted to Makarias, split up, and Bendin ran through the halls back to the room on the other side. On his way he noticed that Hexalexus was, for some unknown reason, still talking to the Vaelift. He noticed all the workers were gone though as Jean exploded into the room on the far side. She was followed by the two men in black.

Once back to the room with Rachel in it, he vifted and found that Callapse and Mez were the only ones there. Callapse was still mumbling miserably to himself. He was holding Rachel's hand in one of his own.

"It's all my fault, Bendin." Callapse tugged on Bendin's arm with his free hand.

"What?"

"I had no idea. I'm sorry, for everything." Callapse sighed painfully. "My sister. She's gone. I . . . did this."

Bendin bent down and held Callapse's shoulder lightly for a second. "We all make mighty mistakes. Please, don't fret forever in despair. Let it grip you. Let it change you. By admitting your own mistakes, you've already taken your first step on the road to recovery and redemption. Our only duty now is to get you, us, her, and everyone of us back to safety. I miss her too. I'm sorry."

Callapse closed his eyes and leaned his head back on the wall.

Bendin watched and waited as Quip vifted in near the top of the foundry section burning bright blue. The intensity increased till you couldn't look directly at it. Shots rang out from the far side and he vifted back. Quip made it back to them before the next person had even arrived.

"Done." Quip licked Bendin and curled up on his shoulder.

"Everything is becoming a major mess out there. I hope we all make it through. Did you tell Jean she needs to lose those two guys before she comes back?"

Mez nodded.

"Quip, can you go and see if you can buy her more time?"

Quip vifted as Bendin saluted the first of the minecarts to come skidding to a stop next to him. Ryan grinned as Pete stopped his cart next to his brothers.

"We're back!" Pete announced carefully adjusting the levers that controlled the motors of the cart."

"I can't wait to see the look on their faces when what we've set up goes off," Ryan said vaulting the edge of his cart and standing next to it.

"What did you do?" Bendin asked curiously.

"Only the most reasonable thing you can in a foundry. Remember how I said this is old industry? I made some adjustments."

"You're not going to tell us?" Callapse said pushing himself away from the wall.

"Let's just say I filched a few shells. Just wait and see." Pete beamed.

"Right, wait till the right moment. I have a plan guys. Gather round," Bendin said quickly waving his arms for them to come close.

"What is it?" Pete asked folding his hands together.

"We are going to escape. We take the cart through the gate."

"Use the cart to escape?" Ryan said disbelievingly.

"Yes, one of the tracks leads directly to the gate. All I have to do is open the gate just before you get there and we've done it."

"But . . . Hexalexus," Callapse said.

Quip vifted into the room knocking everyone but Bendin on the ground. "Sorry, but Jean says that those men can't be lost, but only delayed for a minute when she gets here."

"Great, when she gets here we launch," Bendin ordered. "Mez, get Rachel's body in this cart and take care of the snipers. Pete you drive, as you have the most experience. Callapse please put these bands on and sit behind Ryan. We will probably only get one shot at this."

Callapse put the bands on and everyone settled in.

"Jean will get out on her own. I need her to be a tank masher. Ryan you . . . um . . . smile."

That's just what Ryan did getting in behind his brother.

Mez balanced himself on the back end of the cart.

"What about me?" Quip asked.

"You're with me."

Jean burst through the doorway and asked, "What's the plan? I only have a few seconds."

"Jean, go smash tanks. They are taking the cart to the gate. When the cart passes the middle of the room, head for the gate."

Jean shook her head yes and thumped straight for the middle of the room on the other side.

It was time.

Bendin watched the minecart depart before he followed in Jean's wake. Once Jean came into view of Hexalexus and the tanks, all of them began firing on her. Jean's body was blasted backwards into a large smelting pot. It crashed and clattered to the ground with a loud whump!

Mez shot as many of the students setup for long range as he could.

"Quip, let's see if we can stop some of the Elect and Angels," Bendin suggested.

"Do what you want," Quip replied slyly.

Bendin vifted to Makarias and made his way to the closest one. Bendin vifted in, knocked the Vaelift over with the shockwave, and knocked him out with his Vurfenstaff. Before the rest knew what had happened, Bendin vifted back. Quip did something completely different: Instead of knocking the next man down after vifting in, Quip simply melted the gun's frame. He also vifted back before the others could shoot him. They repeated this randomly causing disturbance and ruckus all along the line, till Hexalexus yelled loud enough to shake the room, "SHOOT THE CART!"

Bendin watched in horror as everyone, tanks and all, blasted at the cart. The cart switched tracks as all the bullets went around them and penetrated the ground behind them. The explosions, however from the tanks wrecked the track all around the cart, effectively derailing them. Pete shifted his weight and started going down a completely different track. Bendin couldn't believe it. Their plan was already ruined.

Bendin vifted in and confronted several of the staff wielding Odge's Vaelift. Quip melted more guns, but was only making a very small dent in the number of weapons in the room. The tanks rolled forward pushing their attack on the minecart. Bendin saw Pete switch tracks only to have the track blown up again and be forced to switch tracks again. At least Pete was trying to get them back on track.

Bendin vifted out of the way of three of Odge's Vaelift as they leaped to pounce on him. They hit themselves instead. Ryan drove off the track and began to drive straight for the end of the room with increasing velocity. Jean plowed into the front line of the tanks as the entire foundry buckled and exploded. Parts, metal, hot cinders, pipes, and large broken fragments of what was once the foundry rained down on everything.

An eerie calm fell for a second before Ryan broke the silence with his yell, "Yeah!"

A substantial rumbling geyser of hot gas burst up through the huge twisted mess where the foundry had been. The burst was strong enough and slow enough to create a tidal wave of broken parts, containers, and hot sticky metal lumped up in a terrible mass.

Everything became a pile of disarray with Vaelift scattering all over to get out of the way of the rolling nexus of hot splinters--a wave of molten death. The sound alone of the rolling mass was Toalt-quakingly impressive.

"Help them at the cart!" Bendin yelled when he saw that Quip had vifted to Makarias.

"Right," Quip's distant yell echoed down the walls to him.

Quip appeared a moment later flying above the cart as the cart caught up with Jean. Bendin moved towards the gate room and watched as the moment of truth arrived, the wave of death caught up and overcame the fleeing cart. The wave began to *push* the cart and consume everything else. Elated, Bendin ran as best he could to the gate room. He was only going to have a few seconds before everything, the cart, the scattering Vaelift, and the wave reached the room.

Hexalexus panting, rushed into the room ahead of Bendin and down to the gate. Bendin vifted into the unchanged room.

Hexalexus sat back and said, "Go ahead, leave. Open it."

Bendin said nothing but sat in front of the door and began to make the motions that Odge had put into his mind this morning. As he made the motions, the etchings around the edge of the gate glowed blazing yellow before staying lit each one in turn. With each flash, sparks flew off wires in all directions around the room.

Hexalexus stood up and clapped his hands excitedly. "Yes, yes, yes!"

The rumbling grew immensely louder and Bendin knew they were almost here. He made the last few motions and the last etching flashed and glowed brilliant yellow.

The last etching lit and the entire gate within the border burst into yellow-white light and faded.

They could see the temple of Makarias mirrored on the other side.

The gate was open.

"Victory!" Hexalexus cheered and then raced to the corner of the room. "Any time you're ready, Bendin." He waved.

The entire wall that separated the gate room from the massive foundry was completely absorbed by the molten-magma-metal-death-wave showering the room with broken bits and twisted chunks.

Pete and Ryan had their hands in the air and were cheering, while Quip was blasting the molten wave with his fire to keep it back. Jean had balanced herself perfectly on the front of the cart and was blocking any prospective attack with her body.

Without any hesitation, Bendin slung Harmon over his shoulder and ran through the gate. He barely got around the corner of the gate as the minecart and everything behind it slammed into the wall with incredible force. The cart sailed directly through the gate!

They were through; they were going to make it! But, Bendin watched in horror as the cart kept going unhindered and flew down into the hole in the center of the room in Makarias. All of those in the cart yelled miserably as it plummeted towards the ground far below. So that was how they were going to go. Bendin felt like everything inside of him had been crushed. All their efforts, wasted. But before he could focus on their deaths, he knew he had to seal the gate shut.

A loud crunching noise erupted from the hole as well as the noise of scraping metal on concrete. Bendin put Harmon down and focused on the gate. He tried a couple of times, but the glyphs were not going out. He sat, sought out Odge and heard a single word. "Mirror."

It dawned on him in a funny sort of way. He did the motions in reverse and the glyphs began shutting down in the opposite order. Once the final one flickered out the gate lit up bright as the sun and flashed closed with a loud thunderous crash leaving the stone etched wall once again in its proper place. The wall severed anything sticking through the gate clean through, and the slab of cooling metal fell into the hole.

Bendin feared for his friends, and he lept to the edge. He knew that there was no way they could have survived that deep of a fall. The noise of scraping continued, and Bendin sadly peered over the ledge into the hole. Darkness.

An uncomfortable feeling came over Bendin, but then there was something.

A bright light slowly rose from the dark hole, and the minecart came into view rubbing up against the wall. Once it was close enough, he realized what was going on.

It was Quip! He was lifting the entire cart and all the people with fire alone. Straining with his might he shoved the cart over the brim and dumped the people and its contents on the ledge. Callapse pulled Rachel's body with him and rolled to safety. Mez grabbed Ryan who grabbed Pete who grabbed Jean. Mez pulled Ryan up, and Ryan pulled Pete up leaving Jean hanging.

"Jean, turn normal; you're slipping," Ryan recommended. "If I drop you you'll probably create a Makariasquake."

She changed and Pete and Ryan pulled her up. The cart toppled over with a loud clang, and fell back down the hole to the bottom with an insanely intense crash. Quip flew to Bendin and completely collapsed in his arms.

Nobody said anything. Nobody moved, and most hardly breathed.

Chapter 25
The Power of Odge

"We almost *died*," Ryan said breaking the silence.

"We *almost* died!" Pete clapped his brother on the shoulder. "I'll get some food and water." He flicked on the lights on his way out.

"Thank you." Bendin felt that was an unspoken need, but was grateful as he knew everyone was on the precipice of complete bodily exhaustion.

Pete returned carrying pills, medical tools, and water from the scrapper. They were distributed and relief spread throughout the group.

"Quip," Bendin said giving him a pill and a drink, "you are a real hero today. Thanks." Quip smiled feebly and fell asleep before Bendin gently slung him on his shoulder. "Mez, thanks again for saving my life."

Mez nodded. "Yes."

"What's going on?" Harmon said stirring. She nervously pressed herself up against the wall in fear. "Where is everything?"

"Harmon," Bendin said sitting down next to her, "You are in Makarias on the other side of the gate."

Harmon gasped. "Send me back!"

"No. I couldn't leave you behind," Bendin said firmly.

"Like I'm supposed to believe that?" She said crossing her arms. She glared at Bendin.

"It's true," said Ryan.

Pete nodded. "I was able to find one of these. It will help," Pete said showing them a silver box. He activated it and helped get Rachel's body up off the ground.

Bendin reached out his hand to Harmon who shrugged him off. "I'll get up on my own, thank you."

"Stay with me, Harmon, or Mez will shoot you."

Mez nodded holding a pistol out for her to see.

Harmon said nothing but followed after them as all of them tried to manipulate Rachel's body back up to where Callapse's scrapper was.

"That was quite the ride, wasn't it, Pete?" Ryan asked.

"Yeah, I can't wait till we can do it again!" Pete said

looking over his shoulder at his brother.

"Mez, please help me with this," Callapse groaned holding his leg.

Mez gave Ryan the pistol, went to one of the compartments and returned with three separate items. The first he used to extract the bullet. The second reversed the damage. The third as Pete said, "seams things up a bit."

Harmon stared at the world around her in complete awe. "I've never seen. . ."

Bendin knew she hadn't been outside either.

"What? It's just the forest and the mountain valleys. No big deal, right?" Ryan said skeptically.

"She's never been outside, Ryan, give her a break," Bendin scolded.

Ryan did a double-take and his jaw dropped.

"I was the same way, we temple-born all are." Bendin waved his hands in front of Harmon's glazed and tearing eyes. Her face hardened slowly.

"I was *this* close to figuring it out, now it's your fault I'm separated from the truth!" Harmon yelled lunging at Bendin and wrapping her hands around his neck. She squeezed and cut off the airflow grinning wickedly. "Goodbye incarnation of Pikuk."

Quip woke as Bendin fell and her hands tightened. He flew up to her face without hesitation. Everyone around them started to move forwards to pull her off, but Quip vifted eight times in quick succession creating a combined, powerful, singular shockwave which launched Harmon straight up into the air. Once she was in the air, Quip followed her vifting every few moments accelerating her body.

"Stop! You'll kill her!" Mez screamed from below.

Quip stopped and Harmon's body smashed into a pine tree and fell being slowed by the branches all the way down to the ground. Harmon yelped on impact, badly bruised, bleeding, but surprisingly conscious.

"Stay . . . off . . . Bendin," Quip breathed in her face.

She nodded hesitantly before tearing up and clawing the ground.

"Harmon," Bendin wheezed. He knelt down near Harmon and said quietly, "I'm sorry you don't understand. You are confused." He showed as much care as he could. "I have not asked you to fight me. I simply want you to listen to me and focus on opening your heart for understanding, your ears to hear, and your mind so that you can understand what is going on. Let Odge do the convincing. Watch."

Harmon tearily looked at Bendin completely confused.

Bendin removed his boots and socks. "Mez, Please bring Rachel's body over here. Lay her here on the ground."

"What?" Callapse interjected. "Haven't you done enough already? She's going to be buried at home, not here."

"Just watch. Quip, it's time." Bendin turned to the others. "This is so you can know that I'm legit. That Odge's authority and subsequent power is greater than Zadok's power."

Quip whispered, "What are we doing?"

"We are going to give her a proper burial. Like we promised. Quip, place your rear paws on her bare feet." Bendin placed his bare feet on her feet. "Quip, your front paws."

Quip put his front paws up against Bendin's palms. He bowed his head. Bendin noticed Callapse skeptically observing, Ryan and Pete respectfully looking on, Harmon still completely confused, Mez and Jean concerned with tears of sadness in their eyes, hand in hand.

Bendin spoke clearly and firmly in the mountain breeze, "By Odge, Rachel, I call thee back."

The mountain wind whisked by all of them.

Breath issued from Rachel's lips.

"Bendin?" Rachel asked from her position lying on the ground. "I heard your voice."

Mez lept forward with tears on his face and asked, "It's you?"

Rachel stretched her hands up and said, "Yeah."

"Really?"

"Yeah."

Mez pulled her up in a big hug.

"Yes, yes, Mez. Thank you. It's me "

Mez reluctantly let her go as Callapse strode over and clasped her hand barely able to speak, "I . . . can't believe . . . you're . . . back!" He then turned to Bendin and pulled him close. "I'm sorry." He then let Bendin go and went and sat down and mumbled, "I can't believe it."

The others all gave Rachel a hearty hug, each in complete disbelief. Except, Harmon. Harmon was the most confused of all of them. Her lips pursed, mouth opened, and she acted as if to say something, but stopped, unable to say anything.

"What did I miss? What happened?" Rachel asked as Pete gave her some pills and water.

"You died," Callapse said grimly.

Everyone solemnly nodded.

Rachel gasped and recoiled. "I . . . was," she turned, "not . . . here."

Rachel grasped Bendin's hand and pulled him close. "Ask me about it later."

Quip flew to her and licked her cheek. "I'm glad you are back."

Harmon stared at Rachel paralyzed with fear. She began to tremble and lifted her hand pointing at Rachel. She said sternly, "I . . . watched you die. This . . . is impossible. You *can't* be real. I don't know what's going on anymore but . . . aaaarrrrrrr!" Harmon raced at Rachel so fast that she almost punched her in the face before Mez dove and held Harmon down. "Don't move or Ryan shoots."

Harmon stopped moving.

Mez lifted Harmon up and forced her over to the scrapper and put her inside one of the compartments.

"That was unexpected. Such a shame, this really is a pretty temple," Bendin noted admiringly.

"Too bad I've got such bad memories of it," Callapse mumbled from behind him.

"I can't believe I died," Rachel said softly to them.

Callapse guiltily didn't say anything to that.

"Jean," Mez said stiffly. Jean obediently followed Mez to his craft.

Bendin jumped into the passenger seat with Quip landing on his shoulder. Rachel, Ryan, and Pete squeezed in the back. Without another word Callapse flew the scrapper away from Mount Desenzo.

Back at the Coils, Bendin pulled Harmon out of the cargo containers. "Promise you will not harm anyone and stay close to me."

"Yes," She grumbled taking in everything in the docking area.

"Good, let's go then," Bendin said wearily.

The whole group split up and Bendin went with Harmon and Quip to the waterfall room. Bendin smirked as he caught Quip catch Harmon's eye, pointed at her with his paw, pointed at Bendin and frowning drew it slowly across his neck. Bendin led her to the place where they could get some boots for easier walking around. Once that was done, Bendin showed Harmon the kid's lounge. Bendin called out, "Starley!"

"I'm hiding!" Starley's voice echoed down from the ceiling. Bendin noticed her braids peeking out from behind the table that was up on the ceiling.

"You know it doesn't work if you say something right?" Quip said using his fire to launch his body up to Starley.

"I know, you funny fox!" Starley giggled tugging lightly on Quip's tail.

"I know, you goofy girl!" Quip hit one of her braids with his paws. Bendin watched them from the floor.

Harmon watched the whole ordeal with her eyes wide, pondering nervously.

"Quip, that makes three of the eight? We're almost halfway there."

"Yeah, because he didn't know we were going to be taking them. See how hard that last one was? He could hide them anywhere now," Quip said.

"Maybe, but let's hope he doesn't!"

Harmon said nothing. Bendin took her to get her wounds dressed by Celeste before they made their way down to the kitchen. When they did, they went carefully pulling their way along. Bendin hoped they could arrange for some more gear. There were only three people in the kitchen: Pete, Ryan, and Rachel. They were already eating up on the ceiling like normal. Bendin pushed off and landed pretty close to his chair, but Harmon missed the table by a meter. Ryan skated over and helped pull her to an empty chair.

"Where is the rest of the family?" Bendin asked.

Starley walked in, skated up to the table, sat in a chair, and watched Pete and Ryan consume food.

"They went out to the jungle to watch Jean show off her new talent," Rachel answered.

"I need you guys to do something for me," Bendin said through mouthfuls of bread he munched on.

"What?" Ryan asked.

"I need you to pray after the manner I will show you. I'm impressed that it's time for some things to change, and I feel very uneasy if I don't do anything."

"Sure," Rachel said seriously.

Bendin explained the simple rules that he had been shown by Harmon and approved by Odge. He gave them the question that they needed to ask, and it had to do, surprisingly enough, with whether he was the head of the Vaelift. Harmon flinched.

"I have no idea why I'm asking you, but you've got to do this every night. At least, till you receive an answer. Please let me know when that happens."

There was noise from outside and Bendin watched as a new face walked in followed by, Tilmon, George, Charles, Jean, and Celeste holding red-belted Destiny. The new face was a girl with jet black hair, dark skin like George's, brown eyes, very tall like Tilmon, and a very shapely body.

"Who is this?" Ryan said suddenly very interested in what had just come through the door.

"It's Tamaira, from the Outcasts. They approved of another one coming over like I was saying earlier. Please make her feel welcome," Tilmon announced.

Ryan pushed off so quickly from the ceiling that his food dislodged from the table as well as his chair and they all floated haphazardly away aimlessly in the air. Regardless of that he skillfully planted himself in a bow on the floor with his nose to the floor.

"I am Ryan Coil. How might I be of service to you dear one of the Outcasts?" Ryan grabbed her hand and kissed the end of it lightly.

Tamaira raised an eyebrow. "Thanks? Ryan, I might need your assistance later I think." Tamaira winked up at the others sitting on the ceiling.

"I saw that," Quip whispered.

Ryan grinned up at his brother who had skillfully gathered Ryan's floating food and was eating it. Pete gave him the thumbs up and smiled too.

At this moment, as Ryan was bowing down and staring up at Pete, a large fireball erupted from his behind and blew a large hole out the back end of his pants. Ryan's face went solid pink as he was blasted forward. He nervously put his rear on the ground and scooted backwards.

"Sorry, Tamaira, I have been temporarily and unavoidably delayed from accepting the pleasure of your company, if you will excuse me." Ryan scooted out of the room. A few moments later they heard and saw the same thing above them with Pete being propelled downwards by a large fireball blasting from his rear end at the ceiling. Pete followed the example of his brother and scooted out of the room, his face pink and his bottom to the ground.

Bendin noticed Rachel trying as hard as she could to not

break her serious expression, but she wasn't doing that great of a job. Finally she couldn't take it anymore and she burst out laughing.

Bendin imagined it felt good that she had gotten back at them for years of pranks.

Tilmon laughed. "Now that, is funny. Rachel! Your cure worked! The Wycliff's have been trying to contact you for days to tell you of your success. They've already sent payment for your services as well."

"Tamaira's already better than George at skating!" Charles declared skating up into the air and in circles around Bendin.

"Oh please, she got lucky today," George said defensively.

Bendin smiled and pushed himself down to Tamaira. "I'm Bendin. It's nice to meet you."

To Bendin, Rachel, and Harmon's surprise Tamaira pulled him close, hugged him, and said in his ear, "Thank you for coming back to the world. Although my people don't generally accept the Vaelift, I do."

"No problem," Bendin said slightly uneasily backing away trying to look as smooth as possible. Quip took the opportunity to introduce himself with one arm flaming red, his head flaming yellow, and his other front paw flaming blue. "I'm Quip."

Tamaira simply giggled.

"Who's that?" Tilmon asked Bendin pointing to Harmon.

"That is Harmon. She's from Toalt, Tilmon. She's with me. I mean . . ." Bendin didn't know how to explain it.

"She came with us," Quip finished

Harmon frowned, but pushed off down to them.

"So she's not a Vaelift?" Tilmon asked confused. "She's dressed like one."

"No."

"Oh. Well . . . welcome then. I assume you are staying with Bendin?"

Rachel watched Bendin curiously as he said, "Yes, Quip and I will take care of Harmon."

"Tilmon, I need your help," Bendin turned to Tilmon. He quickly explained what he wanted and needed. Surprisingly, Tilmon agreed with him and pledged that before the day was out the Tribunal would replenish their gear and even get a special set just for Harmon.

Bendin got Harmon and Quip to come back up to their room.

The room was almost exactly the same as it was when he had left it. A few things scattered about, but it was the closest thing to a home he'd been blessed to have.

"You'll be sleeping there Harmon," Bendin said pointing to the corner across from theirs.

"Mmhmm," she mumbled and sat in the corner putting her head in her arms.

Bendin cleaned up and fixed the room up while Quip took a short nap. Harmon didn't move, but sat in the corner. Pete and Ryan came by to drop off some things for Harmon's bed. Both of them seemed to have recovered from their earlier embarrassment and were babbling together.

Rachel came in a few minutes later. "Tilmon wants to meet you in the sitting room."

"Sure," Bendin said lowering his arm so Quip could run up it. "Harmon, let's go."

Tilmon met them there and held more black cloth bags with yellow ties in his hands.

"Most of this was covered by the tribunal. I tried to refuse them to get you anything nice, but Aspertan wouldn't have it. He really wants your help and approval Bendin. He paid for most of it personally." Tilmon handed Tamaira, Rachel, Ryan, Pete, Callapse, Bendin, Charles, and Harmon one bag each.

Bendin opened his bag to find a new gold belt with silver box, two new cuffs, gold headband, and, to his delight, his own pair of Cleffs.

Pete and Ryan erupted in cheers, tears, and rent the walls with their voices in excitement. "WE GOT CLEFFS!" They shouted it over and over again in a chant.

Tilmon calmed them down. "That's enough boys."

Bendin quickly realized, as the air filled with the Cleffs' twang, that all of them must have been given a pair. All of them were completely ecstatic. Harmon, didn't know what was going on, but that didn't stop her from putting on her gear and testing out her skates.

Tilmon calmed everyone down and everyone sat down in a meditation position of their choice while Tilmon gave thanks. Once done, he revealed a large container of bubbles.

"Bubbles!" Starley cheered.

Tilmon blew the bubbles and everyone watched them ride the air currents around the room. Bendin caught one and found them to be hard, but popped with a loud snap when you pressed on them with your hands. Soon the room was full of loud snapping and thousands of various sized bubbles.

Later, Bendin sat in his bed thinking and pondering about the events of the days past and the sudden and dramatic increase in peril that he had encountered. George was asleep in bed, Harmon was sleeping on a large, but comfortable pillow, and Quip was asleep behind him. He had enjoyed the evening very much and was a nice contrast to the misery of the days earlier. Bendin had replaced his watches, one from Tilmon's shop for Makarias and the other from the temple in Toalt. He certainly hadn't understood the depth of Odge's power. He just wondered if risking your life for one person like Jean was worth it, and which of the pieces he was going to go get next or how he was going to find them. All he could think of for sure was how grateful he was for the help and strength of Odge.

As he was thinking this, a fuzzy warm light radiated from the space in the air directly next to him. A soft but firm and now familiar voice said, "Bendin, I come to you in gratitude for defending my name and have instructions for you. I am Odge." Bendin watched in surprise as a very bright, soft white light got thicker and brighter till a man with white hair appeared next to him, sitting on the bed. The instant he appeared, love flooded the room and he felt beyond a doubt that this person loved him. It was heavy, as if a soft heavy liquid weight filled him up, and the joy was beyond anything he'd ever felt.

Bendin asked, "Odge, which temple am I to go to next?"

"You are going back to Thibracketory, with those whom I shall tell you. You will start a new Vaelift Institute and begin anew. Zadok has changed and accelerated his plans. We will alter our course to gain the advantage."

"Uh," Bendin said.

"Fear not. I will guide you, as I have always done." Odge gave Bendin a hug, and Odge and the light disappeared.

With the heavy weight of Odge's love gone, Bendin fell backwards on top of Quip who woke with a start. "Bendin, I was sleeping here!" Quip wormed his way out from under Bendin, snuggled up to him, and fell back asleep.

Bendin lay there a while longer thinking about what Odge had told him. Even though the light was gone, the happiness he had felt remained.

Then next morning after breakfast and the hard trip

down with Harmon, who was completely new to skating, they went into the family sitting room. He invited Harmon, Quip, Rachel, Ryan and Pete to sit. Callapse was still recovering in his room. He even invited George and Tamaira, but they were busy.

Rachel's eyes were bright and she said positively, "I know you are the head of the Vaelift." She described her experiences and feelings over the course of the night.

Harmon frowned.

"Rachel, that's wonderful. It's exactly what you needed to experience. Now don't forget to keep up with questions of your own and times of gratitude as well." Bendin told her. She smiled proudly and happily and looked at Pete and Ryan.

"We got nothing. I guess we'll keep trying. What's up?" Ryan said.

"I have talked to your father and mother and have cleared it with them if you want to, to receive what I am. So, I'm here to give you a gift. Odge has authorized me to give this to a certain number of people, many whom I haven't met yet."

"Ok, sure! I love gifts!" Pete shouted clapping his hands.

"Rachel, you first, will you become a Vaelift?" Bendin said pulling her towards him.

"Yes," Rachel said nervously.

"Don't worry it doesn't hurt, " Bendin said taking off his skates and had Rachel, Ryan, and Pete do the same. Bendin took her hands in his hands, placed his bare feet on her feet, and spoke a few words, "Rachel, I give you the power of Vaelift. One of Odge's own; may you never betray him."

"It feels so tingly!" Rachel exclaimed excitedly after Bendin had finished and let go of her hands. "And it burns." She frowned felt her stomach with her hands and sat down.

Bendin performed the exact same thing, except with Pete and Ryan's names, without the least variation to Pete and Ryan.

"Now with you guys, you may need to do a few things before it will work. It's kind of like unlocking a gate or discovering cheese for the first time, but promise me you will not go messing around with anything that you might have seen me doing till I can train you properly, okay?" Bendin said.

"Sure thing!" Ryan and Pete clapped their hands against the others in excitement. "We're going to be Vaelift!"

"You already *are* Vaelift," Quip said dryly.

Bendin found himself very excited as now there were more people that were going to be like him. He was also really glad that it had so happened that Odge had decided to include them in the people that were going to be called forward to serve.

Bendin left Harmon with Quip in the Kid's Lounge for some basic skating and took Rachel out onto the special upside-down balcony.

"How do you think I did?" Bendin asked.

"I think you did fine, Bendin. I'm just concerned with Harmon. Are you going to be alright around her?"

Bendin gripped the railing.

"She tried to kill you. . . . I'm afraid she'll succeed. I don't know if I can live with that."

Bendin sighed. "She tried to hit you. I'm not sure I can live with that either. Harmon is confused. I don't know how long it's going to take her to soften her hard heart, or if it's ever going to happen. I don't want to give up on Harmon yet. Please understand that Quip is an excellent guard and keeps her from doing anything. So, don't worry about that part."

"You love her. Don't you?" Rachel's words, though soft, were effective.

"I did."

"Still?"

"I'm confused, I don't know. I think so?" Bendin looked down at the sky and then back up at the ground.

"Bendin, I'm here, if and when you need me. I will not force you to make up your mind, *yet*." Rachel smiled, and then frowned. "I don't know if I'm going to be very good at the whole Vaelift thing. Soladaque was always the one who was athletic," Rachel responded. "Bendin."

Bendin saw her eyes focus.

Rachel continued, "I saw him you know. When I died, I was in a room full of chairs as far as my eyes could see. It was full of people, and we were waiting. For something. Everyone wanted to move, but we couldn't. Then an older man came to me and asked if I was ok. I said yes. He then instructed that when I heard you calling me if I'd accept the call. I answered yes and as he turned to leave he said to me, 'It is enough. Wait for the call.' I'm not sure I was ready for this to be described as death. When you called, I answered and the entire placed dissolved like a dream. Do you think I will really be able to do this?"

"I think you will be fine. Odge wouldn't have offered you a position if he didn't think you were qualified. Zadok is up to something. Odge told me."

"When did he tell you?" Rachel asked gripping the railing

next to him.

"Last night. How would you like to come with me as we go and gather the others that Odge has told me about? I'm thinking about taking you, Harmon, Quip, Pete and Ryan."

"I'd love to. Yes, of course. Please let me get my things," Rachel said skating straight up into the air up at the ground and around the bottom of the house out of sight.

Bendin thought that was, actually, really attractive. He wished he didn't feel so conflicted, but he did, still struggling with the whole Harmon thing. He skated up into the air and followed in the fading trail that was left by Rachel. With sickening speed Bendin did a double bladed stop before hitting the ground letting off a beautiful fireball and popping sound before switching directions to skate into one of the entrances to the house below. He was very excited about the new mission Odge had given him. It was going to be epic.

ABOUT THE AUTHOR

Benjamin Atwood lives in Ohio with his wife and four boys. Benjamin enjoys writing, skating, computers, gaming, game making, family, and friends. Benjamin loves to hear from readers. Email at benjamin@vaelift.com or tweet @vaelift.